LIGHTNING in the STORM

LIGHTNING
in the
STORM

The 101st Air Assault Division in the Gulf War

Thomas Taylor

HIPPOCRENE BOOKS
New York

ISBN 0-7818-0268-7

For information, address:
HIPPOCRENE BOOKS, INC.
171 Madison Avenue
New York, NY 10016

Printed in the United States of America

"Where is the prince who could so afford to cover his country with troops for its defense as that 10,000 men descending from the clouds might not in many places do an infinite deal of mischief?"
—Benjamin Franklin

"The Air Force and armor were the thunder of Desert Storm, while the 101st was the lightning."
—H. Norman Schwarzkopf

CONTENTS

Maps

Dedication

Lightning in the Storm is dedicated to the memory of Command Sergeant Major Walter J. Sabalouski, for whom I delivered this eulogy at Arlington Cemetery in August 1993:

I'd like to first pass along a thought from Hank Emerson, whose health prevents him from attending this service. But as Mrs. Sabalouski can tell you, Hank has been there for her and Sabo all during these last sad weeks.

On the phone Hank reflected on a verse from *The Halls of Montezuema* that goes, "If the Army and the Navy ever look on heaven's scene, they will find the streets well guarded by United States Marines."

"Well, said Hank, "that may be true. We'll have to wait till we get there to see if Marines are guarding the streets. But I know for sure that the honor guard at the Pearly Gates will be commanded by Sgt.Sabalouski."

When I think of Sabo my thoughts return to the first battle of Dak To, and what a *Stars & Stripes* reporter wrote about him there: "I'd heard of NCOs like Sabalouski in previous wars. There was a Sabo at Buna on New Guinea, another at Kasserine Pass and St. Vith. There was a Sabo to hold the Pusan perimeter and fight back from the Chosin Reservoir. Men like Sabo are a vanishing breed to whom the Army is home, and they are the father of their men."

Unknowingly, that reporter was not just using Sabo as a symbol of great NCOs in history, but actually describing Sabo himself. He was a soldier who had indeed fought and won in three major wars, a man among only a few who have ever been awarded three Combat Infantry Badges. Along the way he also won the DSC, Silver Star, Purple Heart, and enough Bronze Stars to build a statue.

So Sabo already had a huge reputation before I met him in Vietnam where he constantly added still more lore to his legend. Some of you have told me that you owe your life to Sabo. My gratitude is of a different sort, stemming from the certainty that nearby in my battalion was one of the greatest soldiers to ever wear a unifrom.

How did he do it? How was he the idol and inspiration for soldiers who themselves were the best in the world? He did it by what is now almost a cliche. He led by example—his own.

But it was an example no one else could match. He was immune to death, contemptuous of wounds. When others were in helmet defilade, Sabo was up and moving. Directing. Ordering his men with words they understood best. Doing what had to be done.

Survival never seemed to concern Sabo. Only victory was important. That attitude, that utter disregard for his personal safety, can not be taught even by example. It is that most rare quality that is born in very few of us because it can't be followed completely—it can only be shown.

And how Sabo showed it! Not with bravado, not like a Rambo, not with any trait or mannerism that is an *appearance* of heroism—but by the core essence of heroism itself. The 82nd had their Sergeant York. The 101st has our Sergeant Sabalouski.

From my conversations with Sabo I know the word "hero" did not go down with him. "Hero" was someone else's description. What he felt he had done was not be a hero but merely his job. The job was what mattered, not how it was accomplished, but that it *be* accomplished. Sabo was not one to bitch about how a job was foolish or even foolhardy. I think he felt that any job performance was supremely important, whether it be policing the company area or repelling human waves of Japanese, Chinese, or NVA. He took it as *his* responsibility that *his* unit do those jobs satisfactorily.

We hardly noticed that his company area was straight.

We watched in awe as he straightened out a battlefield.

Yet I believe Sabo took almost as much satisfaction from the first accomplishment as he did from the second.

Really, the likes of Sabo are not to be explained. We can only be grateful that men like him are there when the rest of us need them—when the need is sometimes desperate. That *Stars & Stripes* reporter may have summed it up: His last sentence about Dak To was, "There had better be more Sabos coming along."

Let that be our prayer, for our army and our country, that there *will* be more Sabos. We can be sure that there won't be many, for men like Sabo come along only once in a lifetime. We on this field have had the unique pirvilege of serving with a legend.

—Thomas H. Taylor

Introduction

Like a green carpet runner, the Mall rolls out between Capitol Hill and the Washington Monument, a splendid assembly area for parades. During the morning, battalions had formed early in the tradition of hurry up and wait, but this was a pleasant period when the author strolled for a half mile by the units, impressed by their appearance, remembering their history. A break in the heat wave favored the occasion; though rain clouds threatened, the feeling on the Mall was that good luck would accompany the marchers, and the day would be as grand as the celebration it marked: the 50th Anniversary of American airborne forces.

The month was July 1990. Fifty years had passed since Hitler's paratroopers conquered the island of Crete, though at such cost that the Germans would never again attempt a similar airborne attack. However the American Chief of Staff, Gen. George Marshall, had envisioned exciting prospects where Hitler saw only future disasters. Marshall directed that the 82nd "All American" Division become the first US paratroopers; indeed, that the 82nd split into two airborne divisions, the second to become the 101st "Screaming Eagles."

Both halves of Marshall's amoeba were prominent at the 50th Anniversary, the two divisions having rewarded his gamble with famous victories in Normandy, Holland, and the Battle of the Bulge. About three hundred men from the 82nd and 101st, each contingent led by its commanding general, stood side by side prior to the parade. The troops carried their 'massed colors'—the flags of every battalion currrently assigned to the divisions, grouped together and festooned with battle streamers from World War I through Vietnam. They were carried by tall, strapping men, selected not only for their appearance but to handle the weight of the flags. Bunched like bamboo, the shiny poles raised a plumed pavilion.

The parade would start on the Mall, swing down Pennsylvania Avenue, turn by the National Archives, through a canyon of federal buildings and finally into Freedom Plaza, passing the reviewing stand and its VIP's, where Gen. Westmoreland was Grand Marshal. Waiting to follow the troops were formations of veterans, most long discharged or retired from the army, but proud and poised to march once more with their units. An astonishing formation was a battalion of South Vietnamese paratroopers, vaguely connected to the anniversary but turned out in crisp period fatigues, sleeves rolled up to sharp creases, and surely the best marching veterans in the parade. A thousand or more had settled around Washington since the fall of Saigon fifteen years earlier. Their families distributed so many yellow flags of the vanished nation that red, white and blue seemed outnumbered on the sidewalks.

There were two uniforms for the American vets. Most who had served in Vietnam could fit into their faded jungle fatigues, so they wore them. The men from World War II preferred slacks and blazers. Before the parade, veterans from both eras infiltrated the color guards to touch and even kiss the flags.

The young soldiers stood agog as living ghosts approached them. Briefly, there was a generational gap to cross—the troops were unprepared to have their forefathers salute them with wet eyes. Television zoomed in on such encounters. With little urging, the vets explained on camera just why their old outfit was invincible in combat. Feats of heroism were recounted, and the basis of legends recalled. The young soldiers stood by, hearing the history of their units from those who had made it: the Bulge, the Ashau Valley were beside them and talking.

They listened with a wistful awe. All were double volunteers, first for the army and then for the airborne. What the vets had done, they were ready to do: a man joins the army recognizing that someday he may be in combat; a man volunteers for the elite of the army anticipating the prospect of combat. Such an attitude does not denote a war lover or Rambo, but rather a willingness, even eagerness, to test himself with the ultimate risk. It is in the makeup of many young men to do so. Across all cultures and millenia this has been true. Talking with them, the airborne veterans could sense that their successors were longing for trial by combat; that indeed they would be disappointed if it never came. In less than a month, unanticipated by anyone, their trial would begin.

With veterans milling through their ranks, the color guards of the 82nd and 101st stood only a few yards apart as if to symbolize their common origin. As the senior division, the 82nd would step off first in the parade. For fifty years the rivalry between these Siamese twins had been keen in the way that only one brother can compete with another.

They jumped together on D Day. The paratroopers were so scattered and intermixed that often objectives were seized and defended by composite forces from both divisions. To this day, Screaming Eagles and All Americans each lay claim for the capture of St. Mere Eglise, an ancient Norman town that added a parachute to its coat of arms—but diplomatically abstained on the question of which paratroopers had liberated them.

In Holland the divisions seized adjoining portions of the highway leading to "A bridge too far." Before Christmas, 1944, they shared a rest area in France where, with everything but firearms, they fought each other for choice bars. Called out for the Battle of the Bulge, they separated at a crossroad, the 82nd to blunt the German offensive at St. Vith, the 101st to reach immortality at Bastogne.

After World War II, the 82nd was preserved as the army's single airborne division while the 101st was deactivated till 1956. However official favor tipped toward the 101st during Vietnam as the entire division fought there, and controlled a third of the 82nd. In the post-Vietnam skirmishes, the 82nd took part in the Grenada and Panama operations while the 101st stayed home at Ft. Campbell, KY.

The reason could be seen in the headgear of the two color guards. The 82nd were still paratroopers wearing jaunty maroon berets, symbols of their light weight and ability to pack up and go. The entire division could load into Air Force transports and be dropped by parachutes virtually anywhere in the world in a day.

The Screaming Eagle color guard wore new Kevlar battle helmets. The 101st had turned in their parachutes during Vietnam to become a helicopter-mobile division, and had remained so ever since. With its own choppers, a third of the 101st could move a hundred miles in a bit over an hour, but for a strategic deployment thousands of miles away the division's equipment required many times more Air Force transports than the 82nd. Though 'Airborne' arched over the shoulder patches of both divisions, for the 82nd the word meant parachutes, for the 101st, helicopters. Grenada and Panama had called more for speed than power so the 82nd received the missions, leaving the 101st to grumble at the anniversary banquet. "But we're going next time." said Steve Weiss, the Screaming Eagles' Command Sergeant Major, "Guaranteed."

He was prescient. Less than three weeks after his prediction, Iraqi Republican Guards would overrun Kuwait.

At the anniversary parade, a bugle sounded adjutant's call. The veterans scrambled to form ranks. The color guards fell in, then the 82nd snapped to attention as the leading unit to march. Their shoulder patch is red and blue with the letters AA in white. Their official march, "The All American Soldier," is perhaps the most stirring music in the army. The 82nd's band boomed out the syncopated introduction, and their color guards stepped off, accompanied by respectful applause from the 101st's vets—but also some good natured jeers like "Almost airborne!" With a composite battalion in uniform and at least as many of their veterans following, the 82nd marched away till only the drum could be heard. Then the 101st's commander—whose novelistic name was J.H. Binford Peay III— called his troops to attention. Peay's command hushed the veterans, projecting their memories like dreams to the last occasion when an order had been addressed to them by a general in uniform. The Screaming Eagles' band sounded off with "Rendezvous with Destiny," the first bars answered by thunderclapping from the vets.

Eleven months later on these same boulevards, the bands struck up again. This time the Vietnamese were among the half-million spectators. The young Americans who had envied the veterans' experience were now veterans themselves. In 1990 the color guards had worn mottled green uniforms, the camouflage of the cold war just ended. In 1991, they wore goggles on their helmets and the sand colored uniforms of the region in which they had won an amazing victory. Once again colors were massed. A year before, President Bush had attended an economic conference in Houston rather than the airborne anniversary. Today, he would be on the White House lawn to award battle streamers to his divisions. The streamers were labeled Desert Shield and Desert Storm.

History would record the war under the latter label, and in the category of easy victories. For the United States it was the swiftest, most one-sided triumph of any war worthy of the name. By historical standards, the effect of Desert Storm ranks with blitzkrieg, a combination of unprecedented technology applied with tactics to exploit it. But while blitzkrieg was principally a breakthrough in ground warfare, Desert Storm, like its name, was more a creature of the air.

At a merging point between air and land warfare were the two army divisions marching in both parades. Desert Storm distinguished the component meanings of 'airborne' in their names as when the cavalry converted to armored vehicles. In the desert, the 82nd's parachutes—symbols of tradition—were as absent as had been the 101st's helicopters in Grenada and Panama. A different theater required different forces, and once more the seesaw had tipped, this time with the weight of the 101st's helicopters. Not since tanks took charge of the battlefield had a means of warfare proven itself so quickly and completely.

Such were the musings in the Pentagon as the 101st marched in Washington for the second time within a year. But for most Screaming Eagles, Desert Storm was a fleeting crescendo, a bewilderingly brief climax of sleepless action, terminating a preparatory ordeal. Of the two new battle streamers, the one for Desert Shield would evoke more memories.

"It's hard thinking of myself as a veteran like the Vietnam guys," said a color bearer, preparing to receive the presidential salute. "The way I look at it, any recognition I get is for Desert Shield. I mean, I worked a lot harder training in Desert Shield than what I did during the ground war. I get real uncomfortable when I hear this 'hero's' stuff. I think heroes are guys who do it when things go wrong. Not much went wrong for us, not much at all."

Steve Weiss compared his two wars:

"Basically the differences were that in the desert we knew what we had to do, we had the equipment and battle doctrine to do it, and the President let us do it. Desert Shield was tough, Desert Storm had some hairy moments, but all together this was a war where Murphy's Law did not apply. In fact, just about everything that could go wrong, didn't. That was the result of long, hard work—plus applied brain power up and down the line.

"If these guys don't think they're real veterans, they're not looking at the right things. They've been through everything in war except the tragedy. They did things right so they didn't have the tragedy. That's their reward, not something they're lacking. They're the best kind of veterans to be, alive and able to teach the next generation what it takes to win.

"So the way we were prepared, we could not be beat. Add to that the support we got from America, and we could not be stopped. If you're going to write a book about it, that's about all you have to say."

The author marched with the Viet vets in the first parade and watched the second from the Lincoln Memorial, camera in hand. There was a photo I tingled to take, triumphantly symbolic, when the 101st wheeled off Constitution Avenue. Just before that turn, a tapering wing of the Vietnam Wall stretched out toward them, pointed at them—so that names of men etched in columns seemed counterparts for men marching in columns.

Unfortunately, throngs of spectators blocked me from photographing the juxtaposition. The moment was lost forever as the 101st marched straight toward the Lincoln Memorial where I stood, then a half circle around it before crossing the bridge to Virginia where this victory parade would halt and disband. My disappointment about the photograph gave way to wistful, intense curiosity.

Wistful in an envious way, for I imagined that the thunderous adulation was overcompensation despite any of the division's hardships during the previous year. It is the lot of few soldiers to receive such public and profuse recognition for their accomplishments; spectacles like this one were as rare as the triumphs of Roman proconsuls.

Curious in an uneasy way, for the 101st's equipment and appearance were disturbingly unfamiliar. The march was preceded by a fly-by of warplanes that had ruled the desert skies. They were odd and futuristicly shaped, all dark and unmarked. The sand hued uniforms and flanged Kevlars of my old outfit seemed more alien than modern. Especially the Kevlars: our 'pots' in Vietnam had been a uniting symbol with two previous wars. It struck me that we Viet vets were now no longer veterans of the last war; instead, we were to the desert vets what the World War II vets had been to us.

But sturdily spanning generational gaps was that shoulder patch, both dark and dashing, the eagle's head, a national emblem. My father had worn the patch while commanding the division in Normandy, Holland, Bastogne. For all his subsequent honors and titles, only the Screaming Eagle is engraved on his headstone, as it had been on his heart. I'd worn it in the jungle where it seemed a talisman and inspiration. Now the patch swung by in unison on shoulders with a background of desert camouflage. I had to learn what new ingredients had been added to the Screaming Eagle mystique—for the reward of reconnecting with it.

Interviews revealed a surprisingly dim afterglow. For the warriors, the Gulf War had started and ended too suddenly for deep level appreciation.

Weiss: "I remember my days in 'Nam, twenty years ago, better than my eight months in the desert. Why's that?"

Time moves slower when you're young, a year representing more of his life than a year when he reached forty. But probably more important was that he left his office to go to war in the

Gulf, then returned to that same office and his previous routine. I heard, "It was like a big FTX [field training exercise]" often enough that it may be the best comparison.

Or the 101st could be compared to an international engineering company like Bechtel. Unexpectedly, a huge project came up in the Middle East. Estimates, plans, site preparation, procurement, production and construction raced through their phases. Under stress of climate and deadlines, the job was completed; then the expatriates went home to resume previous duties, and some scattered to other projects. It's a way of life in which short term memory is quickly blurred, in which the present overtakes the past with scarcely a pause. Many of the soldiers confided that my interview caused their first re-examination of the desert experience. Some called me the next day to relate a flood of details that during the night had emerged from their untapped memory bank.

In contrast, the parallel history from familes on the homefront rolled freely from fresh recollection. Their waiting and worrying seemed to have engraved experiences, whereas the soldiers' toil erased them. A desert veteran would shake his head, wondering if it had all really happened—to be assured by his wife that it surely did.

It happened fast, but that's the way the 101st was prepared to react. The hurry up (deployment to the Gulf) geared down to the wait (Desert Shield) before the march to the Euphrates (Desert Storm). It all happened in less than a year, between two parades in Washington. An outrider for the victory parade was an ungainly helicopter, the Apache, that appropriately had first scouted the hostile sands of Arabia.

Part 1

Hurry up and wait

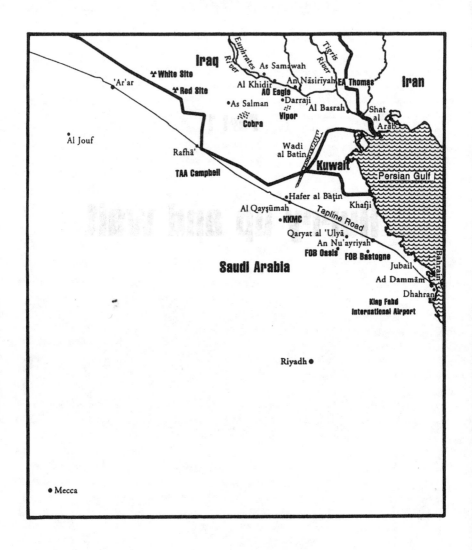

August 1990

2-3: Iraqi troops, armor and helicopters swarm into Kuwait, pushing quickly to the Saudi frontier. President Bush orders a U.S. economic embargo of Iraq.

4-6: European Community and U.N. announce similar embargoes. Saudi Arabia requests U.S. military assistance. Operation Desert Shield begins.

7-8: Bush orders combat forces to the Arabian Gulf, a total of about 50,000. Iraq declares Kuwait to be a province of Iraq, renames it and Kuwait City.

9-10: Saddam interns thousands of westerners. Several Arab League members vote to send forces to join a growing coalition against Iraq.

11-13: Sealift from U.S. begins. Saddam consolidates western hostages in a Baghdad hotel.

15-16: Iraq capitulates to Iranian terms ending their 8-year war. U.S. Navy begins blockade.

18-20: U.N. condemns Iraq for holding hostages. Saddam threatens that they will be used as "human shields."

25-27: Army calls up first reserve units. First sealift ship arrives in Saudi Arabia.

I

In Kentucky fields, the maples grow

From World War II battlefields, the jeep rolled into peacetime garages. Tanks have been converted for earth moving or fire fighting, and the U2 spy plane was adapted for weather reconnaissance. Some police and TV helicopters are modifications of military models—but there will never be a civilian version of the Apache.

Unmistakably this is a war machine, its purpose and arms conspicuous as a gladiator's entering the arena. In a McDonnell Douglas poster the Apache is shown head on, crouched for takeoff, its armament fanned out in front as if everything was fired at the moment it was photographed. The first eight rows of projectiles are 30 millimeter rounds—1200 of them—with the punch to penetrate any armor less than a tank's. They spew from a chain looped into what is called the chin gun, a heavy caliber goatee, a dangling nozzle that articulates as if the pilot is sensing the breeze.

The chin gun seems to be a snap-on-snap-off appendage, designed for easy maintenance, not aerodynamics. The nose above it bulges with oddly shaped components as though McDonnell Douglas forgot the cowling that should conceal them. Instead they protrude like objects stuck on a bulletin board. Two look like memos, one yellow and flatiron-shaped, the other oblong and blue. These, the only dabs of color, are million dollar night sight devices.

Straddling the bulletin board are what appear to be fenders from a 1930's roadster. Beneath but not contained by the fenders are two landing wheels on sturdy struts. The wheels do not retract, as if to emphasize that speed is incidental for the Apache.

Sloping planes to foil radar form the slim tandem cockpit, the pilot's seat slightly elevated behind the copilot-gunner's. Apache aviators are rarely big men. Broad shoulders wedge too close to doors on both sides. The seats are flat and not adjustable. Consoles, switches, dials and instruments crowd the crew at every level, while pedals engage the feet like a church organ.

Low on the fuselage are stubby, narrow wings that provide little lift (that come from the spinning blades). Instead the wing is more a beam to suspend four compact pylons, the 'hard points' for fuel pods, rocket clusters or Hellfire missiles. It all hangs out there like laundry on a line.

Two oversize bug-eyed turbines saddle the tail boom that seems too slender to suport them. The impression is low gear power for the swoop of four long rotor blades, converging in an 'X.' The Apache's predecessors resembled dragonflies. There is no familiar model from nature here: it's a cross between a golf cart and a thysanopteran. It seems pieced together, unfinished, a flying scaffold that should have been enclosed to streamline all those gross working parts.

Appearance counts for nothing. In no other aircraft is form so much relegated to function—and that function is to kill, to strike precisely from great distance in any light and weather conditions. Which makes the Apache a dominator of battlefields, a weapon as much a dreaded breakthrough as the first machinegun.

Flying the Apache is intimate excitement, like racing through mountains in a three-dimensional sports car.

"Gentlemen, start your engines": Switches click under nimble fingers, lights glow on, earphones sound with clips of jargon through a background rush of electrons. Feet pump pedals, turbines thunder, rotors whoosh till blades disappear in faint circles. Protruding between the aviator's knees is the joy stick, his master mechanism, the transmitter of human control.

A shuddering warmup, then the awkward ground vehicle discards the ground. Suddenly the horizon extends from the immediate surroundings without the ski jump sensation of an airliner's takeoff; instead the helicopter rocks as it ascends vertically.

It pivots to scan the new horizon as if the windshield were a wide screen periscope. The aviators seem to be out ahead of the helicopter, for they can see little of it—as if a magic carpet hurtles them toward unseen enemies below. If they fire a missile, electronic sentinels alert the two-man crew. They bend the joy stick, 'yank and bank,' pick out a dune to align it on the missile's path. Watch for it to disappear, or listen through earphones for its departure. Then bob up again and spy out the challenger.

That gully over there might be the origin of the missile. Loop in from another direction and pepper it with cannon fire. Invite the brave ones to shoot back if they're willing to fight for the sky. They get one shot at a darting target. In return their whole half acre is sprayed like a lawn sprinkler.

Then begins the search for tanks. They're the dreadnoughts of the desert, but easy pickings for the Apache. They know it, or soon will, and freeze under their camouflage and berms, fearful to raise dust or generate heat that will mark them for death. Death by Hellfire is sudden and certain. 150 pounds of high explosive homes supersonic, programmed to strike armor at the perfect angle for maximum penetration. A Hellfire could pierce a battleship, and decapitates the massive turret from a tank's hull.

Apaches crisscross the sandscape in pairs, alert to its features. The ground has killed more aviators than have all weapons. Nature's dangers must always be sensed while seeking the enemy. Give them each due respect, but for nature the highest. The enemy can be intimidated, nature can not.

Twist through the terrain, stop and go, hide then seek. When the gunner lases a target the pilot must watch for all else. He can maneuver while missiles are in flight, so long as the gunner has his laser on the target. Either aviator can fly or shoot, and one can do both. When a Hellfire is launched they coach and coax each other—"nose up, steady, steady, right pedal, hold 'er there, hold her..." Their voices overlapping are their minds joined with the missile in flight.

Time of flight spins out numerically on their helmet display. Twenty seconds TOF for a Hellfire to cover four miles. For that period the mental union must be perfect to hold the laser spot on target. A flash too distant to be heard—target destroyed. "All right!," then dash away to hide or seek, reacquaint with other patroling choppers, maybe contact friendly infantry for new targets. It's all dangerous, exhilarating, and fun—but until August of 1990 it had all been training in the Mojave Desert, or realistic but nonetheless mock combat in flight simulators.

Now in August and Saudi Arabia, it was all for real and for keeps. The Iraqis were coming—that was the general expectation—as six of Dick Cody's Apaches crouched on strip alert, ready to dash for the Kuwaiti border. In the heat shimmer of the runway, their rotor blades drooped like withered palm fronds. It was so hot—130 degrees surface temperature—Cody imagined he had strayed into the exhaust blast of one of the taxiing Air Force transports. He plodded toward the shadow of a hangar as heat from the runway invaded the soles of his boots, printing their path across the softened tarmac. For all the military aircraft crisscrossing in and out, the huge airport looked depopulated. The sun ruled, and forced its many subjects into buildings from mid morning till late afternoon.

Like their namesakes, the Apaches would first have to survive the desert before becoming its masters. During this hottest month of the year, routine functions were enough of a challenge to master. Cody had seen a mechanic wince as if scalded when touching a fuselage. How were Cody's pilots even to get in the cockpits? Flying gloves might be the answer. Soaked with sweat, they sizzled upon contact with door handles.

Cody paused for breath, recalling Doc Cornum's analysis of heat affects on the body. Respiration, pulse and blood pressure go way up as in strenuous exercise. When enduring intense heat, this is the body's way to push more blood to the skin surface to be cooled by the air. Cooled? What do you do when the air temperature is 130 degrees?

"Your body doesn't know," the flight surgeon chuckled, "and I don't either. But drink water—eight gallons a day," she advised, to produce sweat, which is the other way your body cools down. Cody swigged again at his plastic water bottle, wondering how he and the other men of 1st Battalion, 101st Aviation Regiment (1-101) could get ready for war in the summer sun of Arabia. He slouched along the hangar wall for a few more minutes. Add some minutes each time out—sort of like acquiring a tan, he reasoned—and somehow we'll acclimatize.

Cody was already tanned. Dark complected, with broad facial features and wide set eyes, his appearance suggested American Indian blood. Fittingly, army helicopter models were named for Indian tribes. At 5'10" and a kinetic 180 lbs, Cody looked cut out for the Kiowa scout helicopter rather than the hard angled Apache.* Like camels of Arabia, his Apaches were not graceful but efficient—and utterly essential in the desert. Gen. Schwarzkopf had ordered them immediately out front where he needed tank killers more than any other force.

That's where they wanted to be: Apache aviators were out to prove that a tank was no longer the best anti-tank weapon, as had been the case since World War II. Instead they were nervous to demonstrate that just as bombers had sunk warships since Pearl Harbor, helicopters would now be the nemesis of tanks. "If we don't stop 'em all," Cody opined on CNN, "we'll kill about 200 before Saddam gets close to Dhahran."

Saddam Hussein swallowed Kuwait in forty-eight hours,

---

* An attack battalion like 1-101 had 19 Apaches, 12 Kiowas, and a Black Hawk.

beginning on August 2, 1990, Cody's 40th birthday. He'd hoped to get home early and perhaps take his wife to dinner for a small celebration; but there was an out of channels project that had occupied him, and kept him at the office late that afternoon. A colonel at the Pentagon had contacted him a week earlier in a way quite abnormal for the army's rigid adherence to the chain of command. This colonel said his job was to monitor the combat readiness of Apache battalions throughout the world, and had noticed how 1-101's aircraft availability rate regularly surpassed similar units. Basically, the colonel wanted to know how Cody did it. This had required him to duplicate and expand on certain information, then transmit it back channel to the colonel in the Pentagon. Such a report tied Cody to his desk beyond quitting time on August 2nd.

Tom Greco, a West Point classmate and an infantry battalion commander in the Third Brigade, finally dislodged him, convincing Cody that he'd miss his only chance for a free beer until age fifty unless he accompanied Greco to the Officers Club forthwith. The beer was a pitcher, half consumed when Cody was paged from the bar. On the phone, Mike Davis, the battalion operations officer (S3), spoke excitedly: there had been an accident at home—at Cody's house. Could he get right over? Cody dropped the phone, raced out of the bar, and ran stop signs as his Corvette careened through Ft. Campbell, Kentucky.

He burst in the front door—to recoil before the cheers and clinking glasses that greeted him. Conspiring with Cody's wife, Vicki, his officers had planned a surprise party, and during his overtime at work they had grown impatient for his arrival.

With a glare at Greco and Davis for their cruel complot, Cody accepted backslaps and kidding. He is a man who unwinds easily, as much a comrade as commander of the men in his battalion. Well lubricated, the party went on till Cody was paged again. This time it was his mother in Vermont, calling with birthday good wishes.

Toward the end of the conversation, she asked if he'd been watching TV. No?—then he ought to turn on a news channel. Something about the Persian Gulf and a war going on. With his mother's admonition to stay out of it, Cody flicked to CNN. Soon the party was grouped around the set as if watching a one sided football game. The time at Ft. Campbell was ten hours earlier than Kuwait's. When news of the invasion broke, it had already been completed.

The news became an explanation for the Pentagon colonel's peculiar interest in the 1-101. "I'd always had a feeling he wasn't just interested in how we did maintenance," Cody recalled. "From the first time he called I had a hunch it was for something operational. I was so sure, I had Davis sharpen up our deployment plans. There wasn't anything going on in the Gulf that I knew of—I was thinking Central America—but I thought a lot about our readiness to deploy anywhere."

The 101st Airborne Division was alerted five days later. 'C' (Commencement) Day, August 7th was called, when 18,000 Screaming Eagles, with their 400 helicopters, 500 vehicles and a thousand tons of machinery, began to move out for the other side of the world. The division deployment plan called for three brigade-size packages, each balanced in ground and air elements, to depart sequentially.

Such was the plan, but Cody suspected early on that it would not apply to 1-101. After C Day, the colonel in the Pentagon began to indicate as much. Schwarzkopf wanted Apaches, even if they were taken out of the planned packages. Consequently, Cody found himself being briefed by the division staff about a deployment plan he knew would be superseded as it applied to his choppers.

"There I was, a light colonel, listening to the senior staff describe how and when we'd be leaving for Saudi Arabia, but all the time I'm sitting there knowing that things were going to be different. It was like watching a mystery movie for the second time with someone who hasn't seen it. I let Second Brigade know that my battalion might move up in priority, but meantime we followed the division plan right down the line."

Cody's forecast came true. Hurriedly, his choppers were stripped out of the division, disassembled and slid into the cavernous maws of the Air Force's largest transports.

"It reminded me of when the starting lineup goes out on the field before the Super Bowl. The rest of the team is coming, but first they form a tunnel to slap your butt while you go out ahead. It was great to get all that support. But we had less time to get things settled at home. That was tougher for our families, but in a way it was easier for the guys. We just shuffled through the processing, then we were gone. It was a couple of months before all the rest of the division got over there."

'Processing' was called P-O-R (permanent overseas replacement), a grim army ritual as unchanged as reveille. In 1990, the Screaming Eagles seemed a continuation of a ghostly queue from earlier wars, the subdued assembly line down halls and between desks where the army prepared itself for the worst by making its soldiers think about it: checking off contingencies in self cancelling phrases like 'death benefits,' or snapping full-mouth dental x rays so that a corpse could be identified no matter how mutilated. Wills and powers of attorney had to be signed, eye glasses checked for use in gas masks. At the end of P-O-R, the chaplain's station was well attended.

Still aching and groggy from a battery of inoculations, 1-101 and Arabic linguists assembled at Ft. Campbell Army Airfield. Driven to their departure in family cars, most of the men found final words missing in action.

Too much had been sudden, the rush and orders and summons to the phone, too many 'final' changes as conflicting requirements overlapped across Ft. Campbell like buckshot fired into a pond. In the past, it had been routine for brigade-size task forces to depart the base but always with the rest of the 101st available to support the send off. Now all the Screaming Eagles were loading up to ship out, pulling in the gangplank as they hauled themselves aboard. There had been no equivalent overseas deployment for the entire division since 1943.

So it was a relief for the first task force to have 'getting ready' be over. Climbing the ramp into an airliner was like crossing a starting line, leaving preparation and turmoil behind. The men felt guilty—the reason their farewells were laconic—about the new tasks devolving to their families. Guilty yet grateful to hand over those tasks. There had been too little time, too much scurry and distraction, even to go over them together. Forgotten details rose in the mind like the climb of the outbound airliner; many first letters were begun while it still gained altitude. But to be en route was no less a relief—we're off, we've begun, and that had to be the beginning of coming back.

Cody's recollection of the battalion's whirlwind departure was how 'hungry' his crews were. Nine months earlier they had stood in readiness on this same tarmac; their destination was to be Panama in Operation Just Cause. He'd hoped they would 'self-deploy'—hop around the Gulf of Mexico from Texas to Yucatan, Honduras, into the Canal Zone. This plan Cody had proposed would have put more Apaches in action faster than the 82nd Airborne Division could move theirs across the Caribbean in Air Force transports.

But high level army politics had given the job to the 82nd. The Screaming Eagles were crestfallen to lose the mission to their arch rivals, hooting "I told you so" when many commentators, in and out of the army, wrote that the 82nd's Apaches did not distinguish themselves in Panama, an opinion which Cody felt unjustly tarnished the reputation of the aircraft. His crews would rather hear their mothers insulted than a bad word about the Apache. Based on the Panama experience, little good had been said about it.

More units moved up to the departure airfield in convoys while the families of 1-101 drove away. The airstream between Kentucky and Dhahran began to siphon a huge vessel to fill a distant one, as part of the most titanic military deployment since World War II. When completed, it amounted to the transplantation of the state of Alaska—a widely scattered population of a half million people, with all their vehicles, fixtures, furnishings and machinery. Hundreds of thousands of tons for the 101st were shipped by air, land and sea half a world away—with round trip mileage more than four times the distance to the moon.

Having gone out ahead of schedule, 1-101 missed the most intense period of the division's deployment, when weight was as precious as space in the sky trains. Both factors were rigidly controlled, a test of discipline as much as logistics.

Every soldier (700 of them were women) had to mount scales at the airfield and weigh in with all the gear he or she was carrying, including weapons. Four hundred pounds was the limit—that included the body. Anything more, even reading material, stayed on the ground. It was a procrustean policy, very unpopular, but enforced without exception for rank or physique. This was a prelude to austerity, as this would be the Screaming Eagles' most austere war.

The boarding troops found themselves in a twilight zone between war and peace. Filing across the runway in full battle gear—everything but camouflage paint on their faces, and weapons in hands (unloaded)—their thoughts blew to and fro amid conflicting rumors. The first one was that Saddam would pull out when he saw what he was up against. The other rumor was that he would have to attack before the U.S. build up. Prior to boarding, clusters of soldiers speculated how they could receive ground fire while landing at Dhahran. Officers reminded them that this was the air assault division—be ready for anything as soon as you hit the ground. Common rumor was that the arrival runway might be under fire like the airport in Grenada.

"So we look like we're going into combat," 'Sarge' recalled,* "but we walk out to a Northwest DC-10 with a stewardess smiling at the top of the steps, just like this was some commercial flight to Chicago. We've each got a regular boarding pass and give it to her. Really weird. You look down the aisle and everyone's trying to cram weapons and helmets into the overhead, but also looking for stuff to read. One guy said, 'Find a magazine?' His buddy looked at him funny and clicked one out of his M16!"

Shortage of transports changed scheduled departures day by day. Convoys converged on the airfield like filings to a magnet. After brave farewells, often a battalion scheduled for airlift arrived to learn their planes were delayed or diverted. Then it was back to unlock their barracks, reopen windows, and lounge on bedsprings till they were called up to the airfield again. For the married soldiers, parting was such repeated sorrow that Vicki Cody told Dick not to come back if his departure was postponed yet again. She had seen his smirk as her husband related how with each postponement the men described 'sympathy sex' that had been bestowed upon them.

---

* All interviewees were offered anonymity, though only few like 'Sarge' preferred it.

So Vicki had deliberately planned their last bedding. Their two sons, Clinton, eleven, and Tyler, nine, had been diverted, the room prepared, the phone turned off, and the union as memorable as hoped for—but that was *it* for Vicki: no more coupling till he returned safely to her arms.

"I wanted *that* to be my memory. No anti-climaxes. If we never touched again—the best would be the last. That may have confused him. He had so much on his mind then. We didn't sort it out at the time. My attitude may have rubbed off on him. When he left Dick was pretty formal with the boys. No tears, no long hugs. I didn't cry either. That really surprised me. It was like this was the occasion when he had to become 'official.' I did too. As the wife of the CO, I was the 'voice from above' for all the other wives in the battalion. It's strange, if you stop and look at it, that the wives were supposed to mirror the military chain of command. Just because I'm married to Dick, does that make me the wives' mentor? Is the chaplain the mentor at a funeral? But that's the army way. I had to take the role, like it or not.

"It was like someone had dropped a cloak of authority over me. I didn't want to wear it, but there it was, draped over my shoulders. At first I looked at it as a challenge, the first opportunity in my life to be both independent and a leader. That didn't last long: the sadness and loneliness took over as soon as he left."

Cody was already wearing the cloak, but now everyone was looking at it—because he was so far out on a limb. In a chapel he had convened 1-101 with their families. There, to all assembled, he'd said, "I'm going to bring every guy back alive." Not that he was going to try. Not that he was going to do his best. Not that he was going to make sure no one was lost unnecessarily. "Nope—it was a *promise*," Vicki recalled the slack jawed reaction, "a pledge: 'I, Dick Cody, hereby go on record, stating that every one of your husbands, fathers, brothers, boyfriends [nearly 400 of them] will come back alive.'"

The wives knew how the Apaches and Kiowas would be way out in front of the division—exposed, the most vulnerable. What they were thinking was that their husbands were the most 'killable' soldiers in the Gulf.

What Cody announced in church was unbelievable, but everyone tried to believe it. They wanted to but wouldn't let on that they did. So as not to embarrass Vicki, they refrained from asking if her husband was serious.

"Everything he did in the war, from what I heard, was driven by that wild ass promise he made in public, in church, that day in August 1990 before anyone had even deployed to the Gulf. I believe in my husband—oh, how I believe in him—but I couldn't believe what he'd said.

"How could I? How could anyone who heard him? We wanted to, so we didn't say anything. Even me, not even in my letters. There wasn't time to think about what he'd said in all the rush-rush of deployment. We thought about it later. I don't know, but if the other women thought about it as much as I did, they thought about it all the time. Our men were over there. We had to believe in something, even if it was an unbelievable promise."

For the next six months there was reason to believe. Some serious accidents in the desert, and a suicide, but the Screaming Eagles seemed to defy probabilities. Then from official sources at Ft. Campbell as well as the flood of media reports, came another promise, that of a ground war. No rumor this time. President Bush said as much. The world was counting down.

And Ft. Campbell braced. The post commander, John Seymour, and the 101st's rear detachment commander, Dan Lynn, consulted over a dreaded contingency plan with the antiseptic name, 'notification procedures.' The procedures had to be explained to the wives' support groups, the details of how they would be advised that their husbands had been killed.

Seymour and Lynn winced, but it had to be done, even knowing that communal memory would flash back to 12 December 1985, a searing day of catastrophe described by another bureaucratic phrase that would once again be whispered all over Ft. Campbell—'mass casualties.'

In 1991, recollection would merge with reality, and Cody's promise of last August be mocked by Bush's in February. The waiting wives could remember how Screaming Eagles perished during an earlier mission in the Middle East, for tragedy,

34

majesty and misery had been written into the division's history:

Sixty medallions—souvenirs of desert service—found melted by burning fuel at a crash site, medallions carried in the pockets, barracks bags and shaving kits of the 248 soldiers who had died together. The globs of metal still trailed wisps of smoke as they were collected in scattered debris.

Eight days later, the medallions lie in rows on a felt-covered table at Ft. Campbell.

"You'll carry these always," the commander tells surviving comrades, formed up in front of the display. Then he calls them forward, one by one, to present each a charred medallion, its original ownership unknown after the crucible of the crash.

There is another paralyzing memento, the molten tip of a company guidon, fire blackened like a poker. Ashen, finger lengths of battle streamers crumble upon touch. There was no way to identify the company either, so it becomes an artifact of the battalion.

A few hours after the presentation, the battalion stands in bitter cold of a Kentucky winter. In hoarse voices they sing "Rendezvous with Destiny," distantly echoed from loudspeakers throughout Ft. Campbell. The Secretary of the Army and Chief of Staff listen as howitzers boom 248 times in slow succession, the name of a soldier read between each salute.

The President witnesses the arrival of caskets. The massive doors of the Air Force's largest transport slowly swing open like a curtain being drawn.

Those were wrenching scenes in the aftermath of the crash at Gander, Newfoundland, but such recollections seemed also a spectral preview. There was also a permanent and adumbrating reminder: a grove of 248 maples, a gift of condolence from the people of Canada, planted in rows near the center of Ft. Campbell.

The maples seemed to grow faster, beginning in August 1990. Families of the Gander tragedy had departed in their grief five years earlier. Now memories of their ordeal returned—crushing, ghostly—and by one measure worse for the wives who had rushed to console in 1985:

In 1985, mass casualities were suffered without any warning.

In 1990, Ft. Campbell was meticulously preparing for them. Whatever else was said, whatever distractions were real or contrived, whatever alarms were subdued and hopes endorsed, the maples grew and spread their shade as if more must surely be added. Many more, because the Screaming Eagles— for the third time in their history—had soared away to do battle. They were gone from Ft. Campbell to a leafless desert, but their families drove under maple leaves every day.

Every day of September, October, November, December, January and February. That was the worst of the waiting; that's why the meaning of worry was almost trivial in the desert compared to its significance in the shade of a maple grove.

August 1990 would be remembered for 'deployment'—the beginning of the beginning—at military bases all over the country. Events were building but not in a discernable pyramid toward an inevitable climax. Events instead were sprouting, independently and unlayered, as if prospects of war and peace grew in competition.

6-8: Saudi Arabia agrees to provide billions of dollars to support Operation Desert Shield. In Helsinki, Bush and Gorbachev meet to discuss the Gulf crisis.

10: To break the embargo, Saddam offers free oil to Third World countries.

17: Air Force Chief of Staff Gen. Dugan is fired for revealing that in the event of war, Saddam and his high command will be targeted for air strikes.

II

A call from SOCCENT

No one in the 101st knew whether there was a deadline for completing deployment to the Gulf. It was the Iraqi army which had a finite period in which to invade Saudi Arabia before enough ground forces gathered to block them, and Schwarzkopf gave no hint as to how fast Saddam's window of opportunity was closing.

A watcher of American TV, Saddam saw about as much as most people knew at Ft. Campbell. The most pessimistic rumors prevailed over optimism in an application of Gresham's Law. All that could be seen and heard indicated commitment of the 101st "for the duration"—a forgotten phrase from World War II, meaning till the war was over. Countervailing rumor was that there would be no war, just a show of force, but all news from the Gulf spoke otherwise.

The media pursued that expectation. Nine TV satellite trucks parked on civilian farmland rented near the end of Ft. Campbell's runway. They shot monotonous footage: airliners and transports poking above the treeline, ascending as wheels retracted, sloping higher with a thin plume of black exhaust, then on to disappear over the northeastern horizon.

"You could tell which unit was taking off," said Chaplain

Kitchens, "by watching the crowd on the ground. Wives of the passengers held each others hands.

"The planes climbed very slowly. Maybe it was because they were so heavily loaded, but I think the pilots wanted to give us one last, long look—something to remember if men didn't come back."

Troops and vehicles noisily converging on the airfield were like the insurge of waves, while the families who had seen their soldiers off were the receding tide. For mothers leading children back to their cars, none of the convoys rumbling through Ft. Campbell could distract them from the silence of the maple grove as they drove home, now single parents.

Many felt a conflicting ambivalence. They wished to be alone with private thoughts, yet in the company of other wives. They sought a new normality, but it was tinged with guilt about the utter abnormality in store for those en route to the Middle East. Most of all, the families were anxious to get things settled, to learn to live with the new situation, to make sure they could handle it.

There was a 24-hour hotline for those who felt they were faltering. The first decision was where to live, a subject incompletely discussed by the spouses before departure. No dependents had to leave Ft. Campbell, and very few did. Some wanted to wait out the crisis with parents. Though that distanced them from the shade of the maples, it also put them in a completely civilian world where no one else was going through the same experience. For the most part, fear was better endured with army friends.

So usually by desire, but sometimes by peer pressure, nearly everyone who waited at Ft. Campbell was soon involved in a support group, often several.* The concept was well developed from previous brigade and smaller size deployments. For years, wives of each unit had organized to meet common needs while their men were far away training. This time, however, family finances presented new problems. Car repairs formerly done by a husband were now an expense for his wife. Soon

---

* Besides support for units, there were specialty groups for foreign wives, wives with problem children, working wives, etc.

phone bills soared when the voice of a loved one in Saudi Arabia was worth any price.

Recent history was prodding the division almost as much as the world crisis to which they were moving. The 101st had been uninvited to Grenada and Panama—so it was said—because their 400 helicopters and impedimenta were too cumbersome for the rapid strategic movement required by these brushfires. Peay, the 101st's commanding general, was not about to let that Pentagonian excuse surface again. After Panama he directed a searching examination of the division, a process called Slim Eagle, to ferret out all vehicles and equipment that could go overseas by ship rather than airplane. Stripping out about a fifth of the 101st's gross tonnage for sealift, he demonstrated that the Screaming Eagles would now be much quicker off the mark.* Nothing was more prominent in Peay's thoughts than to prove his division was light enough, fast enough to go to war in strength and in the lead. His greatest satisfaction in Desert Shield was to do exactly that: the 101st was the first division to 'close' in Saudi Arabia; i.e., deemed to be ready for combat, even before the lighter 82nd or any Marine division.

But to close first, the 101st had to come from behind. Simply collecting the division for deployment was a huge centripetal process. On August 2nd, Screaming Eagles were scattered throughout the western hemisphere: notably a battalion training cadets at West Point, one conducting jungle exercises in Panama, another about to depart for the Sinai, helicopters in Central America, and key officers evaluating National Guardsmen in several states. Peay himself was on leave in Virginia.

TV news was like a bugle sounding assembly, but specific instructions lagged as the Pentagon deliberated the U.S. response. A Chinook pilot in Honduras was impatient for orders, and decided he should talk to his boss about it. He climbed into the sky "till the rotors smoked," high enough for his radio to reach Ft. Campbell some 1500 miles away. There, an unbeliev-

---

* In 1984 on the 40th Anniversary of Operation Overlord, my father wrote a commemorative letter to the 18th Airborne Corps commander, and in it lamented that the heliborne 101st was now too heavy to carry off the same airborne operation it had as paratroopers and glidermen in Normandy.

able call sign came on the air. Yeah, start coming home, the pilot was told—but first get down into your operating altitude.

Already in Saudi Arabia, ahead and temporarily detached from the 101st, Cody's battalion had gone out with the vanguard of the 82nd, both divisions along with the 24th Mechanized Division, comprising the 18th Airborne Corps—abbreviated 18th ABC, or simply 'corps.' With two Marine divisions, 18th ABC was Schwarzkopf's ground force for the Middle East, his military realm called Central Command (CENTCOM), of which he was commander in chief (CINCCENT). Supported by hundreds of fighters and bombers, his divisions began to stream across the Atlantic till there was one ship every fifty miles. The pipeline was open, but like an unused faucet it began to surge with splashes, belches and exasperating pauses. Upon reaching Saudi Arabia, the leading units staked out claims like the first settlers of Oklahoma. "It's a land grab," Brigadier Gen. Hugh Shelton reported back to Peay.

With the 101st still mustering out of Ft. Campbell, Cody's tank killing task force was controlled by the 82nd. He was to head north a hundred miles, beyond Jubail where the 82nd was settling on the coast, close to the Kuwaiti border to back up the thin screen of Saudi forces that would be the trip wire if Saddam risked a second invasion. Cody's Apaches were a component of the aerial armada already assembled to meet the threat. The US Navy's carriers *Forrestal* and *Kennedy* steamed into the Gulf, and CENTCOM's Air Force was setting up in Dhahran and Riyadh. Even at this early date—17 August—the Americans controlled the skies as much as Saddam dominated the sands. Cody's domain was the gritty haze in between.

1-101 leapfrogged up the coast, lifting their supplies with their own choppers, which weren't much good for hauling cargo so it was done in relays. They were to backstop the Saudis but weren't allowed to fly closer than twenty kilometers from the border. Through a molten haze they could see occupied Kuwait, and for practice sighted on Saudi vehicles whose tanks, moving cross country, raised a dust plume the Apaches could pick up right away. Night surveillance was no harder with infrared radar. On the roads, vehicles looked like ants coming down a straw. 1-101 became confident they would score better than seventy percent if the Hellfires worked, but they were too scarce to use for practice.

Cody's optimism became national news when reporters cornered him. He told them his task force would kill about 200 tanks before the Iraqis got close to Dhahran.

"I saw a little news over there, and heard a lot about what was being shown in the States. It seemed to be all gee whiz stuff about how strong the Iraqis were. To me, this was Saddam's psychological warfare to scare America. I thought I'd do a little counter-psychology through the reporters. That's why I called that 200 number."

It drew a reaction. Shortly after Peay's arrival, but before his staff could set up a proper briefing room, CINCCENT himself came down from Riyadh to visit the incoming Screaming Eagles. For nearly a month, 1-101 had improved their command post in an unfinished baggage claim room of the cavernous terminal. Peay inspected Cody's setup, and determined that he had the best accommodations for Schwarzkopf's briefing. Would that be all right with Cody? Peay inquired unnecessarily.

So as the nominal host, sort of captain of the admiral's flagship, Cody was introduced to CINCCENT when otherwise he would have been 'on the wall,' a horse holder with other lieutenant colonels if he were to attend the briefing at all.

"I popped a salute, and sounded off, 'First to fight,' sir!"

That was the motto of the 24th Division, which Schwarzkopf had commanded some years before while Cody served many echelons below him. The general comprehended the greeting, and while taking Cody's hand, slid the other around his shoulder.

"Ah, Cody—glad you're here." Cody tensed as he felt The Bear's hug that moved the two away from the assembled officers. Inaudible to the others, Schwarzkopf continued in a tone less intense than his eyes. "That's great work you're doing up there on the border, son. Just do one other thing for me, OK? Stay away from the reporters."

Though he sat in the front row, Cody remembered nothing from the briefing. "I'd done it again, I guess—raised my profile and got my ass shot. I still think it wasn't such a bad idea, telling the Iraqis that we'd trash their tanks. Let 'em know so they'd worry. That's what they were trying to do to us.

"I couldn't let what Schwarzkopf said get to me. I tell my captains sometimes, disagreement doesn't mean disrespect. I couldn't let even the CINC change my azimuth and power setting."

Though an army man to the core (West Point class of 1972), Cody at times talks more like a fighter pilot. He and the men of 1-101 wore the same gray flight suits as the Air Force; indeed, the Army had more aircraft and pilots.

"We work in the air but we're oriented on the ground. The Air Force likes the wild blue yonder, way up there at supersonic speeds, clear air, one on one against other high performance aircraft, and dodging SAM's. Down near the ground some rifleman can do them in with a lucky shot. They have some great ground support planes, and plenty of pilots who like to mix it up at close range, but the Air Force is mainly oriented on higher altitudes. We stay low and stay a long time around our targets. It's sort of the difference between fighting with pistols or knives."

The Army's pilots are also at another important margin, that of rank. Except for Cody, his principal staff and company commanders, the Apache cockpits were filled by warrant officers, a grade between enlisted men and commissioned officers. In the Air Force, all pilots are commissioned and college graduates, often with advanced degrees, with an average age of thirty something. Chopper pilots typically have an associate degree, with an average age in the twenties.

Cody: "What the Air Force does is pretty much an end unto itself—clear the sky and drop bombs. What our warrants do—and me too—is what an infantryman tells us to do. Aviation in the US Army is not its own boss. We're here for the ground guys and we like it that way. In our flight suits we look like the Air Force but we're not the same breed. I won't say we're a better breed—the Air Force is absolutely super at what it does—but we're a different breed."

It may be an atavistic breed. LIke the Red Barons of the first war in the air, chopper pilots fly slow and low, ever vulnerable to ground fire, down in the nape of the earth. In Saudi Arabia, the nape was the most hostile on earth for flying. From the shadow of the hanger, Cody looked again at his Apaches' rotor blades drooping in the heat like palm fronds. On the forward curve of the blades was a 'war stopper' for 1-101. It was called the leading edge problem.

"Ther're several things about desert flying that degrade performance. First, the extremely high air temperature means less lift, so you can't carry much very far. Second, the dust gets into all the moving parts—thousands of them—and clogs filters."

But the worst effect is abrasion on the leading edge of the rotor blades. They spin at supersonic speed. That's the popping sound when choppers fly—the blades breaking the sound barrier. Whirling through dust is like filing with an emery board. The leading edges wear down ten times quicker. When they're pitted, the whole blade (wing) wobbles, shaking the aircraft like an unbalanced washing machine. When the blade goes, the whole wing must be replaced.

There was no stockpile of Apache wings. If the leading edges became badly pitted, 1-101—and Schwarzkopf's answer to Saddam's tanks—would soon be as silent as the Apaches crouched on the melting tarmac.

There were two miles of tarmac in front of the vast complex under construction, about fifty miles from Dhahran off the highway to Riyadh, called King Fahd International Airport. After seven years of work, King Fahd was about 70 percent complete. In size it already rivaled Chicago's O'Hare, with plans for even a separate royal terminal to accommodate traveling monarchs. When completed, the airport would be the largest in the world.

Almost all the arriving Screaming Eagles would camp out in the desert that surrounded the airport, living in nine-man tents designed by Arabs for Islamic pilgrims to Mecca. High tech aircraft needed less primitive protection from the elements. Without any hangars available to the 101st at King Fahd, Cody had to arm wrestle with the Air Force for ramp space.

1-101 flew in early and parked on the tarmac. The Air Force wanted them off the ramps, but Cody wasn't about to move out on the sand. When a chopper takes off, it's like a vacuum cleaner. On sand, that sucks a lot of dust up into the moving parts. Tom Garrett—a full colonel and the Aviation Brigade Commander—went to the mat so that choppers could keep their squatter's rights. Temporarily defied, the Air Force crowded in around 1-101 as if they were motorboats in the middle of a navy.

The other military tenant at King Fahd was a hush-hush organization called SOCCENT—Special Operations Command for Central Command. Essentially, SOCCENT's mission was to conduct warfare behind the Iraqi lines, and to do so they employed the Army's special forces, the Navy's SEAL's, and assorted Air Force assets. The ultra elite, super secret Delta Force was also on tap, and the CIA represented at SOCCENT.

A Screaming Eagle would have sooner entered a Chernobyl reactor than approach a building set aside for SOCCENT. Anything relating to them was not only top secret but also SCI—special compartmented information. Even speaking to someone from SOCCENT was like an ordinary priest trying to strike up conversation with a Carmelite nun.

Such mutually imposed silence held fast even in the contiguous confines of King Fahd. SOCCENT maintained its own mess halls and latrines, erected its own security barriers and posted its own guards, when cooperation with King Fahd's other tenants would have produced efficiencies for all.

Some interesting looking aircraft were sometimes parked around SOCCENT, but otherwise Cody hardly gave his reclusive neighbors a glance. With many acquaintances from eighteen years in the army, some of them were probably working next door, but he made no effort to find out. It would be awkward, and they were no doubt as busy as he.

Late in another steamy morning, the kind Shelton described as "standing in the boiler room for hell," Cody had been on the flight line where he worked more often than at his desk. The first 'Memorandum of Call' he saw skewered on a nail was from Garrett who had been the previous commander of 1-101, and thus an Apache proponent. Cody rang his extension, thinking that the ramp hassle with the Air Force might not be over.

"What's up, sir?"

"Come on over. We're going to see Col. Johnson."

Bad news. Jesse Johnson was commander of SOCCENT, a position equivalent to a brigadier general's. If he wanted to evict 1-101 from the tarmac, this could be a showdown. As he walked through the heat shimmer, Cody wondered if Shelton could be persuaded to pull rank.

A green bereted sergeant awaited Garrett and Cody at the barb wire. They produced ID cards which the sergeant compared with their faces; then without a word they entered the inner sanctum. Cody's respect overcame his curiosity, so he looked to neither side as if he were walking through a ladies room.

Unfurling a large scale Air Force map of the upper Arabian peninsula, Jesse Johnson acted like a man who needed some answers in a hurry—and couldn't care less about ramp space. Southwestern Iraq was sprinkled with symbols of radar sites.

He began by asking whether the Iraqis could be stopped if they attacked into Saudi Arabia. This was what Desert Shield was all about. Cody repeated his seventy percent kill estimate with Hellfires. But Johnson's brows arched when Garrett cautioned that 1-101 had only two hundred Hellfires on hand—only about ten per Apache.

"I saw on TV that you'd pop 200 tanks," Johnson smiled. "Isn't that about one per Hellfire?"

"Gen. Schwarzkopf classified my estimate, sir," said Cody with a straight face.

The colonels chuckled, then Johnson turned serious: "When are you going to get more Hellfires?"

"When they get higher priority in the pipeline," Garrett replied.

Johnson jotted himself a note. "Well, CENTCOM is beginning to look beyond Desert Shield, you might say. Time may come when we carry the war to Iraq. That'll be an air campaign, at least initially. If there's an allied ground offensive it will be after we soften 'em up from the air."

"Good."

Johnson tapped the picket of radar sites within Iraq's border. "The first strike will be crucial. It's got to take down Saddam's air defense system—which is world class. If we can do that, the Air Force and Navy can go in and bomb at will."

"Roger."

"We'd like to punch a hole in his radar fence. We might want to do it even before—right before—the first strike." Now Johnson was looking directly at Cody. "There are a number of ways of doing that, and one of them could be with Apaches, don't you think?"

Cody sat up straighter, thinking this is SOCCENT, with every weapon in the Defense Department at its disposal—stealth bombers, cruise missiles, plus paratroopers and commandos from every service and several nations on call. Not to mention Task Force 160, reputed to be the best special missions helicopter squadron in the world. But Johnson was looking at Cody, while questioning Garrett about Apache 'reliability.' Undetectably, both Apache pilots bridled. It was the bad rap from Panama again and there seemed to be no way to live it down.

But now, cleverly, Johnson began to hint there might be a way:

"My job is to look at all the options. Let me ask you some things about range and pay loads, OK?"

"Sure." Cody's pulse rate fell. Probably TF 160's gunnery experts were elsewhere, and Johnson wanted some data fast to brief higher ups in Riyadh. "If you need range over the desert, sir, fly at night when the air's cooler," Cody began in a general way. "How far do you want to go?"

"Say, five hundred miles tactical—round trip."

"How are you going to arm, sir?"

"Don't know yet. There're four racks for armament, right? Assume all racks are loaded with Hellfires."

The aviators looked at each other. Johnson seemed to be talking about Apaches—and *he* didn't have any.

"Two-fifty out?" Cody asked, and Johnson nodded. "You can't get there from here. Two hard points have to carry the fuel pods."

"Those have to be dropped before an attack?"

"Affirmative, sir." Cody offered to go back and get the model Apache he kept on his desk so he could demonstrate the problem, but Johnson continued:

"Then I guess we'd need twice the number of Apaches, with two pods each and two Hellfire racks."

Johnson seemed to be mentally calculating when Garrett asked what was foremost in Cody's mind: "How many Apaches were you considering, Jesse?"

"Oh...six or eight. But maybe now we'll have to think twelve or more. That's about all you got, right?"

"Up and running. This sand is a bitch. Leading edges, you know."

"Yeah. Well, we're interested in the minimum number of aircraft to do the job."

"Could I see what the targets are?" Cody asked.

Johnson hesitated for a moment. "All right." He opened a drawer and slid some annotated photos across the desk.

While an air conditioner hummed, Garrett and Cody spent several minutes examining the unfamiliar objects and their labels on the photos. Johnson advised that 'FF' meant flat face and 'SR' meant spoon rest. These, along with 'tropo' for tropospheric scatter, were descriptors for the types of Iraqi radar and radios at a typical site. Additionally there were structures identified as a generator, communications bunker, and barracks, all enclosed by a sand berm.

"Hmmm," Cody concluded his musing, "Can't tell you exactly how to go after a site like this. Covers a pretty big area, doesn't it?"

"About ten acres."

"Tell you one thing, sir: you'll need more than Hellfires. How many troops you think are in that barrack?"

"Fifty. Probably half of them pull shifts around the site, so they all won't be in the barrack at one time."

"Roger. So that means you'd need fleshette rockets, plus a full chain of thirty millimeter in your chin gun. You don't want those troops coming out and firing at you with their individual weapons."

"No we don't. And the raid needs to be completed in about five minutes, so there'd be maybe only one pass at the targets. Figure that in."

"We've never done it, sir, but this looks like you'd have to drop fuel pods for rockets. Do the targets have to be totaled?"

Johnson nodded vigorously. "In that case, duplicate the radar site in the desert here, and my guys will work it over. That's the only way to get a good damage estimate."

"I think we could do that," said Johnson casually. "Think you'd be interested in this sort of job?"

Garrett and Cody glanced at each other. Thoughts like validation and vindication flashed between them telepathically. As the senior officer, it was for Garrett to reply:

"I think we would. Might answer some questions and critics."

With a gulp, Cody recognized the intimation that his Apaches were being volunteered for what would be a SOCCENT experiment. 1-101 was already flying maximum hours in support of the Saudis on the border. What little time was left after maintenance—maintenance much more extensive in this dust bowl than had been required in Kentucky—was needed for desert training with the 101st's infantry who were pouring into Dhahran by the hundreds every day. Cody could picture Shelton's reaction if his tank-stoppers were pulled out to run some hypothetical war game for SOCCENT.

Shelton was as tall and unflappable as Abe Lincoln. Except by the furnace of Saudi Arabia, Shelton had yet to be steamed. When he learned that his precious few Apaches had been volunteered for an experiment, Cody would be the first scalded. And newly arrived from Ft. Campbell was Gen. Peay. Tight knit and tidy, no one had ever seen the number one eagle scream. This could be another first for Cody.

Garrett glanced at his watch. "We need to be getting back."

"Much obliged for coming by," Johnson smiled.

"Don't mention it, Jesse."

Please don't mention it, Cody thought, as he trudged beside Garrett back across the sticky tarmac—don't raise my profile again. Schwarzkopf's disfavor was enough to live down without crossing the stars of two more generals.

But the possibility of the radar raid set his mind into a tug of war. Rehearsals for what surely would be a low level attack meant multiplying sand abrasion on the leading edges. If Hellfires, so scarce throughout the theater, were diverted to him, other Apache commanders would howl and still other generals growl. Yet that might be the least of Cody's dilemma. He imagined himself standing before Shelton and Peay. He could hear their reminder of who he worked for, and maybe a reference to the green beret colonel in Vietnam who thought the CIA was his boss. That colonel was soon a civilian, now running a program called Outward Bound.

That could be Cody's direction as well. But, oh, that raid. Let's see: there was Doolittle's thirty seconds over Tokyo. Not much damage, and all the aircraft were lost, but a big morale builder for America early in World War II. Then there was Son Tay in North Vietnam. Great execution but the POW's weren't in the camp that was so effectively raided. Desert One in Iran—a national humiliation. The radar raid wouldn't be quite on the scale of its predecessors, yet could be more successful by important measures, and equally bold.

Bold—some would say brash—was a Cody adjective. He could make this raid work, make it work better than anyone else—if he got the chance. No one in the army knew Apaches like Cody. It's got to be 1-101, he vowed to the scowling generals in his imagination. Fate decreed it, and Vicki had foretold it:

"When his plane took off from Ft. Campbell, I had this feeling that Dick would do something very special over there. It was like fate was ringing a bell for him. Everyone else heard a fire alarm. He was pumped up for something dangerous, something that would make 1-101 famous."

1-101. Those Apaches crouched on the runway, their rotors drooping in the heat. Apaches and their crews, men whom Cody had promised to bring back alive, each and every one. Dangerous enough was their work now, but Cody wanted to maneuver them into danger of glorious proportions. Volunteers? Hell, they'd swarm over each other to go. Already he began to worry how he could select among them. In spite of the pulsing heat, he felt himself shiver.

September 1990

22: At the Dhahran Officers Club, Schwarzkopf appoints local U.S. commanders to be responsible for good cultural relations with the Saudis.

23: Saddam threatens to destroy Israel and middle east oilfields if the "strangling" embargo is not lifted.

27: The military governor forces Kuwaitis to apply for Iraqi citizenship, and says diplomats sheltering westerners in their embassies will be hanged. Baghdad manufactures license plates for Saudi vehicles in anticipation of the time when the kingdom's eastern province is incorporated into Iraq.

III

The FOB's

Except for SOCCENT, much of CENTCOM headquarters were still packing their bags at MacDill Air Force Base near Tampa. There, Schwarzkopf faced a dilemma that has cost many generals much sleep: whether to commit his ground forces piecemeal and risk their defeat in detail, or first build up complete formations which are formidable once they go into battle, but risk arriving too late, so that instead of defending at odds that favor the defender they must attack with the odds reversed. The greatest Civil War cavalry general, Bedford Forrest, put Schwarzkopf's dilemma in a famous axiom: "Get there first with the most."

The dilemma, of course, is to satisfy Forrest's two conditions simultaneously. Schwarzkopf rushed a battalion from the 82nd to Dhahran in a few days. But these paratroopers, too lightly armed to be effective against tanks, could easily be cut off by an Iraqi thrust down the coast. "Dhahran is Arabic for Bataan," was the first graffito seen in the Gulf theater of war, now called the Joint Operations Area (JOA). Schwarzkopf's own armor force, the 24th Mechanized Division, was slowed by its own weight: 600 tanks and Bradley Fighting Vehicles that would take a month to reach the JOA by sea.

Neither was it simple for Schwarzkopf to determine where "there" was, in order to get there first. With the fourth largest army in the world, Saddam could attack on either or both of two prongs, each capable of collapsing Saudi Arabia. On the coastal route, the destination would be the oil and industry of the kingdom. The second prong could be the road to Riyadh, threatening the throne and capital. Saddam also had paratroopers. If they were prepared to be kamikazes, and jumped on Riyadh to link up with an armor thrust, a CENTCOM counterattack might have to start from the Red Sea rather than the Gulf.

With anticipated mastery of the air, Schwarzkopf decided to move his scanty ground forces up close to the Kuwaiti border where, if the Iraqis invaded, he could trade space for time in which to bring on reinforcements. It was a bold decision, and until late in the fall, something of a bluff. The Saudis remained in their trip wire role, supported by Apaches, while the US Marines assembled behind them to block the coastal invasion route. 18th ABC lined up on their left, covering an area as large as Vermont and New Hampshire combined—plenty of territory to suck in the Iraqis, damage and delay them. Vastly outnumbered, very short of heavy ammunition, the allied army would rely on air power to balance the battlefield.

18th ABC's defensive plan was called Desert Dragon (the corps' shoulder patch is a dragon head). In the plan, the 101st would be the 'covering force,' screening the vast front, locating Iraqi concentrations, and generally disrupting their advance with helicopters raiding tank columns from the air and infantry setting ambushes on the ground.

In late July, before Saddam shocked the world, corps had conducted a two-week map exercise called Internal Look at Ft. Bragg, North Carolina. The exercise scenario assumed an Iraqi invasion of Saudi Arabia, and never has training so well anticipated imminent reality. Some agency at CENTCOM or above was either clairvoyant or acutely attuned to topical events and ambitions in the Gulf. In any case, the 101st had foreknowledge of their covering force mission, and could almost pull the plan from the Internal Look file.

The scenario for Desert Dragon was an Iraqi armor thrust through the Saudi forces guarding the border. The 101st's aviation task force would spring forward to take on enemy tanks as the 3rd Armored Cavalry Regiment, attached to the 101st, moved up to receive the Iraqi attack about twenty miles into Saudi Arabia. The '3rd Cav' would shoot and fall back, allowing the Iraqis to advance down to corps's main defenses held by the 24th Mech, a hundred miles from the border. Here the invaders would be stopped, then counterattacked by the 101st swooping into their flanks.

Because each flight from Ft. Campbell added another company to the division's defenses, Peay's plans had to be adjusted every night to determine what he could bring to the battle if Saddam attacked tomorrow morning. As August had been the beginning of the beginning, September was the first show of any ground force to speak of. It was noticed by the soldiers themselves, like teenage weight lifters watching the mirror for signs of muscle growth.

Peay: "Desert Dragon was a highly complicated operation, requiring close coordination of many combat assets. Besides a tremendous amount of liaison, it featured delaying actions, withdrawals, spoiling attacks, phase lines, and passing units through one another at night—the most difficult maneuvers an army can undertake, and the hardest to control."

No matter how sophisticated the plans, their execution amounted to three fundamental functions for the troops: move, shoot, communicate. As a 'ready' division prior to the Gulf war, the 101st was well drilled in these fundamentals, so it was their special applications to the desert that became the template for training in Saudi Arabia.

And the division's experience in desert warfare was already substantial. In the previous year, four of the nine infantry battalions, and all the helicopter units, had been through 'laser war' in the Mojave Desert. Two infantry battalions had served in the Sinai,* and one brigade participated in the huge multi-

---

* The 1985 Gander crash occurred as a charter airliner was bringing back a battalion from duty in the Sinai. The cause of the disaster has yet to be convincingly determined, and terrorist sabotage—the plane was fueled in Cairo—remains a possibility.

national exercise in Egypt called Bright Star. The G3 (Operations & Training) estimated that some 45% of the division had undergone considerable desert training prior to deployment. Probably even more valuable was the air assault doctrine to fight habitually at night. Over half the 101st's training prior to Desert Shield had been nocturnal. In the furnace of the desert, night training provided more than an advantage, it fulfilled a necessity.

Major Keith Huber ran G3 Operations: "Except in the winter, if you're attacking in the desert, night is the only time when troops can make long, strenuous movements on the ground. You want to get where you're going before the heat settles in and degrades everything. Before vehicles get too hot to touch. Ammunition swells up. Radios lose range. And for this heliborne division, the loss of lift in super-heated air cuts down our capabilities a lot.

"If we'd had to execute Desert Dragon in September, the heat would have been a tremendous factor. One of the most important reasons Desert Storm began when it did was the six-week 'weather window' before the heat got too bad. If we'd had to fight into May, I think you'd have seen almost all our operations at night."

Night fighting doctrine and vision equipment were not developed specifically for desert warfare. It was serendipity: they were developed to counter Soviet anti-aircraft weapons, especially shoulder fired, visually sighted weapons.

Anticipating combat against the high tech Red Army, the 101st possessed very potent radar jamming devices which added to the advantage of darkness, their natural ally. Peay was proud to use the night more than other forces. Screaming Eagles felt they owned it.

Desert Destiny was the division plan to accomplish Desert Dragon. It was updated daily as battalion after battalion arrived at King Fahd. As giant clamshell noses opened, the troops felt the wilting blast of Arabia's heat, and rummaged through their rucksacks for sunglasses to squint into brilliance like that from a permanent flash bulb. Well conditioned and forewarned, there was still no 'adjusting' to these conditions, though advice had been sought from Shelton's vanguard.

"Anything more we can do to get ready for the heat?" Col. Montie Hess, the G3, had inquired in a phone hookup with Dhahran. "Yeah," Shelton advised, "stick your face in a hair dryer all day."

"Yes, sir."

"The good news is you can change clothes a lot—fifteen minutes in the sun, and your laundry's completely dry."

Though there were an insufficient number of hair dryers, Col. Joe Bolt, the division chief of staff, attempted a similar pre-acclimitization experiment, proposing that the air conditioners at Ft. Campbell Headquarters be turned off, and everyone wear T shirts. But visiting VIP's preferred to be briefed on heat debilitation rather than experience it; and female civilians, working alongside T shirted soldiers, demanded equivalent attire of shorts and halters—too informal, Bolt decided—so, to everyone's relief, the AC's went back on.

The Saudi heat and its quick soaking consequence defied all such countermeasures. Water consumption of eight gallons per day was initially enforced, then monitored for two weeks or so after a unit's arrival. Thereafter, soldiers were allowed to rely on their individual bodily reactions. This meant that work was usually divided into 15-minute increments, the maximum period between visits to the latrine. Plastic water bottles were as ubiquitous and emblematic of the desert as insect repellant had been in Vietnam. Soldiers became conscious of themselves as a water circulatory systems, liters in and liters out.

Early photos from King Fahd show everyone with flush faces, regardless of natural complexion. Blood flush on the skin, water flushing the innards. Heat was unconquerable, could not be ignored, only endured. Heat reduced efficiency by roughly forty percent. An endless amount of work had to be done, and less efficiency required more time to do it. For soldiers struggling with the heat, King Fahd amounted to two uncomfortable places, a desk and a cot, both dripping sweat. Towels were valued only less than letters from home.

In time, 'home' took on a double meaning. When brigades manned the frontier, King Fahd began to be considered home;

indeed, a Screaming Eagle was no longer said to be 'pissing stateside water' once he referred to the division base as 'home.' Then, of course, there was ultimate 'home' stateside—'home' and not 'the world' as the same location had been called during Vietnam. Vietnam, for many reasons, had been unworldly in the sense of surreal; but Saudi Arabia during Desert Shield was very much the world because the world was watching it so closely. Screaming Eagles in the desert did not feel at all detached from humanity as had their forebears in the jungle because they were representing rather than rejected by world opinion. Soldiers of both generations coped through a Spartan outlook on equivalently hostile environments: in Vietnam the result was cynicism, in Saudi Arabia, stoicism. The difference was in a commonly misunderstood word, morale. Captain Roger Cotton correctly perceived what morale meant in Desert Shield:

"Too many people think high morale means smiling soldiers skipping around, happy to be here. Nobody is happy to be here. We just understand that here is our duty and obligation, and we won't let anybody down. That's high morale—the willingness to do the mission."

Peay had a 'live' mission in Desert Destiny, while at the same time a vital need to acclimate his troops and train them desert hard. He was able to fulfill the two requirements by combining them, because after real estate was sorted out between the Saudis and U.S. divisions, the 101st could train on much of the same terrain they would 'cover' against the Iraqis.

Thus, the 101st's training cycle began, eventually rotating the division's three infantry brigades and their supporting units, between Camp Eagle II and two FOB's—forward operating bases—far to the north in the covering force sector. One of the FOB's was the ghost town, Qaryat Al Ulya. A few years previous, the Saudis extended their national electric grid into upper Arabia, for some reason running the power lines five miles west of Qaryat Al Ulya instead of through it. After some bureaucratic head scratching, the emir of the province determined it was more feasible to put up cinder block buildings on the power line rather than run a spur to the ancient town. So the townspeople displaced, abandoning their picturesque adobe village to wild camels and passing bedouins. For the 101st, the ghost town provided a perfect site for training in house to house fighting. They named it FOB Oasis.

Hundreds of road miles from King Fahd, Oasis needed an air strip so that brigades could rotate to the FOB in hours, not days. Ron Adams, Peay's other brigadier and his assistant division commander for support, tasked his overworked engineers to find or build one. They did both: discovering a strip abandoned by oil explorers, then improving it to receive the all-purpose truck of the Air Force, the immortal C-130.

The other FOB was near An Nuayriyah, an important road junction if the Iraqis ventured toward either Dhahran or Riyadh. Peay named this site Bastogne, the famous crossroad where the 101st had fought encircled during the Battle of the Bulge in World War II. Though a thoroughly rational man, Peay often invoked the value of tradition, even legend, to remind his division what was expected of them.

Specialist Myron Yancey had found college irrelevant for his freewheeling ambition, so he enlisted to learn how to drive big rigs on open roads, a goal fulfilled in a five-ton truck along the Tapline from King Fahd to the FOB's during most of October. Unrecognized at that time was the importance of this two-lane road, which in Desert Storm would be the most vital in Schwarzkopf's plan.

"Between Bastogne and Oasis, there wasn't much army traffic then—you'd see more camels than Toyotas. Neither of 'em would give you right of way. I couldn't believe it when Sgt. Durham told me the rules of the road. Cars going the other way had priority in *your* lane! That's why the Arabs drive so crazy.

"You got to watch out for camels too. When they decide to move, they do it real slow. And boy do they ever smell! We were driving through fog one time. I was shotgun for a new guy and I smelled this herd fifty meters before we saw 'em. He was really impressed when I told him to slow down.

"From King Fahd to Jubail, you got an idea of all the stuff coming into the JOA. There'd be a convoy every couple of miles—flatbeds, tankers, low boys with tanks, HUMM-V's by the hundreds. The Arabs just weaved in and out of the convoys.

Sometimes a Mercedes got stuck in the middle. They didn't care. They'd smile and wave to us till they could pull around. We'd signal when the road was clear, but usually they'd just go for it. *Inshallah* is what they say—God willing. If God wants them to wipe out, that's OK.

"It got to be that way with us too. If there was a war we might get killed. If there wan't, this was just a long job. Inshallah —maybe that's a good way to look at life. Big things like wars happen or they don't. At my pay grade you never know and it's out of your hands.

"Where Tapline bends it's like time travel into the past. Between Bastogne and Oasis you know how it looked when they talk about 'the wilderness' in the Bible. I'm a Bible reader—my folks taught me. I read a lot of it while I was riding shotgun. I understood why water is such a big thing for people in the Bible. Some of those things I understood for the first time: like Philistines was just an old name for the Palestinians.

"I thought about all the armies that marched back and forth around this part of the world. The Bible is full of wars like this. Now we were driving tanks and planes, but it's still the same. We were big and powerful, and had tons and tons of stuff, but the wilderness is bigger, much bigger. If we bogged down, I could see how the sand could just drift over us like what happened to the army of Nebuchadnezzar.

"I thought of Saddam like him, and the Iraqis like the Babylonians. The Bible shows how cruel they are. It's hard to believe people being so cruel to other people—throwing them into fiery furnaces, and things like that. We were hearing what Saddam was doing to the people in Kuwait. Things hadn't changed at all."

But much was changing for the latest foreign tenants of the desert, their sheer numbers most conspicuously. There had not been a military migration the size of Desert Shield since Eisenhower's armies loaded the British Isles before the Normandy invasion. In Britain they had been crammed and cramped around villages, but Schwarzkopf's army felt more like Daniel Boones of the desert:

Mike Davis (who had lured Cody to his surprise birthday party) was one of the first Screaming Eagles to inspect the lonely outpost of Bastogne, a site the 101st inherited from the 82nd, and promptly named Camp Hell:

"Our Apache pad was an old oil pumping station—something out of the twilight zone. We pushed open this rusty, squeaky door. We had to push hard because drifted sand was deep all over the floor. You'd step inside, and feel you were making the first footprints ever. Creepy, crawly things started moving around because of the light we let in. Spider webs were so thick the walls didn't seem to meet at right angles. Huge, solid looking objects were suspended in the webs. I guess they were the spiders, but they were big as birds.

"I looked at Cody, and he was thinking the same thing: we aren't sleeping in here. We rigged our cots on the roof.

"Some crews came up the next day, and they kind of snickered at us like we were afraid of a haunted house. Then they pushed open some doors. No one wanted to do it, but we had to set up in those places. We needed some shovels before we could use brooms. The snakes and insects were pissed, but they didn't move out, they just slid back into the holes in the walls. Never had any trouble keeping people awake on night shifts. Everyone who worked in there was jumpy all the time."

At first, no ground forces were available to secure Bastogne for the aviators who, in their daily reconnaissance, could still see refugees dribbling out of Kuwait, a queasy reminder that the war was more than a minuet of opposing forces lining up against each other.

"Usually they were on trails with cars and donkeys," said one pilot, "stuff piled so high it looked like a walking garage sale. Farther south, they didn't carry as much. You could see why by the ditched cars and litter. I don't know where they got any food or even water. Maybe the Saudis on the border gave them some, and directions to wells. If they'd been western refugees, I think they'd be wearing just shorts, but Arabs fight the heat by adding clothes. The hotter it gets, the more layers they put on. That prevents loss of body fluid. All bundled up, they looked plain miserable to me, carrying what they'd saved when their world came apart.

"Close to Kuwait, they'd wave at us like they were glad for our protection. Farther south, their heads were down like it was taking everything they had just to get where they were going. God knows where that was. Plenty of them didn't make it. "You could see that when you made a twilight run. There'd be a column out on the gravel plain. Next morning it would be about forty miles south, still straggling along, strung out a lot, and about twenty percent less. I'd pray they could make it to Tapline Road before I went up again.

"Till I saw the refugees, Saddam was sort of a comic book character. 1-101's motto is 'expect no mercy.' That sounded bloodthirsty before, but after seeing the refugees, it was appropriate. It was for a monster like Saddam. For what he'd done he could expect no mercy, and his army wouldn't get any from me."

It was the aviators who first peeked over the confines of Camp Eagle II to comprehend the immensity of the desert, and also its variety. Around King Fahd the sand was flat and white, a gradual merging with the Gulf seabed where, at high tide, the author once walked three miles into the sea before the placid water covered his head. 'Up north,' as the FOB region came to be called, the desert took on features.

A radio team from 501st Signal Battalion, tasked to set up communications with Camp Eagle II, were soon to join Cody at Bastogne, arriving at night. The flight in seemed to be transoceanic. No pin points of light below, but there were widely scattered jets of flame from the desert like giant candles. These were 'flares' where natural gas was burnt off by a kingdom with extravagant energy sources. An Arab adage had circulated among the 101st's chaplains who were developing courteous relations with their Islamic counterparts: Allah bestowed nature's bounty to the world's tribes in equal measure but not equal proportion. To some He gave great forests or splendid mountains, to others mild climate or fertile soil. To the Arabs of this peninsula, He gave His gift in one form—fuel beneath the desert crust.

Soon not even Allah's candles dotted the night. The radio team flew north for so long, through and over darkness, that someone imagined he saw the far off glow of Kuwait City. The pilot knew better. He started down, but the passengers could see no landing lights. There weren't any because this was to be a practice tactical landing with just pathfinders using infrared. The plane came to a stop after three bumps. The radio team got out, and felt a breeze for the first time since leaving America. Bastogne at night seemed so cool that sleeves were rolled down. The new arrivals did not first look around but felt forced to look *up* at a startling transformation.

The sultry haze of the coastal plain did not reach this far inland. Starlights as piercing as lasers seemed to have descended, their sizes clearly differentiated in infinite stillness.

Scorched by day, the radiomen emerged like reptiles at night. For a week, before enough infantry arrived at King Fahd to be sent up to Bastogne, its tiny garrison passed the time pulling radio watch and walking guard. For once the army provided rapturous solitude. Even conversation, the inexhaustable resource, became parched by starlight. Then soldiers walked off alone, sat down on the sand and turned eyes toward night sky, composed of the blackest black and whitest white they'd ever seen.

The early interlude would soon vanish as Bastogne was fortified and converted to a training camp. Sarge came up to provide security for an artillery survey team during the pristine period:

"The FOB's were on a different planet. It was early in the morning when I flew out of King Fahd in a Chinook [cargo helicopter]. Couldn't see much life after we crossed the Dhahran-Riyadh highway. Civilization just stopped like there was a fence nobody could cross. It looked like pictures from space down there. The flats started to show low ridges, and gullies they call wadis, but most of it was rocky plains. They looked real hard, with lots of gravel. Made me think how the armor divisions would love that kind of terrain.

"Then there'd be these beaches where the yellow sand begins. That's what it looks like, a coastline with flat rock islands in huge bays of sand. Some of those bays were like the sea—you couldn't see the end of it, even from a chopper. That's what Arabia was famous for—those miles and miles of long dunes all the way out to the horizon. I mean, we were flying at a thousand feet, and the horizon was *way* out there.

"Those dunes were like ocean waves that didn't move. I

guess they do—the wind moves the sand around a lot—but from the air, they look like the tops of clouds. Mounds and curves blending with each other. In a chopper, you wonder how big they are. Training around Bastogne, we found out."

Cartographers labeled the features in this region 'sand mountains.' The map shows them to have crests of 150 to 1000 feet. From crest to crest was the way the infantry expected to fall back as part of the covering force. Training around Bastogne was for what could happen if two Iraqi armor divisions struck toward the crossroads. Helicopters would track and harass them, and allied bombers would pummel them, but fifty miles from the Kuwaiti frontier, the 101st would have to make a stand at Bastogne.

With no tanks of their own, Screaming Eagles on the ground relied on the TOW, a wire guided missile that requires its operator to be a courageous computer. In the sand, backblast from the missile's launch raises a large puff of dust, alerting the target tank. It had about thirty seconds in which to return fire while its opponent, the TOW operator, guided his missile's flight through a spool of wire spinning out behind. He would be safer if the contest were at night when he could still sight by infrared and his backblast went unseen in the darkness.

TOW's could be hauled around by infantrymen, but the preferred mount was the 'HUMM-V,' the army's worthy successor to the jeep.

"My vote for the war-winning machine in the desert is the HUMM-V," said Brig. Gen. Ron Adams. "It's just the most reliable and rugged wheeled vehicle ever made. Multi-fuel, four drive wheels, and a power train you can almost lubricate with sand—plus a wheel base so wide you couldn't roll one over with a dozer. And in those dunes it seemed anything you drove would tip."

Yancey once drove a HUMM-V that was initially flown into Bastogne by helicopter:

"For the last twenty minutes guys were hardly talking, just looking out at all those hills of sand. They had designs like you see in fancy gardens. The design was one way for a while, then changed to something else. Ridges of sand, bumpy plains of sand, sand S's, X's, T's, and H's. Just about any design you looked for you could see. The thing about it was that it was all sand around Bastogne. Once in a while, there were rocky peaks sticking up like islands, but that just reminded you the rest was sand, sand, sand.

"Harrison said something before we landed, something like he thought he'd see the world when he joined the army, but he never thought he'd see another world! That's the way it was up there, and the infantry was going to be the explorers."

"Getting lost—that was the number one worry," said Phil Jones, an artillery lieutenant who trained around Bastogne. "Our sergeant major said getting lost was easier in the jungle. He'd had a lot of patrols in Vietnam, so I suppose he's right. But the first time you head over a monster dune, the base camp disappears and all you see is more dunes. At night, that's eerie. There's no depth perception with night goggles. You just have to believe your compass, and don't let on to the men that you're worried."

Two men were lost for 36 hours, and 42 helicopters flew over the dunes in search. There was a psychiatric casualty in the division who set out across the dunes with his rifle to "get Saddam." But like a lightship moored in the sand seas, Bastogne's lonely fascinations made it the most popular FOB.

The ghost town at FOB Oasis had repulsively interesting features. Unknown at the time to the Americans, the landing strip at Oasis was still used by the former inhabitants as an animal dying ground. Cpl. Calvin Greer remembered what this meant: "We hopped out of the Chinook into all these mounds. That's where the animals died and the wind blew sand over them. I stepped on this mound, and my foot went in and cracked something. A million scorpions poured out like ants! The lived in the carcass, eat up all the guts, and stay cool inside.

"I think the skeletons were camels and goats. If animals got real sick, the Arabs would just bring them out here, tie 'em up, and let 'em die.

"Snakes and scorpions were entertainment for us. You'd get a big, mean looking scorpion and put him in a jar, and another squad would get one too. We'd shake the jar. That got 'em fighting, so we'd bet on our scorpion. Sometime it would be a viper against a viper. Plenty of them around too.

"The worst thing out there was the black bugs. They looked like beetles—but much bigger and had armor plate. Our first sergeant was really hot on field sanitation, so we dug slit trenches for latrines, you know, just like the manual says—throw dirt on what you do, so everything's sanitary.

"But you'd get up, and these armored beetles dive right down and dig the dirt away. Then while you're going back to your position, these beetles run by carrying your shit. They'd take it down in their holes, paper and all. That kept the slit trenches from filling up, but our first sergeant didn't like it. We had to dig cat holes after that, about two feet deep, and pound the dirt back on top.

"I'd write Dessie about stuff like that, but she still wanted to come up to an FOB just to get out of Division Headquarters. Down there it was like trying to do paperwork in a sauna." Corporals Dessie and Calvin Greer were married less than a year before Saddam swallowed Kuwait. He was an infantryman in the 'Oh-deuce,' the 502nd Regiment that comprised Second Brigade. She worked in G3 Ops, the element of division headquarters that handles war fighting. Consequently, Dessie learned a lot about what the division as doing and planning.

Dessie: "I'd worry about him up at the FOB's. On the situation map, I'd check the position of his battalion every day. Sometime I could find out where his company was. Kuwait was at the top of the map. It was full of these red symbols for big Iraqi units—corps, Republican divisions, tank brigades—top secret stuff, but I knew where they were, all lined up on the border. Then there'd be a few little blue symbols on this side. One of 'em was the 2-502. Just open map between my husband and the whole Iraq army. I wanted Calvin back at Ft. Camel!"

Except for the presence of his wife, Ft. Camel had little to offer Calvin or his buddies. By September, it was clear that the war would not reach the 101st's desert base. That was about all that was clear. War and peace still struggled for hegemony, and Ft. Camel was simply a place, like the maple grove, to await the outcome.

September 1990

28: In the United Sates, the PBS documentary series *The Civil War* is watched by a
record number of viewers horrified by the prospects of similarly bloody war in the
Gulf.

30: The civilian economy around U.S. military bases suffers disastrously because of
absent troops.

IV

Fort Camel

The 101st's military lineage traces back to Wisconsin's 'Eagle
Brigade' in the Civil War.* Now, a century later, Screaming
Eagles were again bivouaced under cotton tentage as they had
been at Vicksburg. Some 2,000 tents, laid out row on row by

---

* In a 1912 issue of *American Historical Magazine*, Civil War veteran Robert
Burdette described the original connection:
   "We got our name from the fact that the Eighth Wisconsin Regiment of that
Brigade carried an American eagle all through the war.
   "Old Abe had the post of honor at the center of the regiment, his perch
being constructed of the national shield, and he was carried by a sergeant
between our two flags, the Stars and Stripes and the regimental standard of
blue emblazoned in gold with the state coat of arms.
   "All the brigade adored him, and secured chickens for him–he was fonder
of chicken than the chaplain, and not half so particular about the cookery. To
see him during the battle fly up into the air to the length of his long tether,
hovering above the flags in the cloud of musketry, screaming like the bird
which bore the thunderbolts of Jove, was to raise such a mighty shout from
the Brigade as would have blown Jericho off the map. Other regiments had
dogs, bears, coons and goats, but there was only one eagle in the Army.
   "Through thirty-six battles he screamed above the trumpets, smelling the
smoke afar off, fluttering to the agitation of the captains and men shouting.
Never once did he flinch, not even as cannons thundered. He was wounded
in the assault on Vicksburg and in the battle of Corinth. At this battle it is said
that a reward was offered by the Confederate General Price for the capture or
killing of our eagle."

artillery surveyors, comprised 'Ft. Camel,' the unofficial name given by the troops to their base on the edge of King Fahd.

Sgt. Maj. Weiss, a tall, almost gaunt South Dakotan with a habitually solemn expression, closely tracked the names and nicknames that arose in the desert:

"The troops are very proud of this division's history, but maybe they wanted some personal identity too. We named some installations here for places in the One-Oh-One's history: places like Bastogne, Dak To, and A Shau. But the troops came up with names of their own like Ft. Camel and Viper. That was fine because this was their war even more than ours.

"But writing home, things could get a little confusing. During Desert Shield, our base camp had all these names: Camp Eagle II, King Fahd, Ft. Camel, and tent city."

The tents of Ft. Camel were made for Arabs, by Arabs, of Egyptian cotton, and sealed the way Arabs had done it for centuries—with loops and wooden buttons. After the war, one of the tents was pitched for permanent display in the 101st Museum at Ft. Campbell.

It was a winter model tent of double thickness and solid white color that replaced those issued in the summer of 1990, the latter translucently thin and woven no tighter than to slow down wind-driven sand. The exterior of the summer tent was a shade lighter than the marl hardpan it stood upon, with half-inch blue stripes vertically spaced about a foot apart. Inside, the tents were lined with native fabric that looked like pages in a carpet catalogue. Bolts, splashes and patches of solid color abutted one another with the impression of a crazy quilt. Melita McGraw, a captain who shared a tent with Dessie Greer, wondered why the Arabs were such psychedelic interior decorators:

"An American civilian who lived here told me the Saudis love color because they don't see much of it outside. He's sure right about that. They can't wear anything but white because of the heat, so I guess they love color in their tents. Up in Jubail, he said they even go crazy on the exterior of their buildings. The city looks like a Persian rug when you fly over."

In purchasing these tents in the nearby cities of Al Kohbar and Dammam, the army relied more on a locally procured item than it had since World War I when the 'French 75' howitzer was adopted as the standard artillery piece of the American Expeditionary Force.

"We did what needed to be done," said an officer involved in purchasing the tents. "To manufacture, then ship canvas squad tents from the States was too slow, especially when priority was for ammunition, rations and mail. Troops were coming in every day. They needed shelter immediately. I lived in a Haj tent myself. It wasn't a Winnebago, but it kept the sun off."

But first the tents had to be pitched, no small problem because in the site preparation of the airport the sand had been compacted into rock-hard marl. Scuffing boots and rolling wheels ground the marl into chalk as fine as that on a blackboard eraser. This dust coated and entered everything: computers, canteens, letters and lungs. It mixed with sweat into rivulets of slurry and dried saliva before each bite so that all food was called 'grits.' Both from heat and the floury dust, Ft. Camel seemed like the inside of a baker's oven.

Tents were raised by Arab crews, closely watched by hair triggered military police. The terrorist threat had been widely proclaimed from both Riyadh and Baghdad, so no Arabs were admitted into Ft. Camel except when escorted by MP's. Conscious of their employers' suspicion, the tent raisers worked fast and rhythmically, swinging huge wooden mauls high overhead while co-workers held the tent pegs. The Arabs had a work rule: if the maul man hit the peg holder's hand, they reversed roles.

Maul swinging is a skill learned over years, and the Americans, despite plentiful manpower, could not replace the Arabs by using the native tent raising technique. Yankee ingenuity was called for, and demonstrated by softening the marl with water, often soaking tent sites the entire night before peg driving began.

The marl quickly rehardened, but the dust was like graphite that lubricated slippage between pegs and marl. The blasting wind could draw pegs like bayonets from scabbards. Soldiers laughed, remembering the skimpy—and elusive—shelter of their tents that blew down regularly. Sarge had a nostalgic affection for his:

"That tent—I think about it like I do my first car—never worked right, always broke down. But I kind of loved it for all the funny stuff that happened when I was in it. You see, when enough wind came up, we were outside the tent when we thought we were in it. Guys sitting around playing cards, trying to sleep or jerk off—then we hear this 'whoo-whooo-whoooo...' We say, 'uh-oh, wind tunnel time again.'

"At night was the worst. Daytime, you could hold the pegs if you saw them coming out of the ground. Nightime—maybe around 0200—you're lying there thinking, should I get up and watch the pegs? If I'm the only one, I can't save 'em anyway. If I wake up the rest of the tent, someone's going to blast my ass. So you lie there and wait to see if it'll take off."

Saudis were sometimes called 'fan belts,' another Desert Shield neologism, naming the loop of thick black chord that holds on Arab headress.

"I'd really like to know how the fan belts keep these tents up. I think it's where they pitch it. Bet they get off behind a dune or in some other wind shadow. We were right out there on the flat. Nothing slowing down the wind for miles."

Thus began the search for artificial wind shadows, and it soon focused on the most plentiful raw material available, sand. Sand in bags; i.e., sandbags. Knee-high sandbag revetments shadowed the pegs and would also be useful in case of terrorist mortar attacks. So back in Kentucky, Adams drained the supply system for synthetic sand bag casings. The Saudi hemp casings leaked too much. Though he was not carrying coal to Newcastle, he surely shipped sand casings to Arabia. *

The 12 by 24 foot tents had two vertical supports but no ridge pole, so the center drooped below head height where this valley was button fastened. Buttons often slipped, especially if the peg ropes were not constantly adjusted for the shifting wind—always a hot wind at King Fahd, that reminded Southern Californians of Santa Annas back home. Left unattended, the tents sagged and tilted until a 'city block,' the home of some batalion

---

* In making concrete, sand did indeed have to be shipped in because the sand around King Fahd had too much salt.

training far away at the FOB's, resembled the jagged surface of a glacier. Until smoking was banned at Ft. Camel, tents regularly ignited.

Sarge: "Didn't a night go by when one of 'em didn't fire up—burned to the ground in a minute. When a tent blew off in the wind, everybody cheered and laughed. Same thing after a while when the tents burnt up. Nobody got hurt that I know of, but just like that there were these nine cots sitting out in the smoke. MRE dressers and stuff, laundry hanging between 'em. Then just like that you were looking inside the tent—but the tent wasn't there. It was down wind, hanging over a latrine!"

MRE's (meals ready to eat—also described as 'mouth-to-rear elements') were highly regarded. As furniture. With hunting knives—much requested as gifts from home—the sturdy MRE cartons could be carved into writing desks; and, by stapling in dividers, even converted into dressers or night stands. Stacked and connected, they became the armoires of Arabia. Ingenious MRE furniture was a mark of distinction, a badge of personality in a world where bleak environmental monotony combined with military collectivity to nearly erase individual identity. But for all these submerging influences, men would be men and women, women.

In spite of the chain of command's constant efforts to keep the troops within the perimeter of Ft. Camel (primarily for security against terrorists), an after hours social life emerged on the outskirts of the tent city. There was a copse of low palms surrounded by brushy hillocks, known to the troops as 'the oasis'—and they didn't mean the FOB. The oasis was their getaway from the division's 'non-cohabitation' policy: an absolute ban on coed tents. The ban applied even to married couples like the Greers. It also discouraged marriages (theoretically possible), as no conjugal relation resulted so long as either soldier remained in the JOA.

Cohabitation was defined as occupation, however temporary, of a living tent (distinguished from a work tent) by soldiers of different sex. Legalistically, 'occupation' meant crossing a tent threshold; ie., penetrating the plane of the tent walls. It was a simpler and different offense for a male to enter a female's tent: that was already off limits to him. The additional offense of cohabitation resulted only if she, then or later, was present in the tent with him, in which case they would both be charged.

A Staff Judge Advocate officer smiled to recall some of the legal nuances of the non-cohabitation policy. His office was involved in all the misgivings predicted about females in a combat zone.

"If he went into her tent, he's violated two regulations and she one. If she went into his tent, there's only one violation for each of them. Interestingly, cohabitation is a crime —the equivalent of a felony—under Koranic law. That's part of the Saudis' sexual apartheid policy. The outcome of conviction, as I understand it, would be that he'd be released with a reprimand and she'd be stoned! I think some of our commanders mentioned that to their women, and it may have been a deterrent."

More realistic deterrences were the harsh surroundings and nearly total lack of privacy that daunted all but the most determined lovers. Agnes, an enlisted woman in the division support command, believed that the officers looked the other way when couples slipped out to the oasis:

"They must have known what was going on out there," Agnes, a female soldier, conjectured. "If they'd really wanted to keep us out, they could've put concertina (barbed wire) around the oasis. It just never got out of control. No girl was ever raped or anything. Beside, not everyone can get it on out there with that sand, scorpions and stuff.

"At night you'd see these pup tents out there like a little mini camp, spread around, about thirty meters apart. It's quiet when the wind's down—and when the moon's up, it can be real romantic. A girl told her guy, 'Look at those pup tents over there: two shelter halves together, two people being one.' Now that's pretty, isn't it? Then you hear a scream. Oops, some lovers just got joined by a scorpion."

For most, love was just another absence in their lives. For them, the only connection to love was mail. An Army Post Office (APO) address for the 101st was established even before the division moved to the Gulf.

Sarge: "Everyone is real down for about two weeks when

they get here. You're not sleeping right, and when you're awake there's the heat that makes you want to stop anything you're doing. But you realize that you're not doing anything to make you sweat. It's just the heat—and it makes you want to lie down till it's over. Trouble is, it never is over till night time.

"You never stop sweating, and there's always that talcum dust in the air. It mixes with sweat, so there's always this film on your skin.

"It takes about two weeks to get a letter saying she got the first letter you sent from here. Then you know the system works—that you got contact back there. You know that sooner or later, your letters will get home and you'll get letters back. That was a big factor in starting life over here."

Initially, there were huge problems with stamps. At first, APO's required U.S. postage for any letter headed stateside, but stamps could be purchased at only a few locations. In the grubby life of Desert Shield, stamps quickly wilted and turned gummy in the heat.

In September, the U.S. Postal Service agreed to accept 12 ounce letters without postage. The soldier needed only to put a return APO address on the envelope and write 'free' where the stamp is usually placed. That speeded outgoing mail, but it went by scheduled airlines that hop scotched west across Europe. Ten days en route was normal once a letter was received by an APO, but APO's were located only at major cantonments like Ft. Camel. At the remote FOB's, visitors were welcome as couriers for mail headed in both directions.

Incoming was always slower than outgoing because Saudi customs went through mail, looking for alcohol and sexy pictures. At first they were so strict that faces of women in magazines were blotted out, and no flatbed mail truck was released till every bag on it was inspected. By October the Saudis realized that the task of thorough censorship was too much for them: they couldn't begin to go through half the loads that were coming in, and resorted to spot checks of one mailbag per aircraft.

Yet there was another huge delay for incoming mail: counter-terrorism inspections.

McGrath: "C-T guys would examine all the packages. I heard

they x-rayed some of them too. People were saying film got ruined, but they couldn't complain because at first nobody was authorized to have a personal camera in the JOA.

"Anyway, everything stopped if a package made noise—and if it 'ticked,' the APO stopped work. You see, the folks at home were sending electronic games over here because they'd heard we had nothing to do. I guess they didn't take the batteries out of some of the games, so they 'ticked.' Standard operating procedure for the APO was to contact the soldier who was getting the package. If he couldn't come right down and claim it, they'd hold it in a pit they dug. But if he was up north, the APO called an ordnance team and they blew up the package in the pit. Boom—there goes somebody's Nintendo game! Happened all the time."

Agnes: "Another thing about the mail was all the lonely heart letters coming over here. You know how people in the States were asked to write to 'any soldier?' Well, it got hilarious. This girl I knew in the APO, she said letters were coming in for 'any 21-year old, slim, white lieutenant,' or for 'any black bachelor from Milwaukee'—stuff like that was written right on the envelope! I think the APO people would pull out the best ones for themselves—perfumed letters, ones with hearts on 'em. That was OK, I guess: they were addressed to 'any soldier,' and the National Guard people working the APO were soldiers.

"And, man, the pictures! Don't know how they got through the Saudis. I knew guys who took leave after the war to visit those girls—the ones that looked so good in the pictures, wearing thong bikinis. There was this sergeant in the 44th ADA who just plain fell in love after he read one of those letters. I told him she was hustling him, but he wouldn't listen. Sure enough he starts writing her and she starts writing back about how tough life is for her. She wanted some money, and Sgt. Evans was just fool enough to send her some."

Sarge: "Just about everybody passed around their letters, photos and cassettes they'd get, so mail call meant news from a dozen homes, not just your own. One mail call kept conversation going for a week. It got so some of us started writing to other guys' families. I thought about how if one of us was killed, his family would get more than just a letter from the CO."

But other sergeants worried about getting too close, thinking about the time when men would be ordered to move out under fire. A squad leader could know his squad so well he felt one or two might be weak in a tight spot. His instinct would be to send his best men when much was at stake, but this raised the probabilities of his best men being killed.

"It was tough thinking about that, and you just can't pre-plan everything you'd do. Some guys want to be point every time. It makes your job easier if you let 'em. Other guys may not want the job but do it real well. And then a lot of people surprise you. Usually they do better than you expected."

But what was to be expected? The Iraqis were miles beyond the horizon, and Saddam's intentions beyond conjecture. War seemed as remote as it had been in the Mojave Desert. Though a civilian, Dan Smith was an official army photographer sent over to take snapshots of life in the JOA for a few weeks in October:

"When I got there, the heat wasn't so bad—just 100 degrees or so, but it still felt like standing in a sauna. All the tents were up, dress right dress, and I didn't see many blown down. The streets were getting paved and the plumbing problems were getting fixed, slowly.*

"But the troops didn't like Ft. Camel much. They'd rather be up in the FOB's training, even living right down in the sand. Once I went up to Oasis with Gen. Peay who asked a staff sergeant if he'd be glad to get back to Eagle II and take a shower. No, the sergeant would rather stay up north. No tents, no cots, no electricity, and just a little drinking water—but no chicken shit details either. It was my impression the officers loved the FOB's because in peacetime they never had so much time alone with their men—that's a kind of luxury that's hard for a civilian to understand. They had all their troops, and all the time was available for tactical training. Professional heaven!

"You see, nobody wanted to go to war before they got a good

---

* Previously, showers drained poorly, attracting vipers, one of which bit a man whose foot had to be amputated.

feel for the desert. Up there they got it in spades. The 101st was well trained before they went over, but that couldn't compare to how ready they were after months in the desert. Then, if somebody got bit by a viper, his squad would just take care of him themselves. Before that they'd call a medevac."

The division's adaptation to the desert followed the pattern Sarge described, the worst period being the first two weeks when jet lag and uncertainty of mail flow combined with the comfortless living conditions, and "finding out where things are." There was no alcohol, a solace and escape for all previous generations of Screaming Eagles; nor was there accessible companionship, so infamous from the bar life in Vietnam. These were someone else's history, memories of pre-desert times, and like all memories, gradually faded, much to the gratification of the chain of command.

Weiss: "If the Saudis had announced, 'OK, you American soldiers are here to protect us, so we'll let you bring in beer,' I think every sergeant major in the division would have screamed! We never knew how many problems can be traced to alcohol and local girls. We found out when we didn't have those problems. Take drinking and driving: not a single fatality while we were in the JOA. In the first week after we got home, three guys got killed DWI."

After the first two weeks established routines, time accelerated. The publicized possibility of troop rotation raised hopes of being home for Christmas, but then the huge 7th Corps arrived from Germany, obviously for an offensive to retake Kuwait. Paradoxically, this boosted morale in the 101st by convincing them that every one was here 'for the duration.' One of the most depressing recollections of Vietnam was arrival in country, to be taunted by veterans about how few days they had remaining before departure. In Vietnam troops arrived and left in serials, each assignment of thirteen months overlapping that of replacements. In the JOA everyone had the same 'end-x'—end of exercise—when Iraq evacuated Kuwait one way or another. The Screaming Eagles would be together and to the end.

Together did not always mean togetherness. In tent city, the heat, grime and discomfort raised tensions higher than out in the open spaces of the FOB's.

Sarge: "Sure, things got up tight at times. You don't have ten thousand guys working, eating, shitting and sleeping up close, and not have friction.

"With a life like that, you had fights. Real fights with plenty of blood, but they were over fast. A couple of swings, and then the guys wrestled and hit the ground. Fights were an outlet for other stuff. Never heard of anything racial, or two guys fighting more than once. They didn't want any serious enemies except Iraqis."

Tense race relations were as remote as Vietnam. The only occasion—less than an incident—Agnes recalled was when Armed Forces Radio Network came on the air:

"The DJ's had to play music for everyone, you see; so when they played shit-kicker songs, the blacks would yell 'ah-ha' like red necks do when they get off on their music. Then the blacks would walk away and listen to cassettes. But the young white guys liked black music. Hey, you could say they were more tolerant than us!"

The chain of command channeled tension and excess energy into athletics, though football disabled more soldiers than all other causes combined. Till the middle of October, the hours between 10 a.m. and 3 p.m. were 'down'—too hot even to do effective desk work, though it went on.

Dessie Greer's work weeks were typical. Depending on whether paper work was constant or came in surges, shifts were assigned in six twelve-hour blocks or seven tens. Night and day shifts alternated weekly, the latter being preferred. Tightly grouped in unfinished hangars, office groups were not divided by partitions to maximize the slight air flow as a few floor fans provided. By night, work conditions were tolerable. By day, sweaty fingers spotted every paper, and brows dripped into machinery to form a paste with the wretched dust. Bold face signs were placed on word processors: "Don't lean over here!"

Offsetting the relative comfort of night work was the impossibility of sleeping in Haj tents by day. Eight or nine tentmates, half with different shifts, could not help but disturb whatever sleep could be caught in cot-soaking temperatures of Arabian summer. Three or four hours, divided between early morning and late afternoon, was considered a good 'night' for day sleepers. Lolling around during the rest of their free time, they were at least spared the ultimate in perspiratory agony when, on the day shift, fans in the hangars had to be turned off to provide enough power for the printers when lengthy documents were published.

Plastic water bottles—courtesy of the Saudi government—stood by every folding chair in the hangar like pins in a bowling alley. When the fans went off, everyone reached for their bottles. Heat debilitation was common at such times, especially for the women, for whom use of the latrine meant a longer walk in the sun than to the men's urinals (though nearby in tent city, latrines as well as showers were unisex). In spite of stern admonitions, many women preferred to limit intake of water rather than broil in order to pass it.

This early period of Desert Shield was in every way the women's baptism by fire. Only in letters were they able to describe the experience until a few women from 'outside' were admitted into the kingdom, accompanying their spouses.* Actress Victoria Tennant was married to comedian Steve Martin. In November, after the Saudi climate had ameliorated, she spoke with Melita McGrath, and turned pale while learning about the conditions.

"How do you stand it?" Tennant asked aghast.

"I don't know, but we did."

McGrath went on to describe that normal army bitching was considered whining when it came from women, so they rarely complained except among themselves. The standard male attitude seemed to be—you asked for it, here it is—this is war, ma'am. The women pretty much accepted that reality, but not the rap that they were rushing to catch the 'baby plane' out of the JOA.

For pregnancy was an instant ticket home. Men were quick to point to statistics showing far higher fertility at Ft. Camel

---

* USO shows like Bob Hope's traditional Christmas visit were not allowed to bring female entertainers unless they were married to someone in the troupe, though women were permitted to perform offshore for the Navy.

than at Ft. Campbell. Wives waiting in Kentucky were also incensed by the comparison. But neither set of critics factored in a medical cause, soon to be discovered: gamma globulin inoculations, compulsory to prevent hepatitis, were found to neutralize the efficacy of popular birth control pills. For women in the JOA, this revelation produced the joke that they had lost their Desert Shield.

For women and men alike, Saddam Hussein was a popular mental dartboard as the suffocating days and humid nights sucked up hours and sucked out sweat. The most revealing thoughts seemed to be expressed in verse. In the very early morning, sergeants chanted to their troops running in formation, who repeated each line and echoed the chorus as feet thudded down rhythmically. Around Ft. Camel, training runs produced such verses:

Lift your head and lift it high,
Air Assault is flying by.

Chorus:
   All the way, (echo)
      everyday, (echo)
   Got to go, (echo) got to be (echo)
      Air Assault! (echo) Air assault! (echo)
   There's one thing I know is right,
   Saudi girls are out of sight.

Chorus

Travel long and travel far—
Desert Shield's like R&R.

Chorus

You gotta' love this sand and dust,
Love it like Madonna's bust.

Chorus

Love those scorpions in your bed,
Saudis with fan belts 'round their head.

Chorus

Saddam, Saddam, it's all your fault—
You're gonna' get hit by Air Assault!

76

But was he, this Shakespearean tyrant? Those who readied to go to war against him knew nothing. No poll was ever taken in the 101st, but by October 1990 they probably would have subscribed to an opinion of Tacitus that "even war is preferable to a miserable peace."

October 1990

3: The U.S.S. *Independence* is the first carrier to enter the Gulf since 1974.

6: About 200,000 troops in kingdom. Schwarzkopf is required to submit an offensive plan for these forces to liberate Kuwait, though he argues the number is inadequate.

12: With Desert Shield deemed fully capable of holding off an Iraqi invasion of Saudi Arabia, but too few coalition forces presently available to mount a successful offensive, a rotation of units in kingdom with others outside is discussed between CENTCOM and the Pentagon.

V

Serving two masters; choosing two teams

October was a month of mixed fortunes for Cody and his Apaches. Peay gave him a nod to train with SOCCENT though the raid remained a when and if contingency—when the air war started, if it did, and don't be late getting back. Cody felt he had dad's car keys, but with stern orders to be home by eleven.

"Garrett and Cody convinced me," Peay recalled, "that the division would have enough Apaches when we needed them [if Iraq attacked at the dawn of the air war]. Maybe they shaded their opinion optimistically, but I wasn't inclined to be skeptical. The Apache had many critics, most of them poorly informed. Pulling off such a raid would restore confidence in the aircraft that never should have been shaken.

"Besides, what kind of commander would I be if I stood in his way? We're the Screaming Eagles. It was a pleasure that on this occasion when a job had to be done, someone asked for the One-oh-one."

Even with Peay's acquiescence, 1-101 had yet to receive a formal requirement to rehearse for the raid—and army protocol had not been observed. The intervening headquarters between the division and SOCCENT was 18th ABC, commanded by Peay's boss, Lt. Gen. Gary Luck, a man who would not be ignored in the chain of command. Moreover, he was a pilot himself, knowledgeably protective of his aviation assets.

Cody: "Starting rehearsals was like taking a car home before you bought it—you'd better drive extra careful. When Gen. Peay agreed to the tasking, we started working on the attack phase of the raid, even before we figured out the other problems. The Saudis gave us a chunk of desert where we shot up some old buses to see if we could get good target coverage. We attacked from the height we would in wartime—about 30 feet of altitude.

"Trouble was, corps aircraft were crashing about once a week in dune country, probably because of depth perception loss with NVG [night vision goggles]; so corps put out the '150 foot rule,' which generally meant you weren't allowed to fly any lower. But hell, in raid rehearsals, we were tight formation flying at 30 feet. If corps found out we were doing that for SOCCENT... well, we'd still be within the rule because we were practicing live fire attacks, which Gen. Luck had excepted, but he still might jerk my leash."

Stubby, crew cut, resembling more a first sergeant than the image of a lieutenant general, Luck was not known as a stickler for command prerogatives. Nevertheless he insisted that SOCCENT follow correct procedures if they wanted 1-101—and with no advance guarantee from him. The correct way (the army way) was for CENTCOM to request an Apache battalion, and if Luck felt it could be spared, he would designate which division would provide it. Choosing the division amounted to naming the battalion.

Cody: "I was nervous, plenty nervous, till the 101st got the nod. Army politics can intrude into things like this. Look at what happened in Panama. I knew the other [ten] Apache battalion commanders in the JOA, and all of 'em would self-castrate to do the raid. Like the attack battalions from Germany—they really impressed Peay while they were working for the division. So I knew 1-101 had strong rivals. You never could tell which of their commanders might be closer to Luck than I was. When we got the job on merit alone, it was a real relief.

"But what we finally got in mid-October was a weak tasking. It said we were OPCON [under operational control] to SOCCENT for training. That did not mean we weren't working for dvision any more—Gen. Peay wouldn't have stood still for that—and I wouldn't have accepted the mission either on those terms; but we were authorized to train with SOCCENT. The tasking didn't exempt us from corps training policies though, like the 150 foot rule. Because we'd been in the desert a month before the other helicopter units, and up on the border doing real world, real war stuff, our desert skills were more advanced. We were out there at high speed and low drag, but that didn't seem to impress corps. Not that Luck's policy wasn't sound. He called it 'crawl, walk, run.' Those crashes were the result of pilots trying to run before they could walk in the desert. Some of his staff didn't want to acknowledge that we could sprint—we were doing it, without a single accident.

"But if I had one... Hey, Cody—ever heard of the 150 rule? I'd be running trucks instead of a raid. I was serving two masters, but that wasn't as tough as making my crew selections."

Cody could put off his final selections until Johnson decided exactly how many of the sites were to be attacked. SOCCENT was studying three targets—Red, White and Blue—and estimated that it would take three Apaches to knock out each site. Consequently, Cody was to provide nine crews. He gratefully agreed to that number because if more were required 1-101 would have to divert too much of the anti-tank coverage he had promised Peay. However if practice for the raid showed that more firepower was needed at the radar sites, other services were eager to supplement or even replace his Apaches. Cody was not only serving two masters, he might have to borrow from one to lend to the other. His credit was good with both, but either could bankrupt him.

He was particularly nervous about cruise missiles and stealth bombers. Highly touted, they seemed ideal weapons against radar sites. He needed to nurture Johnson's confidence in the Apache option, and keep rivals feet out of the door.

"To convince him, I had to get ready fast even though there wasn't even a tentative date for the raid. The diplomats were still talking about a peaceful solutions, and I think bets were about even money that there wouldn't be a war. Sure, I had mixed feelings about that, especially when I started thinking about who would go on the raid."

Cody's first choice was his only easy one. Traditionally, the commander of a unit positions himself with the bulk of his force if the unit is split; and more than half of 1-101's choppers would remain as essential components of the covering force. So the book called for Cody to stay, but to the surprise of no one, he tore out that page.

"I slotted myself to lead one of the three-ship teams. Automatically, that meant Stewmon, my copilot-gunner on the battle roster, was going too. You never break up a crew unless they don't work well together. Bill Stewmon and I were like two men with one mind. Then selection got tough."

Tough at first, then excruciating because of the impact upon morale. There could be a perception that he had divided the battalion into the first and second string. Though untrue, that could be the impression.

There was also the same sort of problem that had come up with Luck. If Cody wanted particular crews, it was not the army way to go around his company commanders and pick those crews. In a way, that was what SOCCENT had done when they'd asked for 1-101 instead of simply requesting a number of Apaches from corps. So Cody followed protocol by telling his three Apache company commanders that there was a special mission on tap and he wanted them to nominate two crews each.

He wasn't surprised when his captains nominated themselves. But Cody just couldn't have all of 1-101's commanders out in Iraq. With the start of the air war, there was a strong possibility that Saddam would counter with a general ground offensive. RHIP—rank hath its privileges—and one of them was to tell subordinate commanders that they could not do what the boss had done, which was to name himself.

"There was a tactical reason too. I had to balance the strength of the battalion: no more than enough to accomplish the raid, with the rest capable of holding off a lot of tanks till we got back from the raid. There wasn't going to be a first and second string: there would be an offense and defense—equally important as they are for a football team."

But unlike football, injuries would not be equally distributed between offensive and defensive teams. The plan wasn't very far along, but all estimates pointed to the loss of at least one Apache. It was naive to hope that the raiders could pitch a no-hittter against the Iraqis' plentiful and modern anti-aircraft defenses. There would be casualties in enemy territory.

"I went over the battle roster for a full day, thinking about that promise I'd made in church. I'd promised all those families that their men would get back alive. Now I was looking at hard facts that indicated I'd be wrong.

"Maybe the main fact was that radars—and the Iraqis had very good ones—are designed to locate aircraft.

"So we had to be invisible. Undetected. All the way in and out. That problem distracted me while I made my selections, but first things first: I had to designate the members of the raid task force.

"I'm a pretty decisive guy, but I kept vacillating. I'd go over the crews again, then it was too hard. So instead I considered a name for the task force. That was easier."

The Screaming Eagles had parachuted into Normandy on D Day, 1944. They took down the Germans' fortifications so the seaborne invasion at Utah Beach could get ashore. That was pretty close to what Cody expected to do: pave the way for the invasion of Iraq's sky. Before he picked its members, he decided to call the raiders Task Force Normandy.

"The first organizational option I looked at for the task force was taking all the raiders from one company. That would give me the right number of Apaches, and men with the greatest experience in working together as a team. I'd've had 'unit integrity' which was very important to me, and came up later at a crucial point in the planning when it looked as though I'd need major support from outside the battalion. I declined that support because I wanted to really know everybody involved."

Three considerations detracted from the advantage of unit integrity: First, the company selected would be split out and isolated from the battalion, with consequent hard feelings in the other companies. Second, the raid was a prize Cody wanted to spread around as much as possible. Third, all the casualties would be suffered by one company. Cody had been the aide to the 101st's commanding general at the time of the Gander crash, almost all the caskets borne by a single battalion. In that winter month of 1985, Cody had seen his boss age ten years.

Tugging in another direction was a huge advantage inherent in the 'single company option.' With equal confidence in his three commanders, he could let them draw straws. Then luck of the draw would take responsibility and recriminations off Cody's back.

"You have to think about those things, but I came to realize it was a cop out. I let sentiment get involved—there's no denying that. Maybe at some level I was dispersing caskets. Looking back, I honestly don't know if that was uppermost or subliminal. What I do know is that the raid was an Apache pilot's dream that I couldn't turn into a lottery. Don't ask me how I got there, but early on I decided that Normandy would be a composite task force."

With himself leading a team of three Apaches against one site, there would be two other team leaders. One of them could be a company commander but the other had to be a platoon leader, because to balance service to his two masters Cody felt he should be able to point to a pair of company commanders back with Mike Davis, handling the anti-tank mission.

"The decisive factor was which two company commanders would work best with Davis."

For a period of six months, around Christmas, 1990, 1-101 had flown extensively at Hunter Liggett, a test ground near Carmel, California, a huge tract of hilly scrub country that had once been William Randolph Hearst's hunting preserve on the Big Sur. The famous tourist attraction, Hearst Castle, stood on a splendid promontory near the southern corner of Hunter Liggett.

1-101 was the army's unit to test Apache reliability and survivability in the aftermath of its suspect performance in Panama. The test conditions were the most rigorous that could be contrived, with lasers substituting for munitions, but otherwise Hunter Liggett was a real battlefield in every respect, and one in which 1-101's Apaches flew under 'fire' while carrying out a gamut of missions by day and night.

A Company's commander at the time was Newman Shufflebarger, who remained at Ft. Campbell as part of the divsion's alert force. B and C company commanders were, respectively, Doug Gabram and Jorge Garcia.

At Hunter Liggett, Gabram and Garcia had worked with Davis for as long and as closely as colleagues ever will in peacetime exercises. The three were a smooth and tested team. That marked the two captains to stay together under Davis, and thus Gabram and Garcia had unwittingly erased their eligibility for TF Normandy.

"I think it was John F. Kennedy who said life's not fair. It was a helluva reward for Doug and Jorge, but they took it like the super soldiers they've always been.

"Of course I wouldn't have selected Shufflebarger if he hadn't measured up to the Normandy criteria. They were: tactical and technical excellence, aggressiveness and courage. After I told my company commanders why Shuff was going, I went over the rest of the battle roster with them, applying the criteria. The three CO's had already made their nominations. I approved all of Shufflebarger's choices, though he had some other great aviators who were hard to leave behind. With Gabram and Garcia, there were several disagreements. They fought like hell for their choices. The crews that weren't selected definitely had advocates. Their CO's went to the mat for them till I thought I'd have to ask them to leave their pistols outside!

"The main strain was that I wouldn't permit crews to be split up. There's a tendency, for a special mission like this, to make 'all star' crews: take the best individual pilot and put him with the best individual copilot-gunner. I didn't think that was the best way, and don't think so now. I bet the Super Bowl champions could beat the Pro Bowl champions every time. It's a matter of working together, knowing each other. That only comes from a lot of experience as a crew. We didn't have time to develop that experience with new crews, no matter how great they were individually.

"What's more, I definitely did not want to give the impression that the all stars were with Normandy and the leftovers with Davis. Balance was what we had to have, and balance was what we got."

The emphasis on crews rather than individuals was also a consolation for those who were assigned with Davis rather than Cody. An instructor pilot (IP) could reason that his partner might be too inexperienced or too new to the 1-101 for the Normandy mission. His partner, in turn, could imagine that the IP might not be sufficiently aggressive for the selection criteria. Cody brooded over this 'blame' rationalization, but there was no way to prevent it.

For all the anguish he put into his selections, Cody's choices were not swallowed whole by 1-101. Some of his best aviators found themselves unwillingly on the defensive team. Cody came to dread the knock, then the closing of his door, as one after another they asked to see him alone. Eyes focused on the wall, the position of attention followed by a formal salute, meant his caller was not there to talk about maintenance reports.

"What made it so hard was that I completely emphathized with them. If Tom Garrett had not selected me for a job like this when he commanded 1-101, I'd have been standing in front of him the same way. Except I probably couldn't have kept my cool. Court martialing a guy is easier than telling him why he can't do what he does best. You're comrades who've gone through a lot together and will go through a lot more. You have the same values, especially professional values, and the top value is your ability to fight an Apache. You know you're the best, and want more than anything else to demonstrate that. The pilot standing in front of me was a mirror. When I said no, I was denying myself. I'd rather send my battalion against Moscow's triple-A than send any of my guys away with the impression that I didn't think they were good enough. Every one of them was good enough to go. The reason I knew that was because I'd flown with them all."

For that same reason, Cody's men subjected him to second guessing. Whatever their rank, all his Apache aviators were air warriors, and judged each other on that basis. This was not democracy, but an aviator's opinion was a valid as another's when it came to flying and fighting their warplane. Colonel, captain, or warrant officer, they were co-equals in the sky. As such, they conceded little to Cody's judgement in differentiating their aerial abilities.

After sounding out his most experienced pilots, Cody's first selection meeting was with the company commanders. Then all the aviators attended the second meeting where the Normandy crews were announced, after a speech by Cody that was both stern and fatherly.

"What I remember saying was that there would be enough war for everybody. The big fight would come after the raid. The most important job for us all now was to ensure solidarity. This was no time to let egos come before responsibilities. I don't know how it went over with the crews, but I expected there would be some hurt feelings."

The communal reaction was disciplined. It was during the days that followed that aviators asked to see Cody alone. "If they hadn't come in to see me, I would have sought them out. I had to let them know that I was the sonuvabitch. If I hadn't, they might have blamed their company commanders for not nominating them.

"It helped to ask them to put themselves in my place. How would they choose? They could always tell me one crew, but they weren't much help with the others!

"I remembered how the astronauts talked about 'making the cut' as their numbers were narrowed for a space mission. This was different. My guys weren't competing with each other, they were assigned to complementary roles.

"It was the toughest leadership problem I've faced or ever expect to. I'll never know how many men were convinced, but some of them weren't. And for all I did to prevent it, there was some division of the battalion into 'us,' the raiders, and 'them,' the stay-behinds. What kept the effort united was the uniform we all wore.

"For all the friendship, the respect and admiration you have for a fellow soldier, the uniform is the ultimate reminder that decisions have to be made by one guy and followed by the others.

It's something more than respective rank. The rank you wear is no more than the official designation of your postion in a hierarchy. It's your uniform that indicates willingness to take your place in that hierarchy.

"The best commanders, I believe, are consensual leaders. I'd like to think that if 1-101 were a battalion in the Civil War when they elected their officers, I'd still be the CO. Anyway, if we'd taken a ballot on who should go on the raid, there'd be two votes for each crew!"

Cody had to be the commander, the decision maker, and everyone knew it. Such authority is sacramental in the army, but in his case for exactly the opposite reason why military autocracy is accepted. The popular image is that if soldiers don't obey orders, other soldiers will die. For the raid, the aviators selected were more likely to die. None of them complained that Cody was putting them at risk—half of them were fuming because he wasn't.

For a few it was more than a complaint. It was a slight so serious that they did what a soldier has to do when an order he receives is intolerable. Cody's selection, of course, amounted to an order. Maurice was one flier who came in to tell Cody he wanted out of 1-101. What was almost worse was that Maurice said he had been defending Cody with the other crews, an indication that there were widespread misgivings about the selections.

Maurice was a chief warrant officer, and even among his most critical peers acknowledged as a—if not the—top gun. His prowess was not a reflection of fighter pilot ego, but rather his mastery of the elements of rotary flight, so that when in the air he magically integrated aircraft and avionics like an Olympic horse and rider. Maurice could talk with McDonnell Douglas as if he, not they, had built the Apache. He could show them feats they had never considered within the helicopter's capabilities. He could have been their test pilot, and may be one day, but his ambition was to fly in unfriendly skies and harm's way. He was an IP, a check pilot who made sure the other fliers knew their jobs.

"Maurice came in and said the worst thing I could have

heard—that I'd lost confidence in him. He asked to be reassigned to another battalion.

"What do I do, throw him out of the office? Chew his ass?
Appeal to him as a soldier, or as a friend? Make a speech or an
apology? Argue with him or cry with him? I'd 've done all those
things to convince Maurice that confidence was why I kept him
with the defensive team. That's where he was most valuable to
the battalion.

"We just stared at each other after he said he wanted out.
Sometimes silence is the best persuader. Maybe he didn't realize that I was at loss for words. The silence had an affect, and
gave me time to realize that I had some wriggle room:

"Maurice hadn't asked to be reassigned if I didn't put him
in Normandy. He wanted out because I hadn't. That was
diffferent than asking me to change my mind. If he could
persuade me to do that, the whole painful selection process was
void. That was impossible, and Maurice realized it. He was
admitting that orders were orders. He was too good a soldier
not to believe in that, so we didn't even mention it.

"Then it was for me to show that I hadn't lost confidence in
him. That was easy because I hadn't, not by any means—quite
the opposite. I told Maurice things about him that we both
knew were true, really high praise that normally is difficult to
express. Much harder than bracing a guy for something he did
wrong.

"I can't remember everything we said, but I felt a tide
turning. He was overwhelmed with disappointment, and so
was I, especially since I was the one who caused it. But he knew,
and I knew, that for him to transfer to another unit meant
leaving either Apaches or the Screaming Eagles. Both alternatives meant terrible sadness on top of the terrible disappointment. I wouldn't allow that. I couldn't have looked him in the
face again if I had."

To renew cohesion in 1-101, and lessen a sense of separate-
ness in TF Normandy, Cody required that all preparations and
rehearsals for the raid be battalion operations in which everyone was involved. Gabram and Garcia, for example, planned
practice routes for the raid though they themselves weren't

going. The armament requirements for the raid remained the responsibility of CW2 McNulty, though he was on the defensive team. Neither were the task force members in any way excused from supporting the division covering force mission. Everyone just worked the extra hours to do both jobs.

Gabram: "Those were 16-18 hour days. We had to be in on every brigade plan in the covering force, and those plans got changed a lot. Every exercise, anywhere: we were there. Then Normandy was always on our plates when we got back to King Fahd. We were flyin' and tryin,' and never caught up. Mercy Six (Cody's radio call sign), kept having battalion formations too. We'd fall out every couple of days, and he'd poop us up on what was happening in the JOA. 'Think war!' That was on all our briefing slides, and he kept hammering on it.

"You see, for the infantry a war didn't seem all that likely. Sure, Saddam was piling more troops into Kuwait, but after October when corps was full strength and operational, no one seemed seriously worried about an Iraqi invasion any more.

"That was sort of the feeling I got around the division. Yeah, we were here, and we'll get good and ready, but not even Saddam is fool enough to attack us. With 1-101, it was different. Cody kept telling us we would fight, and he didn't mean just TF Normandy. He'd tell us all those Iraqi troops in Kuwait weren't there just to occupy the place. They'd only leave at the point of a bayonet. That seems clear now, but at the time Iraqi diplomats kept blowing smoke that made it look like there wouldn't be a war.

"Somehow we kept up the tempo Cody demanded. We were used to long hours. We'd been away from our familes for six months at Hunter Liggett right before the war. It was familiar meeting yourself coming to work. It was a habit. Fatigue was a constant like the heat.

"Times like that you've got to have a laugh now and then. After every formation, Cody would ask for questions, and there'd usually be some bitches—like why can't we keep stuff under our cots? who needs all these inspections? when are we going to get 9 millimeters [pistols] like the division staff? For every question that day, Cody's answer was some more bad news. Finally, a little voice pipes up in the back of the formation: 'When are we going to have a change of command?'"

Garcia: "The CO [Cody] put out for us too. The battalion had some perks unavailable to the rest of the division. The best perk was the trailers way over on the other side of the airport. When Bechtel, the construction contractor for King Fahd, moved out some of their people they left about a dozen double-wide trailers. I think Col. Garrett got 'em for us. Air crews flying night missions had to have someplace to sleep during the day, and that was impossible in the heat and noise of the garage where we lived [Two men to a parking stall].

"The trailers were something to look forward to: showers, carpets, comfortable furniture and—praise God—air conditioning. A guy could get over there once a week maybe, and live like a general.

"Also, once a week, there was 'no boots' day. Everyone could wear just shorts, T shirts and running shoes. Breakfast and lunch were combined in a brunch. Sergeant Longstaff was the best food scrounger in the JOA. 1-101 got famous for pancakes. Cody's friends in Vermont sent over the maple syrup.

"When we got a little time off, we could move around better than most units. Blaine Hodge, the Headquarters Company commander, got a civilian pickup truck from somewhere. Could have been one of those wrecks out in the desert. When the Saudis have an accident, they just pick up the bodies and walk away. When I first saw the Tapline Road, I thought the Iraqis had strafed it. There's a wreck every few miles. Some of them were salvagable, and I guess that's what Blaine did. It was a little white Chevy LUV. It went with us everywhere, even into Iraq. Back at King Fahd, we could get into town sometime or down to the ARAMCO beach near Dhahran."

ARAMCO was a little America, a whole community with shopping mall, western women in shorts, and kids playing softball. It was a compound out on a peninsula in the Gulf, sealed off from Islam. Some of the Americans had been living there for thirty years. The ARAMCO compound even had a grade school, which 'adopted' 1-101 before the division arrived. The children were the strongest reminder that the Iraqis must be halted short of Dhahran, a prospect that tightened the tensor of Cody's aviators who could find few outlets for tension.

Davis: "Maybe it was because we worked under so much discipline that we also did some pretty wild things, stuff that would never go down at Ft. Campbell:

"Poor John Morgan reported in kingdom to be a copilot-gunner with B Company. Everybody at headquarters played it straight. Cody greets him, the adjutant introduces him around, then Morgan meets the Company Commander [Gabram] and his instructor pilot, Zeke Zarnowski. Except they'd swapped flight suits, so Morgan thought Doug was Zeke and Zeke was Doug. Morgan goes down to the flight line to meet his crew chief, a sergeant—but he's another impersonator, Warrant Officer Turberville ['Turbo'], who's actually one of the best fliers around. Morgan's got more mistaken identities than an Italian opera, but that's just the setup for what's coming.

"'Sergeant' Turberville walks him around the Apache, pointing out this and that, and says, 'Sir, let me show you how she taxis.' Crew chiefs are only allowed to warm up a helicopter—never, never to roll it around—and much less to fly it. That would be like a stewardess taking the controls of an airliner.

"Morgan's plenty worried; but here's his new crew chief—the mother hen of the aircraft—someone every pilot respects to the utmost—indicating it's OK for the crew chief to taxi Morgan's Apache. Well hell, he thinks: this is the war zone; maybe stateside rules are relaxed over here. Besides, Tuberville is his crew chief. He'd never put a new aviator in hot water. Oh, no.

"So Morgan looks around, climbs in front, and Turbo hops in back like he's always wanted to be a pilot. 'We'll just go out on the apron, sir,' he says over the intercom.

"They're out there, then Morgan feels the bird lift off! He can't override the controls because Turbo's in the pilot's seat. 'Just once around the pattern, sir!' Turbo sounds like he's about to fulfill a fantasy.

"If that isn't enough, Cody comes up on the radio: 'WHAT THE HELL's GOING ON, 935?' That's the aircraft tail number. Turbo tells Morgan on the intercom that he'd better respond—Turbo's too busy trying to fly the Apache. Morgan stammers something to Cody about 'a temporary emergency, sir...' It sounded like he felt his assignment with 1-101 would be very temporary! Cody, Killian, the battalion safety officer—everybody in headquarters is running around, tearing their hair, when 935 finally comes in for this wobbly high speed landing, bumps a few times, and stops. A couple of us duck like the rotor blades are going to hit us. On the flight line, the real crew chief is being punished by doing pushups. Cody stalks up to the Apache: stands there with his hands on hips while Morgan and Turbo unbuckle.

"I've seen some guys come out of some pretty awful crashes, but none of 'em looked as white as Jim Morgan when he climbed out of that cockpit."

October 1990

13: U.N. Security Council unanimously condemns Israel for killing 19 Palestinians at Jerusalem's West Wall.

29: Ten sailors of the U.S.S. *Iwo Jima* in the Gulf are killed in the explosion of a steam pipe.

VI

New Age: the tether and the telephone

Initiations like Morgan's provided what litle relief there was for the aviation community that was beginning to fall from grace. In spite of Luck's 'crawl, walk, run' policy, crashes continued more regularly than the ground commanders would tolerate. Not only the heliborne 101st, but the 82nd and 24th divisions as well, relied on the moblity of their choppers to shrink vast desert distances and watch for the enemy. The high accident rate, elevated by only a few units, brought down official wrath upon them all. The aviators felt themselves singled out as a class for a form of collective punishment: one after another, the helicopter units were subjected to the dreaded 'IG,' a top to bottom scrutiny by inspectors general.

In peacetime, 'an IG' is cause for all other work to stop, as the unit puts its records in order, rearranges its affairs to comply with the book, spits and polishes all equipment for a once-a-year facade. The annual IG is to be endured as part of army life; a special IG is an unmistakable sign of displeasure from above. The aviators resented it to the point of alienation from the rest of the desert army.

Davis: "There was a basic unfairness about this whole safety purge. Sure, there were crashes, but there was no safety baseline for desert flying in conditions like this. It had never been done before. The inspectors didn't know what to expect any more than we did. All this was taking a lot of time from what we needed to do to support the infantry."

While corps cracked its whip, Cody's other master required a different performance from 1-101. On the firing range south of Dhahran, SOCCENT arranged a fleet of junked vehicles to approximate the layout of the radar sites. On a moonless night, the kind desired for the actual raid, TF Normandy took to the sky. Briefly, the nine ships orbited King Fahd, ended radio contact, then split into three teams, disappearing from each other to make separate runs on the mock targets a half hour away. Red team, Shufflebarger leading, struck first. Observing the 150 foot rule en route, his Apache and wingman 'went tactical' for the approach, descending to thirty feet to open up with Hellfires, rockets and 30mm cannons.

The rockets were 'fleshettes,' slender projectiles that burst into myriad slivers to spray enemy troops in the open.

Davis: "During Desert Shield, you could also call them fleshettes because they were as scarce as chorus girls. Everyone was screaming for 'em, but we had priority from SOCCENT. McNulty went down to draw sixty from corps. He got 'em, along with some very dirty looks."

Cody had given Shufflebarger a maximum of four minutes to complete his attack. Through the eerie display in his helmet visor, the vehicles slowly disintegrated, sand puffed from cannon strikes, and blossoms spread on his screen as Hellfires bored through their targets. His wingman did the primary work. Shufflebarger stood by to finish off incomplete damage. Tensely, tentatively satisfied at Red team's results, he broke radio silence and ordered his team to pull off.

Blue and White teams followed to chew up adjoining targets. It was a light but no sound show for the aviators. Acoustically insulated in their headsets, they watched missiles strike inaudibly. 'Nintendo war,' reporters were to call such uninvolved destruction, and the teams admit a resemblance to electronic games. The Apaches fired salvos with detached deliberation, sliding in the air only to focus on new targets. All completed their attacks in the alloted four minutes.

Garcia: "It's a little abstract, but that helps you concentrate on what has to be done. It's different from an artilleryman firing a howitzer. He never sees his target. It's also different than an infantryman shooting his machinegun. He sees his tracers reaching for a target, and that's pretty personal from what I've been told. Attacking from an Apache at night is both remote and real, and hard to describe. Sort of like putting a tennis ball in play, seeing if it will hit where you want it to, and the opponent's reaction. If you've surprised him, you soon realize he doesn't have much of a chance to get the ball back to you. That's something about New Age that needs explaining."

Davis: "We were really hot to see the videos. Snapped 'em out of the nose while the rotors were still spinning. This was something we had to practice too—getting that film out and on the way to SOCCENT pronto. They had to know the extent of damage right away, even though we'd give a spot report when we pulled off the targets in Iraq. All those Air Force birds were waiting to hear if they had a clear path to Baghdad on opening night.

"Right after the shoot south of Dhahran, we were dying to see the target coverage. Cody and Killian were looking right over my shoulder, saying 'Yeah!' and 'OK!' Coverage looked pretty good, but physically inspecting the targets had to wait till morning."

The videos were good enough for Jesse Johnson. He viewed them, rewound the cassette, and set up the VCR for Schwarzkopf who had reserved for himself the decision whether or not to use Apaches. When his boss had sat down, Johnson froze the first frame to explain the readouts and symbols on the pilot's display. Then he pressed the 'forward' button.

As if some underwater camera was exploring a seabed, sand dunes began to undulate on the screen. This was the terrain before the junkyard. Then the trucks emerged, dark silhouettes on the chalky desert. Shufflebarger's voice announced the code word to engage the targets. From the top of the screen, a coruscating ball homed in on the largest wreck. Numbers began to count down on the screen, indicating the missile's time of flight.

"Is this actual speed?" Schwarzkopf inquired.

"Yes, sir."

To produce a picture, the infrared camera compares the relative heat of objects. The first Hellfire strike sent out jets of white light like a Roman candle—hot metal flying off the wreck.

"Wow," said CINCCENT, as rockets and cannons added pyrotehnics. The sound of firing was muffled thumps. "That looks pretty easy."

Johnson nodded, glancing to perceive Schwarzkopf's expression. Easy, or too easy to be convincing? CINCCENT seemed to scowl throughout the four-minutes of demolition, then the screen turned into a rage of white lines and static. Johnson got up and punched 'rewind.'

"Right good coverage, general. We'll have a walk-through damage assessment in the morning." Schwarzkopf's mouth remained downturned, but Johnson recognized that as a thoughtful, not necessarily skeptical, visage: the natural set of the CINCCENT's face in contemplation. "I recommend we keep Apaches primary," Johnson concluded.

"OK. Give 'em a go. You're sure they'll get 100 percent? Is it all going to be as smooth as the video?"

"There're navigation, range and rescue problems, sir, that we're just beginning to work on."

"Keep me informed."

Johnson had scheduled the damage assessment briefing for five minutes, and that's what it took. He left the room as the next briefer entered.

"The next day we were go!" Cody elated. "We'd proved what we could do once we got on the targets. After that, everything was about how to get there, and what happened if anyone got hit. When Schwarzkopf chopped, this was our high. But what went up, sure came down..."

The downer arrived as Thanskgiving was approaching. Already the menu had been announced for what would surely be the most gratifying meal since the Screaming Eagles left home. Garcia's was the Apache company on strip alert, ready to scoot up to the border if Saddam decided to spoil the American holiday. With Gabram, Garcia headed out to the flight line where his Apaches' avionics systems were being checked.

Garrett and Cody were huddled at Aviation Brigade headquarters, discussing how sister service relations had soured still more, specificly with AFSOC, the Air Force component of SOCCENT, who were crowding out the 101st's helicopters by sheer weight of size and numbers. Hostility had become so open that AFSOC mess halls had posted signs, 'Army personnel keep out.'

The Army aviators had dual cause to feel unsupported. Under the prewar CENTCOM plans, the terminal and nearby hangars had been allocated entirely to the 101st. SOCCENT was to be in Riyadh, and originally was, but then deemed to have too high a profile in the Saudi capital, and had to move out. For their new home, they selected King Fahd, arriving early and with plenty of money to requisition space from Bechtel who had no knowledge of CENTCOM's plans.

Moreover, AFSOC's adverse possession was not challenged by Peay, who wished to live and let live—better to keep his mind on the covering force mission. Protecting his peace of mind was Bolt. Typical of chiefs of staff, he had responsibility to order the importance of matters which should be brought to the attention of the boss. The space squabble with AFSOC apparently did not rank high among Bolt's priorities.

Then there was the irony that TF Normandy was doing a job for SOCCENT—AFSOC's job, really, and perhaps their most dangerous job in the war. Yet now, except for alert crews, the Army aviators could not even chow down in SOCCENT mess halls.

The 101st's aviators remember the moment the way they do a Kennedy assassination—where they were, what they were doing. The unmistakable sound is the first memory—*whoosh* —a Hellfire leaving the launching rack.

Garcia: "I froze. It was a couple of seconds before I could glance at Doug. He was in a freeze frame too."

Garrett: "Dick and I looked up at the same time. His face said he didn't want to believe it. That must have been my appearance too. We both came out of our chairs together. Cody was gone for the flight line. I didn't even see him blast out the door."

In the ten seconds between the launch and explosion, Garrett raced for the top of the parking lot, somehow with the presence of mind to grab a pair of binoculars.

"I had no idea where it would hit—not even the direction—but while I was taking those stairs three at a time, I remembered Garcia's Apaches were pointed toward AFSOC."

Apache 383 was 'cold': no power systems running, and every passive safety feature checked out and in place. Fred Pieper and Dave West, C Company's armament and maintenance officers, were running inspections for each Apache on strip alert, and had just moved on to the next one when 383 did the impossible—fired a Hellfire while sitting on the ground.

The officers' backs were turned. Like a scream, the whoosh spun them around. The Hellfire rose slowly—Pieper remembers some of the numbers on it—the booster rocket ignited, and the missile continued its impossible flight, curving rather than holding a straight trajectory, as if confused in search of an absent target. Hellfires aim only for objects illuminated by lasers separate from the missile. No lasers were on, so flight in this case was random, though the unguided missile seemed to recognize an acquaintance and considerately avoided the nearest Apache.

Next in its path were the army's largest helicopters, Chinooks, one of whose crew chiefs stood atop, working on the rotor mast. The Hellfire whooshed by him between the fuselage and rotor. Angling to a peak of a hundred feet, the missile hesitated. Receiving no commands, it took an indifferent glide path toward the AFSOC ammo dump.

The boom was muffled, the secondary explosions deafening. The Hellfire struck a bunker full of warheads and fuses, stored separately from AFSOC's bombs. Half a million dollars of munitions spurted, roared and skyrocketed in an audio-visual display not witnessed again until the victory day celebration in Washington, D.C.

Sirens wailed all over King Fahd. Assuming a terrorist attack, the 101st's security company turned to charge the ammo dump. "Accident! Accident!," someone screamed to them. Dropping their weapons, they joined in fire fighting.

For Garrett watching through binoculars, the scene had the

unreality of a horror movie. Cody leaned against an Apache, needing its support for his legs that seemed a blend of lead and rubber. Dark complected, Garcia was whiter than the ubiquitous dust. He was new to Apaches; to check out as a pilot Garcia had required a waiver to enter army aviation so late in his career. As AFSOC's ammo dump boomed and burned, he wondered if he would be allowed to return to the low tech rigors of the Rangers where he had served for the last four years.

Cody was the first to revive. He raced to find Garcia, to ensure that every failsafe system had been in place and operating. If so, there had been either incredibly sophisticated sabotage, or something had gone wrong with the Apache's black boxes—manufacturer's tech reps in the JOA could decide which, but for now Cody had to believe that it was either one or the other. He *had* to believe it, then convince his shaken battalion that despite waves of stern-faced investigators that would surely engulf them, the truth would out.

What churned his stomach was the likelihood of investigations so protracted that 1-101 would lose the Normandy mission. Reverberation from the ammo dump explosions would reach every other Apache battalion in Saudi Arabia. The echo would be their applause.

This caused Cody to reflect that for the raid to succeed in Iraq, everything would have to go right; but even more so, before the raid nothing could go wrong or rivals would step in like eager understudies. The army's first war since Vietnam was so internally competitive—it reminded him how the New Age army was sometimes in a tug of war with its Vietnam-era leadership.

For example, the blasts from the ammo dump rocked 86th Evacuation Hospital, a cluster of prefabs adjoining the terminal complex. Working her shift there was Lori Gabram, an army nurse, a lieutenant married to Doug, B Company's commander. Someone in her ward shouted that the army fired a missile at the air force—prepare for mass casualties! She did, but in an hour the conflagration was under control with no one injured. Yet her anxiety remained high:

"It might have come from one of Doug's Apaches! I knew

this could be an awful incident for someone's career. I had to find out who shot the Hellfire, but the Apaches were parked about a mile away, so no one knew and no one at the hospital cared much except me.

"This was still my shift so I couldn't go out to get more information. Then an orderly said the crew had turned in urine specimens for drug testing. He told me which refrigerator they were in.

"The racks were full of pee bottles for a lot of reasons. I read every label, looking for names I knew. Pieper. West. Those were the only ones I recognized. I felt terribly sorry for them, but so relieved that B Company wasn't involved. If they were, I knew that it would be one strike and you're out."

That result would shatter the Gabrams' lifestyle and status as DOD DINK's (Dept. of Defense, Dual Income, No Kids), though now, to be married in the desert was to be harried. They had met while students at Bowling Green University (Ohio). Doug took an ROTC commission while Lori finished nursing school. To qualify for the army's 'joint domicile' program, the couple had to be wed, and therefore they were in 1986. Hoping to be posted to Germany, they found the army had no position there for Lori. The sole joint domicile assignment was at Ft. Campbell, with no assurance whatever they would be near each other in time of war.

Only lovers' luck reunited them in Saudi Arabia. The state-side military hospital to which Lori was assigned did not deploy to the Gulf, but she was sent to 86th Evac as a replacement. Originally it was was to be set up in Dhahran, but to the joy of the Gabrams, moved to King Fahd.

After three months of separation, Doug had stood by his idling HUMM-V at the bottom of the ramp when Lori debarked. Grimy from the cramped 15-hour flight and reeling from jet lag, she staggered into his arms. Through her fatigue Lori could not understand what he was saying: In a half hour, he informed her, she had to be at the hospital for an orientation briefing; now just get in the HUMM-V, and let him take care of the details.

One eye on his watch, Doug roared across the runway for Cody's vacant trailer. Twenty minutes, and the Gabrams, were well spent when Doug checked the time again. Someone was covering for him on the flight line. He opened the trailer door and pointed her to the hospital: she should walk over and find the briefing room. Lori barely comprehended the instructions. In a moment she heard the HUMM-V drive away. There had been no time for a shower but she had to put on some clothes other than those she had flown in half way around the world. Groping in her duffle bag, she pulled out a T shirt, running shorts and sneakers.

Soldiers and airmen seemed to be looking at her as she trudged across the tarmac. Someone pointed her to the briefing room. Lori was the last new arrival to enter the room. All the rest were in the prescribed uniform: desert camouflage, harness, weapon, boots, and gas mask strapped to the thigh. There was a collective gasp as behind the podium a colonel—the hospital commander—stopped in mid-sentence.

Lori: "That wasn't a good way to start! The colonel kept close track of me from then on. You see, there were several of us married to guys in the 101st. The colonel seemed to think we were beating the system whenever we saw them. He put a 10 p.m. curfew on the nurses tents—which we named Camp Chastity. It got so the 86th Evac could be made into a sequel for MASH—that's where this colonel's mindset was, back in the Korean War."

In tent city too, married love in the New Age army was finding a way through and around the non-cohabitation policy of the old. Dessie and Calvin Greer were able to obtain intimacy in exchange for information. An order from G3 wasn't an order till Dessie typed it up on her computer; consequently, information often reached Calvin before the order came down the chain of command.

Before long, officers in 2-502 became aware of the corporal's back channel and exploited it. When his battalion pulled guard around division headquarters, it seemed that Calvin regularly drew the duty. The sooner he got the word from her, the sooner his battalion could begin planning for what division would send down.

Beholden to the Greers, Calvin's officers provided a form of consideration. In 2-502, policy was that an enlisted man could not leave the battalion area alone. That made it difficult to arrange rendezvous, but Calvin found his squad leader to be very accomodating when Dessie had some free time in her tent—a tent, as everyone knew, was off limits to any male. Nevertheless, Calvin's squad leader invariably obliged him: the two wound through Ft. Camel as Dessie finished her shift at G3. Her four tentmates made themselves scarce. An improvised partition was in place, and while his squad leader snored on the other side, the Greers enjoyed privacy.

Dessie: "Rest of the time we had to write each other, just like one of us was back in the States. When the Oh-deuce went up north, he might as well have been back in the States. I was worried about him up there. He worried about me too—said he had himself to worry about, his squad, and me too. Scuds, terrorists and gas—that's what worried him about me back here.

"The most scared I was was when they had that drive-by shooting up at Bastogne."

This was a murky incident, apparently a terrorist attack, about which accounts still vary. In any event, one night while 2-502 was training at Bastogne, a truck or maybe two approached their camp with headlights off. They were challenged by sentries and stopped. They may have returned to Tapline Road, but if so, someone first got out and fired off a few bursts at the Americans. Helicopter and ground search turned up nothing.

The next day, Saudi police combed through outlying villages and interrogated itinerant bedouins. Rumors reached the 101st that some Iraqi sympathisizers were responsible; but then again it may have been Saudi nationalists, resentful that an American outpost stood on their frontier.

Keith Huber was Dessie's boss and ran G3 Ops, where the New Age army interfaced with an ancient culture:

"The drive-by shooting set off a lot of worries that we'd been expecting. We could not just seal off our FOB's and training areas. This was the Saudis' kingdom, and they—not us—controlled who went through. We weren't allowed to stop them even if they went up to every position we dug for the covering force. That made us very uncomfortable at first, but cooperation with the local emirs proved to be good. They were the ones who could find out who had legitimate business in an area we were in. Anybody else they ran out real fast.

"Up around Oasis, for example, the emir was super friendly. His territory was closest to Iraq, and he knew we were in his province to stop an invasion. We really won him over when Col. Garrett took him for a helicopter ride.

"All those rumors that we'd have cultural clashes never materialized. Anybody could wear a crucifix or even a Star of David. We still got ham in our rations. The aviators wore American flags on their flight jackets. Chapel services were held in tents or out in the open. It was division policy to have a male ride shotgun with female drivers, but that was our only real concession to Islamic customs.

"The religious police hassled for a while about women like Dessie running in shorts, but Gen. Peay brushed that off. At first, Vietnam veterans were deeply suspicious of Arabs, but gradually came to realize this was a different war."

Peay was the 101st's most prominent Viet vet, the foremost 'connecting file' between two wars united by heat but otherwise as different as their respective eras. He had served in Vietnam for two years as an artillery officer, first in 1967 with the 4th Division, then in 1971 with the 1st Air Cavalry. Vietnam was no distant memory for him, but rather a constant reminder of how badly a fighting force could deteriorate if morale and discipline began to slip.

He rarely spoke of his Vietnam experiences, though they had resulted in a Silver Star and a fine war record. For Peay it seemed Vietnam was like a childhood trauma, with an effect buried deep in his psyche yet close to the surface of his motivations. His Purple Heart did not commemorate his real wound from Vietnam, one that remained raw for twenty years: in Vietnam, Peay had seen not only men but an army die.

It was his army, that of his classmates at VMI, the West Pointers who were his colleagues, and a wide coterie of officers and sergeants whose dedication withered in the scorn of the 1970's, and very many abandoned the uniform—for the army had been a light that failed.

For those who remained to remove the curse of Vietnam, the

light slowly began to glimmer again. First when the draft was abolished, then by degrees as a new and purposeful meaning for a tired and cynical term, professionalism, became defined by a new generation of soldiers recruited by the slogan, "Be all that you can be—you can do it in the army."

America hardly took notice. Viet vets in the civilian world would often mock the possibility of such a transformation. *Yeah, be all that you can be. If you can't do it in the army, you can't do it anywhere.* They weren't listening closely to a change in self-designation. In the 60's and 70's they were GI's; in the 80's and 90's people in the army called themselves soldiers.

The transformation occurred quite quietly around 1977, when much deadwood was chopped away, and a multitude of time servers pensioned. The army became a near brother/sisterhood of like minded people willing to serve certain unselfish ideals that amounted to a calling. Their values—instilled rather than imposed—were validated through the benefaction of Reagan defense budgets, providing the HUMM-V's, Abrams tanks, and Apaches that were the envy of the world.

And like a calling, like the wellspring of a religion, the unjust martyrdom of America's army from Vietnam remained vivid in the memories of the desert army's commanders, participants in starkly contrasting wars. Said Peay, addressing the 101st's veterans at the first Division Association reunion after the desert war:

"[There was an] intangible that was constantly in the minds of us who had fought in Vietnam. We remembered you who fought with us. Our experience in the jungle was with us in the desert. Mentally, we swore that victory would never again be taken from us after it was won on the battlefield. With this sentiment, Camp Eagle II, the division's base in Saudi Arabia, was named in memory of Camp Eagle in Vietnam."

Camp Eagle II (Ft. Camel) hardly resembled the decadent army bases of late Vietnam. Peay made sure of that. Soldiers, on or off duty, would be presentable. Even sweat bands tied around the head were banned.

"We're Screaming Eagles, not pirates," growled Weiss, perfectly expressing Peay's convictions. Philosophically, the commanding general and his sergeant major (a former drill instructor) were as one: discipline was dogma, and appearance, like faith, was the substance of things unseen. In short, Peay would have his division not only win the current war but expiate and exorcise the last one—like a poor but proud parent, pep talking a son through college.

At the time of the Hellfire incident, both the 101st's brigadiers and the colonels commanding brigades were Viet vets, but none of the lieutenant colonels and very few sergeants. 'Veterancy' was something between a club, a priesthood, and kitchen cabinet; but for the rest of the soldiers, Vietnam was not on their conscience, so they did not empathize with how embedded it was in Peay's. It was at their middle management level that his policy of 'get ready for war but keep garrison standards' jarred with colliding priorities.

Pre-Vietnam, the army lived by a 'zero defects' philosphy. Later recognized as stifling initiative along with individualism, zero defects gave way to 'the freedom to fail.' Now, for good reasons as well as bad, the former philosophy seemed to make a comeback, with Bolt the most ardent backer.

Typical were the onerous inspections that set Aviation Brigade's teeth on edge. Similar was the insistence on immaculate briefing charts and intolerance for even typographical errors, implying coequal emphasis on show and go.

Such rationalization did not go down smoothly in the New Age army whose discipline disguised differences with the disciplinarians. At the troop level it was expressed in their preference for the FOB's over Camp Eagle II. Up north, they lived in open desert, training hard and long, but under the eyes of only their unit officers. Mail, showers, and better food awaited them at Ft. Camel, but so did garrison regulations and numerous inspections.

"Trust me on this one," was Peay's reply to a remonstrance from one of his brigade commanders. On rare occasions when he had to buck up individual soldiers, Peay told them this: "We love ya' [and he meant it], but we're Screaming Eagles. We're different from the other divisions."

It was tough love, and comparative differences for the most part resulted in no advantage for Screaming Eagles. Ft. Camel was intermediately comfortable between the 101st's sister divisions in 18th ABC. Upon their arrival, the 24th Mech had trundled right out into the desert, and lived throughout the war under conditions equivalent to the 101st's FOB's. The 82nd, by contrast, had relatively sumptuous quarters by the coastal town of Jubail. King Fahd had been allocated to the 101st, SOCCENT's usurpation nothwithstanding, but Peay could have opted for the desert had he so wished.

But before he went to the Gulf, Peay read up on the North African campaigns of World War II. Famous German and allied commanders alike wrote of the necessity for a 'tether' in the desert: a base from where supply lines radiated, and to which the fighting forces connected with their administration; a place of permanence and a place to return. That Ft. Camel was unappreciated as a tether can be marked down to three causes: the aforementioned irritants of its management, the less than obvious necessity for a tether (well understood only by Peay and his logisticians); and most importantly, the relative deprivation Screaming Eagles felt vis a vis soldiers from other commands with whom they had contact.

Rear Echelon Males & Females (REMF's) have always been held in contempt by front line soldiers. It was not REMF's and their comforts that Screaming Eagles resented, but rather soldiers like those of the 24th Mech who, for all the austerity of their desert domicile, had more liberal access to the ultimate luxury and addiction of the war—the telephone.

Phone calls in Saudi Arabia were analagous to heroin hits in Vietnam. With the right contacts, they were widely available, affordable, a much sought escape from an alien environment; and like the drug, the more you used it, the more you wanted. Spurring the addiction was an additional craving: to get no less than the other guys. For the first few months, phone calls were largely unauthorized if not illicit. By world standards, Saudi Arabia's telecommunication system was well developed, but concentrated in cities which only REMF's regularly visited. It was because the 24th Mech was allowed to use civilian phones that the 101st felt relatively deprived.

In another carryover from Vietnam, Peay was nearly phobic about terrorism. He would not let his troops form long lines in front of unguarded phone booths where drive-by machinegunners could mow them down. He made a high priority of installing phone banks at Ft. Camel, but technical and contractural problems delayed them till Thanksgiving. Meanwhile, the Screaming Eagles demonstrated the truth of a jingle heard in AT&T ads: 'when you gotta' talk, you gotta' talk.'

To call or be called from home was more than a pleasure, it was a mark of accomplishment no matter what rank the soldier. It involved either slipping away to a civilian facility, or patching through the military network to connect with a commercial trunk. Most prized and prestigious of all was knowledge of the 101st's 800 numbers, intended for official calls to the States. In one brigade, in one month, the 800 bill was over a million dollars. Shortly, access to military phones was virtually denied, and every call logged. But the 101st was designed and trained for night operations. In the darkest hours its soldiers knew how to find what they were looking for. This period was perfect for calls to the States where midnight in Arabia was mid-morning in Kentucky.

Moreover, though outgoing calls were forbidden, the army could do nothing about incoming. At night Garrett kept his official phone by his bed, both to safeguard it and for notification if there was a helicopter accident or outbreak of war. Neither emergency ever interrupted his sleep, but rarely a night passed without the phone ringing for some soldier in his brigade.

Col. Tom Hill commanded First Brigade:

"If the 60's and 70's were the age of instant gratification, maybe the 80's should be called the decade of instant communication. That's what our young guys expected. They were brought up with touch tones, cordless phones, cellular phones, calling cards, satellites and beepers. They'd watched Just Cause [Panama] on TV, and seen the 82nd calling home while under fire! So calling home from Saudi Arbia was no big deal. Three bucks a minute, but what else was there to spend your money on? And it was fun for them to get over on the chain of command. They were in a guerrilla war with the chain of command, and winning."

It was the only war being fought that fall. All else were preparations, vigil, anticipation and speculation. The mission of Desert Shield, to deter an Iraqi invasion of Saudi Arabia, had obviously succeeded, but the occupation of Kuwait continued with scant prospects of ending. Go home or to war?—someone had to tell the Screaming Eagles.

November 1990

2: Iraqi radio announces that Saddam's foes will "curse their destiny" if they attack.

8: 200,000 additional combat forces, including 1,200 tanks of 7th Corps in Germany, are ordered to the Gulf to provide Schwarzkopf with an "offensive option."

13: At the Dhahran Officers Club, Schwarzkopf outlines the Hail Mary plan for his generals.

16: Secretary of State Baker rejects Soviet initiative to link Iraqi evacuation of Kuwait with Israel's evacuation of Palestinian lands.

19: Saddam reinforces his occupation of Kuwait with 250,000 additional troops.

27: U.N. tentatively approves "all necessary means" to eject Iraq from Kuwait. Saddam given till 15 January 1991 to withdraw.

28: Two former chairmen of the Joint Chiefs of Staff publicly advise against an offensive; that instead sanctions be allowed to take effect.

VII

Waiting it out

In November, after the Pentagon hinted that 18th ABC units might be replaced by fresh troops—a process called rotation—the Third Brigade CO, Bob Clark, began a message for his troops almost plaintively:

"Rumors are everywhere! But none of them are true, so far as I know. There have been no changes to our status in Saudi Arabia and, while rotation plans are being discussed, no decisions have been made. We will let you know just as soon as we know anything."

Rumors were indeed everywhere. Back in Kentucky, instant though sporadic communication tended to disrupt the support groups, infecting them with rumors, some good, some bad, almost all false. The 101st retained a presence at Ft. Campbell where each unit had a 'rear detachment,' a handfull of soldiers who were either very recently assigned or otherwise excused from service in the Gulf. Rear detachments were the official conduit for news from the JOA, but despite the best intentions their information was often useless and always outdated by 72 hours. The 'real' news came, and the rumors spawned, when some wife's phone rang.

Within hours of their arrival at Dhahran, Doug Gabram's company was assembling their Apaches outside a warehouse owned by a kindly Englishman. "Ring home if you like, lads," he said, gesturing to the phone in his office.

So as not to run up his phone bill, the aviators decided that their wives should use a phone tree to call back to Dhahran. Doug planted the tree by telling Lori (still at Ft. Campbell at the time) that when they finished their conversation, she should call a platoon leader's wife, giving her the warehouse's number. That lady, in turn, should tell the next, and so on till everyone in the warehouse had talked to home. The unexpected hookup gratified the parties on both sides of the world.

But only B Company had been putting their helicopters together by the good Englishman's warehouse. After the calls, their wives were bubbling with excitement—but wives from the other companies fumed with disappointment. Why had B Company alone been so privileged? In their indignation, they turned on the head of the battalion support group, Vicki Cody:

"I didn't know. I didn't receive a call either. I got a hold of Lori, and she told me how the tree happened. I passed that on to the other women, but some of them were still pissed. One officer's wife said Doug Gabram had compromised the life of her husband by saying where he was calling from! Just ridiculous. That was a very bad scene, and there were others that always came up when someone talked to her man in Saudi.

"We weren't a bunch of dingy, hysterical females—far from it. But this was something no one had ever experienced. We were absolutely starved for believable information. I can't think of any people who went through what we did except the wives of POW's, especially Vietnam. My God, I can't imagine how they survived it—how they held on to their sanity. Five, six, seven years without getting any news, without hearing a voice.

"But the Gulf network sure had a down side. A couple would get to talking on the phone, and he'd say something like 'Billy

Benson almost died.' Well, Billy may have caught dysentery from the water and had been pretty sick, but that's not what his wife hears from another wife.

"He'd probably written her that he was in the hospital, but for a while letters were taking a month to get back here. So the first thing she heard was that Billy was almost dead. Naturally she wants him evacuated, brought back here right now. I'd ask the rear detachment to check it out. That took a week or more, while Billy's already returned to duty. But the system got clogged with messages like that. While one supposed emergency was getting tracked down, the phone calls created others, and they all got stacked up.

"There were real emergencies, most of them on this side, most in the first couple of months, and most of those financial. I mean real emergencies.

"Our first support group meeting after the battalion left was in September, at the chapel. We had about a hundred people, and a clinical psychologist there—I think his name was Walt. He told us what happens to us during separations like this. It was very informative, and at the end there were questions. This lady raised her hand like she was embarrassed, and said some rambling things we didn't quite understand. Walt nudged me, and said we had to talk to her afterwards.

"When the meeting was over we approached her—asked how she was doing—it there were any problems. She just looked at the floor, and tears started down her face. Her husband was enlisted. He only made about 800 a month, and he took the check book with him. He left her with $20 cash, three kids, and an empty fridge. I just hugged her till she could get over it. She was terribly shy, and didn't want to be a bother. Bother! That's what a support group is for!

"It really hit me how some enlisted wives were living on the edge. For some screwy reason, the troops weren't getting a separation allowance. If Desert Shield had been a training exercise, they would have gotten an extra couple of hundred bucks per month for being away from their homes. But along comes Catch 22: the division headquarters was now in Saudi, so the troops weren't away from 'home.' By the army's reasoning, home is where the division flag is.

"This took a long time to get sorted out. Eventually, we got back pay through some trade off for the separation allowance. I forget what it was called, but I didn't get mine till January.

"But right here in front of me was this mother of three with a bare fridge, a fist full of bills and no credit! I'll tell you who came through, and that was the civilian community.

"Sgt. Cantrell said start with the chaplain's office. They'd begun to receive donations. By the time we checked them out, they had a room full of canned goods and ready-to-eat food. That wasn't all. We got calls from people in Clarksville [TN] and Hopkinsville [KY], asking where they should send their checks. We didn't ask them for anything; they asked *us*!

"Those were calls to the battalion, but it was happening all over Ft. Campbell. The chaplain's office became the clearing house so the neediest got what they needed regardless of their unit. That lady was saved, and it was from the goodness of the hearts of average, hard working people who had never met us, but who loved us and what our men were doing over in the Gulf. I still get teary thinking about it.

"Payday was when I'd really find out how people were doing. Money problems outnumbered all the others ten to one. I'd sit there, sometimes right at Dick's old desk, and say hi to everyone coming in to pick up her allotment check. If a wife was hurting, I'd talk it over and usually connect her with Sgt. Cantrell. He arrived in October to be the senior NCO for the battalion rear detachment. He was absolutely dedicated to winning the war on the home front. And he was a miracle worker when it came to cutting red tape. I'd tell him what the problem was, then he'd drive the lady all over post, getting the paperwork done.

"If she had a debt problem, Sgt. Cantrell would talk to the merchant. Every one of them stretched out payments as soon as he asked. They'd do that even though the economy here was devastated when the 101st moved out. It was just so heart warming. It made you think, what if people were this nice all the time? It would be a different world."

Lori Gabram had the dual experience of being in a support group, then when she went to the Gulf, becoming one of the soldiers supported: "Doug and I had bought a house in

Clarksville. When I got orders for Saudi Arabia, my neighbor found out and said he'd watch the house—and not to worry. He was Sergeant Major Oates, a retired Vietnam vet from the division. He didn't just watch the place, he secured all the windows, and had the police to patrol around there. When we got back, our lawn was mowed, and the refrigerator stocked. Oates wouldn't take a penny for what he did.

"There's a saying that the army takes care of its own. We thought that meant just people in uniform, but the army includes communities of civilians too. In peacetime they love our business, but in wartime they show they really love us. Americans are the kindest people in the world. When they appreciate what you're doing, they show it with kindness that makes you choke."

During the weeks before she deployed, Lori underwent much training for treatment of chemical casualties, and how to protect herself from these feared substances that had been banned internationally since World War I; and not used since even by the likes of Hitler, but threatened by intimations from Saddam. In her support group, Lori's NBC (nuclear, biological, chemical) training produced a dip in the emotional roller coaster ride to Thanksgiving. On the home front there were fewer undulations, because from the now reliable mail and occasional phone contacts, they sensed a sort of stability developing in the desert. But stability also implied the calm before a storm, a feeling that things were too quiet, that something big was brewing over there. For the soldiers in the desert, the prospects of peace and war whipsawed the emotions.

Weiss: "Every peace initiative went up like a balloon, then popped. We'd hear from the media that this statesman or that head of state was hopeful after he saw Saddam. Just as regularly we'd get intelligence that he was revving up his war machine another notch. G2's [intelligence experts] would rather be wrong than surprised. We'd react, usually with aviation, to every report. That got old when it happened over and over again. Uncertainty was Saddam's best weapon in psychological warfare. He fought that war pretty well. Would he invade or wouldn't he? Would he pull out or stay put? Would he use chems [chemical warfare] or not? Every possibility put you in a different state of mind."

It was a constantly speculative state of mind, in which rumor and routine eroded readiness. A Third Brigade soldier wrote a hundred word article, "Attitude Check," for the desert news letter. In it he facetiously advised that one had been in the desert too long if one looked forward to the next concert by the 'horny horns,' a small brass ensemble from the division 'band in the sand'; or if camels started to flirt; if three minutes was plenty of time for a shower; that flies over a latrine were welcome company; that skipping stones along crests of sand dunes was a sport of science, skill and pleasure.

Spoofing an after action report for Desert Shield, a Second Brigade soldier listed among 'lessons learned':

"Clicking your heels together three times and repeating, 'There's no place like home,' won't get you there.

Optional gear is stuff the insiders know you will need but won't tell you to take so they can laugh as you suffer.

You'll always send your family 'hate mail' one day before you receive a care package from them.

Bedouins think we look funny too.

100% security means one man awake, watching for the XO.

Mail is a form of riot control."

Such commentary on Desert Shield by the shield holders was less petulant than wry; a sort of sparring with the air by prizefighters in their corners awaiting the opening bell. Except the fight was subject to cancellation at any time. War was not so much in the air as in the background, and death was another remove. The desert lexicon had no synonyms for killing, as had the Vietnam vernacular; e.g.—zap, waste, grease. Desert Shield resulted in no combat deaths, a merciful mark of virginity for troops who readily accepted themselves as 'cherries.' It was higher in the chain of command where death and virginity were contemplated by Viet vets who knew both states.

Weiss: "It's hard to get ready when there's other information that says you're getting ready for a false alarm or the wrong thing. How we operated depended a whole lot on whether Saddam used chems. Flying and fighting in rubber suits is a world of difference than what we were used to. In MOPP 4 we could do about a fifth of what we were capable of.

"Before the war, the nickname for NBC was 'Nobody Cares.' Our NBC people had the toughest job of all: to make us think about what we dreaded most."

There were four degrees of Mission Oriented Protective Posture (MOPP) when facing NBC attack. MOPP 1 was wear of the gas mask—loathed for its humid confinement and resented for its necessity—with the rest of the gear near the soldier. But the mask alone was a mere annoyance compared to the complete regalia required to withstand the range of chemical agents suspected to be in Iraq's gruesome arsenal. MOPP 4 included an impermeable hood, gloves, boots and coveralls: the soldier's full coat of armor against chemical attack of all types and duration. For biological agents, MOPP was supplemented by innoculations, based upon guesswork about which among hundreds of viruses Saddam might spew undetectably on the battlefield. However, division doctors were hardly worried that he could deliver and sustain dangerous quantities of germs.

The experience of the full MOPP 4 ensemble is like suiting up for a scuba dive, then staying out of the water. Names and rank are covered up, faces replaced by identical rubber features that seem modeled from a science fiction magazine.

U.S. troops were required to have their masks within reach at all times, and the rest of the MOPP gear only a sprint away. The most convenient way to comply was to strap the mask case around the waist where it could rest bulkily on the hip or thigh bone. Once removed, the mask is not easily repacked, so it came out only for drills and, later, whenever there was a Scud alert.

During alerts and drills, business was to go on normally; but the mask made face to face communication difficult, and voices thin on a phone or radio. Drinking through a straw required a special cap on the canteen. There was not even a theory on how to eat while wearing a mask, and if the attack employed a nerve agent, bodily functions as basic as voiding were impossible without some skin exposure.

"NBC was Saddam's ace up his sleeve. He had the capability and he'd used it against Iran. People didn't want to say so, but NBC could be the war stopper. You could see it on their faces after a long gas drill. The gas wouldn't get you but heatstroke could. Imagine trying to fight a war in 155 degrees. That's how hot it got, exercising in MOPP 4. Fortunately for this division, once we went into action we could not easily be located for gas attacks. That's because with air assault tactics we move around so much.

"That was another reason we wanted to get started if there was going to be a shooting war. We'd feel better once we were a moving target."

At King Fahd they were a stationary target for Saddam's secret weapon, terrorism. Bechtel's construction crews were TCN's, third country nationals, meaning neither Saudi nor American but mostly from the poor third world. By agreement with the Saudi government, Bechtel was permitted to continue building King Fahd even as it was used as a U.S. military base (Bechtel did not pull out completely till the air war started in January 1991). TCN's had little business in Tent City except for a few barbers and, initially, tent raising crews. These did their work under the eye of the 101st's military police. But in the terminal, parking and hangar areas, TCN's with identity cards hung around their necks moved about freely. Thais, Filipinos, Pakis, Omanis, Yemenis, Jordanians and Sudanese could be found in numbers almost anywhere in and around the aviation facilities. If there were terrorists, they would have been recruited from these TCN's.

There was a Beirut syndrome afflicting the aviators, who worked and slept in the passenger terminal and its parking lot. The Marines' casualties in Beirut were horrific because the carbomb's blast was tamped by the enclosure of a building. Ever since, the Marines have preferred tents in open spaces where a blast would dissipate.

Garrett: "We were sleeping in a parking lot, three stories high just like any stateside airport has. Usually there were two cots in a bay large enough for one car. The lot was well built, with plenty of reinforced concrete, so we didn't worry much about the structure falling down on us the way the building did in Beirut. Just the same, guys would feel around under their cots before they got in it."

Saddam had promised a terrorist offensive, and many of the

big names in terror were headquartered in Baghdad where he supported and supplied them. The 101st was not alone in taking the threat very seriously. In the States, security measures were causing passengers to arrive hours early, and cut down on air travel.

Peay: "I saw it in Vietnam: if you're not constantly conscious of the terrorist threat, you'll have casualties. They're the most demoralizing kind because they don't result from straight up battle but from lack of vigilance. In other words, they're someone's fault, not the enemy's. Sure, the enemy set the mine or drove the car-bomb, but someone was off guard if the enemy gets in to do it.

"This was one of the toughest tasks for leaders up and down the line. When we train we train hard, then expect to go back to a secure area and relax. That's fine, it's necessary, provided relaxation doesn't lead to laxity. Security consciousness can never sleep.

"Subconscious vigilance is hard to develop, and harder to check on, but everyone in the chain of command must check, recheck, and check again—then start over tomorrow. It's tiresome; it can be annoying. It could mean you're unpopular, but there's no higher responsibility for a commander.

"I'd like to think the 101st was targeted by terrorists. We were certainly a lucrative target with all our aircraft lined up, and our troops in a tight cantonment. But I think the terrorists looked us over—looked on a number of occasions—and saw we were alert and suspicious. We may have offended some Saudis, but I think we deterred some terrorists."

The background terrorist threat was a constant reminder that though bullets weren't being exchanged, that this was a war. Then 7th Corps from Germany began to roll ashore with so much armor it seemed the Arabian peninsula would tip. 7th Corps was an army in its own right, more than double the size of 18th ABC. Augmented by the 1st Mechanized Division, the 1st Cavalry and other hefty reinforcements, 7th Corps was larger than the American army that had been defending western Europe against the Russians. Obviously, 7th Corps was overkill if Schwarzkopf's intent was merely to continue the defense of Saudi Arabia. 7th Corps' arrival in the JOA spawned congressional debate in Washington over what was called 'the offensive option.' Garrett described the development to his brigade this way: "7th Corps is here to join us, not replace us," killing a diehard rumor that there would be troop rotation.

That truth pushed the emotional roller coaster up rather than down. The government clearly had a plan now to settle scores with Saddam. Stalemate, stand off and sitzkrieg were worries of the past. Then speculation began on what the offensive option could cost.

Estimating the cost in casualties was an inexact science. Most of the conjecture reached the JOA by way of letters and calls from home, the ultimate source being TV commentators, and sometimes medicos from the armed services who were their guests on the air. Reaching the troops third hand and consequently distorted, they wondered what were accepted figures when Saddam spoke of how the allies would "wade in their own blood."

A divison surgeon discussed the casualties question. "There were tables, most of them going back to World War II, that gave casualty rates for troops attacking or defending. From Vietnam we had experience with the kind of wounds produced by the Iraqis' Soviet weapons. We had to go all the way back to World War I for figures when gas was used. For desert warfare, there were data from the recent Arab-Israeli conflicts, but these were mostly armor battles, not too relevant for the air assault division.

"We knew there would be a lot of burn injuries when choppers crashed. We'd lose more people from shock in torrid desert conditions. We assumed medevac choppers could not be used as close to the front lines because of the Iraqi army's air defenses.

"But that was about all we had to go on in forecasting casualties: very old empirical data, and some scientific guesses. What we did was safeside everything upwards. If we were going to err, it would be on the high side. Worst case, in other words.

"My wife saw a lot of widely differing figures on TV about what the total losses in a war with Iraq might be. The range, I think, was from ten to fifty thousand dead. As a rule of thumb, there are about three wounded for every KIA. Numbers like that are very distressing, not only in military medicine, but to families waiting for a war to begin. We didn't like the idea of talking to the media about casualty projections, but we weren't told not to. Actually, the media were not a presence in this division, so I never had what would have been a very uncomfortable interview on the subject of casualties."

Uncomfortable interviews simply did not occur in the 101st. That was a feature of the New Age army that Peay recalls with a smile of satisfaction. The slogan, 'No more Vietnams,' intended by anti-interventionists who coined it, for application to Central America, resonated instead in the Gulf. Indeed, no one followed the slogan with more conviction than Schwarzkopf's command. The ethos of Vietnam would not be duplicated in the desert, and that difference included (probably emphasized) media coverage.

Weiss: "The policy of this division toward reporters was suspicion. We were polite, we did what we said we'd do for them, and we didn't tell them lies. But until they showed us that they were trustworthy, and not just out to create a story, I had a Missouri attitude toward reporters: you show me you're OK, then I'll believe it."

Weiss's attitude drew nods throughout the division. This was an attitudinal orthodoxy of the Vietnam-era leaders that was readily accepted by their New Age subordinates. With the prospect of appearing on TV or in a newspaper back home, any soldier was happy to be interviewed; but there was no inclination to 'go to a reporter' with gripes, or even feelings about the war. The presence of an escort officer with the reporter was no doubt an inhibition, but the spools of pool footage reveal no sense of restraint on the part of the troops. The restraint was in the questions—as if the reporter accepted the permissible scope of his inquiry, or at least was conscious of what the CENTCOM censors in Riyadh would release for transmission back to the States.

Weiss: "I've always heard that the media are supposed to be suspicious and skeptical. That's great stuff about the free press guarding the interests of the public. Isn't it right in the Constitution? Well then, why should they bitch if we're suspicious and skeptical too?"

Sarge: "Rumor #4,276: Word came down that some CBS reporters got lost near the border and were missing. Rumor was the cav [aerial cavalry] would have to go out and find 'em. We were up on covering force with First Brigade, so we were the closest. The Platoon Sergeant shrugged—said it would be a good mission. A squad leader said he'd be damned if he'd go out to save some reporter's ass.

"That was bullshit—he'd go wherever the CO sent him, but it got a good argument going. One guy said he hoped our troop got the job—we'd be the first into Kuwait. Another NCO sided with the squad leader: 'That'd be hairy up there. I'm supposed to risk my men to save some fuckin' reporters? They weren't even allowed on the border, right?'

"Nope, they weren't. The way we heard it, they made an unauthorized trip up there without an escort. Used their own vehicles. That settled it for this NCO. Someone mentioned Erroll Flynn's son who was MIA in Cambodia the same way. The Army didn't go looking for him. I don't know if they did or not. If these CBS reporters were women, that's different, but the guys can look out for themselves. They went off limits. A couple of them were foreigners too, someone said.

"'But what about the Americans? You'd just let the Iraqis take 'em? The answer was we'd pick 'em up if we didn't take any casualties. Well how would we know that? We talked about a lot of situations: if it was night, we'd go in; if the reporters were under fire, we wouldn't; if they were wounded, yes; if not, no. Back and forth like that. Someone said the reporters could start a ground war, and that shouldn't happen before the Air Force softens up the Iraqis.

"It was a real good discussion—took a lot of the afternoon—anything that killed time was time well spent. I'd say the general feeling was that the shooting war shouldn't start because of these guys, but if we could get 'em out without casualties, we should try."

What was worth casualties, and how many seemed acceptable in the kill-but-don't-be-killed army? That heavy question appeared as a mid- point in the emotional roller coaster when the offensive option loomed. The divison was ready to fight, and its soldiers longed to fight for the reasons young men join the army to test and establish their manhood. But like the way it surfaced in the debate about the worth of the reporters, fighting for fighting's sake was not the wish of everyone.

What other motivations were there?—nothing as strong as the feeling that "We've come this far, let's finish the job." "Let's not have to come back again in a couple of years," was a corollary slogan. Strategic purposes were ethereal, even among officers, for national war aims seemed more ambiguous in the offensive option than they had been in the clear rationale for Desert Shield. Manhood validation had to be coupled with a collective cause before the two became reinforcing.

The collective cause (distinguished from unit pride and group identification) was never defined to a motivating level, but as substitute there was the literally mountainous evidence that the home front believed in what its soldiers were doing and preparing to do.

Cody: "A catch phrase around that time was, 'The road home leads through Kuwait.' That was as high a motivator as there could be to go over on the offensive, but still didn't answer the question of why we had to liberate Kuwait. That's for other people to answer, and I won't try. But it must have been OK because we were reading what America had to say about it. I mean, you could read all day and not get through the mail America was sending us.

"Each day a mail clerk dumped another mountain of 'any soldier' letters on a big table in the orderly room. That was in every other battalion too. When you had the time, you could reach in and take letters at random. It just blew your mind. This was all fan mail. I tried to be conscientious about answering it, but I really couldn't keep up.

"The letters—not to mention the packages of goodies—said everything and anything. Some were brilliant, some were dumb, and most in between. But what they all said was that whatever we were doing, they were with us all the way—pulling for us, praying for us."

There was never a more prodigious 'any soldier' letter writer than Lettie Gingerich. From her cottage in Redondo Beach, CA, she hand wrote an average of four letters per day, starting in August when the deployment began, not ending till her correspondents came home in April. Over a thousand letters, all told. She was partial to the 101st, as her husband, Eldon, had been a Screaming Eagle in World War II.

She asked to 'adopt' each anonymous soldier she wrote; asked that they send her a picture and tell her about themselves. Many did, till Lettie's desk, scrapbooks, and walls filled with a gallery of her foster family. She made myriad phone calls for them, got to know many of their families, and visited several when they returned. A regular at the annual reunions of the 101st Airborne Division Association, she wrote to all the soldiers at Ft. Campbell she knew who had left for the Gulf. Generals, sergeants major, majors and privates—Lettie invited them equally into her extended family, which already included a score of Vietnam veterans. But not even a battalion of adopted children could fill the void left by her youngest. Never married, he would be forever young in his mother's memory, for those on the Vietnam Wall never age.

In one letter she learned how he could have evolved, if he'd had more years, but not many more than a New Age soldier different in gender and military occupation, but in some way a spiritual peer of her son.

Dear 'Mom' Lettie and 'Dad' Eldon,

Hi! My name is Luanne and I'm with the 101st Air Assault band. I've only been in the Army for 18 months. This is my first time overseas.

I'm 22 years old and a white female. I'm originally from Atlantic Highlands, NJ. My mom lives in Portland, TN where she raises parrots, African greys and Amazons. Before that she was a trainer, exercise rider and groom for race horses.

In the band, we played at the 50th Airborne Anniversary celebration in Washington, D.C. You must have heard us. The reaction and pride of former 101st members was overwhelming! In Saudi Arabia, we've been playing music ranging from 1940-1990, country, rock, pop, Motown and big band sounds. Over 30 concerts so far. We get tired, our morale suffers, but we raise it for others, so the show must go on.

So far, it's not too bad. We get along pretty well and days are passing, but loneliness can take over. I can't wait to get back with my family! So many times you hear about married soldiers separated by the war, but what about us single soldiers? We have as much heartache and questions as the married people but no one seems to know it. I'd like it if someone understood our point of view.

Keeping musical instruments clean in the desert is as hard as for weapons. Music keeps me occupied and also those who listen. If we're here at Christmas (God forbid!) I might play 'backup' for some big stars they send over here. I hear Bob Hope's coming.

But if there's a war first, the band has a military mission. I'm not ready for that, but most of the troops are. I just pray that they take care. I want to watch them listening to us till we go home. That's when we'll really play like never before! God willing. That's what the Arabs here say—in allah—God willing.

Well, I better go. Thanks very much for your letter and I'd be proud to be your adopted 'son'—but is it OK if I'm a 'daughter?' Thanks again for your care. You take care too, and God bless. I'm so grateful to you both.

December 1990

6: Saddam promises to release all hostages.

8: U.S. evacuates its embassy in Kuwait but leaves flag flying.

15: Iraq agrees to direct talks with the U.S. but, only in Baghdad and on a date set by Saddam.

19: Schwarzkopf's deputy, Lt. Gen. Waller, admits to media that the coalition will not be prepared to mount a ground offensive by the 15 January U.N. deadline.

22: Iraq threatens to use chemical weapons if attacked.

VIII

The best laid plans

The President and senators, the comedians and athletes, all departed with Thanksgiving; but the shouting and tumult from the Hellfire misfire continued to roll around King Fahd. Cody hunkered down to receive investigations from each tier of command. Division assembled the basic facts and personnel involved; corps expanded the scope a bit but witheld its report, awaiting the premier investigation from ARCENT.

In answer to them all, Cody had two bastions: his own encyclopedic knowledge of the Apache's firing systems, and support from the manufacturer's tech reps. Their testimony corroborated that human error was unlikely in the misfire because all safeguards were inspected immediately after the accident, and found to be in place.

Cody: "Suppose you drove a car. You put it in 'park,' turn off the ignition, set the hand brake, get out, and lock it. If that car starts by itself and runs into an ammo dump, you can't be blamed for the explosion.

"That basically was my position. I could show any inspector that Garcia's guys had taken all the safety steps—the Apache was right there just the way they'd left it—I had it roped off and under guard."

Eliminating human error somewhat deepened the mystery. Cody didn't advance a causal theory, but suspicion narrowed on the black boxes. Perhaps the unstoppable dust penetrated even their seals. Maybe the heat scrambled their electronic brains. Only Rockwell International could tell for sure, and their diagnostics were in California. So in a couple of weeks, the investigation was pushed out of the JOA. 1-101 was neither blamed nor exonerated, but understandably shaken.

"It was vital that they kept confident in their aircraft and the armament crews—and not feel they were in the division dog house. I don't know how well I reassured them, but things started to lighten up after I went over to SOCCENT one day, and Col. Johnson had a sign over his desk. It was like a scoreboard—Army 1, Air Force 0. I rogered, and said, 'Sir, that was just a warning shot.'"

Johnson was ready to move along with the Normandy planning. In about six weeks, the air campaign had to be 'go' under the assumption that peace maneuvers would fail. Cody learned that his raid was not included in the campaign but was rather the precursor for it. Indeed, the raid had no name, coded or otherwise. Because they were self designated as Task Force Normandy, unofficially the raid came to be called Normandy.

Iraq's vital infrastructure—its communication and transportation network—was enclosed by a radar 'fence' roughly concentric with its borders, and set back from them to protect the fence with a territorial buffer and a screen of ground forces. At the heart and hub was Baghdad, where radiated all military C&C (command and control) essential for any nation at war, but even more so for a highly centralized autocracy like Iraq. It was a poorly kept secret that allied air forces would go after Iraq's C&C before undertaking any other operations. If successful, they would decouple Saddam's chain of command, and cut contact with his armies. This would be soonest accomplished by silencing the switchboards and transmitters in Baghdad.

To do so, the allies had suficient weapons to knock out power sources in and around the capital. Devastating accuracy was likely if the warplanes were not distracted by Iraqi interceptors or anti-aircraft fire. Neither of these threats would arise if they were taken by surprise; and they could be if Baghdad was not alerted by the radar fence.

Cruise missiles could streak over the fence too suddenly for Baghdad to react. Fired from US Navy ships in the Gulf and Red Sea, cruise missiles were used to great effect; but there were not enough of them to assure complete disruption of C&C. Stealth aircraft were unproven against the sophisticated Iraqi radar, and had shown to be unreliable in Panama. Pilot-guided weapons in aircraft visible to radar were therefore indispensable. For them to reach Baghdad undetected, there had to be a hole in the radar fence.

Cody: "The hole would open what the Air Force called a 'black corridor.' Bombers could come down the corridor in about twenty minutes—too little time for Baghdad to realize what was happening."

How big a hole, how wide the black corridor, was one of the first questions Cody and Johnson had discussed. The fence was a picket of sites about forty miles apart, with overlapping arcs of radar coverage. Knock out three adjoining sites, and a hundred bombers could pour through with plenty of room for two-way traffic (the corridor would also be their route of egress). Knock out two pickets, and the gap narrows to the minimum necessary. Knock out but one, and the overlapping coverage of the adjoining sites plugs the gap.

The early Normandy rehearsals demonstrated that three Apaches firing on each site could total them. Complete destruction was necessary because the sites contained an array of complementary radar. Any one of them could provide Baghdad with the early warning for which the sites were designed. Searching the sky on different frequencies, the radars reported speed, altitude and azimuth of approaching aircraft; and from knowledge of these characteristics advised the aircrafts' likely identification and mission. Twenty minutes warning was sufficient to scramble interceptors and focus surface to air missiles (SAM) near Baghdad. If Iraq had the advantage of such warning, the Air Force estimated 20% casualties for their first wave of bombers.

The pickets' job was not to down the bombers, only to warn Baghdad of their approach. However, the sites did have shoulder fired, heat seeking anti-aircraft missile launchers called Grails, similar to the American Stingers with which Afghan rebels pretty much cleared the skies of Soviet helicopters. The sites were also protected by rapid fire anti-aircraft guns called ZPU-4's and S60's.

An Apache raid to take out a radar picket is like a military mugging. First, the target must not suspect that it is being approached. Then the purse is snatched before the target reacts. The mugger sprints away before the cops can be called. Hit and run: surprise compensating for overwhelming force.

The purse snatching phase had been well rehearsed. It was the unsuspected approach that set Cody pondering with AF-SOC's intelligence officer, Capt. Jamie. Through high tech hush-hush wizardry, Jamie had 'interrogated' the target radar sites and could brief the Normandy pilots on the Iraqis' electronic routine, the most favorable feature of which was the nature of their radar.

Cody: "They were designed to spot fast movers [supersonic attackers], so they looked up to cover the farthest horizon. Their radar cone included surface coverage, but there the 'ground clutter' can confuse them. Down where we'd be flying, the cone reflects off the dunes, showing the radar operator a lot of returns that he has difficulty sorting out. Sand storms and haze give him more trouble.

"Radar also notices speed, so we planned to fly slow. Of course we'd be in a tight formation in order to present the minimum reflection. We'd also come right down the middle of his cone, so that we'd be the weakest possible signal for the sites on his sides. Our other advantage was that the Iraqis were unfamiliar with what an Apache looks like on radar. We have a very different signature from fast movers."

Cody had an additional advantage—experience. As a captain in 1979, he helped develop a light combat helicopter to take out radar sites defending Teheran. This project was begun in the aftermath of the Desert One disaster. Had he been re-elected, President Carter was apparently prepared to try again and free the hostages in Iran by force.

127

"In '79, we tested that chopper against our own I-Hawks (the improved Hawk anti-aircraft missile launcher) at night, flying NVG, in the Arizona desert. I-Hawks were also one of the main weapons the Air Force was up against in Iraq. Another valuable thing I learned from the LCH tests was how fleshettes tore up radar. That's why I insisted we use them for Normandy."

With his approach method in mind, Cody studied what armament he'd need, and the attendant problems of weight. To provide redundancy of ordnance on every structure at each site, the Apaches would be loaded to the teeth, indeed overloaded by peacetime safety standards. All told, there would be 68 Hellfires, 150 fleshette rockets, and 8000 30 millimeter rounds for the cannons. Topped off with fuel, the raiders were sure to lumber along at the slow speed Cody desired to foil the searching radars. But because of weight, the engines would be working near capacity, a fact requiring tip top pre-flight tuning. Perfect mechanical performance no one could guarantee. One of his toughest decisions was what magnitude of malfunction would justify a mission abort for any of the Apaches.

Cody remembered Desert One in detail. Sea Stallions (cargo helicopters) on the first leg to Teheran developed a problem in the auxiliary hydraulics—or at least instruments were showing the pilots a problem. Holding safety first, they felt justified to abort. Another Stallion aborted because of weather. After a C130 collided with a chopper, the raid had no backup aircraft. So the aborts contributed to the disaster that developed—two wrecks and eight American bodies charred out on the desert for the Ayatollah to kick and curse.

"Something like that wasn't going to happen with Normandy. I've always felt you lose more by being too conservative than too bold. I wanted my pilots to drive on to the limits of the aircraft. By adopting that policy, I was imposing on them my personal faith in the Apache. I felt it had limits none of us had ever reached. I was so sure of that I permitted a pilot to abort only if he experienced total engine malfunction, a fire, or hydraulic failure. Otherwise, press on with the mission.

"Coming off the targets, he had more discretion, but going in I asked him to be almost a kamikaze pilot. Better to die heading for success than a corpse after a failure like Desert One."

Mechanical failure was only one of myriad possible hazards from the time TF Normandy took off in Saudi Arabia till they returned hours later. They might receive ground fire when crossing the border, which could at least alert the Iraqis that helicopters were intruding. Saddam's fighter planes and anti-aircraft artillery (triple A) would be at full strength and un-scathed because the war had not started. Two types of dangerous interceptors could be looking for Cody before he was half way to his targets: MIG's and Hinds.

"Our bombers wanted a moonless night to attack Baghdad and so did we. With no moon, border guards could only hear us when we flew over—and we picked a stretch of desert where we thought they'd be the fewest. If the Iraqis scrambled fighters [four MIG bases were plugged into the sites], we'd know when they had us on their acquisition radar, and scatter like quails when they see the shadow of a hawk.

"Then he'd have plenty of trouble locating any of us. An Apache poking along in the dark at camel height is very hard to find from a MIG. Even if he picks me out his high speed is a disadvantage. I can dart like a water bug; he makes wide sweeps even in his tightest turns. We tested our survivability against fast movers at Hunter Liggett. We had some tricks for MIG's—if he lined up for an attack, we'd fly straight at him and pass under before he could get his nose down.

"It would be cat and mouse out there, but we could still get the cheese."

But before they did, not only MIG's but heavily armed Hind helicopters might join in search. This meant TF Normandy would have to fight its way to the targets, for Hinds could not be eluded like MIG's.

"That was the worst scenario, no doubt about it: MIG's upstairs, Hinds on our tail, and triple A below us. To even the odds, I could have gotten CAP [F15's] to stand off and help out if we called. Trouble was, the CAP had to stay outside radar range of the fence or else they'd tip off the raid. That meant they couldn't enter Iraq where we'd need them right away. For those reasons—and the fact that every fighter was going to be thrown against Baghdad that first night—no CAP was on call for Normandy."

Ground fire, MIG's and Hinds meant casualties. TF Normandy pilots were not kamikazes though they would be as persistent. The problem of downed Apaches was addressed by attaching four AFSOC choppers, called Pave Lows, to the task force. These Pave Lows from the 20th Special Operations Squadron were used for electronic warfare, but could also rescue pilots on the ground; and for that purpose were armed with 50 caliber machinguns in case survivors were surrounded as had usually been the case in Vietnam.

The Pave Lows were flown by Air Force crews that the Army aviators had never met, or really ever heard of. This unfamiliarity, and the depressing precedent of Desert One, was like an unidentified blip on Cody's radar screen.

'Interoperability' was an ominous term appearing frequently in after action reports from Grenada and Panama, describing the problems inherent when two or more services try to work together. In those mini-wars, interoperability was rarely better than tolerable, often much worse. As a consequence of interoperability fiascos in Grenada, a major four-star joint command, USSOCOM, had been staffed by all four services to integrate special operations worldwide. In the Middle East, SOCCENT answered to Schwarzkopf, but was the creation of USSOCOM similar to the way General Motors would form a team of engineering specialists to support Buick. SOCCENT worked quite well in the capacity for which it was designed.

One of the reasons for that success was the well tested relationships between the service components represented within SOCCENT. Soldier, sailor, airman, marine—they all answered to one boss, Jesse Johnson. It was he who rated their efficiency, and thus wrote a chapter in their careers regardless of the color of their uniforms. They therefore had a major stake in making interoperability work, and smoothly.

However, the Normandy mission was outside this established setup for special operations. Cody's raiders were 'borrowed' from the 101st. The Pave Lows he needed for support were AFSOC's. Johnson did not write Cody's efficiency report, nor did Cody write the Pave Low commander's. Indeed, he was the same rank as Cody, Lt. Col. Comer of the Air Force. Thus, many ingredients of Desert One's fatally flawed command structure seemed present for the first strike against Iraq.

Cody: "When Rich Comer and I sat down for our first heart to heart talk, I noticed one thing that set the tone for the rest of our relationship: we were wearing identical gray flight suits. That sort of said it all. We both flew rotary wings, we'd both be going on the same track, exposed to the same dangers. There was a lot to coordinate—really basic stuff like how we'd do commo checks—but from the get go we were more than just working together on a mission, we were brothers in the sky."

En route, just before the attack, Pave Lows would fall behind the Apaches by about ten miles: close enough to reach a crash in minutes, far enough back so as not to receive ground fire directed at the raiders. Comer would have to keep his distance from Cody by dead reckoning because use of onboard radar would be picked up by the Iraqis. So too would the ships' radar jammers, so they would remain off unless signals indicated that the Iraqis were tracking them. There would be no other friendly aircraft in the sky that night until the sites were attacked; consequently, TF Normandy's identification friend or foe (IFF) signals would also be silent while the raiders were inbound to their targets. Coming out, streams of bombers would be grim shadows overhead, streaking for Baghdad. They would 'paint' the choppers with bursts of radar, and IFF would respond that it was TF Normandy headed home.

An equally important service of the Pave Lows was navigation. They had satellite positioning (GPS) capability; the Apaches had only doppler and a target locator. Cody would use them all for cross checks, but GPS was the most reliable and precise. Therefore the Pave Lows would lead until the flight was ten miles from the targets.

Cody: "I couldn't have too much redundancy when it came to navigation. If I could have stuffed Loran on a ship, I would have.

"Of course we'd be on radio silence inbound. Under Murphy's Law we could get split from the Pave Lows so their GPS would be worthless to us. Rich Comer came up with an idea. He said he'd carry a bunch of 'chem sticks.' These are like the luminous batons you see when aircraft are guided out to taxi at night. Rich said he'd toss 'em out at any coordinates we pre-select. We're flying nearby so we'll see 'em on the ground. That way we can double check our position with GPS as long as the Pave Lows are with us."

If misfortune or enemy action did not separate them from the Apaches, the Pave Lows would drop a bundle of chem sticks at the release points (RP), some ten miles from the targets. By GPS, this crucial location would be accurate to within ten meters. As they crossed their RP's, the Apaches would load the GPS coordinates into their computers and target systems. From satellites, the target's locations were known with great precision. With the RP's located with equal accuracy, the raiders' weapons would be perfectly sighted and programmed, even before the pilots saw their targets.

Expedients like the chem sticks emerged as 'what ifs' permuted in Cody's mind through November and into December. He found himself awaking late at night and early morning with some new contingency mulled by his subconscious during sleep.

"Every bad possibility had to be thought through, then considered in light of what was already planned. It always meant a change, small or large. Like losing a ship just over the border. Does his wingman stand by—that's the time honored practice since World War II—or does he continue and let the Pave Lows pick up his buddy? What if a Pave Low goes down? Does another one divert, or do the rest continue the mission? They can probably take care of themselves, but if there's Iraqi armor around, they'll need an Apache. Or should USAF fast movers come in for anti-tank work? They're already targeted on strategic stuff in Iraq. Find an answer and it creates a couple of more problems.

"Probably the worst one was if we lost a ship at the target and the radar site's still working. The fast movers have to finish the job. One of us crash where the bombs are going. Maybe a Pave Low too. Maybe his wingman and one for the Apache are still shooting around the target because the Iraqis are closing in. What do we do? How do I plan for it?"

Such questions were for Cody's solitary contemplation. Because of Normandy's ultra secrecy, he could consult with virtually no one in the 101st. Not even the Normandy pilots knew where the targets were or under what conditions they would be attacked, or when. Their consent to be in the raid was uninformed. Cody found himself staring at them as they went about training for the covering force mission. In his eyes they seemed surrounded with an aura of innocent unreality.

They didn't know what he was planning for them. They couldn't agree and encourage him, or express opinions if they didn't. Davis began keeping a book on Cody—how he looked as well as what he did—and the resemblance was to 1-101's logo, a snarling gargoyle. Understandable when his 'Normandy day' began after dinner when the ordinary exhausting day ended.

In his cubicle of an office—the claim room for lost baggage at King Fahd—Cody rolled back a canvas curtain from the Normandy map. In his notebook were thoughts that had intruded during the day. He poured over the map, measuring distances, jotting coordinates, calculating fuel loads, balancing weights.

No one could join him in his mental inner sanctum. By phone he might consult with McNulty on some nuance of armament: whether there could be a mix of fleshettes and armor piercing rockets. The question had to be hypothetical. No one can know what he's contemplating. No one can be shown reality. Midnight, one a.m., two a.m. The coffee pot is charred when Cody flings himself on his cot. Uneasy rests the head that thinks alone.

Reveille is at five, followed by another full day supporting the division.

Davis: "Yeah, this was his hard ass period. It's a wonder he didn't lose it with three hours sleep night after night. I'd see him biting someone's neck off—it wasn't petty stuff the guy didn't deserve, but Cody would've handled it differently at home or after Normandy. One time it was Jody Bridgforth in the barrel. Looking back, I can't imagine what must have been going through Cody's mind while he chewed this guy whose life he'd been planning in the middle of the night.

Garrett: "Aviation Brigade grew into a huge conglomerate

once we got all our reinforcements and attachments. 1-101 was one of nine battalions I was responsible for. Dick was experienced and competent; his battalion was all top notch people, so I was grateful not to have to give them much attention. I didn't ask Dick about Normandy because of my implicit confidence in him, but I assumed he knew that I was there if he needed my counsel."

Though previously a professor of Military Psychology & Leadership at West Point, Garrett never encountered such an acute case of 'command loneliness' as had infected Cody.

"I should have been more alert to the unique stress Dick was going through, but I guess there was too much else on my own mind. Tentative plans for the offensive option were starting to surface, and I was in the catbird seat all the time.

"I remember Dick sort of tugged my arm—wanted me to see something. Sure, I said, lead on. He started pacing around this sand table. This was the IP, there's White Team's RP, Pave Lows back here. I was getting the full brief on Normandy!

"I still didn't catch on why. It's like Joe Montana telling you his next game plan. You're flattered, but the last thing you'd assume is that he wanted your input. I mean, there's just no one better than Dick Cody at his game.

"I made a few sensible, but I guess not very useful, remarks and waited to hear the point of this walk-through briefing. Dick seemed to be waiting too. Expectant. I think I said something like, 'That's nice, Dick. Any problems?' But whatever it was he wanted from me he held inside. I wish I'd sensed that at the time. He'd been talking to himself for so long about this, he was deathly afraid he'd overlooked something. It's clear now that he wanted an understanding ear, someone knowledgeable to reflect on his plan. I'm sorry I wasn't able to provide what he needed at that stressful time. I may have even added to his anxiety by not hearing his silent plea."

Without counsel from above, neither did Cody have input from below, though lateral communication with Comer was valuable and essential. Besides GPS, the Pave Lows had terrain-following radar to check the Apaches' navigation during rehearsals. Light signals were devised so that while Pave Lows led, they could indicate turns or changes of course without breaking radio silence. Yet all that the pilots knew was that they were practicing to fly somewhere, sometime, and hit a target someplace.

Shufflebarger led one of the attack teams:

"Those were tough flights, all blacked out and low to the ground, but they got to be routine. If I'd known we were practicing to start the war inside Iraq, I wouldn't have slept as well, no sir."

Gabram: "What Lori was that no one else had, except me, was somebody to talk to, confide in, and let everything out. That was a great pressure valve for me. Cody was solo—he had to keep pushing more things inside. The further along a plan like this goes, the more details he had to remember and coordinate himself."

The pressure valve for the rest of the battalion was athletics. A backboard was erected in the parking lot. Inter-company volleyball was hotly contested. Mental fatigue seemed to dissolve in sweat, and football was a popular expression for pent-up aggression.

Jamie Weeks was scrambling. Bobby Gunter was blitzing. The sack was heard in a crack, as Weeks crumpled on his folded knee.

Cody: "Boy, I knew how he felt. I blew my knee at West Point—that medically disqualified from the combat arms. It proved a blessing for me in the long run, but Weeks' injury was worse because I had to drop him from Normandy.

"It looked like we'd have to bring in a substitute crew and make another tough selection—but just about then the Blue site went off the scope."

One of the three radar sites had gone off the air. Capt. Jamie searched and probed all the frequencies to find it, but Blue remained silent. The most plausible theory was that Blue was being repaired or updated. In the interim, adjoining sites would pick up its coverage.

Now with only two targets, TF Normandy had four Apaches and a pair of Pave Lows for each. It was just as well Blue had taken itself out of the picture. Jesse Johnson's recurring question was, "Can you get 100%?" With an extra Apache to mop up, Cody could more firmly answer yes—every radar would be taken down.

Cody: "In the back of my mind was the possibility that Blue might come up again just before we took off. That would have been a nightmare, and I was having enough of them in my sleep. But Blue coming back didn't seem to bother Johnson. He must have known something about it that I still don't."

An extra Apache on Red and White—good news—one less route to rehearse; each raider could take off a little ammunition; fuel consumption wouldn't be as fast. Fuel. Each chopper would gulp it down at about 150 gallons per hour. The refueling plan was the last phase of the plan to be rehearsed.

"Tactical refueling is a routine exercise for army helicopters. We call a battlefield gas station a FARP—forward area refueling point. You roll in the HEMIT's [rough terrain tankers] or drop in some blivets [huge gas bladders], hook up the hoses, and fly in the thirsty birds. On occasion, we'd refueled all nineteen Apaches in fifteen minutes. A FARP can be broken down just as fast."

What would make the Normandy FARP perilously different was its location, not within friendly lines, but on the Iraqi side, or even in Iraq itself, for the task force would have to be topped off close enough to the targets to hit them and return, not to the FARP, which would be long gone, but to an air base twenty miles within Saudi Arabia. Like Doolittle's raid on Tokyo forty-nine years earlier, TF Normandy would try to sneak up as close as possible before taking off with full tanks. And like the cause of Doolittle's fate (loss of all his aircraft), enemy detection of the fueling point meant disaster.

For Cody, a desert FARP also meant new units and personalities involved in the raid. TF Normandy took off from King Fahd in December to meet them. This was going to be dress rehearsal for refueling, and take place 500 miles away near King Khalid Military City (KKMC), a 20th century fortress astride the road to Riyadh thirty miles from the Iraqi border.

For the first time the raiders moved toward their targets. All previous rehearsals had been held near the Gulf so that spies along the frontier would never see Apaches and arouse concern along the fence.

Shufflebarger: "Flying up there we noticed how different the desert was. No more flat nothing. There were wadis, mesas—pretty rugged country compared to the coast. Plenty of sand but a lot more features. But I didn't see them on our maps! The maps really weren't much good for navigation. I really snuggled up to my Pave Low."

Johnson had laid on the FARP rehearsal. It would be run by SOCCENT who would test two possible refueling options: tanker helicopters called 'fat cows,' and HEMIT ground vehicles. At night, TF Normandy flew to the site. To Cody's dismay, it was a deep dust bowl that caused brownout for any descending chopper. Fat cows were parked along one side of the FARP, HEMIT's on the other. In darkness the Apaches orbitted, unable to contact the ground on a prearranged frequency. On another channel, the problem was worked out, and the Apaches instructed to land on a certain azimuth—180 degrees opposite the one called for in the plan. After some shouting in the desert and weaving in the sky, TF Normandy headed down.

SOCCENT was expecting fewer than nine Apaches. Several were waved back into orbit. Those that came into the billowing brown curtain were halted two hundred meters from their pumps, and signalled to ground taxi the rest of the way, raising the worst dust conditions the aviators had ever experienced.

Engines coughed, gears ground, and compressors shrieked complaints in the darkness. Cody could see nothing in the maelstrom but he'd heard enough. Refueling was aborted before it had scarcely begun. Spitting sand from their exhausts, TF Normandy climbed back into the night. What was to be a dress rehearsal for the first strike into Iraq was instead a reprise of Desert One. When they flew back to King Fahd, Task Force Normandy no longer believed in Santa Claus though red and green paper was sprouting around tent city as Christmas approached.

Vicki Cody: "In Dick's letters I saw a lot of tension growing between the lines. I thought it was because Christmas was coming, and that always stirs up thoughts—another year passing, and emotions about people you're close to—plus this year it was the first Christmas we were separated—and by a war.

"A big morale lifter was a video the guys made and sent back here. All three hundred of them had thirty seconds on film. They said about the same things—hi... love to the wife and kids. Didn't matter what they said. Just the voice was enough, and to see them looking healthy, smiling, laughing, joking on camera. Every wife wanted a copy of the video. If it had been for sale, it would have definitely outsold everything at Blockbuster! We'd passed it around for copying, and wives got impatient for their turn.

"The video went with us to show relatives when we left Ft. Campbell for Christmas. Most of us did that—visited parents over the holidays. Somehow we knew the war wouldn't start while we were away. When it started we wanted to be here, together for support, but we needed a break before then.

"We made sure anyone who stayed wouldn't be alone for Christmas. Civilian families volunteered to have them over—more volunteers than we had wives who needed them.

"I was able to be with both my and Dick's family in Vermont. We were minor celebrities. A grade school had me over to tell about being a desert widow. It seemed hard for people in Vermont to understand how we were handlng things at Ft. Campbell. We'd just been doing it and not thinking about it much, but it made me realize how different our lives were from the rest of the country. People couldn't understand why we weren't worried to death. Well, we just couldn't be—that was all. I worried plenty but I couldn't let it rule my life. Worrying was almost a luxury, something I had to ration and not keep me preoccupied.

"Dick called Christmas morning. That's when I really felt myself sinking. I'd been holding it off till I talked with him. I must have swelled up because I said we'd call him back when we got over to his father's house later in the day. It would be more cheery then with a lot of people to talk with him.

"Dick left a number where he could be reached. We placed the call late in the afternoon. It rang a couple of times, and there he was. This was a phone the Air Force put in for him. It could only receive calls, but that's all we wanted.

"His parents, sisters and brothers all had a chance to talk with him. The bill was hundreds of dollars—his father still won't tell me how much. To hear the others talking and cheering him up cheered me too. It made me realize I was just the first person in his life who was supporting him. There was his family, then Montpelier, the state, and America itself.

"I didn't want to leave that kind of environment. It was hard packing up to return to Ft. Campbell and the support group responsibilties. I didn't want the phone ringing and wives asking me the same old questions. I almost dreaded it, and really would have if I'd known what was coming up in the new year. When we got back, the rear detachment was ready to brief us on the 'notification procedure.' That's what would happen when our men got killed."

Christmas was a half holiday for Cody. The rest of the day he worked on what alternative could be devised for a FARP. Somehow TF Normandy had to reach and return from their targets without refueling. The glimmering of an answer began in a story told to him by Lt. Tim Devito who had experienced a fuel pump problem last year on a routine flight from Ft. Campbell to Ft. Bragg.

January 1991

9: Geneva talks between Secretary Baker and Foreign Minister Aziz accomplish nothing. Aziz vows that if Iraq is attacked, they will "absolutely" attack Israel.

12: Congress adopts resolution allowing Bush to go to war. In favor: House 250-183, Senate 52-47.

13: After meeting with Saddam, U.N. Secretary General Lopez de Cuellar declares that "God only knows" if there will be war. Saddam reiterates his determination to keep Kuwait.

IX

The Apache gets new legs

It had been an administrative movement of several Apaches. For the 500 mile flight, two hard points carried auxiliary fuel tanks of 200 gallons each. Somewhere over Tennessee, Tim Devito noticed that one outboard fuel line wasn't working. The other tank sufficed to reach Ft. Bragg, though as it drained, the full but unusable tank caused the chopper to list and required that Devito trim to balance weight. He landed, logged the problem for maintenance, and thought no more about it then or after he flew back to Ft. Campbell.

But a year later, the FARP fiasco reminded Devito of the one-tank incident. He was a supernumerary for TF Normandy, keenly aware of Cody's refueling problem. Initially, it didn't appear that 'aux' tanks (also called pods) were a solution because they were not designed for tactical flying. Pods were flammable, unprotected by armor, and not self-sealing if punctured by a bullet; they were intended solely for administrative long hauls like the one Devito had flown in peacetime.

About all Devito knew was that TF Normandy had to fly beyond the range provided by inboard fuel. He assumed that two aux tanks were not necessary—with that much fuel his buddies could round trip from KKMC to Baghdad—and he doubted even Cody would have volunteered for a venture of that scope. Moreover, with two tanks, only a pair of hard points remained to carry munitions. That, Devito knew, was not enough firepower for whatever it was TF Normandy had to do.

If its vulnerability were not a consideration, he speculated that one tank might be enough to take the raiders half way to Baghdad and back without a FARP. He hesitated to mention the possibility to Cody because flying with a single tank—much less flying into war that way—was not in the book. And as a result of the safety purge, the book was gospel. Nevertheless, Devito dared to intrude one night on his boss's Normandy hours.

Creased with stress, Cody's face remained set, but his eyes narrowed till they seemed to look through and beyond Devito as he nervously related his experience with one tank. Then Codys' questions came quickly: what about the lateral center of gravity, the handling in a quartering wind, holding in a hover, reaction of the firing systems? Devito had no answers, only the memory of an untroubled, straight ahead flight across Tennessee. He left Cody drumming fingers on his desk, and with a contemplative look.

Cody: "I was battle rostered with C Company, so Garcia looked after my ship. In the morning I asked him to go up with me with one aux tank. We'd just hover while I fiddled with the firing systems. I didn't want anyone else to test this because it wasn't within regulations."

Garcia: "With a little trim, the ship responded real well. The only thing out of the ordinary was the firing computer. It only recognized a pair of either aux tanks or weapons. You couldn't tell it that there was one of each. I was thinking, if Cody wants ordnance where the other tank should be, he'll fire off the fuel pod! Well, maybe a little napalm on the target is what he's looking for."

It wasn't napalm but new 'legs' for TF Normandy that was on Cody's mind. Two hundred gallons would take him from the IP with enough fuel for twenty minutes over the targets. That was a wonderful cushion. The first strike should cripple the radars in five minutes—that was SOCCENT's requirement—but if only partially successful with the first attack, TF

Normandy would go after the targets twice or three times. And again if necessary for the 100% destruction Cody had promised Johnson. With an aux tank, he could re-attack the targets *five* times. If the radars weren't dead then, he'd tell the Pave Lows to call in fast movers.

It had been determined that the attacks could be from a hover. Therefore, the Apache's performance as a stable, stationary platform was all important. To provide such a platform was the pilot's job. He brought his ship to the optimum elevation and direction, then complied with the copilot-gunner's requests for small adjustments, which were usually "steady, keep her steady..." For all the amazing capabilities of GPS and firing systems radar, the flight of the missiles would be guided by the front seater's eyes, focusing on the laser spot reflected from the target. He could hardly miss if his pilot kept him level.

Cody: "It was a little harder with an aux tank. You worked the tail rotor pedals more than usual, but it was about the same as fighting a wind. The mechanics alone was no big problem. The problem in attacking with an aux tank is what's coming off the outboard hard point next to the tank. If it was rockets out there, their ignition could set off your fuel pod."

Satisfied with his Apache's performance at hover, Cody tried some maneuvers, duplicating those anticipated for the flight into Iraq. They proved to be well within a good pilot's capabilities. Soon one-tanked Apaches from 1-101 soared away from King Fahd like lopsided bumble bees—and set other helicopter units buzzing.

Davis: "'What's crazy Cody up to now?' That was the kind of stuff we'd hear on the flight line. After the safety purge we knew we'd be hearing things from higher headquarters too. You can't just go flying around in ways that aren't in the regulations. It would be like an airline deciding to use just three engines instead of four to save fuel: the authorities aren't going to allow it. Cody needed to get an AWR real fast."

An Air Worthiness Release was authorization to fly in a way not covered by regulations. The only place that issued AWR's was Aviation Systems Command (AVSCOM) in St. Louis, Missouri. Cody fired off a request to AVSCOM, requesting general permission to fly tactically with one aux tank. Recognizing

1-101's wartime status, AVSCOM's answer was remarkably prompt. In effect they said no, because it wouldn't work—Apaches weren't designed to do that except on straight, long haul flights. That response put Cody in the ticklish position of advising them that it *did* work—he'd tried it.

AVSCOM's second reply was slower, and indicated to Cody that they were stroking their chins. OK, they said, if you have some empirical flight data to prove your point, we'll give you an evaluation. But forget about shooting ordnance with aux tanks: beside the fire hazard, the target computers won't work (the problem Garcia had perceived).

Cody was ready for that response. At a Saudi test range he had indeed fired a Hellfire from alongside an aux tank. In so far as rockets were concerned, AVSCOM was right—they had checked with McDonnell Douglas next door in St. Louis—the computer recognized what was on the inboard hard points only in pairs. Cody proposed that because fleshettes were the rockets to be used, the computer was unnecessary since he wanted 'area coverage'—metal sprayed all over the place—rather than pinpoint accuracy. By cranking distance to target into the computer, it would allow him to fire rockets as Cobra gunships had in Vietnam—like shotguns rather than death rays.

Cody was as pleased as surprised when AVSCOM came back with permission to go ahead if you have to. Keep us advised.

Garrett: "This was the solution Cody needed, and became known as 'the Devito option.' But the consequences went beyond Normandy, and indeed were very far reaching. Apaches now had new legs that transformed their capability. With an aux tank, their range was doubled. So was their operational time because they no longer needed to refuel at some browned out FARP, but could instead fly all the way back to hard stand so their maintenance problems were greatly reduced. Then the Apaches could go way out again, far deeper than where the Iraqis expected them, and stay there till they ran out of targets or ordnance.

"I imagine the Iraqis felt like the Nazis did when P-51's with belly tanks started providing fighter cover for our bombers all over Germany. It amounted to strategic surprise. It was also similar to our development of skip bombing against the Japanese navy, and a jury rigged plow we put on tanks to bust through hedgerows in France. Improvisation and ingenuity are great intangible advantages for the American army. The Devito option is only the most recent example."

With an AWR in hand, Cody advised Johnson that thanks to all concerned, but a FARP for Normandy would not be necessary:

"He just said, roger, proceed with your plan. Nobody's feelings were hurt. Del Daly got a hold of me, and offered his fat cows just in case. I took him up on that. If for any reason, one of my ships ran out of fuel in Iraq, Del would fly a fat cow up to him like roadside service. I started sleeping a lot better after the Devito option was approved. The 2-229 [a sister Apache battalion at King Fahd] still laughed at us flying around with one tank, but you know what? before long they were doing it too."

Doug Gabram: "We started flying one tank before Christmas. It wasn't something we'd done in the simulator [a multi-million dollar interactive video environment at Ft. Campbell], and we talked about the vulnerability a lot. If just one tracer hits that pod, we're crisped. Doing all our flying at night was high stress, but if we had to fight with an aux tank hanging outside the door, the best time to do that was in the dark.

"Lori and I had our second separation just before Xmas. In August I'd left her in Kentucky when I came to King Fahd. She joined me by November, but now she was leaving me behind! December 20th Lori was transferred to a hospital at KKMC. That put her about fifty miles from the border, while I'm back here 300 miles in the rear!"

Lori: "That was funny, looking back on it. I'd worried about him flying border patrol, but now I was up there and he wasn't. KKMC was not at all what I expected. It was like a five star resort.* My hospital was set up to support the coalition forces. It was interesting to see so many foreign uniforms around the complex: Saudis, Syrians, Moroccans, Egyptians, Kuwaitis— someone said there were even some Afghans—plus British and French.

---

* KKMC had been built for the Saudis by the Idaho construction giant, Morrison-Knudsen, at a cost of $10 billion.

"That was December, and we were both still in Saudi Arabia, but I didn't see Doug again till after the war was over, almost four months later. We found that we couldn't even write each other within the kingdom. There was just nothing set up for that. We had to write our parents, and they relayed letters back and forth between us."

In early January, Cody appeared at KKMC, hand carrying a letter from Doug. But what Lori expected to be a happy get-together with Cody was not. Normally sociable and voluble, he was not the man she remembered. Though she did not know it, the reason for his visit was final coordination for Normandy.

Cody: "Yeah, I ws preoccupied because things started rolling toward the starting line when Bush set the 15 January deadline. If Saddam didn't start pulling out, TF Normandy would start the war. Russ Stinger was keeping a full time watch on the targets, and started to advise me on the two week weather forecast. We'd have no illumination from the moon, which is just the way we wanted it for a FLIR attack—we could see them but they couldn't see us. The only weather that could really bother us was major sandstorms. It was a little early in the season for them, so the clock was ticking down nicely."

Lt. Stinger was the 1-101 intelligence officer (S2), trained to locate tanks, accustomed to dealing with enemy tactics in ground combat. The groundwork for Normandy vaulted him into the rarefied space technology of strategic intelligence, an atmosphere he found both awesome and congenial:

"This was my first experience with SCI. When I reported in to the Air Force [AFSOC, though Stinger will not acknowledge it], they advised me that disclosure of anything I learned was punishable with ten years and/or a $10,000 fine. That really got my attention, plus the lie detectors they could put me on at any time.

"But after that, everyone was as friendly and helpful as they could be. The Air Force, of course, is air minded—more so than the Army—so they understood exactly what we needed. All I had to do was ask my contact man. No written requests, no channels, no bullshit or red tape. He'd refer me to someone who had the answer: 'Go up and see Ted in Riyadh.' That's all. I'd walk in, ask for Ted, and explain the situation. CENTCOM was a madhouse getting ready for the air war, but Ted would get right on it. If it was going to take a few hours, he'd invite me to to use his hotel room or go out and buy stuff we'd never seen at King Fahd. And they had phones right and left. That was sure one of my perks—I probably called home more often than anyone in the battalion.

"What they showed me about the targets was like being perched right over them. Actually the satellite pictures were better because the photo interpreters spotted and labeled stuff I probably wouldn't have noticed if I'd hovered over it all day. And of course the Air Force's ELINT could practically tell you if it was Akhmed or Ali manning the tropo scatter that day. It would have amazed the Iraqis how much we knew about them. It sure amazed me."

Indeed the Air Force knew that at the generator for target Red, the Iraqis had a pet dog. Photo interpretation even produced an opinion about the dog's sex (male), and he was labeled Jammal, appearing on the target folders alongside missile names like Grail, and with a notation on how Jammal would appear on FLIR so that he would not be mistaken for a fleeing target.

Beside weather, Stinger asked mostly about finding the best concealment for the routes, and any items arriving or leaving the targets. For example, a new trailer coming on a site was very important. If it contained a triple A, Cody had to know it. The interpreters could determine the capacity of the trailer down to a cubic foot, compare it to the size of all Iraqi triple A weapons, and tell Stinger if there was anything to worry about.

"Maybe the most important thing the Air Force showed us was that the targets could be attacked from hover. Cody's original plan assumed that we'd have to make gun runs—sort of a slow version of fighters strafing the targets. But after studying and monitoring the radar sites, we became almost certain that they had no triple A that could reach beyond our stand off range. That meant we could hit our targets with Hellfires from farther out than their triple A could reach us. That meant, if we got in undetected, we could just hover out there—stand off and accomplish the mission with only MIG's and Hinds to worry about."

Cody: "When Russ confirmed that good news, I started feeling much better. Up till then, I wondered how I'd keep that promise I'd made to the 1-101 families: everyone comes back alive. Hell, I wondered why I'd said it! It just came out of my mouth back in Kentucky. I certainly hoped we'd all get back alive, but I'd had no rational military reason for my promise. Now, step by step, little by little, it began to look like the odds were improving.

"There was never any doubt that we'd take out those radars. Otherwise, I wouldn't have told Col. Johnson we would.

"Casualties were something else. Anytime there's metal in the air where you're flying, each piece means a potential casualty. Casualties happen. They just do, no matter how good the plan is. But with our stand off range longer than the triple A's identified at the sites, a big risk factor was reduced. The other thing going for us was that the triple A at the sites weren't guided by infrared. We could see but they'd only have radar. When we popped up as a big blip, we'd be too close for radar to save them."

The first week of January, Cody eased off. All that could be rehearsed had been, the last being a 'bandit break'—how the two teams would atomize and reassemble if jumped by MIG's en route. Zeke Zarnowski, a former Air Force paramedic in Vietnam, now a pilot in White team, was taken back when the Iraqi aircraft for the rehearsal were said to be MIG 29's. These top of the line interceptors were equipped with 'look down, shoot down' radar from which there was no escape by the Apaches, even in sudden dispersal.

Zarnowski mentioned the enemy capability to Tim Roderick, another Air Force veteran, now flying with Red team, and 1-101's expert on Soviet aircraft. Roderick's reply was a twitch of his mustache. Tom Drew, White leader, got into a quietly growing discussion:

"We're gonna' go in, do the job, and nobody gets hurt," was his dismissive prediction. Drew was a second generation chopper pilot—his father had commanded TF 160. For Jody Bridgforth, a front seater with Red, the bandit break drill set off a jingle:

"Look down, shoot down,
Do it all around town."

Cody watched Bridgforth's casual finger popping but could not interpret TF Normandy's mood. It was as though Cody had a pile of surprise Christmas packages to open for his men, and could not predict what their reaction would be. Nothing yet could be disclosed to them, not until the night before the raid. Till then, Bridgforth became an attitudinal weather vane for Cody. When Bridgforth was deadly serious, Cody knew everyone else would be.

Twenty-five years old, a junior college dropout, with a mustache that looked like film from a vanilla milk shake, Bridgforth would be the lamb if there was slaughter. His Virginia accent was as faint and disarming as his perpetual smile. Jody Bridgforth came to the army from central casting, to die in John Wayne's arms on the sands of Iwo Jima.

His back seater was Jim Miller, another TF 160 alumnus, and a former enlisted soldier in special forces. Cody wished everyone on the raid had Miller's survival abilities in case they were shot down. At the Red target, Miller would hover next to team leader Shufflebarger with Tim Roderick in the back seat. 'Captain Shuff' was the head of a flying family—his wife flew Hueys in the National Guard. Laser sighting was child's play for Shufflebarger who found more challenge in skeet shooting.

On Miller's left would be the crew of Tim Vincent (front seat) and Shawn Hoban. Vincent was 1-101's basketball star in the King Fahd hangars. He was also a Ranger who could find his way home from the fence on foot if necessary. Saudi Arabia had been especially trying for Hoban whose loneliness for the many women who missed him was like the forced withdrawal of Desert Shield's alcoholics. On the far left flank of the Red raid was Lou Hall, a standardization pilot, which meant he checked out the instructor pilots. He was also a Vietnam veteran on gunships, and Cody's confidant: if there was anything seething among the warrant officers, Hall would champion them to the colonel. In Hall's front seat was Jerry Orsburn, A Company's prankster.

Except for Shufflebarger, Red team was all warrant officers. Each had accumulated over 8,500 hours flying Apaches, though their average age was mid-twenties. If one team was stronger than the other—a suggestion that would be hotly disputed—it was Red because they would be on their own, forty miles from where Cody could get them help.

The lineup for the White site was Cody on the right flank with Bryan Stewmon who had crashed in the mid-air collision at Hunter Liggett, then pulled out his stricken pilot, surely saving his life. Jorge Garcia was awarded the Soldier's Medal for his part in the rescue. As a demonstration of confidence in Stewmon, Cody put him in the front seat. Working close to the ground was in Stewmon's blood—his father was a retired crop duster. On Cody's left was the Red leader, burly Tom Drew, once a warrant officer in 1-101 who went to officers candidate school and returned a second lieutenant. He was front seater for Zeke Zarnowski.

Next was Ron Rodrigues piloting Lee Miller. In early 1991, Rodrigues had left 1-101 to be an Apache test pilot for the army. When the war broke out, Rodrigues pulled strings, coattails and rabbits from a hat till he won reassignment with Cody, and teamed up again with Lee Miller to become the winning crew in the battalion top gun competition. Cody had served through the years with almost all his pilots and gunners; e.g., with Lee Miller way back in the 24th Division, and with Lou Hall, off and on, for nine years. Cody did not have to guess when he foresaw how everyone would perform.

On the left flank was 'Tip' O'Neal shooting for standardization pilot Dave Jones. Jones had stepped from a recruiting poster. Slim, serious, serene, he looked like he should be the general's aide—but there was no better instructor in the battalion. Where Jones stood with hands clasped behind him, O'Neal had his hands on hips, regarding the world as if it were one of the black boxes that fascinated him. A representative of the computer generation, O'Neal absorbed himself in how things worked, how maps were made, what was the master program for the entire Apache environment. He easily understood the rehearsed plans to such detail that if the firing sequence were followed, his would be the first shot, albeit first by only a second at most.

The attack plans for both teams were the same. Iraqi radar sites were laid out identically, so each crew would spew a fan of fire to cover a sector of his site. Within the sectors Cody had assigned primary and secondary targets; the fans overlapped so that from hover one team could attack adjoining sectors if his wingman was shot down or missed his target.

Behind the two firing lines, the rest of TF Normandy would be positioned at three locations. Two Pave Lows for each team lurked back at the release points ten miles from the targets. Across the Saudi border, seventy miles away, was a spare Apache crewed by Tim Devito and Mark Ivey; accompanied by a Black Hawk helicopter, piloted by Terry Seanor and Dave Parker (son of a former commander of the Army Aviation School), carrying Russ Stinger and an emergency maintenance team under crew chief Bobby Gunter.

Cody had flown with them all. He knew their approaches and attitudes the way a madam knows the idiosyncrasies of her girls. Now, as the second week of January began, Cody prepared his men to become prisoners of war.

Which meant the crews were 'sanitized,' stripped of all personal identification save military ID cards and dog tags. The Screaming Eagle patch was removed from flight suits, and tail numbers erased from the Apaches. Five months of letters from home were stored in footlockers or destroyed. According to the Geneva Convention governing treatment of POW's, captives were required to tell their captors only name, rank, and serial number; but the Iraqis were expected to extract more—and they did by torture. To prevent exploitation of loved ones, no one in TF Normandy wished to reveal the fact if they were married, so the letters from home were stored or burned.

Vicki Cody: "They shipped Dick's footlocker back. I got it just before the ground war. I didn't want to open it. It sat there by the door for a week as if it were a casket. When I finally opened it, there was the feeling that he was dead and these were like his remains. Everything I touched—his clothes, papers, jewelery—was like his spirit coming out of the footlocker.

It was eerie. I got rid of most of it or put it out of sight and burned some of the papers.

"When Dick got back he was mad because I hadn't saved his Doonesbury strips with those Desert Shield characters. He'd cut the strips out of Stars & Stripes every day. Well, I was mad too because he hadn't saved my letters—he burned them when he was sanitizing for Normandy!"

Sanitization complete, Cody asked Garrett to request a briefing for Gen. Peay at SOCCENT. Jesse Johnson and his Air Force deputy, George Gray, were the only others present. Up to this point, Peay knew nothing of the mission's specifics, nor did Garrett. Finally, the map from Cody's tiny office in the baggage claim room came out for view.

Without a glance at notes, Cody talked through the runup for the raid and its execution: A seven hundred mile flight across Saudi Arabia to KKMC; there to refuel and continue on to a small AFSOC airfield at Al Jouf where TF Normandy would at last be shown the targets and routes for their mission. They'd stay the night in AFSOC quarters, sleep late because takeoff for Iraq would be around one in the morning of January 17th. If all went well, they'd be back by dawn, refuel at Ar Ar or KKMC, and immediately proceed to King Fahd where Peay would find them ready for duty on 19 January.

This last point was the most important purpose of Cody's briefing. Commencment of the air war was expected to draw a retaliatory ground attack from Saddam. Peay had to know when all his Apaches would be available to start killing tanks. Cody explained how his defensive team could hold the fort while TF Normandy was away.

Cody lowered his pointer, turned from the map to invite questions. Peay deferred to Garrett who asked when division would be advised of the raid's results:

Mike Davis would be with SOCCENT right next door. When Davis got the word, he'd notify Garrett. Expect a call around 0400 on the morning of the 17th.

Garrett had no further questions. "Well," he said, joshing Gray, "it looks like air superiority is going to begin on the ground."

As the briefing concluded, Peay had angled forward in the chair, fingers interlaced between his legs. He nodded at Garrett's comment. Peay realized the occasion called for something more.

"You're going to do it, Dick. The 101st legend continues. Start the war, but don't be the first casualty, OK?"

Peay's handshake was short and firm, as was Garrett's. Johnson clapped him on the back. Cody watched them leave together, rolled up the map, and stared a moment at the empty door. This was it. This was unreal reality. He heard his silent laugh, an inward chortle of almost vengeful satisfaction, coupled with amazement at what a weird, wild world it was, putting him in the back seat of Apache 977 on a secret flight to Al Jouf.

His 40th birthday party—that was strange enough—but his memory vaulted back to graduation at West Point nearly eighteen years before. No, earlier to his days as a cadet. Glib, apparently rash, irreverent and unstudious, Cody had seemed least likely to succeed. Indeed, his classmates had rated him as lacking apitutude for military service, and he was nearly boarded out of the academy for that reason, saved only by testimonials that his worth should be judged by less rigid standards.

Hobbled by his basketball knee, Cody could not even qualify for the combat arms of the army, much less wear the standard merit badges of paratroopers and rangers earned by West Point second lieutenants. Instead, he was relegated to the low speed Transportation Corps where he gained his advancement through unique expertise in helicopter maintenance. From the Vietnam years (too early for Cody), helicopters were where the action was in the army, but helicopters were no use to the bold tactician if they were down for maintenance. Cody kept them flying. Therefore, high ranking tacticians wanted Cody around.

But then he seemed to be in the wrong places at the right times. Others won renown for trifling accomplishments in Grenada and Panama. Hotshot pilots gravitated toward TF 160 for special operations. Along came the maligned Apache in 1985, and interest was elsewhere. Cody became the Apache's voice against a host of critics:

"It wasn't sleek like the Cobra. I loved the Cobra and Corvettes too, but they can't compare with the boxy Rolls Royce. The Apache is like that. It doesn't look flashy, but it does things no other ship can come close to."

Cody's father had a large Chevrolet dealership in Vermont, and specialized in Corvettes. The oldest of seven children, Cody was to inherit the dealership, but his basketball prowess as a shooting guard drew the attention of Bobby Knight's scouts and got Cody an appointment to West Point. The dealership could wait till he fulfilled his five-year military obligation, but not a 30-year career. The army was to be a chapter in his life, not he a chapter in army history. That would be written by well marked classmates like Tom Greco or the first captain of the Corps of Cadets, Bob Van Antwerp, both ranger-airborne and wearing Screaming Eagles at King Fahd.

But now it was Dick Cody buckling into his helicopter early on the morning of January 15th; Dick Cody watching the men of the defensive team gathered with upraised thumbs. The nine Apaches lifted off, Red team following White. Tent city sprawled below like the crowded peaks of a snowy mountain range—18,000 soldiers oblivious to the history makers flying off to the north. A slight breeze ruffled the division flag, as if to confirm that the legend continues. For it was to Normandy the Screaming Eagles had flown forty-seven years earlier, Normandy on D Day. Now Task Force Normandy flew toward its own D Day to start another war.

As a second lieutenant, Cody had explained a small anomaly brought up in his security clearances: his family name had not always been Cody. It had been anglicized by his grandfather, Rashid Oude, an immigrant from Lebanon. In January 1991, this historical quirk gave Rashid's grandson another chuckle: the opening battle of the war between Arabs and Americans would begin under the direction of an Arab-American.

January 1991

14: TV pans on CENTCOM's stateside headquarters near Tampa, Florida, where the Super Bowl is played after a tingling rendition of the national anthem by Whitney Houston.

15: U.N. deadline expires, then Baker rejects a last-minute French peace plan because it links Kuwait with Palestine.

X

Soft porn and popcorn

Transmission lines and buildings soon passed under the powerful throb of Apache rotors, then roads below scattered into wispy trails as TF Normandy headed northwest across Arabia's central badlands. Half a million soldiers were marshalled beyond the horizon, but what could be seen now in the silent vastness was neither a theater of war or even life. An extension of The Empty Quarter, an abyss larger than Texas, sprawled in dreary monotony beneath the arrow of helicopters. This was the wasted domain of the desert, where tiny gnomes of gray-green vegetation seemed to kneel, seeking permission to exist. This was winter, when the sovereign sun, hoarding water like Midas, hibernated behind a steel wool overcast. For the first three hours, they flew above it, crossing the web of gullies jagging through the barrens, practicing identification of vague descriptors on their maps like 'numerous mounds,' 'desiccated terrain,' 'sand ridges,' and 'gravel plains.'

Dune country was the most dangerous terrain for low level flight, yet low was how TF Normandy had to fly as they approached the range of enemy radar. Cody would give the fence no radar signatures to study, no inkling that Apaches might be close to the frontier. Leading the flight, he eased down into the overcast where only altimeters revealed the distance between a landing and a crash.

His Apache stuffed in the steel wool fog, Shufflebarger's instrument panel went blank.

"Generator failure!"

"Roger," Roderick replied, and broadcast an emergency, while Shufflebarger angled toward the ground like a submarine searching for a soft seabed.

"Smoke!"

Jim Miller followed him down, reading Shufflebarger's altitude till they settled on a rocky plain. Bridgforth sprinted over with a fire extinguisher, as Shufflebarger and Roderick moved a safe distance away, while TF Normandy orbitted overhead in the fog. Seanor's Black Hawk landed with Gunter to investigate the problem. It was indeed the auxiliary generator, smoking but not afire.

Cody awaited a prognosis from the ground, thinking how 1-101 had the highest operational readiness rate in the army; but here on their most important mission, along came this mechanical failure. Murphy's Law had been suspended since the Hellfire incident; now, combining with the law of averages, would things start to go wrong? Something will go wrong, he was sure. This might be it. He hoped so. Never exorcised from his mind had been the fear of the forgotten, some slight oversight with fatal concatenations: some nail for want of which the horseshoe of luck could be lost. Well, better that a glitch now in the Saudi wilderness than over Iraq.

Banking in long curves, Cody waited for the report from Shufflebarger. If his Apache was seriously disabled, should Devito become Red team leader? If so, there'd be no further backup. If another Apache went down, could three handle all of Red's targets? That had been the original plan...

Reprieve. The message from the ground was that Red Six could make it to KKMC, *inshallah*. The sick Apache made it.

The stop at KKMC was to have been no longer than a self serve fill 'er up. On previous visits, Cody had seen many multinational Arabs around the complex. Cagey and uncertain allies, they had radios. If any also had sympathies for Iraq, Cody wasn't going to give them a long look at nine mysterious Apaches. "Regas and haul ass" had been his plan.

But now Red Six was down and perhaps out. There was no

repair shop for Apaches at KKMC. Only TF Normandy's experience and expertise would do the fix, if it could be done. The Black Hawk—code name, Good Wrench—disgorged tools, then its crew scrambled in and under Shufflebarger's turbines.

Cody's forte is maintenance. He could almost tell from the intent expressions of his mechanics that the generator was going to work again. The question was how soon. He glanced around the tarmac for figures in Arab headdress.

The aux generator spit a few times, then roared into a reassuring throb. Gunter stood back listening. At belt buckle level, his thumb shot up. Everyone was already refueled. Like scrambling fighter pilots, the crews hopped into their ships. They'd been on the ground an hour and a half. In a minute they were gone.

Their destination was Al Jouf, an AFSOC air strip four hours west. In ancient times, Al Jouf was a point of departure for caravans crossing The Great Nefud, 400 miles of Arabia's most spectacular desert featuring steep revetments of sand a hundred meters deep and a mile across. For TF Normandy too, Al Jouf would be the point of departure, called the IP. The Pave Lows, and the final briefings awaited them there.

Zarnowski: "We flew nape of the earth between KKMC and Al Jouf. I don't think even AFSOC's radar picked us up, because when we arrived no one seemed to be expecting us. We hadn't called them on the radio—maybe that was the reason. Anyway, we got out, stretched and pissed, and parked just the way we'd take off for the mission. We still didn't know what it was.

"After a while this unmarked truck comes out and takes us to a compound where civilian contractors used to live. We got a kitchen and bath but just two little rooms for all of us to sleep in. No beds or cots, but it was great to sit on a flush toilet. We cleaned the place up best we could, and started cooking MRE's on the stove. Pretty soon Cody comes in, looking like he wants to tell us something. I thought maybe he'd say we could get chow with the Air Force. I knew they'd be living a lot better than this."

Roderick: "Cody's carrying a lot of maps and folders—target

folders. When he spread 'em out on the floor, I realize we're finally going to find out where we're going."

Bridgforth: "Sure, I'm real interested in what he's showing us—but there's something in my mind that says, hey, there hasn't been any shooting yet! When I hear the colonel talking about IP time, it dawns on me that we might *start* the shooting."

Jones' thoughts focused the salvo sequence. Either O'Neal in the front seat or his counterpart on Red team should send the first round down range.

Shufflebarger: "What impressed me was that my target folder was just like our rehearsals. In practice, we were told we'd be shooting at 'structures.' Now in the target folders, the structures had labels like 'radar mast' or 'barracks.' Their positions were exactly the same as we'd rehearsed. The layout was in my mind already. I could have loaded my target data in the firing computer right then. Stinger and Cody had done a super job planning this thing, no doubt about it."

Cody watched his teams absorbed by their target folders. To him, the atmospherics in the room seemed to waver between blase and impatient. Their entire Desert Shield experience had been one of 'let's get started,' transformed now by TF Normandy into 'let's get it over.' But Cody had promised them, by promising himself, an interlude for reflection. He was not going to assume they had volunteered for a mission that had been unfolded to them for only a few minutes. Anyone who wanted out now, could. He announced loudly that he was going outside to smoke a cigar. Anyone who wished to join him, should.

He stepped into the patio, and patted his pockets. No cigars. The tensions of the runup had overridden even the strongest physical addiction. As a substitute for nicotine, Cody began pacing when he heard the door open and close. Without turning, he tried to imagine who it was. His last guess would have been Zarnowski.

"How's your cigar, sir?"

"Zeke, I'm out."

This was not news to Zarnowski. He had provided Cody a cigar at KKMC, and now pulled out two more. They lit up together. As the match flared, Cody searched his friend's face for an indication.

"Good mission." That was all Zarnowski or anyone else had to say about it.

Now, barring a startling pullout by Saddam, it was going to happen. Gen. Powell and Secretary Cheney had flown into Riyadh the week before Christmas to review Schwarzkopf's war plans. Jesse Johnson, on that occasion, had to stand up before them and guarantee what Cody had guaranteed him— 100% destruction of the vital radars at each site.

This was more than reassurance for VIP's. For Powell, especially, it was the opening key of a symphony composed under his supervision, to be conducted by Schwarzkopf. The first shots would be fanfare for the volleys to follow. This war, he insisted, would begin with an intimidating bang so as to ensure it would not end with a whimper. Vietnam had both begun and ended with uncertainty. Desert Storm must start as it should finish—decisively, with no doubt who won.

Powell was gratified that 100% destruction meant more than required for Cody. In reviewing the target folders with his men, Cody set the standard for mission success to be what Johnson required, *plus* destruction of the sites' external communications. That is, the radars were to be liquidated in such a way that Baghdad would not even know it till too late.

Additionally—and beyond Johnson's requirements—all permanent structures and triple A were to be taken out, so that the Air Force could virtually forget the sites for the rest of the war. When the Apaches peeled off to rejoin the Pave Lows, Cody wanted only ghosts in ruins left behind. Only Jammal would be spared.

That was how Cody defined success to the task force, and it was to be accomplished in under five minutes. Moreover, there was but a twenty *second* window in which the two sites, forty miles apart, must be hit simultaneously by the first Hellfires. Such was the stopwatch timing for starting the air war that certain radars had to come down within twenty seconds for optimal coordination with cruise missile and stealth strikes elsewhere on Saddam's C&C network. Blank screens, dead phones, and roaring static were to be Saddam's introduction to Operation Desert Storm.

Retrospectively, Roderick shrugged. "It was do-able. We realized that because we'd practiced it so many times. Getting in and out could be tough—we expected it would be—but if we got lined up and locked on the targets, they'd be history. Hell, we'd run a lot harder attacks on the simulator."

Johnson had moved TF Normandy up to Al Jouf to await H Hour, now that D Day was set for January 17th. Fatigued by their 14-hour flight and the impact of comprehending their mission, Cody told them to sleep in the next morning, a step in 'reverse cycling' their bodies to rest by day and fly by night. Crew fatigue was a significant factor in his plans, not so much for the raid, but for the high speed return to King Fahd in expectation that the air war might precipitate an Iraqi counteroffensive on the ground. As important as his guarantee to Johnson was Cody's promise to Peay: when the Screaming Eagles needed Apaches, 1-101 would be there at full strength.

To coordinate TF Normandy's transition from radar raiders to tank killers, Mike Davis moved over to SOCCENT's building at King Fahd as a temporary liaison officer. Green Berets were going to war with the Air Force, slipping teams into Iraq to lase targets, as well as other SCI activities that Davis could only guess. He knew people in TF 160; they and all of SOCCENT were in D Day mode, a grim bustle of taut faces, many streaked with camouflage.

Cody's mission was but the first item on SOCCENT's immediate agenda. No one asked Davis about TF Normandy, and no one knew. With difficulty he was able to get a phone connection with Al Jouf. Had the Apaches arrived? Wait one... What Apaches? After investigation, Al Jouf confirmed that yes, there were some Apaches now parked out front. Whose were they? Wait one... Can't tell: all the tail numbers were sanitized.

Davis could assume that if there were nine Apaches parked in group up there 700 miles away, they were Cody's. Davis did not know if Shufflebarger's defective ship had left KKMC. He asked the airman at Al Jouf to please go out and count the Apaches, but the phone lines were too busy for Davis to hold.

Should TF Normandy guard their ships all during this night before the raid? This was a command decision for Cody. He decided no. If the Air Force didn't have the strip secure, this was going to be a bad war. His men were really tired—how else to explain the yawns and subdued conversations? Even if they couldn't sleep (Cody doubted if he could) they should rest through the night rather than walk sentry posts.

But the Air Force had stuck them in this compound a couple of miles from the strip, the only place where lights were on. Not even Cody had ever seen Al Jouf; no one knew what was around here, and in the dark there wasn't any way to tell. TF Normandy couldn't just close the door and go to bed. Grumbling at the Air Force's indifference, the warrant officers set up two-hour guard shifts to secure the compound. They had M-16's for the job. There would be one in each Apache, to fight their way out of Iraq on the ground if necessary.

Rolling out slim futons, the crews practically carpeted the two small rooms. Lights would go out with the sun. Bridgforth sprawled on his sleeping bag, and wrote letters while waiting to pull guard. "Don't forget to mail 'em," Jim Miller muttered, "unless they're for Saddam."

Miller had a secret under his flight suit pocket. In some New Years roughhouse, his knee had bent the wrong way. He had concealed the pain that walking caused him so as not to be dropped from the mission as Weeks had been. Bridgforth, however, knew Miller's condition and it worried him. The only flash of a dream he had that night was that Miller was on his back, a crushing weight Bridgforth could not carry out of Iraq.

Except for Cody and Stewmon, all the White team crews were from B Company (Bearcats). At twilight, Zarnowski passed the word for them to join him in the patio. The Bearcats back at King Fahd had given him a package to be opened this evening. Drew, Lee Miller, Rodrigues, O'Neal and Jones gathered around him. Paper tore—a note fluttered out. It read, GET SOME! Unaware of the bon voyage package,* Cody heard the Bearcats' chuckle recede into a dark corner of the compound.

---

* A six-pack of a beverage, the contents of which the Bearcats would not reveal to the author.

With his task force put to bed, he rode down to the air strip with Stinger to study any updates for weather, routes and targets. Comer greeted them, and Cody brought up the matter of security for the Apaches and the compound. Comer apologized—some air police would relieve the aviators forthwith.

Stinger gawked to see AFSOC's facilities at this remote outpost: A VCR was playing a soft porn film still popular in stateside theaters. Microwaves dinged periodically as airmen—wearing Florida State Seminoles baseball caps and Hard Rock Cafe T shirts—passed by to remove toasty popcorn. From five months acquaintance with AFSOC, Stinger had become a convert. This was the way to begin a war. To hell with the army's monasticism. The Air Force had the right philosophy: it only makes sense to provide as much pleasure as possible when the most possible pain was in prospect.

The routes were not yet 'curved.' What AFSOC had to show Cody was the theoretical maxima for avoiding radar detection, lines as jagged as lightning with abrupt and acute angles. It was time to smooth them out, to show Comer what final adjustments to make in the actual track. There were Iraqi border guards reported in that grid square. Did Cody want to bypass it?* No—the detour would take them too far out of the way.

But what about the Saudi border guards? It was doubtful they could tell whether the sound of helicopters was coming or going. Cody and Comer agreed that they'd take their chances with friendly fire rather than advise the Saudis that there would be an outbound flight tomorrow night.

H Hour was still bracketed by Bush's deadline for an Iraqi withdrawal and sunrise. Though Saddam had occupied Kuwait in 48 hours, there was no indication he was preparing to leave as quickly. Comer opined that H Hour would be close to 3:00 a.m. on the morning of the 17th (in the Mideast time zone). The Pave Lows were ready. The Apaches were ready. If Comer were right, they would start for the border in about twenty-eight hours.

When tense, Cody clips his syllables, a reversion to his New

---

* West of KKMC, the border was a 30-mile-wide belt of no man's land patroled by both countries

England accent. "OK," he said with noticeable clips, "let's do it. When's the joint briefing?"

With the stern 101st, the hour would have probably been at daybreak. With the relaxed Air Force, it was proposed by Comer for tomorrow evening. Cody was silently grateful—he had told his crews they could sleep in.

With blacked out lights, Cody and Stinger drove back. They tiptoed into TF Normandy's quarters, but the subdued sounds they heard convinced them that few were sleeping: resting, keeping silent so as not to wake the other non-sleepers, but there were no snores. No real slumber till nearly daylight when sleep finally crept up on men who tried not to show they were awake.

As light seeped through windows, Cody noticed the hands outside sleeping bags. Nearly everyone had removed all jewelery, even wedding bands. Sanitizing had been the worst phase in the countdown, the step that prepared for the possibility of failure and capture. He was glad sanitization was behind them. More reassuring would be the final check on the flight line—examining links in the chain guns, pulling arming tapes from the Hellfires, pins from rockets. Till then, thoughts would draw away into soltitude even while the men were together enduring the morning.

When everyone could see that the others were awake, they started to roll their sleeping bags quickly—then paused, realizing the time to pack them was hours away. Bags were unrolled and rerolled, each wrinkle smoothed out with the deliberation of a tea ceremony, as minds tried to focus on something beside waiting.

A pot boiling water to heat MRE's bubbled unnoticed: Eggs Benedict would not have tempted appetites. Someone had heard that you shouldn't eat before combat because food in the stomach was a bad thing if you were shot in the gut. Hall and Zarnowski were the only Vietnam veterans, but they offered no opinions.

"If you're hungry, eat. If you're not, don't."

"No, you ought to eat now. It's all going to digest, and you'll dump it before takeoff."

"Right. You need energy from food."

"I got chocolate. That's energy, and keeps you awake too."

"No, man. That's just a rush. You need good, solid food."

"So why aren't you eating?"

"Maybe in a couple of hours."

Such discussions were extended for the sake of distraction. When Cody departed for the strip, crews hoped he would send for them soon. Amid the Air Force's luxuries was the way to spin out the hours, not here in these bleak rooms with the lonely ambiance of a deserted bus station. As a pale sun enriched the patio, TF Normandy tried to invent a game like soccer with MRE cartons.

The Air Force was watching a taped football playoff game. Cody considered sending for his men to join them but forgot as he became absorbed with the air campaign that would follow the raid. Not a good idea to become too acquainted with it—if he were captured, he wished to know nothing—but the Air Force didn't mind him seeing the events planned for the first night:

Carrier strikes from the Gulf and eastern Arabia were not included, but the waves of attacks from the Red Sea and Riyadh were enough to fill several single spaced pages for just H Hour alone. As TF Normandy peeled off their targets, all hell would start coming the other way. Cody noticed that several Tomahawk cruise missiles were scheduled to cross his return route, and wondered if a collision were possible.

"About the same chance as being hit by a meteor," an airman told him.

Lounging and chatting were the Pave Low personnel who, like the Apache crews the night before, had just been informed of location and probable time for the raid. At nine that evening—if the intervening hours ever passed—all participants from both services would gather together for the first time. To help his men while away the time till then, Cody asked for a couple of decks of cards to take back to the Normandy compound.

Vicki Cody: "Everything after New Years was really new. President Bush announced the deadlines, and you could feel Ft. Campbell tense up. Last year everything was 'if' and 'maybe'; now, at the beginning of 1991, something was going to happen for sure.

"It was just like the football playoffs that were going on at the same time—just like the countdown for the Super Bowl. One day closer, another day closer. We were ready to pop.

"For some reason, I felt more anticipation than fear. Then I'd catch myself, and realize I should be more afraid.

"I don't think there's ever been a war started like this—with everyone knowing when the kickoff would be."

TF Normandy filed into the Air Force suite like cowpokes reaching a saloon after weeks on the range. Brushing their sleeves set off puffs of dust and a certain amusement with the airmen. Nods and hellos were exchanged without much enthusiasm. Bridgforth looked around as he had at Hearst Castle:

"I don't live this good at home," he drawled for no one in particular.

Only Zarnowski found an emotional element in this first full meeting with the Air Force. He squinted at one of the 'PJ's' (aero-medics) curiously familiar features. Only the Pave Low pilots, not their PJ crews, had participated in the rehearsals.

"Hey..." Zarnowski started to ask, convinced he knew the face, but unable to conjure the name.

"Yeah..." The PJ experienced the same recognition. They had been aero-medics together in Vietnam, twenty years before, and had not seen each other since.

Zarnowski's memories flooded back, merging his first war with his second. Flying out of Danang and Thailand, he had raced to the calls of pilots descending in parachutes. Now he was a pilot; it could be his call that set 'SAR'—search and rescue—in motion.

SAR was what this first and final joint briefing concerned. Cody had nothing inspirational to say to a group so quintessentially professional that 'brief backs'—narrations of what everyone would do on the mission—were now redundant. His points were that everything to be done had been practiced to perfection. The plan was sound, the people and planes were sound, so the chance for failure was small enough not to distract anyone from concentrating on what they knew they could perform, and indeed had performed.

Cody's laconic remarks—all the more unpretentious with a country music cassette playing in the background—affirmed the workaday mood of the briefing. It was, after all, a chat among themselves, not a presentation for VIP's. Comer, sensing the lack of any historical content, sought to add it, beginning, "Right behind us will come the greatest aerial armada in history...," continuing with a few stirring words about the importance of the mission.

He put it in human terms. Not counting the two dozen lives at risk in the task force, scores more in the armada were nearly certain to be lost if the fence was not thoroughly cracked. This, to be sure, was a destructive raid, but destruction for the purpose of saving American lives. Yes, Iraqis would no doubt be killed—perhaps a hundred of them if the garrisons at the sites were annihilated—but as Gen. Patton once put it, "Your job is not to lay down your life for your country, but to cause some other bastard to lay down *his* life for *his* country."

Nearly a year later, Gen. Powell reflected on the unique character of the Normandy mission, when asked to compare it with three other famous raids—Doolittle's bombing of Tokyo, the attempt to liberate American POW's in North Vietnam (Sonh Tay), and the Desert One debacle:

"There is a significant difference between TF Normandy's efforts and [these] three operations. [They] were directed at single objectives, and when they did or did not accomplish those objectives, events moved on. TF Normandy's mission, on the other hand, was an integral supporting part of a larger air operations plan which, in turn, was an integral part of a still larger overall campaign plan."

Comer's remarks put a new tone on the briefing, an emphasis on what the two services would do for each other. The keynote was 'don't worry about your wingman': aviation speak meaning 'we'll be there if you need us.' For the Air Force that meant if an Apache went down, a Pave Low would be on the ground beside it immediately.

The PJ's added that a standard practice of SAR might be waived for this mission. Bridgforth: "This PJ stands up and says, 'if you're hurt on the ground, two of us are going to come over, one guy with an aid kit, the other with a gun. We'll stop your bleeding, then tie you up and load you in the Pave Low.' They'd keep us covered on the flight back too, in case we're Iraqi agents. I guess something like that happened once or twice in Vietnam.

"The way they said they'd treat us sort of blew my mind, but then an officer said if the PJ's saw us go down, they'd just come over and rescue us like friendlies instead of EPW's."

After the joint briefing, TF Normandy re-inspected their Apaches, then more blank hours held them in their two-room compound. They were driven to the flight line around ll p.m.

They went through their final checks in darkness, pin points of red and green light signalling the status of flight systems. The squatting shadows of four Pave Lows had joined the string of eight Apaches. Stinger's Black Hawk and Devito's spare Apache were the last in line. Al Jouf was on higher, colder desert than at the Gulf. The crews began to stamp feet and rub themselves through their flight suits.

In Washington, at 1:30 a.m. Al Jouf time, President Bush put in a call to President Gorbachev. Thanks, was the message, for your efforts to achieve a last minute peace, but the war will start in a couple of hours.

There were still some 1,200 Russian advisers in Iraq. Bush did not want any of them to be casualties from American bombs. He also advised the president of CNN to warn his reporters, notably Shaw and Arnett in a Baghdad hotel.

CENTCOM was not altogether surprised to intercept increased electronic traffic between Moscow and Baghdad, considering that a lot of Russians in Iraq needed to be told to get their heads down. But ELINT also picked up a reply from Saddam's headquarters. This was indeed alarming. AWAC's and radar watchers tensed to see if the fence became more alert.

Apparently a Gorbachev message was for Saddam's eyes only. Apparently Saddam, constantly and secretly on the move between hideouts, could not be located by his staff. Apparently one of his deputies was asking Moscow if he should decode the message in the dictator's absence.

A midnight breeze blew across the blackened air strip at Al

Jouf. For warmth, Cody and Stewmon sat in their helicopter for a final talk. A blacked out sedan approached the line of Apaches, driven by an Air Force colonel who asked which ship was Cody's.

17: After initial air attacks, Bush announces that Operation Desert Storm and "the
liberation of Kuwait" have begun.

XI

For all you do...

The colonel drove top speed across the tarmac. "Gotta' talk
to you!" he shouts.

Cody climbs down from the cockpit, goes to the car, leans his
hands on the rolled down window. "What's up, sir?"

"It's go, Dick. Your mission is go. Time on target, 0238. That's
straight from CINC."

Cody passes the word down the line: takeoff for White team
at 0100: twenty minutes. Ground generators kick in one after
the other—too much noise for a last word with his White
teammates—so he walks rapidly back to Red team, whose
takeoff is six minutes behind White. But their generators too
are attached and whirring. It's extremely dark; Cody really has
nothing more to say anyway, so while passing each Apache he
just thumps its fuselage like a jockey might pat his horse before
the Kentucky Derby.

He feels this will be a night of the Apache, as much so as for
their crews. Not long before, a video from Ft. Campbell arrived
in the mountainous piles of Christmas mail. A wife had taped
a portion of *60 Minutes*, a hatchet job on the Apache. She had
been hesitant about sending the tape, for fear her husband
might lose confidence in his helicopter; but she wanted to know
if it was the problem machine *60 Minutes* had depicted.

The answer would be in other videos, eight of them, taken
by TF Normandy's FLIR cameras. Let Morley Safer show this
to the folks back home, Cody told himself, and they'll watch

the wrath of God. Speedy, stealthy, invisible and invincible: everything an attack helicopter should be. Prime time, Cody fumed, prime time—as he returned to his Apache.

Bearcat crews shout to each other, "Get some, baby!" Someone around the Black Hawk recognizes Cody as he turns back up the line and calls, "Here we go, Commander."

With no pitch in their blades, White team's wings whoosh almost silently, warming for takeoff. 0100, the H Hour, is not to be calibrated by Cody's wristwatch but by atomic clocks, such is the importance of the twenty second window at the targets. Comer's Pave Low had taken the 'time hack' from a satellite. Over the radio he passes the official time to the flight: "At my hack—zero, zero, forty-eight. Six, five, four, three, two, one—hack."

Fourteen helicopter pilots zero and release the second hands on their cockpit clocks. Shufflebarger does something more. He did not want even to glance down at the clock when his eyes were on the target. He'd tied a chem stick to his wrist so he could read the time by raising his watch to his face.

Bridgforth stands close by his Apache, craning to watch White team depart. He sees only small ruddy glows from six manifolds. They flare with blue and yellow; then the quietly whirling wings catch pitch and begin to thump. "Yaaaah-ha!" Bridgforth screams into the night as he unzips, and pisses flowingly on the runway.

There is nothing more for him to see till Comer flies low over the end of the runway and drops a chem stick. It looks like a luminous baton as it falls then bounces off the tarmac. As White team passes over this point—the IP—they crank designated map coordinates into their computers, coordinates accurate to ten meters. This is the first known point of reference. The Pave Lows with their GPS lead, but the Apaches will check every landmark en route, verifying the team's navigation.

White's four Apaches lift off. For Drew, the familiar sensation of becoming airborne has a momentary novelty, as if his Apache had risen over the curtain between preparation and execution, the cusp of training and mission. From then on, deja vu is confidence: "We're night people. We'd flown completely blacked out at night before—many, many times. FLIR is like an invisible headlight. I lined it up on Cody's ship, and started watching the scenery for the landmarks that should come up."

In flight, the aviators watch three worlds. In the front seat, the copilot-gunner wears night vision goggles but they aren't much help without a moon. Scudding clouds pass between him and the sparkle of stars, but occasionally their amplified reflection from smooth rock outcrops show him some crude outlines. In the back seat, the pilot keeps one eye naked to watch his fluorescent instruments. Over the other, a lense the size of a half dollar perches on his helmet visor as though he were wearing a monocle. This is his FLIR—the infrared sensor connected by servo-mechanisms to a football-size zirconium plated pod, gimballed on the Apache's nose. From the front, the sensor looks like the face of a huge flatiron. The flatiron costs about a million dollars.

When the pilot moves his head, the flatiron mimics his movement. Where the pilot looks through his monocle, FLIR sees the thermal image of objects at which it is pointed. Using a selector, he can have 'white' heat that shows the hottest objects as the brightest, or 'black' heat which reverses the contrast. Except in fog, smoke or sandstorm there is sufficient contrast, because FLIR has nothing to do with light, only relative heat. FLIR is not a beam of anything but rather a thermal sensor. What the pilot sees in the monocle are images about as sharp as those on an oscilloscope. At fifty feet altitude over fairly flat desert, his range of view is about ten miles. But his field of view is tunnel vision—as Drew said, like driving on a pitch black night with one headlight—yet he can guide that tunnel through utter darkness at 120 mph, skimming terrain in a wilderness he has never seen before. Like high speed bats, White team wings toward *terra ingognita* at the border.

Radios are set for listening silence: an inadvertent transmission could be detected by the Iraqis, and they have the technology to locate the transmitter. Listening silence will be lifted by only two signals: when any Apache has lased his target, or by Drew's ten second notice ("party in ten") to open fire. Intercom between pilot and gunner is secure from enemy detection, but en route there is sparse intra-crew conversation except to note landmarks and exchange navigational opinions.

Through FLIR, the terrain below appears as peninsulas of shadow and washes of brightness. The weak winter sun had not warmed the sandscape enough to produce stark thermal contrasts between valleys and ridgetops; but knowing what to look for, the pilots check off the first two landmarks before the border—a deep gully (wadi), and a dry lake bed (*sabkha*), both too insignificant to have names on the map. The next landmark should be a sheepfold, reported to be abandoned. In case herders are still nearby, the route has been offset from the landmark. Cody searches for it even before the clock predicts its appearance: spotting a man-made feature will be as welcome as finding a sunken ship when exploring the depths of the sea.

Cody enters the grid square of the map where AFSOC, in the final briefing, suspected the presence of an Iraqi border patrol. He can see the Pave Low in front of him as spurts of white from its turbines and manifolds, as dark shadings on its cooler metals. Comer's Pave Low, leading the procession, shows itself smaller as spurting roiling light, the signature of its exhausts.

Cody swivels his helmet; the flatiron slaves. Below, he detects right angles not found in nature. Vaguely, faintly—on the margin where Stewmon can corroborate Cody's identification—a sheepfold seems to take shape.

While he confirms it, a flash bursts from the desert. This in fact is the first shot of the war, and aimed at the intruders. The Apaches react instinctively, tense for a 'JC maneuver' (Jesus Christ, here comes a SAM!)—a climb for the sun, the ultimate heat source toward which heat-seeking SAM's can be deflected. Except there is no sun at 2:00 a.m..

The streak of heat peters out like a cheap flare. Cody guesses the SAM is a Grail, probably aimed at where its crew thought they heard helicopters. The missile's arc is roughly across White team's track, but the Pave Lows fly straight on. Maybe they didn't see it, or decided it wasn't enough of a concern to make a time consuming change of course.

Telepathically, Cody agrees with Comer: 90 miles from Al Jouf to White site, with a twenty-second window at arrival. There is no slack in the timetable, and who knows what's ahead?

The Grail's challenge goes quickly out of mind. Cody does not regard it as a threat, only an indication of alertness by a border patrol. If they have a radio, it would be a small one and FM, with not enough range to call the fence.... unless there is a relay between them. Cody studies the map for elevations along the route that might be relay points. There are several.

They cause him to gulp. But, OK, what if they were discovered?—that's 'within the parameters.' The plan assumes the fence will be alerted. This danger is within the plan. Just work the plan. Just work the plan and it will work... So in his mind the Grail is an amber, not a red light. Besides, there's much more to think about as the route rolls out through the FLIR, similar to a travelogue he had studied during rehearsals.

The route generally follows a watercourse, a serpentine of ephemeral streams that rushed through wadis after the rare rains of winter. The watercourse snakes through flat-topped elevations higher than White team is flying. Cody called them mesas and dangerous. They present the flight with a succession of sheer-walled baffles, around which White team slaloms like a game of follow the leader. The leader is Comer, whose sophisticated radar shows him the shape of approaching terrain. The helicopters are a couple of hundred meters apart, each pilot intent to notice the first indication of bank or turn by the one in front of him.

Presently dry, the watercourse itself is a continuous landmark. There are points where White team had predetermined to take short cuts over its meanderings. These are danger points where the flight rises into view of radar cones on the fence. Momentarily, beeps sound in the cockpits: White team has reflected Iraqi radar beams.

That was to be expected. The trick is to disappear before operators on the fence could study the radar images or set up triangulation to locate the bogies. Before they hear repeated beeps, the flight dives back into the wadis.

Now there is not a structure, not a sheepfold, not a sign of life below. AFSOC and Stinger had picked the most uninhabited route. It looked as though FLIR were exploring the deepest trench in the uttermost parts of the sea; the flight seems headed into only more remote desert.

But Cody has been checking off the miles with the ticks of his clock, all the while canting his ship to compensate for the aux fuel pod. Fuel consumption: as expected—and the heavily loaded Apaches become lighter by the minute. Air speed: a little faster than expected. They had accelerated while in the watercourse, decelerated while in Iraqi radar because the slower moving an object, the less information it gives the fence.

Forty miles to the fence... thirty miles. Weather? No way to tell till they rise out of the watercourse for the last time, when they'd leave it on the final heading for White site. Then there should be a panoramic view of the northern horizon and its cloud conditions. They'd break out of the watercourse at twenty miles.

Cody fidgets. He's calculated nine seconds till Comer breaks left to leave the watercourse. Thirteen seconds pass, and Stewmon looks back in his mirror. Then the second Pave Low banks. "Yup," Stewmon hears Cody's clipped assent.

He rotates his helmet up, down, and side to side. Tongues of cloud are strewn above the northern horizon, and look to be a good thousand feet above the desert, and nearly as high over the flight as it hugs the ground to slither up to the fence.

The airspeed indicator turns counterclockwise... a hundred knots, ninety. Time: 0226. Estimated distance to targets: twenty miles. Only twelve minutes left to get in position.

Cody's head moves in shortening arcs. The heat sources at White site should appear as a faint thermal glow on the horizon. He is looking for it, he is staring at where it should be, he's almost imagined it, when a chem stick (visible only to FLIR) tumbles through the night to a soft landing in sand.

The RP. The second known reference—the release point where Comer is to peel off ten miles from the target. The Pave Lows have led the flight perfectly. Now it's the Apaches' show, time for them to emulate their namesakes and sneak up in the dark on an unsuspecting settlement in the desert.

Heading: 255 degrees. Air speed: fifty knots. Cody does not sense he is providing much power, yet the fuel pod feels more cumbersome as if the Apache were flying slower than fifty knots. There must be a tail wind coming up this wadi, Jones conjectures, as he joins the vigil for White site's thermal appearance.

But it is Stewmon who first sees White site, not by FLIR but through his NVG. The Iraqis have some *lights* on! Shortly beyond the RP, he can perceive a luminous spot out in the dark desert, a pallid ember—a miniature glow like that of a city at night, seen from an airliner hundreds of miles away.

"Light source at two-sixty," he whispers on intercom, as if the Iraqis might overhear him.

Yes, now Cody picks up thermal radiation. Target! The word forms on pilots' lips. Whoever fired that Grail back there didn't send a warning to the fence. They're not going to know what hit 'em. They don't know a thing. This realization lessens fear and hones killer instincts. Payback time, payoff time is at hand. White site is going to be blindsided. When they are seven miles out, eight pairs of eyes begin to study the radar site's acreage, laid out just as it had been in the target folders, but appearing on FLIR like a film negative.

They knew the site would be big and it is, resembling a middling dairy farm with machinery and tools scattered in clumps without too much concern for space or order. A two-story barrack is the main barn; the site's power generator is the garage; the tropo scatter radio shed is the size of a small farmhouse; various radar vans are the farm's tractors and trailers.

The Apaches creep closer, so low that dust devils swirl on the sand.

Cody slowly banks right, sidling to the far flank of the firing line. Drew slides in beside him, still separated by a safe hundred meters; Rodrigues moves into the slot beside Drew, and Jones takes his station on the other flank. Their line extends about a quarter of a mile; long enough for the firing fans to cover the site like invisible spotlights; short enough so they can all see each other with NVG. As if on Cody's silent command, White team swings around, making a left face in unison, their individual targets directly ahead, but partially masked by the small mesa on which the structures stand.

The Apaches are still about six miles out, far enough not to be heard, close enough to lase their targets as soon as they bob up to a hundred feet of altitude.

But they are early. Ninety seconds early. Fighting the tail wind drifting them toward the targets and the tilting weight of the fuel pods, the pilots lurk at dune height, billowing the sand of Iraq as they wait out the final minute of the last five months.

Ninety miles south, orbiting in the blacked out Black Hawk, Stinger had imagined Cody's flight passing each landmark. Stinger's watch was also set by the atomic clock. Seanor, his pilot, has the only FLIR aboard. Stinger advises him to study a narrow arc of the northern sky, the sky above White site far away. This is like a World War II movie for Stinger, watching the luminous sweep of his second hand.

At 0237—plus a few seconds—Seanor's head jolts back. "What happened?" Stinger calls through intercom.

"Whoo-wee!" Seanor gasps. Undetectable except through FLIR, a giant fireball had lit up in Iraq.

The blast of the 1,000 lb. cruise missile, destroying an air defense command center behind the radar fence, went unnoticed by White team. Their tunnel vision is focused on their firing fans.

The blast must have been too far away to be heard by the Iraqis at White site—their acquisition radar continues calm rotations like the beam of a lonely lighthouse. Even as low as he hovered, the radar beam pings against Jones' cockpit, setting off a beep.

"We got sweeped!"

"We gotta' shoot, man!" O'Neal responds. But they hold back. Four Hellfires are to salvo from the firing line at 0237 plus 50 seconds.

Miller broke radio silence a half minute before: "Target Bravo," he announced triumphantly. His laser had locked on his primary target, whose coordinates are stored in all the Apaches' computers. The other gunners can electronically reference their targets from Miller's lase.

Ten miles away, Comer begins a planned maneuver. The two Pave Lows rise on an azimuth offset from the Apaches' firing line—rise high enough for White site's radar to detect them, drawing attention from any returns pinging off the Apaches. This is the finishing touch to Cody's plan, the polished end play—to blindside the radars as they looked elsewhere. A thought flashes back to his lonely cubicle at King Fahd, and the moment late one night when the idea for Pave Low decoys came to him.

As the team tenses for Drew's ten second warning, they discuss their targets on intercom: "That's the spoon rest...roger...there's the generator...hottest thing out there... yeah...got constraints?... negative...okay... left pedal... bring her up, bring her up...not yet, man."

Gunners coax their pilots to 'get constraints': align the Apache to put the laser within a narrow arc covering the first target to be hit. The pilots struggle with the overloaded and unbalanced Apaches; struggle also against the yawing effect of flying backwards against the tail wind that pushes them closer to the range of the Iraqis' triple A. Altitude remains fifty feet; firing altitude will be a hundred. When the four Apaches bob up together, constraints will have to be regained.

What they want to see now is a solid box on the FLIR screen. No box means the Apache is not aligned on the target. A box with dashed lines tells the pilot to make small adjustments till the lines become solid—then he has constraints. Lee Miller had already lased Target Bravo, so all the gunners could offset to their targets, but first the pilot must swivel his ship till he has constraints. His gunner can hardly wait. "Party in ten," says Drew over the air, as if he were a butler announcing that dinner is served.

The Apaches rise like the Four Horsemen of the Apocalypse cresting a hill. Attack altitude: a hundred feet.

Lasers switch on. The lighthouse radar beam sweeps around once more, unsuspecting. The Iraqis apparently have not even picked up the Pave Low decoys. The only change Rodrigues notices is his better view, and that someone has flicked off the light in the barrack.

With lasers on, a reticle centers on the FLIR screens. Rodrigues has constraints on the front door of the barrack. If an Iraqi had emerged he'd have seen nothing, but the pencil-thin laser beam would have burned out his eyes before he could blink.

Reticles slew slightly because of the tail wind—gunners mutter for their pilots to hold steady. From each target now, lasers reflect a tiny ball of twinkling light like the faraway exhaust of a jet.

Jones had been thinking about the first Hellfire O'Neal would punch off. The long-tried patience of America's desert army—their dislocation and discomfort—it all seemed to have arrived at a point of vindication; as when after a laboriously lengthy trial, sentence is pronounced on a mass murderer. For all you do, Jones thought, then says on the air:

"This one's for you, Saddam."

From within the cockpits, the Hellfires' ignitions sound like soda bottles opening. Instantly, 'TOF' appears low in the right corner of the screens: time of flight for the missiles. As Stewmon's TOF runs down from twenty seconds, Cody glances at the cockpit clock. The first observed shot by the Gulf war coalition will hit seven seconds into the window prescribed by CENTCOM.

The Hellfires' trajectories are outside the scope of the FLIR screens. Launched at an upward angle, they reach supersonic speed and are only caught on film an instant before impact. Till then, White site reposes in quiet darkness. Not a single sentry stands guard.

O'Neal's primary target is the generator, glowing among the other heat sources like the moon among stars. TOF: zero—the generator shed bulges into a fat ball of brilliant light; hot smoke sweeping up like a cape in the wind. The explosion, six miles away, is inaudible in the cockpit.

What follows is a silent movie on the FLIR films: a surreal tableau of carnage and destruction, with sound effects provided only by the crews' comments to each other, and the regular ignition of Hellfires. When these missiles are all launched, the rockets firing sound like the rapid drawing of swords. When the rockets are expended, the 30 mm cannons complete the three-part performance, pumping out shells in the slow tempo of World War I machineguns.

"Yes!" O'Neal exclaims, as the generator shed becomes a

lightbulb. Jones guides the constraints to frame an auxiliary generator. "Hold her steady... steady. Aha!" The structure comes apart like a flash fire in a house of cards. Jones-O'Neal develop a rhythm, swinging constraints, walking Hellfires to the far left of the the radar site. Twenty seconds TOF, another target knocked down. Do it again, do it again eight times.

"You asked for it, Iraq." Jones intones, "You got it, baby," He swings the nose over to the right of his fan. On the ground, it seems an ant hill is being probed. "I see people running around now."

The people look like tiny animated paper cut outs. A few jump out of structures near by O'Neal's initial two targets. It appears that when the generator went up, the Iraqis thought it to be an accident, and ran over to fight the fire. When the second target blew, more joined them and scattered to the right, but like a wavelet they washed back again because hell was also erupting in Lee Miller's fan. Only Jammal seemed to sense the direction of safety; he streaked across the bottom of Miller's screen and out of everyone's picture.

In the first minute of the attack, Miller guided three Hellfires into his assigned targets: Primary, a command post—lock constraints, reticle on, missile away, TOF, zero. The held breath instant when what looked like a football poised over the doorway—flash, target afire. Shift constraints, a word to Rodrigues, but he's already sliding the nose toward the secondary target. "Looks good, looks good..." PFIZZss—Hellfire away. TOF, zero, football, flash... do it again. Fiery debris arching through the air from Drew's fan.

Drew's FLIR camera didn't work. Later he was kidded that the blank was because he never acquired a target—'Maggie's drawers,' the red flag signal from the old army's rifle range, meaning no hits. But overlapping film from Lee Miller and Stewmon proved that Drew went seven for seven—witholding his eighth Hellfire because the entire radar site was obscured by the smoke of its destruction.

Smoke is Cody's growing concern. He'd given Drew operational control of White team. Cody is there for overall coordination of TF Normandy, though for now Red team is forty miles away and beyond his influence. Here at White, the site becomes a billowing cauldron. Cody has Stewmon do his shooting rapidly, so Cody can turn attention to the general situation at White.

Accordingly, Stewmon strikes his primary target with rapid fire, the equivalent of 'fanning' a pistol—putting two missiles in the air at the same time. His primary is the tropo scatter radio link with Baghdad, a big building deserving two Hellfires.

His attention focused on external radio trafic, Cody loses Stewmon's TOF.

"Where are they?" is Cody's clipped question.

"In the air." Two seconds later, "Hit one."

"OK," clipped. "OK."

"Sliding left." Five seconds later, "Hit two."

"OK, OK."

Perceiving Cody's distractions as commander of the raid, Stewmon begins a running narration of what he is doing on the firing line. He hits with the third missile, but his report is the first disappointment:

"We lost that one."

The Hellfire was a dud, skipping off into the sand like a dummy torpedo. The wasted missile produces a paradoxical relief for Cody. His abiding fear was that he had forgotten something in his preparations, and now he is sure the result of his oversight was this dud. After the Hellfire incident at King Fahd, Cody had the battalion's entire stock of Hellfires rotated, suspecting that long exposure to dust and infernal heat had caused brain death in the errant missile. Perhaps somehow one of the old stock had rotated around to Cody's Apache.

"OK, OK," he gladly concedes. Stewmon re-lases the target and destroys it. As planned, and without further comment from Cody, he begins a gun run with rockets and cannon, breaking off a mere 800 meters from the shattered barrack.

"End of mission, Commander," he advises Cody. This Apache has done what it came to do.

"Breaking right," Cody announces to White team.

The other Apaches have a few more Hellfires to launch when they hear him advise that he is leaving the firing line, a reminder to everyone of the elapsed time they had forgotten. The raid seems hardly begun, when Cody's transmission indicates that it should be nearly over.

The sound track from the FLIR films catch an instant anxiety. Pilots impatiently ask their gunners to shift to rockets. Rodriques tries to shoot some, but Miller still has the firing system working on Hellfires.

Intra-crew communication becomes staccato. No one wants to be last to leave the firing line, the Apache on which the others will have to wait before racing home. It seems Cody is rushing them, but he might know things they do not. On O'Neal's film, a fast moving object sped horizontally across the top of the screen. Flying debris, or a far away MIG?

"You want to go rockets?" "Do it." "Fuck it, put a missile in there...." "Bring it up, bring it up..." "Thirty mike-mike. Git some..." "OK, we're all over the target area." "Break off! Break off, big time." "Whatsa' matter?" "We're too close, man."

Transfixed by bursting targets, Lee Miller has drifted into range of triple A. The air defenses have been silent, stunned like everything else the Iraqis had on the ground, but now Miller is well inside the Apache's stand off range. With a burst from O'Neal's cannon, Miller breaks left into the moonless night to find his place in the procession back to the RP.

Cody is already orbiting his flock like a mother hen. The radio sounds like O'Hare's control tower on Thanksgiving weekend, except that transmissions keep interrupting each other:

"White Five, White Six, seen Four?" "Negative." "Six, this is Three, breaking behind Four... I thinks that's Four." "OK, OK! White Two, White Six..." "Six, eight k from RP." "Anybody seen a Pave Low?" "Damn it, clear the net—Four, Six, over..."

Behind them, smoke spews from the radar site as if it were a city dump burning trash. Cody transmits "California A-A-A" to Comer who relays the message to CENTCOM that destruction at White is 100%, with no U.S. casualties.

Then Cody tries to reach Red team: "Red Six, this is White Six, over." He calls again, every minute, but static is the answer.

XII

For all they did

Bridgforth feels the termperature drop as his chopper rises. Oh no—he and Jim Miller forgot to tell the crew chief their thermostat was stuck. Now it would be a long, cold ride to Red site.

White team's exhausts had long since disappeared in Bridgforth's NVG. He is following Shufflebarger, who is right behind the Pave Lows. A few bullets are fired their way as they cross into the border badlands. Not a good omen: a new reason to be nervous about Bush's deadline. They felt it was like telling Saddam, heads up, we're coming. "Look down, shoot down..."—the silly jingle keeps repeating, as gunners scan the skies for shooting stars, the appearance of MIG exhausts. Red team's mood is that they'll have to fight, either on the way in or out. The patter of ground fire at the border as much as confirms it.

Roderick recalls Cody's critique of the 'bandit break' drill: if a MIG is lining up, tilt the Apache and salvo fleshettes at him—make him attack through a hail of metal slivers. Roderick knows better because he knows MIG's better. They'll not have to dive that low—they can stand off with their missiles just as the Apaches expect to do at Red site.

Shufflebarger can not fly too low or slow for Roderick's liking. The only way to foil MIG's is to fool them into thinking Red flight is a bedouin caravan or Iraqi convoy; therefore, merging into ground clutter is foremost in the minds of the fatalistic Red crews.

Without a lengthy watercourse to guide them, their landmarks are few, but they believe in the Pave Lows guided by satellites rather than *sabkhas*. So Red team hunches behind each other like the crew of a bob sled, while eroded wasteland rolls out palely in FLIR monocles, as if skimming the dunes the choppers are speedboats dashing across waves.

Is everyone still with him? Under radio silence, Shufflebarger can only assume they are. Not until they rise on the firing line will he be able to confirm it. Till then, the exhaust of a Pave Low is his guiding star.

A dot of heat way off to the left. It moves; a smaller dot nearby rises slightly. Camels. Hopefully wild camels, but maybe that second movement was a Bedouin roused from sleep. Wonder what he thinks? A far away convoy? —but he knows there is no road for many miles. Thunder? —too early for rains.

Then he recoils at the sound of an express train hurtling overhead. It's there, it's gone—a roaring arrow pointed north. In the next weeks the Bedouin will remember a sonic apparition, associate it with what began that night of Allah's olympian wrath. Into the next century, the Bedouin's story will probably be told around campfires.

The Apaches' radar detectors are silent, but this is no solace for the nervous, who take it to mean the Iraqis are waiting. They're only being smart, when threatened by the US Air Force across the border, to leave radars off so as not to attract homing missiles. The pessimists are sure the enemy was alerted by Bush's deadline. They try to imagine Roderick's thoughts. What does he, the expert, think about the electronic silence?

It's an indication of nothing for Roderick. Cool, mature, quietly intent, he knows only that the flight is in the air. What's going to happen, happens. They're working a damn good plan. If you want the job done, send the One-oh-one. He'd heard that from Vietnam. OK, the One-oh-one has been sent. The job's going to get done.

The aviators take heart from the sound of their Apaches. That's Indian country outside the cockpit, but in the turbines' steady throb they hear accompanying protection from Good Wrench and guys at King Fahd—like a hearty sandwich packed by mom to nourish and sustain a long trip. Makes you remember there're a lot of very competent people behind you. They've done their job—McDonnell Douglas, Maintenance Platoon, tech reps, the crew chiefs—the job's going to get done.

Red's format dittos White's: a chem stick dropped by the lead Pave Low at the RP, Apaches slinking single file up to the firing line, rise on Shufflebarger's ten second notice ("Joy"), lase, and open up on targets. But first they must fly, fly down that dark twisting tunnel to the target.

The absence of Cody is tangible in Red team, which means pluses and minuses. The commander is not there to observe each crew's performance, though he will critique the results recorded on FLIR cameras. Cody has done things a certain way, most often the best way, but nevertheless a constriction on individuality—and individuality in combat is the special satisfaction of men who fly Apaches. The fewer commands heard in their earphones, the more they'll savor this raid, and the better, they're sure, it will be performed.

But absent too is the knowledge that the CO is sitting right out in the night with you—that what could hit you could happen to him. If there's a danger differential between Red and White, it is with White, slightly more distant from home. He's there and you're here, so no one is thinking that Cody took the softer mission. Good or bad luck will be the only real difference. But some people in Red team would have preferred that when the sky lit up at 0238, they'd have the colonel, not the captain making the calls.

Shufflebarger is the captain, and he likes it that way. He and Cody have vast mutual respect, but they also thrive in a rivalry about how best to fight Apaches. Shufflebarger is a protege of Garrett, Cody's predecessor commanding 1-101. Gabram and Garcia were brought in by Cody and thus were more in his stamp. Consequently, it was seen by some as almost reverse favoritism that Shufflebarger got Red lead, such were Cody's scruples in selecting TF Normandy. Whatever influences resulted in his selection, Shufflebarger is flying this night with a second mission: to prove he was the right choice, indeed the best choice.

So determined that he never briefed Cody's draconian abort criteria—because Shufflebarger simply won't have any aborts.

In a way he is Cody's son, the independent one, setting off to start a business in his father's field; in another way, the Black Prince, setting off on an expedition for his king; in a third way, Cody is Lee and Shufflebarger his Jackson, embarked on his own Valley Campaign. It is shrewd psychology that has placed him in the nose of Red Six. As determined as Cody is to vindicate the Apache, Shufflebarger is to vindicate Cody's selection of him.

This is Cody's plan, but Shufflebarger's calls from here on out. A three-sided connection is also closing its last apex. The first line was drawn when Garrett handed Cody the SOCCENT mission, the second when Cody gave Shufflebarger the Red mission.

In personality, Garrett and Cody contrast as much as Cody and Shufflebarger. In important respects, Garrett is to Cody as Cody is to Shufflebarger—a triangle of ambivalence with Cody at the right angle. He would acknowledge them, and they him, to be first class; then take stylistic differences indicating that first class did not mean classy, by admittedly subjective standards. There is an undertone, an undertow, when they speak about a bilateral relationship that includes Cody.

But all three are demigods to Bridgforth, hunched in the cockpit, wriggling his feet in the cold, munching chocolate for warmth. What to do with the wrapper concerns him—Cody might come over when TF Normandy is back together again, open the door, and have a stern word about trash if he sees some. Bridgforth decides to litter Iraq when he dumps his pee bag, a bundle of absorbent (developed for astronauts) stuffed in a thigh pocket.

Red team is thirty-five minutes into the mission scheduled for forty-five. The terrain seems to be rising. Wadis open in the direction of flight. A chem stick from the Pave Lows topples through the night. The Apaches veer into the final azimuth. With the RP behind them, they know they're on their own now. Vincent feels sweat oiling his flight gloves: the hardest flying is ahead as the four raiders head for a deep wadi winding up toward a long bluff, the edge of a plateau, and the line of the fence.

Jagging and craggy, the wadi cuts deep into the plateau.

Some switchbacks are too sharp—the flight hops over them. No radar pings when they rise, but no sight of a thermal glow either. They dive back into the wadi, anxious for some sign that Red site is where it should be. Less than a minute remains before 0238.

The bluff before them is so steep, Shufflebarger cuts airspeed from sixty knots to almost a hover. Red team bunches behind him like an accordion. The rim of the bluff bristles with radar masts.

Masked by the bluff, Red site's generator and other hot objects had been undetectable. The raiders have only forty-five seconds to spare. Backing off from the bluff, Shufflebarger takes them up for a look at their targets.

Radio silence breaks with "Three talley alpha," the Pave Low's announcement that they are performing the decoy maneuver. Engines strain to lift the heavy Apaches—the four rise simultaneously, as Red site unfolds like the view of the hotel lobby from a glass elevator.

"Joy." Red team's timing is better than in any of the rehearsals.

On the far left, Orsburn aligns his reticle on the team's primary target, the generator for the entire site. He zooms in on it to triple magnification, just to make sure. Hoban glances over the site through NVG. One light is on. The scene is as quiet as Christmas Eve. What else is there for the lonely garrison to do except sleep at 2:38 in the morning? Through FLIR, the triple A positions are dark and cold.

Low on the horizon, six miles away, beyond the distance where Apache engines are audible to the Iraqis, Red's lasers flick on. No tailwind yaws their hover; only the ponderous weight of fuel and munitions cause them to wobble. No one has words in mind, no "This one's for you, Saddam," before trigger fingers tighten—but Orsburn's thinking this might be how the Japanese felt when they looked down on slumbering Pearl Harbor.

From the desert, the opening salvo of Hellfires appears as four small flashes. The missiles fly for twenty seconds, so fast they strike before their supesonic boom reaches the ground.

The thunder of their detonations sets off a hair trigger reaction by one Iraqi awake in the radio van:

"Nahnoo taht hogoom..!" "We're under attack...!" are the first and last words transmitted from Red site.

When he sees the generator bulge into a fireball, Bridgforth is so transfixed his thumb freezes on the trigger button until three other Hellfires burst their targets into flame, soundless explosions for the Americans. Then pilots and gunners converse freely, coordinating like the crew of a racing yacht, tacking and trimming for advantage:

"Gimme some nose." "Sliding left..." "Bring her up." "OK, comin' up, comin' up." "We're real heavy, man." "Steadee...lookin' good." "You ready with rockets?" "Do it." "Roger, roger." "Gonna' put fleshettes out there?" "Look left, buddy." "They all off?" "Yeah—open up the good eye." "We're too far for cannons." "I got 3700 nav range." "OK, punch 'em off."

"Excellent," says Hoban, as if he were still instructing and Vincent was his student gunner.

For rockets and cannons, the Apaches move up as close as 3,000 meters from their targets. Blown up in early Hellfire fusilades, the only thing triple A puts in the air is smoke.

Yet flashes from the ground seem aimed at the raiders. Cody had warned of this effect when enemy ammunition and fuel exploded. As Iraqis scatter for cover, Red team watches for weapons turned toward the sky. But in their panic no one is even carrying weapons. To look up through the conflagration is the same as staring into the night beside a bonfire. What's comprehended is what is heard: Hellfires booming, rockets bursting, cannons stuttering—and screams from their targets.

In the video replays 1-101 saw fate in the night: the first Hellfire crumpled the generator shack, but one Iraqi escapes. He rushes to warn his comrades or receive first aid. The fleeing figure reels across the sand, arriving at the next door simultaneously with the second Hellfire. In the instant before his body is consumed, it's framed by the fireball.

The cloud from destruction is now Red's only real problem. With a tertiary target obscured by smoke, Jim Miller asks if anyone saw it hit. Yes, Vincent broadcasts, the radar mast fell.

Barely five minutes since Orsburn lit up the generator. He is also first to finish his job: "This is Red Three. I'm clear of target area, headed south."

The announcement, like Cody's at White site, spurs the others to hurry. Cannons pound continuously till chain guns empty. Fleshettes salvo, appearing on FLIR as schools of wriggling silver fish. For long, impatient seconds the targets squat unharmed—then spurt with flame, and the ground around them sprouts bushes of dust.

One by one, Red team break off. It is for Shufflebarger to fly down the firing line, assuring that they've completed what Cody had sent them to do. A score of fires, large and small, merge in smoke. Minutes earlier it had been as dark and quiet as a dairy on Christmas Eve. Now it lookes like the national Boy Scout encampment with bonfires everywhere.

As the raiders flee, they become scattered. Through FLIR's tunnel vision, Shufflebarger can only pick them out one by one. He calls for the others to locate themselves with reference to Apaches he already has in sight.

A new voice breaks in: "Accident! accident!"

A red cluster flare soars above the RP—the signal that a helicopter has crashed. Bridgforth's back presses against the seat. Lou Hall imagines a mid-air collision, the doom of Desert One. How could that happen with all this space to fly in? Most probably it was a Pave Low, rising to join the flight. An Apache and a Pave Low, like mating dragonflies, falling grappled together, men and metal fused in flaming fuel. FLIR sweeps the ground for what would be the brightest fireball of the night. It's a Pave Low. He has *accidently* fired a red flare. Stomachs resume normal size; curses cut short in rueful gratitude.

Shufflebarger feels forgiving. The Pave Low is his voice to the world, and he has a report: "Nebraska, A-A-A!"

"Roger."

The Pave Low switches to UHF with range to reach all the way to King Fahd, 700 miles away. His message, 100% destruction at Red site with no U.S. casualties.

At King Fahd, Mike Davis is groggy from the fatigue of his vigil. Cody's 'California' report had spelled one half of relief; now 'Nebraska' completes it. Jesse Johnson grips his shoulder.

Already (a period of less than ten minutes), reports from the opening attacks on Baghdad glow with success no one had dared imagine. As Gen. Powell put it: "The performance of Task Force Normandy blended into the mosaic of what was a huge military operation with numerous successes that came so rapidly, one after the other, that now it is difficult to remember the separate pieces."

Indeed TF Normandy's success is almost ancient (and largely unrecognized) history, even as the Apaches escape from Iraq. But Johnson knows what they did, what they did first and did while the enemy was at full strength, with all its assets intact and its vaunted might undamaged. "Tell Gen. Peay," says Johnson, "the Screaming Eagles' legend grows."

Davis does not use these words when he wakes Garrett, but instead advises that the task force could be expected back at King Fahd in about twelve hours, if all goes well.

All is not going well. Cody and Shufflebarger fail to reach each other on Apache radios, and the Pave Lows are now out of the communications loop. What Johnson, and indeed Powell, learned within minutes of the task force's success is known only in part by the team leaders. For all either of them know, the other was wiped out at his site.

Both teams see more danger coming out than going in or at their targets. They had carved a channel in the dike, and a tidal wave thundered toward them. Radar sweeps the Apaches like police spotlights at a burglary; IFF lights flash, scant seconds before huge shadows appear ahead and rush over them. The Air Force is piling onto Iraq like an avalanche.

They come in narrow waves of three and four, confining themselves to the black corridor. They come on the deck at 200 feet, supersonic and totally blacked out—while the Apaches crawl in the opposite direction at a hundred knots and sixty feet. F-15's, gorged with bombs and missiles, hell-bent for Baghdad, set off huge bow waves of compressed air in which the choppers bob like row boats.

This phase of the mission had never been rehearsed with the Air Force. A hundred feet of vertical separation was AFSOC's offhand guess at what would be a safe margin. "Get out of the stratosphere!" Vincent tells his pilot, when the altimeter inches over a hundred feet. But in places they have to rise that high to clear the terrain. The roaring stream of bombers is rocking Bridgforth to the point of sea sickness. He asks Jim Miller to level their chopper, lest they tip and crash.

White team's egress is similarly buffeted. Zarnowski has an additional problem. His rotor blade had been hit, probably by a flying fragment from his target, but maybe by an Iraqi bullet. None of his red lights went on, so he does not report the problem to Cody; but the nicked blade stirrs up turbulent air on the leading edge, setting off a vibration that makes flying rough as a washboard. The Apache's unrelenting shudder amplifies the post-tension fatigue that begins to infect Zarnowski when he realizes what a long, tooth rattling ride it will be back through Saudi Arabia. He resolves to tough it out for the next twelve hours, and not broadcast an emergency unless the fuel pod acts like it might come off. Otherwise, he won't bother Cody who keeps calling and calling for Shufflebarger.

Shufflebarger is equally anxious to hear from Cody. The two teams are converging on a rally point just over the border where Stinger's Black Hawk and Devito's Apache wait for them. But the team leaders keep calling each other en route. The distance between them lessens to fifty, forty, thirty, finally twenty miles. If there were a moon that night, they could see each other with NVG.

Stinger hears them calling each other. He's as relieved as they will be in a few more minutes. He slumps back and runs his thoughts on fast rewind. It all worked. It was all there. All his informaton had been correct. It all worked.

Red leaves Iraq with a sendoff of ground fire. Isolated border patrols finally noticed that a war had begun. Cody leaves by dumping his pee bag on Iraq. Had it all happened, or had he imagined it? It seems both vivid and long ago, technicolor but monochrome. He always flinched to hear the war compared with a Nintendo game, but that was how it had appeared through FLIR at two posts on the fence.

Perched near the border, Seanor is ready to relay the good word between White and Red—then his radar detector flashes.

"MIG!" he exclaims to Stinger, whose stomach rams his chest as the chopper drops to the deck at free fall speed.

Like a field mouse under the shadow of a hawk, Seanor dodges for cover, plunges into a wadi as his passengers grope to tighten their seatbelts. No matter how he maneuvers, the detector flashes and beeps. A superb pilot, Seanor twists, turns, hovers and sprints, but the radar follows implacably. Stinger's stomach can not keep up. He prepares to vomit between his legs.

Shoving the stick to and fro, working the panel switches for electronic countermeasures, Seanor feel he is a tennis player trying to defeat a backboard. This MIG is just too good—and this Black Hawk's going to be the first one shot down in the war. He reaches up and flicks off the radar detector. Now the sound of death will be the continuous audio signal that a missile is headed for them. The MIG had looked down, now he would shoot down. Bridgforth's jingle had been an omen after all.

Through another minute of evasive convulsions, the cockpit is silent except for the sound of wretching. Then Seanor hovers as he switches the radar detector off and on. The first night of the war has filled with a cacophony of electronic impulses. Some combination stuck the detector on a false alarm.

Stinger raises his head from between his legs. He'd been preparing to die, and now he feels he has. He expresses his resurrection in a stream of obscenity, added to Seanor's oaths. Trying to elude the phantom MIG, he has raced all over the frontier countryside, and it seems a long time till he relocates the rally point.

There, he and Devito rise in the darkness to meet twelve choppers approaching at a shallow angle. They do one turn in the sky together, then the four Pave Lows break off for a post on the border where they will stand ready to rescue any Air Force pilots downed over Iraq.* Cody is tempted to do a victory roll to see the Pave Lows off, but the aux pods and crew fatigue restrain him from aerobatics—the Apaches have many more miles to go that night before they sleep.

---

* Such was the shock and weight of AFCENT's onslaught, Comer had no further work that night.

Their mission for SOCCENT was over when they recrossed the border. From then on, Cody is on his own to make it back to King Fahd and fulfill his promise to Peay. The return plan called for refueling at Ar Ar, but because so little time and gas has been spent over the targets, the task force could reach Al Jouf.

That night the lonely airstrip has transformed into one of the busiest in the world. F-15's which buffeted TF Normandy on their way to Baghdad, are already back and preparing to launch again. Al Jouf is their recovery airfield. The army choppers are like little leaguers trying to get into the stadium for the first game of the World Series. Low and carefully, they orbit Al Jouf, requesting permission to land: "Hey, guys, remember us?"

Dawn seeps into the sky as they seek fuel pumps. Stiff, cold and cramped, they descend from their cockpits, shake hands woodenly, and exchange a few subdued questions with members of the other team. Some sort of congratulations must have gone around, but none are remembered amid the scream of F-15's landing and departing. Fatigue is already erasing memory.

Cody has trouble focusing on what to do about Zarnowski's damaged blade. The Apache will have to remain at Al Jouf; someone says the Black Hawk should stay too. A new blade can be flown up from King Fahd in a C130; Good Wrench will install it, then the two fly back together 700 miles by way of KKMC. These are all Devito's recommendations. Cody accepts them without understanding. He's been awake for eighteen hours, and is numbed by the prospect of many more in the air.

After a scald of coffee, TF Normandy closed their cockpits once more, slipped out beneath the Air Force landing pattern, and headed for KKMC. There, the garrison was muffled and masked in MOPP gear. REMF's gawked to see the aviators casually refueling without gas masks. An officer strode over, asked them if they knew the war had started, and ordered them to mask.

Listening to the air war helped keep them awake over the last dreary leg of their aerial odyssey. Tuning into AWAC frequency, they heard bombers report, Iraqi interceptors downed, and a British Tornado pilot exclaim he had lost his wingman. The air campaign was on, big time, prime time. Vincent tried to revive himself by thinking how he had been part of starting it all:

"I always wanted to be part of something like this. I always wanted to be on the cutting edge. What we did was about as sharp as the edge can get."

And he could almost watch what he had begun on instant replay. At Al Jouf and KKMC, TV sets were blaring with footage of the new war nearly as quickly as it was being fought.

Such fascination, and satisfaction of accomplishment could but momentarily stop the head-swimming crush of fatigue. The Apaches wavered through the sky. Pilots and copilots traded off on the stick. Cody ordered the man resting to watch the other in the mirror, talk to him, open cockpits and blast their faces with air. He spread the interval between choppers to avoid collision.

Some men sang to their partners, annoying them enough to keep both awake. Others focused on their families, traced details of their features, concentrated on remembering, held on to vivid thoughts when the mind floated off toward oblivion. But they could not hold out against their bodies' demand for rest, for sleep. They'd pushed the physical envelope; it was elastic, and having expanded with adrenalin, it shrank with lysergic acid. An epidemic of narcolepsy swept through TF Normandy. When heads found a point of equilibrium on the neck, there were stuttering moments of unconsciousness. Then a shout on the intercom: "Godammit, we didn't fly into Iraq to crash in Saudi!"

A squirt of adrenalin, as when there's almost an accident on the highway. Nose up, look around. Check your partner, check your wingman. Where'd he go?! He'd slewed off, losing altitude, dreaming of sleep. Half way to King Fahd, TF Normandy had not slept for thirty-six hours.

At first when IFF beeped, the crews forced themselves to revive. They were flying over allied triple A, manned by green and nervous gunners expecting an Iraqi aerial counterattack. Soon the beeps were disregarded, and merged with the constant ringing in the aviators' ears. They exhaled forcefully; tried hyperventilating to infuse oxygen into occluded brains.

But nothing could hasten the minutes crawling through the morning, the hours nudging past noon, and the day's glacial creep into afternoon. ETA was 1600. Somewhere on the edge of infinity was King Fahd.

Davis called them at maximum radio range; Cody's reply was grumpy and short. TF Normandy had been gone for two days. Davis had spent most of the time awake himself, so could imagine how tired they must be. He called Aviation Brigade and Division to ask that the debriefing be postponed twenty-four hours. That was fine with both headquarters. All the Screaming Eagles were loading to move up to the border tomorrow; no one had much time to hear about yesterday's mission.

Davis decided there should be no organized homecoming celebration within the battalion either. The only thing Task Force Normandy would appreciate was their cots. From over the clustered peaks of tent city, the Apaches wobbled into King Fahd as though the pilots were cherries making their first solo landing.

A month later, the division was fully deployed on the Iraqi border, in the final stage of preparation for the ground war, clearing the decks for the intense combat ahead. Administrative matters were hurriedly processed—there would be no time for them once the balloon went up. Aviation Brigade was busier than anyone. Garrett had few minutes for his personnel officer (S-1), but Division had asked if there would be decorations for TF Normandy, now disbanded, with the crews serving again with their companies.

Yes, Garrett decided, there should be a little ceremony and medals awarded. Ask Cody what he thinks they should be.

Cody's only firm opinion was that what anyone got, everyone should. He did not know it, but AFSOC had already awarded the Pave Low crews Distinguished Flying Crosses (DFC). A year later, the Air Force would induct Cody into The Gathering of Eagles, what they call their hall of fame, alongside the likes of Doolittle and legendary World War II aces. But in February 1991, the raid was considered by the 101st as no more than a collateral mission accomplished in a way that met the division's high standards. Screaming Eagles always accomplished their missions, and thus were notably stingy with high ranking medals (known as valor decorations). Excellence was the expectation, not the exception.

Moreover, before the ground war there was no baseline for heroism. Soldiers would surely die in the weeks to come, some heroically, and most, presumably, in the infantry. One of Peay's 'never again' anathemas from Vietnam was inflation of decoration, abused most often by officers who merely cruised over battlefields in helicopters. So in Iraq, the high end of valor decorations would be reserved for the ground fighting. Cody was not inclined to argue otherwise. Furthermore, with impending events on everyone's minds, the ceremony would be expedited if the medals were such that Peay could authorize, rather than higher ones requiring corps or ARCENT aproval.

Moreover, Apache aviators remained the most 'killable' soldiers in the JOA, with the ground war only weeks away, and dangerous missions already scheduled. Better that TF Normandy have medals pinned on their chests now; that was better than higher awards presented posthumously.

The result was the Air Medal, with a 'V' for valor, to all the crews. The Air Medal is two ranks below the distinguished Flying Cross.* For all they did, TF Normandy got a passing pat on the back.

It didn't bother them, and they took the pat as a shove to get back into the war, though a war in which they would not see action again for more than a month. What TF Normandy had started would take that long for the Air Force to finish. Air superiority, as Garrett had chuckled, began on the ground; but now, for the next month, superiority on the ground would be determined from the air.

So Desert Shield was over and Desert Storm begun, but with the same question as before—would Saddam's and Schwarzkopf's armies collide?

---

* In Vietnam, the author was awarded the Air Medal for simply being a passenger on a number of helicopter missions, most of them no more dangerous than the shuttle from JFK to Manhattan.

Part II

Go deep

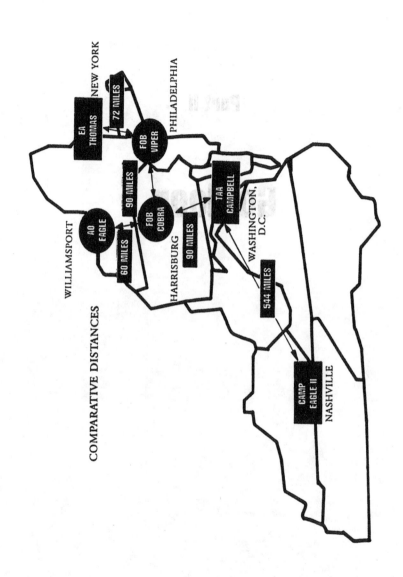

COMPARATIVE DISTANCES

WILLIAMSPORT

AO EAGLE

EA THOMAS

NEW YORK

72 MILES

FOB VIPER

PHILADELPHIA

90 MILES

FOB COBRA

60 MILES

HARRISBURG

90 MILES

TAA CAMPBELL

WASHINGTON, D.C.

544 MILES

CAMP EAGLE II

NASHVILLE

18: Scuds fired at Saudi Arabia and Israel. The Patriot missile apparently intercepts its first Scud.

19-21: Patriots airlifted to Israel where some are manned by U.S. crews. Bush calls up another 20,000 reservists as Gulf forces grow to 472,000. In contravention of Geneva accords, Iraq displays captured airmen on TV and threatens to use them as human shields.

XIII

Watch this...

Task Force Normandy had "plucked the eyes" of Iraq's radar, said Schwarzkopf in a famous televised briefing; and the first surge of air attacks completed the blinding, so that his ground forces could deploy en masse to the border undetected. His subsequent strategy was to convince Iraq that if there was an allied counter-invasion it would be a thrust up the coast, supported by amphibious landings from the Gulf.

This was only to deceive: his main attack was always intended around the enemy's western flank, a turning movement that became known as the 'Hail Mary'—an inappropriate term borrowed from football, suggesting a desperate, last second play. To the contrary, Hail Mary was methodically planned, meticulously detailed, and a feat of logistics matching its spectacular strategic success. To revise the metaphor, Hail Mary was instead a power sweep that capped a drive developed in pre-season. It was the big play, designed to move and support a juggernaut where it would be positioned to, in Gen. Powell's words, "cut off [the Iraqi army] and then kill it."

The 101st's role would be in the cutting off. As the only heliborne force of its size in the world, the Screaming Eagles were to leap into Iraq and sever Saddam's main supply route (MSR) between Baghdad and Kuwait. The evolving plan had the 101st initially far ahead of allied ground forces, operating for the most part independently. Only some French light armor, supported by the 82nd Airborne, would protect the 101st's left flank. On their right, the balance of 18th ABC would swing up parallel to the Kuwaiti border, while 7th Corps—Schwarzkopf's Sunday punch—struck toward the Iraqis' center of gravity, their mechanized reserve of Republican Guard divisions. Sandwiched between 7th Corps and US Marines on the coast would be the Pan-Arab allies attacking across the Saudi-Kuwaiti border.

This was the grand plan that underwent several iterations, beginning in November when the offensive option became possible with the arrival of 7th Corps. The changes for the 101st arose from questions about its unproven capabilities. Powell: "The unique characteristics of the air assault division were finally going to be tested in combat. Fast moving, deep operations over a wide area were the purposes for which the division was designed." Designed, but never before deployed.

How deep into Iraq could it strike, and how fast? The answers hinged on how far the division could operate from its logistical base. Logistics, more than anything else, meant fuel—fuel for the HUMM-V's, the mules of the infantry—but most signifcantly, aviation fuel for its fleet of helicopters comprised of Cobras, Kiowas, Apaches, Black Hawks and Chinooks. Kiowas were two-seater scouts, so light and few in number that their fuel consumption was a negligible. With the Devito option, aux fuel pods were now an accepted (though nonetheless dangerous) expedient to double the Apache's range. But Apaches were fighting machines. Of different but equal importance were the troop carrying Black Hawks (capacity: a fully loaded squad of 12 men), and the cargo carrying Chinooks (capacity: 20,000 lbs of bullets, beans, vehicles, howitzers, or anything else the front line troops needed).

So above all other considerations, fuel ruled—an ironic hegemony on the sands of the world's foremost petroleum producer. Indeed the fuel which powered the allied forces came from under those sands: first to be pumped, then refined, then transported to use. The devil was in the transport.

The basic problem for Schwarzkopf's logisticians was as

simple as it was stupendous: move an army of some 400,000 soldiers plus their million tons of equipment and supplies over distances up to 600 miles. Move them for the most part on a single two-lane road through a wilderness so desolate that it provided not even water. Having moved them, sustain their encampments for at least six weeks, the first month being the estimated duration of the air war, the following two weeks the estimated period for the ground war. Keep the titanic movement and the encampments secret from the Iraqis on the border, at some points a mere twelve miles away.

The only feat comparable in scope was the allied invasion of France in 1944. The only obstacle not present in the Arabian desert was the English Channel which, however, provided Eisenhower with a curtain from enemy reconnaissance that Schwarzkopf did not have. As a substitute, his air power constantly blew sand into the eyes of Iraqi intelligence. Under a monsoonal torrent of bombs and missiles, their reconnaissance forces could barely raise their heads, much less move forward and look around.

For Yancey, whose 5-ton truck had already logged over a hundred thousand miles supplying the FOB's in Desert Shield, the rumble of far away bombs added an audible dimension to the Tapline Road where he had lately traveled in silent solitude. The lonely highway on which he'd had time to re-read the Old Testament became the busiest, most crowded two-lane road in the world.

"I think all the trucks supporting corps were put into a pool. They called it the Dragon Express. At King Fahd we'd load up till the shocks were straight, then head up Tapline to Bastogne bumper to bumper. We'd drive with lights that far—about eight hours—then get five hours rest. Usually someone else picked up the truck for a night haul, but sometimes we drove it the next morning. We'd do another stop like that at Hafer Al Batin, take a break, and do it again to Rafha.

"Past Bastogne, we'd go on blackout. That was tough staying the right distance from the truck in front of you, and also hard to stay awake. Convoy speed was supposed to be 45 all the time, but I think we averaged more like 30. Coming back we'd usually be empty.

"The road wasn't wide enough for two flatbeds to pass in opposite directions. They'd always hit their mirrors. This happened so much we loosened the screws so the mirrors wouldn't break.

"Worst part though was when you got to the drop off point at night. You had to find a unit if guides didn't pick you up. No roads in there, so you could just be driving off into the desert and run over some guy sleeping. It's a miracle that didn't happen.

"Past Hafer, you started hearing the bombs. The jets were way up there, so you didn't hear them. Daytime you saw their sky trails. Nighttime when the clouds were low you could see flashes off the ground way to the north, so far off you couldn't hear anything. Daytime they'd bomb closer to the border.

"Me and my shotgun didn't talk much about the bombs. We'd say, 'Hey, look at that one,' or something like that, but we didn't think about Iraqis getting killed. But you could imagine what it was like being under those bombs. No, I guess you couldn't, not really. I was in a plane that went through some awful turbulence one time, shaking and dropping. Must have been like that in the bunkers. I bet the Iraqis did a lot more praying than when they ran over Kuwait. It served them right—that's the way I look at it. Didn't bother me that they were getting buried alive. 'Vengeance is mine,' saith the Lord. We were doing His work."

After the air campaign started, Yancey found the road over crowded. Convoys were too much like commuting in a 24-hour rush hour. He had been a janitor at Yankee Stadium—all winter he'd been working by himself, now all these people were jamming in and raising hell.

"But time sure went fast. January was like a week. The same road, the same stops, the same punchy feeling over and over. I didn't think there was this much equipment in the whole army, but I felt like I'd moved it all."

Yancey's transportation battalion logged a million vehicle miles during Desert Storm, setting the ground war in motion like the preliminary uncoiling of a python sizing up its prey. The 101st had the longest distance to move, and they started at night:

At 2:00 a.m. on the morning of January 17th, minutes before TF Normandy struck, the rest of the Screaming Eagles began moving out when the night shift at division headquarters received a call from corps, announcing that Operation Desert Storm had begun. The division was already packed, and by dawn two brigades were loading into C130's that flew into King Fahd every fifteen minutes. Their destination was called a tactical assembly area (TAA) which Peay named for Ft. Campbell, the 101st's home straddling the Tennessee-Kentucky border.*

The remaining brigade, the First, was deployed on the front edge of the covering force, so its commander urged Peay to let him make the short move into TAA Campbell rather than return hundreds of miles to King Fahd, and then retrace his steps. But Peay said no—before manning their TAA for the ground war, First Brigade needed to connect with their administration at King Fahd, the last opportunity they'd have to do so. From the time Schwarzkopf finalized the details of Hail Mary, things were to proceed step by step in an order Peay had established in his mind.

Like "Now hear this" from the captain to the principal departments of a warship, Peay spoke his mind through three outlets. First was the 'command group' comprised of himself, Shelton, Adams, Bolt and Weiss. Bolt overlapped with the second outlet, the division staff, and also the third, facetiously called 'the council of colonels.'

Within the council were Peay's tactical lieutentants. These were the commanders: Garrett (Aviation), and the infantry brigades, Hill (First), Purdom (Second), and Clark (Third). The indeterminate start time of a ground war had inconveniently revamped the main knights of Peay's round table, with the result that the last two brigade commanders were new to their jobs, a baffling irony in that the army had put into effect a 'stop loss' policy as soon as 18th ABC was alerted for deployment to the Gulf. Stop loss meant that everyone was frozen in their jobs.

---

* Though most of Ft. Campbell is in Tennessee, the post office stands in Kentucky which is therefore the official address. Screaming Eagles joke that it is easy to determine which state they are in by looking at the grass: green on one side, blue on the other.

It only made sense that soldiers who had trained and worked together, in many cases for years, would continue established relationships in combat.

Stop loss meant that retirements were postponed, schools cancelled, and the normal career moves suspended for the sake of continuity. Military careers, after all, were designed to put the right people in the right jobs at the right time—and the time for the army was war time.

Except there was an exception for the jobs that probably mattered most. Full colonels, the best and the brightest from which the army's generals were selected by the most exacting standards, were not to hold command of brigades beyond their normal tenure of two years, war or no war. The last ghost of Vietnam had not been exorcised, that of 'ticket punching'—visiting all the jobs necessary to be considered for general, war or no war.

Brigades were few, and competing colonels many. The army reserved such 'command slots' years in advance, and there could be no deviation from the regular rotation of colonels, war or no war. Consequently, colonels Gile and McDonald lost command during Desert Shield for jobs outside the JOA. Both had been with their brigades for two years, during which they hand picked their staffs and mentored their battalion commanders. For Second and Third brigades, their coaches would be replaced between the end of the season and the Super Bowl. Otherwise, their lineups would not change, thanks to stop loss.

Gile went out in October: "It was called 'relinquishment of command,' but I felt I was being relieved." i.e., fired. It was no consolation that the policy was being applied to colonels throughout the desert army; nor was it in Peay's measured nature to see the policy as pernicious. To do so would have violated a professional tenet, that of implementing policy from above whether or not Peay agreed with it—indeed, acting as if he did in either case.

Peay: "I had two great O-6's [colonels Purdom and Clark] waiting in the wings, and remember the changes of command were before it looked like there'd be a ground war. Gile and McDonald were going on to important jobs, so no one could infer that I was casting them off."

Of course in his position at the head of a unique division poised for war, Peay could titrate the command chemistry of the 101st as he pleased. But as if the decision resided elsewhere, he permitted Gile to appeal to the source of stop-loss exceptions, the Chief of Staff of the Army, Gen. Carl Vuono, who visited the division in the fall. The three rode together in a HUMM-V, en route to Second Brigade's training site. Wedged between six stars, Colonel Gile had to couch his plea in terms that did not imply that he was indispensable or even better than any successor. He made his case with the strongest argument: that lives of troops could be saved through a chain of command thoroughly familiar with all its links, starting at the top. Vuono answered without looking at him:

"Gregg, you're going to be chief of staff for the 10th Mountain Division [at Ft. Drum, NY]. Division chiefs of staff are harder to find than brigade commanders."

Replacing Gile was another of Peay's long time colleagues and one-time division G3, Ted Purdom, a tall and talkative Oklahoma State alumnus (MS from Georgia Tech) with a resemblance to Moses. A former division G3 himself, Gile had not been reluctant to challenge G3's directives; thus, the classic line-staff tension was taut between Second Brigade and G3. Now Purdom was 'switching sides,' and in so doing he introduced himself to his new staff by pointing up the brigade's defects he had perceived in his last job. The criticism did not go down easily, and was interpreted as a knock on Gile to whom his staff had been devoted.

Third Brigade's change of command came a month later when Bob Clark took the colors from John McDonald. The outgoing commander was a genuine whiz kid, promoted ahead of his contemporaries to lieutenant colonel and colonel. Cerebral, demanding, and astute, McDonald went to be chief of staff at SOUTHCOM in Panama, a prestigious job of high responsibility, but he too left the Screaming Eagles with sentiments similar to Gile's—that they'd rehearsed their orchestra, now someone else would conduct its performance.

The new conductor at Third Brigade was Bob Clark, a Texas Tech graduate whose uncle had survived the Bataan Death March, and with military ancestors dating back to the War of

1812 when stars began to appear on Clark's family tree. His great grandfather was promoted over Andrew Jackson, even after Old Hickory won the battle of New Orleans.

Clark had rejoined the 101st from the Army War College after commanding a battalion in First Brigade, and previously Clark had worked near Peay in the Pentagon. Gen. John Wickham, a former commanding general of the 101st and Army Chief of staff (now retired), was somewhat a father figure for Peay, Clark and Hill; they had all served as his aides in 'the building' and won their spurs in that crucible of careers. Thus pedigrees developed. Major figures do not move in and out of the 101st randomly.* Clark was a marked man in that he was expected to make his mark now that he had made his opportunity—and Peay would give him more.

First Brigade remained with Tom Hill, now the most established and experienced of the big four commanders. As a lieutenant he had fought with First Brigade in Vietnam, qualifying him in the desert as a rare 'double eagle' (or less honorifically, a 'turkey sandwich'), entitled to wear the 101st patch on both shoulders. Another Texan, Hill had worked under Peay/Wickham for two years, and attributed the division's proficiency to the standards that Peay demanded.

Peay's career branch was artillery, and the 101st was predominantly an infantry division, so his standards were not shaped by personal experience but rather his sense for positioning. His concept of positioning derived from the incomparable ability of US artillery to 'mass fire'—to promptly bring down an irresistible volume of steel on specific terrain. Peay extrapolated from his experience in massing fire, to concentrate all combat power in the 101st with similar speed and flexibility. Like a howitzer barrage, he expected to concentrate heliborne infantry and attack helicopters like the division's artillery— concentrate and then devastate. He saw postioning to be his

---

* There is a similar familial/fraternal network in the 82nd, among the armor divisions, and to a growing degree within special forces. Choosing which family to join is an early career decision. At the top end, mixed pedigrees can come into play; e.g., after the Gulf War, Shelton was named CG of the 82nd, the military equivalent of a descendant from both the York and Lancaster lines. When branch and functional affiliations are factored in, individual career pictures become intricate; e.g., Adams' logistics-aviation background.

primary job, then the infantry brigade commanders would begin theirs—maneuvering troops onto objectives. With full confidence in Hill, Purdom and Clark (all virtually hand picked by Peay), he was content to let Shelton overwatch the division's tactics.

So Peay deferred to his brigade commanders in how the infantry would fight, but woe betide the colonels if they fell short of his standards in how they got into operational positions. A large scale night heliborne exercise had gone off sloppily soon after Peay took command. He said nothing at the time, but Hill still cringes in recalling the gathering of commanders in the aftermath.

"It wasn't an ass chewing—I'd call it the silence treatment. When Peay's pissed the most, he says the least. I'm the other way. I cuss and storm, and get it all out. With Peay you feel you haven't heard the worst he thinks about you. But by not saying much he gets you to remember what's on his mind. I think everyone at that critique remembers operational standards. AIR ASSAULT STANDARDS! That was sort of a silent shout in the room."

Standards of appearance and deportment were specified and ardently enforced by Sergeant Major Weiss, right down to the correct wear of chin straps on the desert hat. For significant matters, Peay's standards were somewhat to be inferred because he considered them not so much his but rather those of division tradition.

He is quick to point out that the Screaming Eagle patch is recognized throughout America. A man of undetectable emotion, he nevertheless describes the 101st reverentially as a "national treasure," seeing himself as a steward of the division as much as its commander. His standards then were those of history and almost legend, difficult to explicate but all the more powerful for their underlying mystique. At the division's last homecoming celebration, and after Peay had relinquished command, he put it this way:

"Tonight the eagle on my shoulder looks back at this supreme experience of my life. You here tonight [101st veterans of Europe and Vietnam] know best how I feel. There must be a benevolent virus that infects us from the time we first sew on the patch, producing an unknown electricity that stimulates whatever it is that makes a superior soldier. Then there is a contagion of excellence when such soldiers work together. That's what happens, and that's how this division made history whenever it has fought. You can't describe it except in metaphysical terms, but you feel it and you know it."

Peay's standard, essentially, was to ensure that the infection was epidemic throughout the division—that the surpassing excellence that was the Screaming Eagle tradition would continue and even reach new heights. Even in the internally turbulent cauldron of Desert Storm.

Straddled in 18th ABC by the 82nd and 24th divisions—the former cocky from Grenada and Panama, the latter commanded by a Schwarzkopf favorite—Peay would not outdo them with razzle-dazzle or show. Instead he turned to his planners for the way to translate tradition into action.

As a former Screaming Eagle himself, Luck was prepared to give Peay loose reins for the division's charge to the Euphrates. Peay was the antithesis of Patton, but felt he could produce the same result without blood and guts, and even exceed it by a quantum leap. The proof would be in the plan. With the substance but not the trappings of audacity, the plan would reveal a boldness unsuspected in Peay's reticent personality.

Garrett: "Gen. Luck was willing, but his staff had some unbelievers when it came to air assault. They couldn't openly scoff at what we were planning—they knew better than that—however, you definitely had a feeling they thought we were dreaming up something impractical and maybe impossible. I think they were waiting for some general at CENTCOM to step in and bring us down to reality. Drop a brigade on the Euphrates in 48 hours? What've you guys been smoking?"

Neither was there a truce in the forty year rivalry between the 101st and 82nd, and in the eyes of Peay's staff, corps continued its favoritism toward 'America's guard of honor.'

The 82nd were paratroopers desperate to use their parachutes. But behind the mechanized Republican Guards was no place to drop the All Americans with little more than TOW's to defend themselves. Schwarzkopf himself squelched two proposed drops. The golden day of the classic airborne, with the sky filled with thousands of 'chutes, grew cloudy in Korea and ebbed to twilight in Vietnam. But these limited wars were considered the exception by paratrooper proponents—Iraq was a different beast, one more like the Nazis snarling behind their defenses. The 82nd had jumped into Fortress Europe, and were eager to repeat the feat behind Fortress Kuwait. But Schwarzkopf said no—hell no—perhaps remembering 'a bridge too far' when the British First Airborne Divison was annihilated when surrounded by German armor in Holland.

Prohibited from unfurling their parachutes, the 82nd Airborne sought rapid conversion to heliborne. Some forty new model Black Hawks reached corps and were promptly turned over to the 82nd for general use despite the 101st's crucial mission to get to the Euphrates first with the most. To Peay's staff, it was apparent that the incestuous relationship between corps and the 82nd had moved into a desert tent. Both had lived together at Ft. Bragg, exchanging officers back and forth in a regular rotation that almost merged the aims and personality of one with the other. Garrett, in particular, seethed about the new Black Hawks diverted to the 82nd:

"The feeling around here was, 'watch this, you guys.' We were going to show people at corps some things that would pop their eyes. We were going to do stuff they'd never seen before—in fact, nobody had. The plan was the thing. If we did our calculations right, we had the men and machines to carry it off.

"I've never been involved in planning like we did during January. I doubt if I ever will again. Everyone's heads were together. I had a special planning cell just to compute fuel, weight and distance templates. Every battalion built a huge sand table [some double the size of a football field] where they'd walk through each step of the campaign. It was awesome. We'd come to a problem and stop, look it over, walk around it, peek under it—try to see how we could get from here to there.

"Sometimes it took a major change, and that vibrated things up and down the line. There were a lot of blind alleys and red herrings too. Some things simply did not look do-able, and took original innovations like the Devito option to move forward.

But step by step, piece by piece, it was coming together like a jigsaw puzzle.

"That's just what it was. We had a picture of what the final result should look like. We were all holding pieces of the puzzle and trying to get them to fit. Sometimes we had to reshape pieces, maybe even make new ones, but that was even more fascinating—and really exciting."

Garrett's acquaintance with Peay went back to Vietnam when they had served together in the 1st Cavalry Division, the original forerunner of the air assault division. To be bold amidst the vicissitudes of war, Peay characteristically surrounded himself with known quantities, Garrett perhaps the foremost example. While Peay was Assistant Division Commander, Garrett was XO of the Aviation Brigade before commanding 1-101 for three years, turning it (and the new Apaches) over to Cody. Garrett then attended the Army War College for a year, returning just in time to lead the Aviation Task Force to the Gulf within weeks after Saddam invaded Kuwait. All told, during the previous decade, Garrett had served seven years in the division:

"Hell, I felt like 'Old Abe' [the original Screaming Eagle from the Civil War]. Tom Hill was the only colonel I didn't know well when we got to the desert, and I'd served, over the years, with many of the battalion level commanders throughout the division, especially the key ones supporting Aviation Brigade." Garrett was saying history was destiny. New guys—what few there were—had to be known by old guys to be accepted into the scheme of things.

The basic scheme was a double leapfrog. One infantry brigade would land in Iraq about midway to the Euphrates Valley wherein ran Highway 8, the MSR between Baghdad and Saddam's garrison in Kuwait. The next brigade would fly up to snip the MSR, returning for fuel at the mammoth FARP created where the first brigade landed. The last brigade prepared to leap frog from the FARP, either to reinforce the brigade blocking the MSR or in the direction of Basra or Baghdad, depending on developments elsewhere in the Hail Mary strategy.

If the basic scheme were accomplished, never would so many helicopters fly so many men, so much equipment, so far in such a short time. The first phase alone—to be accomplished in but a few hours—involved an area the size of the three southern New England states. The next two leapfrogs would vault distances as long as the mid-Atlantic seaboard. Gen. Luck gave Peay the real estate he asked for, with an option for more. Except for political constraints from CENTCOM, the air assault division could push itself to the limits, and these would be self imposed.

As they settled into TAA Campbell, the planners started work with sheets of paper as blank as the desert. For once they could challenge their imagination, a resource underutilized in army careers. Tom Hill's mind almost cavorted with possibilities.

He had already succeeded with one maneuver. As the most experienced of the infantry brigade commanders, he was the betting choice for the first jump into Iraq. But toward the end of Desert Shield he nailed down the job for First Brigade by rehearsing them in a large scale FARP exercise with Peay observing.

"When Gen. Peay thought FARP, I wanted him to think First Brigade. Yeah, I was getting up on Purdom and Clark, but I don't think we saw this as a rivalry. We sort of had a gentlemen's agreement about trying to ace each other out for missions, and I don't think I violated it by lobbying for Cobra [as the FARP was to be named]. Third Brigade would be first to the Euphrates, so why should Clark complain, and Ted... well, along came Hafer Al Batin, and for a while it looked like the hottest mission in the JOA."

January 1991

26: Iraqi fighter aircraft flee to Iran. Saddam sacks his Air Minister.

29: An Iraqi brigade seizes the abandoned Saudi town of Khafji on the coast.

31: Coalition forces recapture Khafji.

XIV

Hail Fatima

On January 8th, Peay and brigade representatives flew up to KKMC, from there to do a ground reconnaissance of TAA Campbell—an area larger than Rhode Island—for the purpose of dividing it among the division's units. Here on the frontier was a different desert from that around King Fahd. It was higher and colder, all the more noticeable in the Arabian winter; but the difference most evident from the air was color. Rather than graceful dunes of pale sand, this was Martian desert, ruddy, dotted with stunted brush. The ground was a rubble of slate, hard enough to break entrenching tools. The wind blew as on a mountaintop, a steady moan, even heard over the radio. TAA Campbell was bleak and depressing. It gratified the visitors only in representing the final stop before the war that would get them home. This was the last waiting place.

Subdividing the featureless TAA would be easy: just lay out plats and mark them with signs made from MRE boxes. Good thing, the visitors agreed, that training at the FOB's had been so austere, hardening the troops for this windblown wasteland.

Landing back at KKMC was like arriving at Palm Springs from Death Valley. As Lori Gabram had learned, KKMC was in many respects a resort. "Let's attack from here," someone joked, as Peay's group began conferring over maps. They were interrupted when he was called to the phone. It was G3, 18th ABC.

Though 7th Corps had been piling ashore and moving up to the border as fast as possible, a longshoremen's strike in Germany, inadequate sealift, plus all the unique requirements of outfitting for the desert, had set the heavy armored formations behind schedule. Now, with the air war a week away, they were not yet in position to repel an Iraqi counteroffensive if such were triggered by allied bombing.

Consequently, 18th ABC would have to cover a portion of 7th Corps' front until it completed its deployment. The stopgap looked to be a brigade-size job. The call Peay received at KKMC was instructions to send one up to Hafer Al Batin forthwith. He selected Second Brigade quickly. First Brigade was slated for Cobra, and already involved in rehearsals. Third Brigade had just returned to King Fahd at the end of the covering force mission. Second Brigade was already rested and refitted, so they were the obvious choice. Peay called Shelton to get 'em on the road and into the air.

Neither Hill nor Clark had reason to envy Purdom, despite the apparent importance of the Hafer Al Batin mission. No unit looks forward to removal from its parent organization to be temporary help for another; sometimes in a status of second class citizenship, working with new people, learning new procedures. Moreover, Second Brigade had attack plans to develop, preparations in which Purdom's presence was vital for input and influence. As in any large organization, the component which is not represented usually has cause to regret it.

But cross-attachment was a common army practice; indeed the air assault concept would not be fully tested during the war unless it was combined in some proportions with armor, thus demonstrating the division's versatility and 'synergy.' Resolved to make the best of necessity, Purdom launched a migration in Air Force transports, Chinooks and Black Hawks, line haul trucks, buses and tactical vehicles.

As always, Dessie Greer in G3 was first to know the future for her husband's battalion. "They're movin' you," she confided, "over to 7th Corps!" Calvin reeled, assuming that he alone was about to leave the division. But in six hours, nothing of the entire brigade remained at King Fahd except empty haj tents flapping forlorn in the winter wind.

They'd be used again, but the procession of convoys rolling north to the border foretold an indefinite absence. An expression coined in the fall was heard again, this time in buses jammed with troops: "The road home goes through Kuwait!" Iraq was to be substituted for Kuwait in the case of the 101st, but this was still a secret for all but high ranking Screaming Eagles.

With a vehicle every twenty feet for 500 miles, Tapline Road was already overcrowded, so some Second Brigade convoys were routed by way of Riyadh and KKMC, an eleven hour journey. A Chinook crash-landed and was destroyed by an engine fire, along with a howitzer it was carrying. Otherwise, except for its speed, the move was unremarkable compared to the bizare situation at its destination.

Hafer Al Batin, and its environs, was an international hodge podge of support troops, all the more perplexing because the allied MSR (Tapline Road) ran not from the rear to the front but laterally; i.e., southeast to northwest. The Pan-Arab legion had moved up from KKMC and sprawled out north of Hafer Al Batin, an oil town some forty miles from the border. Much too close to the Pan-Arab screen were supporting installations like hospitals (still being erected), an airfield, and supply dumps which would be overrun in a trice if the Iraqis came down the Wadi Al Batin in strength.

The wadi was the most significant terrain feature in hundreds of miles: a formidable canyon of varying depth running on a straight azimuth from KKMC, some thirty miles southwest of Hafer Al Batin, to the tri-border junction of Saudi Arabia, Iraq and Kuwait. The wadi was the best and obvious invasion route for an Iraqi preemptive strike: it would cut Schwarzkopf's MSR, then force evacuation of KKMC, the only permanent military installation in north central Arabia, and politically important (like Stalingrad) if only for its name. Such an attack would also hit the allies at their weakest point, exploiting their unfamiliarity with each other, their differences in ammunition, communications, and indeed language and military philosophy. Few Americans were confident that Egyptians and Syrians were prepared to fight their Arab brothers to the death. That was not the Arab way.

Another ominous feature of a full scale attack down Wadi Al Batin was that it was a canyon, a very wide one, bounded by bluffs rather than walls, but still an escarped corridor providing some neutralization of the allies' ultimate advantage, their mastery of the air. With triple A positioned on the edges of the escarpment, fighter-bombers might have trouble getting down into deeper sections of the wadi for low level strikes necessary to knock out moving tanks. Moreover, two good roads paralleled the wadi, offering a supply line adequate to support a mechanized corps. The Iraqis would need to be bold and favored by poor flying weather, but if ever they were to initiate a test of arms with Schwarzkopf, the Wadi Al Batin was the place, and Hafer Al Batin their first objective.

Purdom was shocked at the situation he found there. The endless convoys rumbled down Tapline Road without a thought for their vulnerability from the wadi. Commanders of the administrative units, including a British Air Force hospital, looked at him as though they thought him mad when he said they ought to move out of danger. What danger? "And, Colonel, would you tell us why you're here, and who sent you?"

Purdom could cite his orders from 7th Corps: to "retain" (defend) the airfield at Al Qaysumah, fifteen miles from Hafer Al Batin, and thereby deflect an Iraqi thrust down the wadi. He worked now for Maj. Gen. Tilelli, commander of the 1st Cavalry Division (armored) , the lead element of 7th Corps. Second Brigade's relationship with them was TACON, meaning that Purdom was to act on Tilelli's orders but otherwise take care of himself. That meant Second Brigade had to get its supplies from the 101st which was still at King Fahd, 600 miles away, preparing for its own move.

Purdom saw something like Bastogne coming along. Not Bastogne, the FOB, but the original Bastogne—the famous Bastogne the press called the hole in the donut when German panzers washed around it in the Battle of the Bulge, and where the Screaming Eagles told the Nazis, "Nuts!" in reply to a demand for surrender.

He was recalling Bastogne because of how the Iraqis were massed on the border, just the way they had before they invaded Kuwait, and this time they were pointed right at Hafer Al Batin.

"You don't think we were looking over our shoulder [at the 101st's history]? You bet I was, when we got that CENTCOM intelligence report on 12 January."

This report was graded "probably true, usually reliable source," an endorsement from CENTCOM to take the information most seriously. Purdom did. He began thinking about Bastogne, Belgium, when he read the size of the attack predicted.

"Three armored divisions were coming along the wadi, with the Tawalkana and Hamurabi Republican Guards divisions in the second echelon. For a minute I thought some guy in G2 was pulling my leg. Then I get a call from 7th Corps headquarters. Gen. Franks is in the air, en route to Al Qaysumah. If the corps commander was coming to see me, it was time to start worrying."

As he waited for Franks, Purdom reviewed what little other intelligence he'd received concerning enemy intentions. What came to mind was his personal impression while riding through Hafer Al Batin. In contrast to the friendly indifference of the Saudis on the coast, the Arabs here were sullen and surly. Before the war, the town was the junction for oil pumped down from Iraq into the Trans-Arabian Pipeline, thence to the Mediterranen and world markets. When sanctions were imposed, Saudi Arabia closed the nozzle and threw the townspeople out of work. Hafer Al Batin, with a large populaton of Jordanians, was believed to be full of Iraqi sympathizers. Purdom put it off limits to his troops. Then came the surest sign that there would be battle: Hafer Al Batin's population began to to leave town, first in dribbles, then in a flood reminiscent of refugees from Kuwait.

The Iraqi attack, larger than any they'd launched against Iran, was forecast to kick off no later than the morning of January 14th—a day away. There was no time to spare, and Franks didn't waste any.

"What do you need, Colonel Purdom?"

"To get all the support troops out of the battle area, sir."

Franks promised Second Brigade control of all tenant units in

Garrett, left, and Cody.

A Black Hawk is winched into an Air Force C-5A for the flight to Saudi Arabia.

Apache armament. The four largest objects are external fuel tanks. *(McDonnell Douglas)*

Material bound for Saudi Arabia is loaded on a C-5A.

RIGHT: Tent city.

BELOW: Pictured is about half of Camp Eagle II (Ft. Camel, tent city) at King Fahd International Airport, Saudi Arabia. *(Pratt Museum)*

A camel and a Screaming Eagle share some Evian.

ABOVE: Camouflage netting protrudes on the bleak landscape of TAA Campbell.

BELOW: The ultimate letter-writer, Lettie Gingerich. Behind her on the wall are some photos and return correspondence from soldiers in the Gulf. *(Lettie Gingerich)*

ABOVE: A howitzer crew training near FOB Oasis.

LEFT: Training for house to house fighting at FOB Oasis. *(Pratt Museum*

BELOW: Apaches begin a night mission.

ABOVE: An Apache launches a Hellfire missile. Note silhouettes of copilot-gunner (front) and pilot (back) in cockpit. *(McDonnell Douglas)*

LEFT: Contrails filled the sky when the air campaign began.

BELOW: An Apache about to refuel at FOB Bastogne as a Kiowa hovers nearby.

ABOVE: Black Hawks land First Brigade soldiers at Cobra on G Day. *(Bill Gentile)*
BELOW: Soldiers of Second Brigade await their lifts into FOB Cobra.

RIGHT: Cobras
approaching
Toad.

Top: Generals Schwarzkopf and Peay in front of war maps at D-MAIN.

Above: Chinooks hauling howitzers.

Right: A Chinook landing fuel blivets at FOB Cobra. *(Tom Garrett)*

RIGHT: A
CHINOOK lifting
a 155mm
howitzer.
(Tom Garrett)

BELOW: Two
Black Hawks
browning out.
(18th Airborne
Corps)

RIGHT: Several
Chinooks
brown out.

ABOVE: Border watch: A TOW anti-tank weapon, mounted on a HUMM-V, points into no man's land between TAA Campbell and Iraq. *(Pratt Museum)*

ABOVE: A desert patrol goes out from TF Citadel.

LEFT: Eagles on the Euphrates: A Third Brigade soldier in an ambush on Highway 8.

ABOVE: EPW's. *(18th Airborne Corps.)*

BELOW: Soldiers of the Third Brigade loading for their air assault into AO Eagle.

BELOW: An Apache atop a mesa in Iraq.

ABOVE: Sergeants and officers of Third Brigade around a sign greeting visitors to the Euphrates valley. Behind them is a wrecked Iraqi truck, to the left front of the sign is an Iraqi helmet. Col. Bob Clark is fourth from left.

RIGHT: Cease fire! Cody (in baseball cap) spreads the word to 1-101 at FOB Viper. *(Dick Cody)*

LEFT: Rhonda Cornum, her elbows still in casts, with daughter Regan. *(Army Times)*

BELOW: Redeployment: A Chinook in a cocoon to protect it against storms at sea is off loaded after its return voyage to Jacksonville, FL. HUMM-V in foreground.

BELOW: Screaming Eagles from this 747 form up to march into the hangar of joy.

ABOVE: Returning the colors to Ft. Campbell.

RIGHT: Welcome offboard. Pan Am stewardesses join celebrations in the hangar of joy. The one on the left has helped carry this Screaming Eagle's M-16!

BELOW: Hangar of joy: Left to right, Mrs. Weiss, CSM Weiss, Mrs. Peay, MG Peay.

ABOVE, BELOW AND LEFT: Hangar of joy.

LEFT: In the Hangar of joy.

RIGHT: Doug and Lori Gabram are greeted by Lori's mother. *(Doug Gabram)*

BELOW: Dad's back!

Welcome home Dad!

BELOW: Dad's Kevlar becomes Ryan Peay's souvenir during homecoming at Ft. Campbell.

any size area he needed. Purdom turned to his XO, David Wood. "You heard the general, Dave. Clear that airfield."

Wood made for the door, wondering how to explain to disbelieving doctors, airmen and logisticians that the corps commander had just approved their immediate eviction.

"What else?" Franks asked impatiently.

"I could use earth movers and barriers."

"You got it." Franks reached for his phone; it was instantly connected to his chief of staff. "Landry—Franks. Strip out all the engineer battalions. Put 'em on the road up here." There was a question from Landry. "Make Tapline one way if you have to. Get 'em up here now.

"What else?" asked Franks again, turning to Purdom. This was his chance to get any assets in the inventory of the mightiest corps the US Army ever fielded. He tripped off hastily compiled requirements: Hellfires, TOW's, mines, barb wire...oh, yes, his supporting Apaches would need additional fuel. Purdom could imagine Brigadier General Landry scribbling down the wish list as Franks converted it into orders.

"You'll have four heavy engineer battalions tonight. Anything else can I do for you?"

"1st Cav, sir. They've got other missions besides backing me up..."

Franks raised his hand, and gestured for the phone again. In a moment he was talking to the 1st Cav's CG:

"Tilelli—Franks. How soon can you get up here behind Purdom?" Tilelli apparently asked what size force he should send. "Your *division*, John... Good. Move out."

Purdom's mind was awhirl. He was certain that unless someday he became a corps commander himself, never again would his requests become instant, unquestioned commands, summoning forces from near and far. Franks turned to him once more. Purdom was afraid he had forgotten something he might need later. Already this three-starred fairy godfather had multiplied Second Brigade's defensive capabilities fourfold.

"Last call," said Franks with a small smile.

"Well, sir, my Apaches come from the 229th [a battalion like Cody's, attached to the 101st from 18th ABC] They're about 60 miles up the road..."

"I'll get 'em closer."

Franks was stretching his authority because to move closer the 2-229 would have to relocate into an area controlled by the Saudi Army. Nevertheless the Apaches moved.

Franks flew away like Santa Claus, having emptied his bag under Purdom's tree. Second Brigade's staff was wide eyed when they heard the scale of support headed their way—then blinked, hearing that the 7th Corps commander felt such a massive defensive effort was called for. On the night of January 17th, radar picked up bogies at the tri-border. Like an anvil chorus, the darkness rang with the clank of Second Brigade battling the shale.

They had broken many an entrenching tool when heavy engineering equipment rumbled toward them from Tapline Road. There were cheers—but the arriving backhoes were for digging in the TOC and artillery, not foxholes, which remained the work of infantrymen. Then the rain began.

Calvin Greer: "We were soaked, soaked, soaked. Water got so deep in the holes, your E tool just brought up thin kinda' mud. We tried to bail 'em out with ponchos. I didn't know it then, but this was the longest, hardest work we'd do in the whole time we were over there."

Greer's battalion, 2-502, and 3-502,* dug in around Al

---

* For the sake of preserving historical lineage, the army had adopted (and frequently changed) a system for equating brigades with regiments, both numbering about 2000 soldiers, divided into three maneuver battalions. Certain regiments had won renown in America's wars through Korea. The 'equating' system can be as complicated as the British peerage; but in the 101st, First Brigade was comprised of the 1st, 2nd, and 3rd battalions of the 327th Regiment, Screaming Eagles who went into combat from gliders in World War II, and helicopters in Vietnam. Similarly, Second Brigade was the 1st, 2nd, and 3rd battalions of the 502nd Regiment, originally paratropers, with campaigns identical to the 327th's. Thus, Greer's battalion was the 2nd of the 502nd, abbreviated 2-502.

Third Brigade's historical mirror, the 187th Regiment, had no connection with the Screaming Eagles in World War II; but when Gen. Westmoreland commanded the division in the 1950's, he added the 187th, his old outfit from Korea, where they acquired the nickname 'Rakkasans'—umbrellas—which is how the Japanese saw descending parachutes to be. The 502nd (read Second Brigade) had two nicknames, the 'Oh-deuce' and 'Strike Force.' The 327th (read First Brigade) never acquired a distinctive nickname, instead using mottos from its battalions like, 'No slack' or 'Above the rest.' Mottos and nicknames were not dead letters, but rather the expected greeting when

Quysamah airfield, the position anchoring Purdom's east flank, while l-502 entrenched around a quarry near the town. In the six miles of wadi between the two positions, there was nothing to stop or even hinder the Iraqi corps, reported to outnumber Second Brigade twenty to one, and in tanks a thousand to zero. Three armor divisions were reported in the first attacking echelon; in the second was another, plus two mechanized divisions of the Republican Guard. The expected attack took on the name, Hail Fatima, Saddam's go for broke gamble. It was an onslaught Purdom could only hope to deflect, delaying its advance down the wadi and on to KKMC, the Iraqis' ultimate objective.

But Purdom's (Tilelli's as well) orders were not to delay but to retain, terms of art with explicitly differentiated meanings in the army. Delay meant, essentially, to shoot and fall back—not to become 'decisively engaged' with the attackers. Retain, by contrast, meant stay where you are—'die in place,' colloquially. If this was not to happen to Second Brigade, if Hafer Al Batin was to be a Bastogne rather than an Alamo, Purdom needed a whole lot more help than what he saw in his vicinity, Gen. Franks' largesse notwithstanding.

True, the lst Cav was rolling north to back up Second Brigade, but their mission was to counterattack if Purdom was in danger of being overrun. True, the lst Infantry Division (Mechanized) was assembling twenty miles to the east, but they were unready for close combat. That was why Second Brigade had been thrown into the breach. The lst Division's tanks had not yet received their ammunition, though their artillery could be of some help. Salvation had to come from the air, from 2-229th's Apaches and the Air Force's A-10's. For a time, Second Brigade could hold up the Iraqis, forcing them to gather where their tanks could be killed quickly and in huge numbers. If Second Brigade didn't go under, it would be because of a plausible but never tested premise: that state of the art air power, exclusively, could stop armored forces unstoppable in previous wars.

That remained to be seen, and Second Brigade would be both witnesses and guinea pigs for the test. Air support would be a

---

salutes were exchanged, sometimes to the amusement of an onlooker: it took a Dick Cody to call out to Gen. Peay, "Expect no mercy, sir!"

godsend, but Purdom recalled that God helps those who help themselves. The infantryman's greatest help has always been from the earth on which he marches and fights. Second Brigade turned all their efforts to reshaping it into a subterranean strongpoint.

Purdom: "It comes as a surprise to a lot of people outside the army that a TOW has a longer range than a tank. We definitely exploited that differential in positioning our TOW's behind the tank ditch, which was our next major engineering project. But if the tanks advanced inside our standoff range, and there's nothing but desert between the TOW and the tank, the TOW had better hit first or he won't get a second chance. We dug a primary and alternate position for every TOW [sixty] in the brigade. That way they could shoot, and hopefully scoot, to another hole before they received counterfire."

Greer: "We dug in the TOW's first before we dug our own foxholes. That was OK. Tanks was the big worry. Even with the rain, guys would hear 'em comin'. Got so the sergeant told 'em to shut up—we'd get plenty of warning before the Iraqis got here.

"We dug day and night. We did it in shifts. When we got picks and shovels, we'd dig and dig, and then just hand 'em to the next shift. Dig four hours, pull guard four hours, sleep four hours. And, oh yeah, it would rain for twelve hours. There was a guy in my platoon that said it was all over for us because our air support couldn't hit nothin' in this rain. Another guy was pissed at that kind of talk, 'cause he knew Apaches could see tanks, rain, nighttime or no. He went to the platoon leader—he came down and said that was right about the Apaches, and didn't want any more rumors like the other guy was spreading.

"Whenever there was a break in the rain, Apaches came over our position like they wanted to cheer us up. It was sure good seeing 'em. Made us think division hadn't forgotten us.

"We had some funny things you'd hear about, and we were so tired the silliest little thing would get guys laughing so we'd have to sit down and cry. Like there was this Jewish kid, you know, in 3rd batt.? His squad said he didn't have to dig because they were going to give him to the Iraqis like a hostage—so the rest of the squad could get away.

"And you know, we had a couple of Moslems too?* They got some kidding at Ft. Camel—stuff about the haj tents, and how that's the way they wanted to live. Out on the perimeter at Hafer, they got their payback. They'd say things in Arabic like they were reporting to the Iraqis that overran our position. They'd salute like Iraqis do, with their palms out. When things got up tight, someone would tell 'em to knock that off."

Without a tank ditch to protect the TOW's, they would get only one shot. In 48 hours, a ditch was dug, six feet deep, fifteen wide, and six miles long. Guinness has no record for such a feat of field engineering but Second Brigade claims it, with a deep bow to the 7th Corps and 1st Cav engineers who moved most of the shale, sand and soup, employing forty dozers.

For maximum effort they had to work all night, every night, so they asked if they could use lights. Purdom said, hell, use 'em. The Iraqis would find the ditch soon enough anyway, though in the mucky sandscape a tank could roll up to twenty meters from the ditch before he saw it.

No doubt Saddam sympathizers in Hafer Al Batin tipped off the Iraqis about the daunting ditch, information even more valuable as a deterrent than a defense.

Next priority was getting the artillery batteries and battalion CP's dug in. The work was so fast, they looked like they were on elevators descending into the ground. When Gen. Franks came up the next time, there were just muzzles sticking out. Second Brigade went underground—under water, like otters. Franks was impressed—pleased and surprised.

Greer: "We were wrapped around the airfield. There were still a lot of REMF's milling around and moving out. I saw troops from a lot of nations that I never knew about. Most of 'em spoke some English, and we got to trading. The British had pretty good rations but didn't want ours. Everyone would trade berets for our desert hats, and I got one from Syria.

"We got the best offers for our [Kevlar] helmets. We jacked

---

* There were originally 35 professed moslems in the division when it deployed to the Gulf. In the cradle of Islam, fifteen more Screaming Eagles converted with the encouragement of the Saudi government who provided free transportation and accommodations in Mecca, as well as Arab dress for this holy pilgrimage of haj.

the price because they'd always ask about the situation—why were we bustin' ass digging in? We'd say, don't you know this big Iraqi corps' coming down the wadi?—it'll be here tomorrow. We'd make it sound like a real serious situation—and I guess it was. That's when they'd ask about our helmets. It's the best one in the world for stopping bullets, and they wanted it bad."

Purdom never got a follow-up on CENTCOM's intelligence report, but until Franks told him differently, the Iraqis were still coming. Second Brigade even started taking pills to pre-treat the effects of nerve gas, and activated their chemical alarms. That's how seriously 7th Corps still viewed the threat.

Purdom was like a seismographer, watching precursory ground distortions unknown to the public. He is a worrier by nature, meticulous in preparation, supervisive in execution. If the flying weather wasn't too bad, he hoped to shunt the Iraqi corps over into the strength of the 1st Cav. That was the best Purdom could do—hold his position long enough to force the attack into a killing ground for others to counterattack. 7th Corps started working on that plan.

"But out front of us were the Pan-Arab forces. They had to be in on our defense and counterattack plans. By all military logic, they should provide early warning and be our covering force, then head south before the Iraqis blasted through them. I sent liaison officers out to coordinate with them about this, but they didn't want to talk to us. No one had told them about the threat or our mission.

"I guess that should have alerted me that the threat might not be all CENTCOM had made of it. You'd think the Pan-Arabs—and they included a Saudi brigade—would be well informed about a threat as serious as that in the CENTCOM intelligence report. Besides, they were much closer to the tri-border than we were, and therefore probably had good intelligence of their own."

Purdom's was not to reason why. His greatest concern was fratricide—headlines about Screaming Eagles shooting up Arab allies. It very nearly happened. In fact, it did happen in reverse when the Egyptians fired on the 1st Cav rehearsing a counterattack plan.

The basic problem was that there was no overall allied commander in the border region. Questions had to be resolved 200 miles away in Riyadh between CENTCOM and the coalition commanders in chief. Coordination was a foreign concept to the Pan-Arab forces strewn around the Wadi Al Batin. Each nationality (Egyptian, Kuwaiti, Saudi, Syrian) held jealously to their turf—turf allocated to them under the Hail Mary plan—almost as an expression of national pride.

The fratricidal incident that was Purdom's most vivid recollection involved the Egyptian Commando Brigade (their self-designation—they bore no resemblance to the western understanding of the term, 'commando'). They were under orders from their headquarters in Riyadh to retain their sector, and scoffed at Purdom's suggestion to move or even allow U.S. forces to operate adjacent to their sector. The attempted coordination also suffered from inadequate translators.

The CO of Greer's battalion undertook an embassy to the Egyptians when, by chance, a mechanized company of the 1st Cav cut across a piece of the Egyptians' turf. The Americans in armored vehicles were taken under small arms fire. Ignoring it, they drove into the sights of the Egyptians' MILAN anti-tank missiles. The Americans' turrets swiveled to stare them down. The MILAN's prepared to open up. Luckily, Purdom's ambassador was able to intervene in time.

Twelve days after CENTCOM's report, the Wadi Al Batin threat dissolved in misty rains. Was the threat another clever insertion of disinformation by the Iraqis, or did their informers in the town report Second Brigade's dogged preparations and the formidable tank ditch? On January 17th, the air war cancelled any opportunity for Hail Fatima. Yet there is certainty that Saddam had a spoiling attack in mind, and one was attempted, on a much reduced scale, when Iraqi armor thrust down the coast into Saudi Arabia, temporarily occupying the town of Khafji, from which the marines expelled them on January 31.

Purdom was eager to turn over his inundated fortifications to 7th Corps, and return to the 101st which was now settled in TAA Campbell, coiled to attack into Iraq. Second Brigade pulled out of Hafer Al Batin on January 25th. Already signed, sealed and delivered to Purdom was 101st DIV OPLAN 90-5. As Purdom had feared, he, the absent brigade commander in the final formulation of the plan, got the least appealing mission: Second Brigade, to whom had befallen the most dangerous mission of Desert Shield, received the equivalent mission in Desert Storm—to seize a fortified airfield called Tallil, an objective that loomed as the Verdun of the desert.

Greer and his comrades were too soaked by rain and fatigue to care. Bouncing along the Tapline, their heads jerked in sleep. Each time heavy eyes opened, the scene on both sides of the roadway was the same: men, vehicles, weapons, tents, camouflage nets, repeated endlessly—for two, three, four hours between Hafer Al Batin and Rafha. Greer could hardly believe the army was so large; but this was not more than a third of it, assembled and absorbed in preparations, remote and distracted spectators at the execution of the Iraqi Army as the air campaign concluded the first of six devastating weeks.

3: Air campaign reaches 40,000 sorties (approximately one fighter-bomber strike for every ten Iraqi soldiers in Kuwait).

8: Grating under CENTCOM restrictions, a team of American reporters crosses the Kuwaiti border, returning with interviews of some Iraqi soldiers.

12: Near Baghdad, 400 Iraqi civilians are killed in an air raid shelter that CENTCOM avers was used as a military command complex.

14: Imprecise and conflicting battle damage assessments from the air campaign perplex Schwarzkopf who wants the Iraqi army rendered 50% ineffective before he launches his ground campaign.

XV

Chattanooga—via Cobra

The first Scud alert came on January 18th, while the division was marshalling at Ft. Camel. Suddenly everyone was faceless, nearly voiceless, in their masks. The great dread was coming —contrails pointing down from Iraq, a spectral warning not to approach. But nothing more appeared in the sky that day.*

The first seven Scuds were launched against Israel, Saddam's attempt to convert Desert Storm into a religious war. He failed, but these Scuds did upset the air campaign by diverting almost a third of the fighter-bombers to search for mobile launchers. This change was known only at Peay's level, and caused him misgivings that tactical targets would drop in priority. At the final generals' conference in Dhahran, Schwarzkopf had prom-

---

* The author, at that time a colonel in the Army Reserves, had been corresponding with Gen. Peay in an effort to be assigned to the 101st. From Dhahran Peay called while I was watching football on TV. He excused himself in order to put on his mask because this first Scud alert had just sounded. Simultaneously on my TV screen, the football game was interrupted by a reporter in Dhahran with the same news.

ised them the mother of all air campaigns to soften up the Iraqi army before it was attacked from the ground.

Stateside commentators speculated that Saddam might succumb to air power alone; and a ground attack, if he did not evacuate Kuwait sooner, would be 'mopping up.' Not from conviction but only to deceive him, Gens. Powell and Schwarzkopf made no efforts to dispell this notion, while all preparations in the JOA were to the contrary. Iraq's veteran army, the fourth largest and among the best equipped in the world, had been digging in for five months. Though some of it could be buried by bombs, the rest would be dislodged from Kuwait only by bayonets. No one in the 101st seriously thought otherwise.*

Third Brigade closed into TAA Campbell on January 23rd, followed by First Brigade three days later, and Second Brigade rolled in from Hafer Al Batin on the 29th. The newly relocated Division headquarters (DMAIN), division historian Cliff Lippard wrote, "was a maze of tents, sand bag bunkers, camouflage nets and concertina," slowly taking shape in the middle of a dry *sabkha*. The thought occurred to him, what would happen if rain here came down in quantity as it had at Hafer Al Batin? DMAIN would need Noah's ark: all the trucks that hauled it in would be useless to get it out.

To move the 101st had required 358 flights by C 130's and 1,910 vehicles like those in Yancey's convoys, plus vans rented from Saudi contractors—whose drivers pulled over and parked whenever they saw bombing in Iraq. No one was at all certain what the Saudis would do when the shooting started.

Tom Preston had an early glimpse of Saudi attitudes, even before the 101st got underway for TAA Campbell. He was chaplain for 326th Engineer Battalion. According to the army table of organizational equipment, there was no military vehicle assigned to him. But the Japanese government (on December

---

* Screaming Eagles were not in a position to judge the relative contribution of bombs and bayonets to the Iraqi collapse, principally because enemy forces were few and scattered in the 101st's AO, and therefore not hit by the Air Force nearly as much as the Republican Guards massed in Kuwait. The question is unlikely to be resolved whether body blows from the air enabled the knockout punch on the ground; i.e., that the outcome of the fight was determined more in the first round than in the second.

7th!), in a gesture of support for Desert Shield, had donated a fleet of Mitsubishi 4x4's to CENTCOM. One had trickled down to the 326th, and became Preston's temporary transportation to the front. Despite its enviable features like stereo, air, power brakes, seats and steering, the Mitsubishi was designed for economy, burning low octane gasoline unavailable from the army. So Preston had to pay his way to the war. As his convoy formed for the 350-mile journey, he sped off to a Saudi gas station.

"The highway was jammed with refugee families who had fled south from the border. The gas station overflowed with pickup trucks loaded to the axles. One man had his wife sit on the household goods piled in the truck bed, while his goat rode in the cab!

"Finally, I was able to maneuver the Mitsubishi up to a pump. I offered U.S. dollars to the attendant but he shook his head—no Riyals, no gas. Then I noticed two veiled Saudi women sitting on a truck across from me. One gestured for me to come over. This I did not want to do. In that crowd, my uniform with a Christian cross on the helmet made me conspicuous enough. Several Arabs began to point at the cross.*

"An older man joined the two women and gestured for me again, so I approached them. In English one of the women asked what I wanted. I explained my predicament and she translated to the man. He was her father and said he would pay for my gas if the attendant wouldn't take dollars. I thanked him profusely and told my driver to start pumping. We were already late for the convoy and would have to catch up on the road.

"No sooner had he started pumping than I was grabbed from behind by both elbows and spun around violently. I looked into the muzzle of an AK-47, complete with banana clip. This Arab was grinning while he mimiced the sound of his assault rifle on full automatic: 'eh-eh-eh-eh-eh...' I felt I was getting closer to Jesus than I wanted to be at the moment.

"Then this Arab pulled the AK out of my face and beat his

---

* Before the 101st deployed to the Gulf, the army's Chief of Chaplains recommended that all religious insignia be removed from uniforms. Peay overruled him, directing division chaplains to wear their crosses or even Stars of David.

chest with his fist. 'SADDAM BAD!' He pointed north and made a cutting motion across his throat. 'GOOD AMERICAN!' he exclaimed for everyone at the station to hear. People came over to shake my hand, pat my back, and reproached the attendant for not accepting my dollars. He relented. I started to pay, but the father came over and told me this tank was on him. Actually, he made a little speech that his daughter translated, 'Thank you for what you're doing.'"

From a chopper, Lippard saw TAA Campbell as a scattered range of dunes sprouting on endless flats. The low dunes were camouflage nets draped over whatever was under them: truck parks, maintenance shops, artillery batteries, command posts:

"They were as conspicuous as a circus camp. Occupied positions were clusters of activity with acres and acres of nothingness between them. If the Iraqi Air Force ever got down here, they'd see plenty, but wouldn't be able to tell what the nets were hiding. From ground level, you could just see tiny humps on the horizon. There were three constant sounds: wind, choppers, and shovels hitting rocks. You could dig a couple of feet easy, but from there on down it was all solid rock."

It took a full day to drive a HUMM-V from one end of TAA Campbell to the other. First and Third Brigades guarded the northern periphery, which was the international border. But the de facto border was several miles north, where Saudi and Iraqi outposts faced each other. Hill and Clark pawed the sand to send patrols into Iraq. Until they did, the 101st would have to rely on satellite photography and radio intercepts to determine who and how much they would be up against. But Schwarzkopf had forbidden any physical reconnaissance, though his corps and division commanders pressed him as much as they dared. He finally and partially relented, promising that patrols into Iraq could commence seven days before the ground war ('G minus 7'), though G Day remained unspecified. Till then, his Hail Mary force was to remain under wraps and away from the unwary Iraqis.

He had taken some measures to keep them that way. 'Dummy' divisions, including one simulating the 101st, were left where 18th ABC had been. The dummies were only a few special radio operators who busily imitated normal radio traffic of the units they were impersonating, but division commanders like Peay felt the ruse had a short half-life. With bedouins roaming through TAA Campbell, he feared his enormous bivouac would soon be discovered and reported to Baghdad. Already there were reports that Iraqi brigades were beginning to migrate west from the Iranian border.

But like the bear which was his nickname, CINCCENT, having set his will, was immovable. No army reconnaissance into Iraq before G minus 7. Schwarzkopf conceded that bedouins would detect a gathering force on Iraq's western marches, but even if they were Iraqi agents their reports would be microscopic, incapable of providing the big picture of his western maneuver, a picture—by reason of its immense scope—only discernable by aerial reconnaissance, impossible while he ruled the air. So Schwarzkopf remained adamant: no army reconnaissance into Iraq before G minus 7—and stop asking him when that would be. Three other men had to sign off on that date. Their names were Powell, Cheney and Bush. The corps commanders could bite their lips, but till then, Schwarzkopf made clear, don't come around any more with requests to patrol into Iraq.

Against this backdrop of a dropped curtain, Peay honed his plan. It was honed rather than formulated—that had already been accomplished at King Fahd—and on January 26th Peay required his brigade commanders to backbrief their roles in the 101st's plan—tell him what they were going to do as the deepest receivers in the Hail Mary play.

The play as diagrammed was a second major iteration, formally named OPLAN 90-5, known better as Desert Rendezvous II.* Desert Rendezvous I was Tom Hill's brainchild to block the Euphrates valley west of As Samawa after establishing a *covert* FARP in Iraq. This recommendation represented the ultimate

---

* Rendezvous is a buzz word for Screaming Eagles. In 1942, when the division was activated, its original commander, Bill Lee, wrote his men that they had no history, but "a rendezvous with destiny." That phrase became the title for a book relating the 101st's exploits in World War II, for which Eisenhower wrote in a foreword, "I sent the 101st on many important missions; never once did its fighting men fail to add new luster to their reputation as one of the finest units in the Allied Forces."

in radical employment of air assault forces, but the improbability of concealing his brigade, plus all the helicopters and equipage required for a giant FARP, strained the imagination of the corps G3, and propelled logisticians out of their chairs. Moreover, if the 101st struck so far west, all the divisions back down the line would also have to displace. Furthermore, Hill's ground tactical plan envisioned considerable house to house combat in sizable towns like As Samawah. This portended high casualties, and nullified the principal advantage of the air assault division: the speed and flexibility of its helicopters. Then too, from his Vietnam experience Peay had developed a horror of mixing U.S. soldiers among indigenous civilians. For these reasons, Rendezvous I was shelved.

Desert Rendezvous II, usually shortened to simply Desert Rendezvous, was proposed and adopted as the conservative alternative, but conservative only when compared with its predecessor. Desert Rendezvous was a two-inch thick document, replete with annexes, tables and overlays—printed and signed by January. All times in the plan were based on G Day, so that the blanks were filled automatically when CENTCOM confirmed that date. But Desert Rendezvous contained another blank, one on the map—where was the crucial FARP going to be?

Wherever it would be, the site had to have a name. Lt. Col. Montie Hess, a slim version of Yul Brynner, was Division G3 and responsible for naming objectives. For the FARP and its defensive perimeter, he decided on '7-Eleven,' an apt name for what the site would be—a gas pump and convenience for people in a hurry. 7-Eleven appeared in early planning drafts till one day Peay heard it used, and took Hess aside. Henceforth please consult me, Montie, before naming significant operational areas. Peay had a categorical system of names in mind, and it started with snakes. He directed that the first division objective be called Cobra.

Hess erased and edited with alacrity. He was very much an exception among the key players, all the more so for being in the exceptionally important position of G3. Though he, like Hill, was a 'double eagle,' Hess had last served with the 101st twenty years earlier in Vietnam, so he was largely unknown to the inter-war fraternity. His sponsors were Shelton and Bolt for whom he had worked elsewhere. Peay had brought him in on their recommendation barely a month before the war started.

So Hess was the new guy, subject to critical observation. Hill in particular, as commander for the landing on Cobra, had reservations about a G3 unschooled and inexperienced in air assault. With much to prove and scant freedom to fail, Hess drove his staff to exhaustion and sometimes distraction. But he worked himself as hard and with even less rest. Peay did some of his best thinking at night, often after his staff had gone to bed; but he needed a nocturnal interlocutor, someone not so much with opinions or original feedback but with objective answers for simple questions from Peay's mind which seemed to hold more compartments than a beehive. For plans and operations now Peay's consuming concern, Hess (sometimes it was Bolt) was the general's nighttime sounding board and answer man.

Hess: "[Peay] sort of set two shifts for himself. The first one was the normal duty day that ended after the evening briefing. Then he'd catch some z's, get up and start working the phones to the States. I don't know who all he talked with, but they included veterans from the Division Association because he really liked to keep connected with our history, keep continuity with our past while he planned our future. Around midnight, he was ready to start picking my mind."

Working for Hess was Major Randy Mixon, G3 Plans, the staffer most focused on the division's future. Mixon was exalted—but more often kidded—for being a Knight of the Jedi (a sobriquet from a famous Lucas movie), one of a select group of middle management officers from a postgraduate department at the army's Command and General Staff College. Jedi Knights had come over from Ft. Leavenworth to polish the theater plan to nearly Napoleonic brilliance. Mixon plays down his knighthood, but its standards were evident in the brainwork that evolved Desert Rendezvous:

"My first guidance was to get a brigade onto the Euphrates. No time limit—just propose all the ways that could be done. Among the possibilities were 25-mile hops which would take at least two days. The command group scrapped that alternative before I had to give it any more thought. Word came down to go deep—we want that brigade on the Euphrates ASAP. Maximizing aircraft range, we figured it could be done in 48 hours if all went well.

"The pace vehicles for the 'go deep' plan were the cargo helicopters. As heavily loaded as the Black Hawks and Chinooks would be, their range was absolutely critical. Considered together, this meant the FARP must be no farther than eighty nautical miles from where we were. Cobra had to be that close to both TAA Campbell and Third Brigade's objective on the Euphrates if we were to get there in 48 hours.

"Everything in the plan jiggled around that range restriction. It meant the possibilities to site Cobra were confined to a chunk of desert no more than a few miles wide in an AO bigger than Connecticut. A couple of miles north, and you couldn't complete the first round trips between Campbell and Cobra. A little farther south, and you'd come up short on the triangle between Campbell, Cobra and the Euphrates. Aviation Brigade wasn't doing fuel estimates in hundreds of gallons—they were figuring down to single gallons. Backup was zilch. If the Iraqis could knock out the gas station with artillery, Desert Rendezvous would be Desert Gallipoli.

"It was tantalizing when we moved the template around on the map. I couldn't just put an 'X' with a pencil and call it Cobra. The Black Hawks, and especially the Chinooks, had to land where there would not be brownout. Before we picked the site of the gas station, someone had to fly up there, land, and check out the surface conditions. But with the CENTCOM restrictions on reconnaissance, this wasn't permitted."

The 'template' was First Brigade's defensive perimeter for Cobra, to be established if the largest helicopter assault in history succeeded. Hill's mission, essentially, was to secure the 100,000 acres around the FARP—known as 'the gas station'—to be set up within the perimeter. When the gas station opened on G plus 1, Third Brigade would fly that night from TAA Campbell to the Euphrates, cutting Highway 8 in an area called AO Eagle. The Black hawks that delivered them would fly back down to Cobra from Eagle and refuel. This would complete the first and most important vault in Pey's leapfrog maneuver.

Hill would command both the aviation and ground forces allocated to establish Cobra. He back-planned from what he wanted in the template to determine how 300 choppers could get him there. During the long wait (eventually 44 days) at TAA Campbell, Hill came to realize that everything he would need at Cobra could not be flown in and still meet Peay's timetable.

"I was looking at 5,000 men, 50 howitzers, with tons of vehicles and ammunition. None of that meant diddly if we couldn't bring in enough fuel for Third Brigade's birds. Gregg Gile used to say, 'Any helicopter may be useless after two hours.' He's right. If the chopper fleet couldn't refuel, we'd have the biggest aviation parking lot in history. I could be the greatest commander since Hannibal, but I'd fail if we couldn't bring in gas fast enough to Cobra."

The logistics to do so remained a 'war stopper,' ranking second only to finding the precise location of the template. Peay couldn't look for that location till G minus 7, but his logisticians pored over the fueling problem as soon as Desert Rendezvous was approved. Hess felt himself becoming a logistical adjunct rather than the tactical director, as most of his time was devoted to fuelers' estimates.

Hill had to rely that they'd come up with a solution as he dealt with the tactics of securing, then defending, 100,000 acres with 5,000 men. A battalion, 1-502, from Second Brigade was added to his task force for that purpose. If he were to string his four battalions along the perimeter, each man would be about a quarter mile apart; however, the Iraqi forces suspected to be in the vicinity of Cobra made such wide dispersal foolish. There just weren't that many Iraqis around. Their center of gravity remained near the coast, to hold off an amphibious invasion of Kuwait from the Gulf.

Saddam was fond of American movies; among his favorite potboilers was *Sands of Iwo Jima*, from which he evidently derived his understanding of American warfare. Thus, Saddam loaded up his beach defenses, and kept the Republican Guards in reserve close by, prepared to hurl the marines back into the sea that he vowed would "bubble with blood." Yet there must have been some of his generals who saw a greater threat from the exposed desert flank. By the new year, apparently they had convinced him to spread some forces in that direction. In a few weeks, the air campaign interdicted sizeable troop movements, but despite nonstop bombing, Iraqi battalions infiltrated into the 101st's AO.

This resulted in dispersed defenses arrayed against Schwarzkopf's westernmost force, led by a brigade of the 82nd Airborne (mounted in trucks) and French light armor.* On G Day, they were to race for the airfield of As Salman, seize it, then screen the allied west flank.

Disregarding border patrols, the only other threat of any significance in the 101st AO on G Day was a heavy brigade near As Samawah. In total, there were some 10,000 Iraqi soldiers to reckon with, a very skimpy force to defend an area that, as Mixon noted, was larger than Connecticut.

Planning for the worst case, Hill assumed his airhead could be attacked within three hours by as many as five battalions (maybe 7,000 men). Obviously one Screaming Eagle positioned every quarter mile on Cobra's perimeter was not the way to stop them. Hill had to rely on the Air Force to hamper their movement toward Cobra, then his attack helicopters to strafe the Iraqis as they drew nearer, then artillery to hit them, and finally strong points with TOW's whose overlapping fire could fill wide gaps. It was no more than a tertiary worry whether the Iraqis could penetrate the perimeter: Hill had more than sufficient firepower to stop them. His secondary worry was to hold them off at such distance that they could not hit the gas station with artillery. Just a few lucky rounds could mean catastrophe in Cobra's huge stores of ammunition and fuel.

But any enemy action was not the primary concern. The implacable problems were the same as had been pondered in December at King Fahd: where could the FARP be placed? how could there be enough fuel for Third Brigade's Black hawks returning from the Euphrates?

These remained the questions that kept officers and NCO's

---

* The French, in contrast to the other allies, excepted themselves from the requirement to take orders from Schwarzkopf. The French did, however, agree to 'cooperate' in Desert Storm and so, to reduce problems of coordination, they were set out on the extreme left flank.

pacing in tents while their troops were introduced to the novelty of war, albeit on a small scale.

First and Third Brigades kept watch on the border. The Saudi outposts had pulled back, so now at last Iraqis and Americans faced off, though at long distance. Peay, his mind focused long range, wanted no distractions from close-by skirmishes. His policy created a situation reminiscent of the sitzkrieg phase of World War II, or the prowling along the Iron Curtain in Cold War Germany—continuous reconnaisance, stopping, watching, listening, reporting—but rarely shooting.

Before G minus 7, no patrols were to intrude much beyond the American outposts, widely separated in a speckled line running fifty miles along the Iraqi side of TAA Campbell. Typically, a patrol asssembled at dusk. Depending on the distance to be covered and the stealth required, a squad would set out in the dark on foot or in HUMM-V's mounted with TOW's. Their mission might be to reconnoiter ('recon') a gap between outposts that had not been visited before, or perhaps respond to a report from a Kiowa which had observed suspicious activity in a map grid square close by in Iraq. None of the recons promised much excitement; but this at least was real; this was war, this was why most of the infantrymen had joined the army. As if to add realism for patrols, there was sometimes the far away rumble of a B-52 strike.

Lt. Col. Greco commanded one of the patrolling battalions, 3-187. It was he who had lured Cody to the officers' club for his 40th birthday, and now felt retribution every time Cody came visiting in a chopper—landing so close to Greco's tent that the rotor wash blew in walls, pulled up pegs, and sent his staff diving for papers. It had happened so often that Greco stationed a 'Cody spotter' outside, prepared to load sandbags on the tent skirts.

Cody most often was flying a Kiowa rather than an Apache these days because scouting, not fighting, was 1-101's mission at TAA Campbell. Its sister battalion was the 2-229, commanded by Bill Bryan, a long time acquaintance in the helicopter community. He and Cody divided the clock, 1-101 patrolling the skies at night, 2-229 by day. The arrangement worked well despite inherent problems: 2-229 was not 'organic' to the 101st, they had joined the division from Ft. Rucker, Alabama, and did not wear the Screaming Eagle patch on their shoulder. They were attached to the 101st, somewhat as Second Brigade had been attached temporarily to 7th Corps at Hafer Al Batin. Garrett took pains to assuage any impression that 2-229 was a stepchild, and by January Bryan felt his boys were part of the family.

So was his 'girl.' By Congressional statute, women were not to serve below brigade level. Attack helicopter battalions were considered too combat oriented for females, but 2-229 had a flight surgeon who was so exceptional she was made an exception. Major Rhonda Cornum M.D. was known as 'Doctor Apache.' She had, in a sense, raised the original crews when the flying tank-killer was introduced in 1985, and she conducted the psychological testing to evaluate the cockpit environment. Cornum knew aviators the way they knew their ships. If Congress had tried to take her away, there would have been FLIR on the Capitol dome and Hellfires in the rotunda.

Like Bryan's Apaches above him, Greco had a ground version of FLIR for his patrols. It was called a thermal telescope, a sort of infrared searchlight that saw most of what action there was in the shadow war on the border. Vehicularly mounted, it lacked the mobile perspective of 2-229's FLIR, but it was the best eyes the infantrymen had.

At sand level, far off infrared images were amorphous. An Iraqi flashlight could be distinguished from a campfire, but a herd of camels resembled a motorized Iraqi patrol. The scope shot out a laser beam: the distance to the unknown heat source appeared on the screen.

Report it to the company commander; he reports to Greco who requests a Kiowa scout to investigate. TF Normandy had lived the night of the Apache. Now, as G Day approached, these were the days of the Kiowa.

Spec. Stu Suchland wondered if the war had really started: "We crammed ten soldiers fully loaded with ammo and anti-tank weapons into the back of HUMM-V's. It was a very tight fit. The weather was damned cold in the mornings, so we'd kid each other about how hot it was when we got here [at King Fahd in September].

"The HUMM-V's covered each other when we left the l-187 perimeter. One would stop in a firing position while the other went forward about a thousand meters, then he'd do the same thing. Everybody dismounted and zeroed in on the front when we stopped. The patrol would do this leapfrog right up to a long ridgeline that was probably the best physical border between us and Iraq.

"On top of the ridge were outpost buildings that Iraqi border guards used to use. We could see their soldiers out there, at most 3000 meters from the buildings. I guess they could see us too. My company called for close air support. A few minutes later six ships joined us. They made passes but didn't fire on the Iraqis. This went on all morning, and we sat there watching and eating lunch with the enemy in plain view. Eventually we loaded up the HUMM-V's and headed back for our perimeter.

"This incident got me confused about what war was supposed to be like. I never expected to sit still and watch the enemy eating their lunch! Especially when we had him so outgunned."

Peay's plan at this time was to thwart counter-reconnaissance—to prevent Iraqi scouts from learning what was going on in TAA Campbell or indeed that the 101st was there at all. To push the Iraqis off the border risked the capture of Screaming Eagles in combat, so Peay's policy was pretty much shoot only if fired upon. He was so successful that Iraqi intelligence believed that patrols like Suchland's were Syrians.

Suchland and Yancey were members of the same PTA in Tennessee. While the infantryman's war at TAA Campbell resembled sitzkrieg, for the trucker the same period was the most hectic of all.

Yancey: "We were hauling nonstop, around the clock, for the G Day build-up. Getting the troops up to the border was just the beginning. Everything they ate, drank, shot and put in their gas tanks had to be loaded, trucked, and unloaded. Suchland said he was getting bored? The truckers sure weren't. We were afraid there wouldn't be enough time to move up all this stuff.

"Then along comes February 14th. I'd forgotten this was Valentine's Day, but the folks back home sure hadn't. All of a sudden [instead of rations], the flat beds are hauling mail bags full of valentines! No one planned for this, but for morale I think it was a good idea getting those special messages to the troops before the war started."

The Screaming Eagles had already gotten a collective message from America; indeed had received it back in August, and it was now in their thoughts as they pondered the Iraqi horizon from the wind-swept desolation of TAA Campbell.

Most of the 101st's vehicles had been driven from Ft. Campbell to Jacksonville, FL to be loaded on ships for the Gulf. In the States, a military convoy is a monotonous sight, unnoticed by the public except when freeway traffic is slowed. But those convoys to Jacksonville became transformed—a spontaneous cavalcade of patriotism that still rolls on in the memories of those who drove and those who watched.

From state highway patrols, the people of Tennessee, Alabama and Georgia became aware of the convoys. The word also got around on the teamsters' CB band: the army wanted every flat bed truck in the Southeast at Ft. Campbell, and would pay for the empty return trip from Jacksonville—a bonanza for the truckers because usually there is no compensation for such a deadhead run. Profit was not the truckers' only motive in driving the 1800 mile round trip, often in twenty hours. Many of them were Vietnam vets. At least one had served with the 101st, and displayed a large Strike Force decal on his bumper. They were resolved to get the division's equipment to port and on time.

On the afternoon of August 15th, Chattanooga media began encouraging Tennesseans to come out to the interstate and show support for the passing soldiers. Hundreds of people did, most of them standing on the overpasses. When a radio station learned of this, they sent a news car with American flags to wave at the troops. During the hours the convoys went by, the crowd grew till the overpasses were jammed. The overflow moved to the embankments of the freeway, offering their hands for the troops to touch.

These scenes were shown on local TV that night, so the next day (a weekday) the crowd grew to thousands and the flags grew bigger. Several 6 x 8 footers were draped as banners from the overpasses, brushing the tops of army vans. Like flowers in a high wind, the freeway embankments seethed with red, white and blue—a scene picked up by national TV, and a further stimulus for the next day when the demonstration closed one lane of traffic.

That night a flag thirty-five feet long was unfurled. Next day, the highway patrol estimated the number of people at over 8,000 lined along miles of freeway. "The sun was hot and the sky was clear," said an observer, "but every time a convoy went through, there were so many flags raised that we all had shade."

Whether it was a howitzer or dumpster being transported, the people gave it an equal cheer. Often commercial flat beds carrying division equipment overtook a convoy; they too were cheered, and responded with blasts on their air horns.

The next night was Saturday. Ten thousand people turned out. Many were children whose parents wanted them to witness and remember this outpouring of love and emotion. For the troops, the normally humble and boring convoys would be one of the deepest memories of Desert Shield. They felt they had to react, to reciprocate the appreciation showered upon them. One serial slowed to 10 mph so that troops could slap high fives with the well-wishers. Soldiers and civilians seemed to be in a photographic fire fight, both sides snapping pictures of the other as fast as they could.

During the tumultuous evening, a charter bus returning aviators from Jacksonville pulled out of their convoy. The officer in charge apologized to the highway patrol and asked permission to thank the people packed onto an overpass. A policeman readily cleared a path for the bus. When the door opened and men in flight suits got out, the crowd rushed them. "They hugged the air out of us," an aviator remembered. "It didn't matter that we were sweaty and stunk, they hugged and kissed us like we were rock stars! I wish I'd been wearing my shades because I was crying."

Everyone had to have a picture taken with the aviators. Addresses were exchanged, then when the bus finally got under way again, the crowd began chanting, "USA! USA!"

For some battalions that experienced the exhilaration of the Jacksonville convoys, 'Chattanooga' became a rallying cry in the desert, a shorthand expression of encouragement when spirits were low, when there was occasion to grumble, "What the hell are we doing here?" The answer was, "Chattnooga, man." At TAA Campbell, an officer had a message for his soldiers on the eve of battle:

"In the days to come you will be tested to your limits, but you must go beyond them. With this in mind, the word I'd like to leave with you before we start is Chattanooga. Those people who stood by the highway are with you now. When you're too tired to think about anything else, think about them. Say it to your buddy. Chattanooga!"

A member of the crowd who had been on "convoy watch" the entire three days, wrote to Peay: "I know there will be some rough times ahead for your division, but you can rest assured that when you get back we will all be on the other side of the interstate, welcoming you as you pass again through Chattanooga."

At TAA Campbell, Screaming Eagles began to search for a route that would lead to that interstate, a route 500 years old.

February 1991

16: *Newsweek* features a map depicting the Hail Mary plan. Iraq does not react, probably because so many magazines were publishing speculation about how a ground war would look.

21: Through an exchange of personal envoys with Saddam, Gorbachev tries to arrange a ceasefire coupled with Iraq's unconditional withdrawal from Kuwait. Bush tentatively agrees if the withdrawal commences no later than noon, 23 February, and coalition forces move right in.

23: Saddam rebuffs the above terms.

XVI

Route of the Pilgrim

By any standard, 'Binnie' Peay is an eminently self-contained man; but as the floating date for G Day drew nearer, he had trouble containing himself because Cobra was still a template poised over a thousand maps, and would remain so until Schwarzkopf consented to reconnaissance deep into Iraq. What Peay needed to find would either confirm or contort the Desert Rendezvous plan. If the latter, time might be too short to effectively readjust, and certainly to rehearse, a new scheme of maneuver.

The worst case that eleventh hour reconnaissance could reveal would be no suitable LZ's within the area planned for Cobra. It was surface conditions that would make them unsuitable—loose sand, persistent dust, and the word most dreaded by the air assault division—brownout. Peay was warned of helicopters, their altimeters deceived by dust devils, crashing in the desert or into each other; helicopters on the ground, their fuel pumps fouled with fine sand, lifting off into a dense curtain impenetrable even by FLIR or NVG. Peay's flying flotilla, the largest ever launched, would have to turn back, stranding Pathfinders who had managed to land. Drawing nigh was the possibility of Desert Gallipoli or a reprise of Desert One. This was Peay's Gethsemane, an implosion of anguish with no pressure valve, nothing that he would allow to break out on the surface.

Weiss: "I guess his nightmares were about brownout. Gen. Peay felt a lot more than he showed. He cared as much for the soldiers as they did for each other, but in a different way. There's love between guys in the foxholes: they're like brothers. If you ask me, that's where you see the greatest heroism, when one soldier does something incredible for the guy beside him. But there's also something like a parent's love in the chain of command. I hope I have it. People said I looked worried all the time. I was. I was worried about lives.

"Gen. Peay felt that way double or triple. What I did wouldn't affect many lives, but what he did affected us all. Like the MOPP decision. He had to balance the risk of not going into MOPP against the efficiency we'd lose if we did. We'd seen those pictures of Kurds who'd been gassed. They looked like bodies floating in water, all bloated and their eyes open. You never know what's in a man's imagination, but I think Gen. Peay could see his Screaming Eagles twitching out on the desert like that.

"What I do know is how he tensed in briefings when the subject of casualties came up. It got pretty gruesome as G Day got closer. 'Contaminated bodies'—that's what I'll never forget. What do we do with casualties covered with gas like a powder or mixed with blood from their wounds? Do the surgeons have to operate in MOPP gear? Was that possible? Then the bodies. Bury 'em in the sand, or risk contaminating a chopper to get them back to the morgues? You didn't want to hear about details like that, but it was someone's job to consider them. Gen. Peay heard them out and thought them through.

"He could look around during those briefings and see young soldiers near the tent, smiling, moving around, doing their jobs with faith—living as if death wasn't in their future. Gen. Peay knew it was for some of them. I think for him it was like watching a son who had been diagnosed with incurable cancer but hadn't been told. Gen. Peay knew, and he felt it as deep as anything can go.

"He prayed—you can take my word for that. He keeps things like that way inside. You have to know him a long time before you see that they're there and powerful. We were all praying that we'd find a FARP site for Cobra, but he had more other things to pray for than any of us."

Prayers in the military mind are prioritized and logical. Until touchdown reconnaissance of the Cobra FARP site was permitted, other prayers would be offered.

They began to be answered from unexpected sources. Benevolent fallout from TF Normandy's raid provided more of a glimpse of Cobra than was otherwise available. For topographic information about any area in Iraq, the established army channels were from division through corps to ARCENT, the army component of CENTCOM. These levels did their best, but seven other divisions (not to mention three more in the marines, plus special forces) pressed their intelligence requirements with equal urgency. It was for the Air Force to get it.

Russ Stinger retained a back channel to the Air Force. "They owed us one," Cody noted, and had Stinger call his marker. On a first name basis with the strategic intelligence people at AFCENT, Stinger asked that they take a close look—really close—at the general area for Cobra. We'll do our best, they agreed, and this meant sliding a space satellite a bit for microscopic coverage, and perhaps fifteen minutes of photography. The photos, both visual and infrared, were the next best thing to hovering over the desert or landing some scouts to check out surface conditions.

Aviation Brigade knew what to look for in the satellite photos. From five months experience flying the desert, they'd learned that 'gray areas' meant either a rocky surface or a dry sabkha with hard caked mud on the surface. These conditions generated the least dust and loose sand when churned by descending rotors. Acres of such conditions, within the template for Cobra, had to found before G Day.

February was assuredly the month, but which day was as unknown and anticipated as a winning lottery number. So secret, so close held, was G Day that it was not transmitted by even the most secure electronic means. Twenty-four turned up to be the magic number: 24 February 1991, a day to be inscribed next to 29 July 1965 and 6 June 1944 in Screaming Eagle history. From Luck's lips, Peay learned the date two weeks before, and with it came authorization to commence helicopter reconnaissance of the division's AO in Iraq on 14 February, St. Valentine's Day.

February 11th, 12th and 13th were a shuffling series of meetings, consultations, and updates of plans. Besides the overriding importance of siting Cobra, the question of weather in the Euphrates Valley rose like one of the rain clouds predicted. Peay grew groggy, traveling and listening to one operational briefing after another from his brigades, in addition to comprehensive briefings at DMAIN. He cracked his knuckles during the weather forecasts, but seemed to nod off—took what his staff called 'long blinks'—whenever Hess became long winded. Peay revived for Huber's presentations on operations, but relapsed again when logistics were the subject. His logistics expert, Ron Adams, was the best in the business, so unless he raised a logistical problem, Peay gratefully left the field to him.

Adams' problems had been many and serious; but by G minus 10 some had been solved through the initiative and innovation of his subordinates. As there was an aviation community in the army, cutting across divisions and corps in a worldwide network of officers who knew each other and their respective specialties, so too was there a logistics community. Wherever there there was a problem, someone, somewhere had encountered it before or could refer to an experience he'd heard of.

A smaller scale logistical network thrived in the 101st. Faced with identical problems, the 'XO's' and logisticians attempted many improvisations from which Adams, overwatching the network, could pluck promising ideas. Almost all successes meant defying the book, or regulations applicable to peacetime and installed for safety considerations. Safety had not been discarded—it was a visceral subject for Peay—to accept the perils of war, but in order to establish and operate a unique gas station eighty miles deep in Iraq required a new perspective toward safety. 'Solve the problem,' became the new philosophy, 'then make the method safe as possible.'

The basic problem was too much stuff needed with too few

aircraft to lift it—despite the 101st's unprecedented aviation assets. Adams himself was an aviator, thus holding cross membership in two army communities. He realized that the solution was either to lift more with the same number of helicopters or make more round trips between TAA Campbell and Cobra. Despite heroic efforts and economies, the latter option turned out to be a non-starter. Tom Hill was adamant that there were too many troops and too much essential equipment needed in Cobra right away that none could be moved back to later lifts, which anyway were scheduled to turn around as fast as they could be refueled. Moreover, Garrett had already scheduled his choppers to fly at maximum speed for the loads they were to carry.

The answer, then, had to be in the loads. Could they be made lighter, or could the choppers perhaps carry more than they were rated for? But the slack already had been drawn tight on the lightening option. Hill said his brigade would all piss before they embarked, but he wouldn't let them leave with one less round of ammunition.

He agreed to shave safety by removing the seats from troop-carrying Black Hawks. This was a serious decision: in a crash, seats and their belts would save lives, but without them one more soldier could cram into a Black Hawk. That meant a couple more platoons to defend Cobra on the first lift alone.

Any significant weight savings would have to be in the Chinooks, the moving vans of air assault. Artillery, heavy engineering equipment, and of utmost importance, the gas containers to support Third Brigade's leap to the Euphrates, all had to be carried in pendant slings called external loads—towed, as it were, through the air.

With G Day approaching, the Chinooks were loaded, unloaded, reloaded and reconfigured permutedly, but to no avail. In fact, test landings proved to be a setback for the load planners. Setting down anywhere else in the world, the pilot could find height references on the ground; but over flat desert in brownout there were none, so he had to rely on his altimeter. However, the altimeter was blocked if he were descending with the typical external load of a howitzer and HUMM-V. Thus, on top of the vertigo of brownout, his instrument was useless to tell how close he was to the ground. Safety could be stretched but not defied, so the result was a load carrying capacity about half of that expected from a Chinook.

Adams: "We couldn't live with that. We had to look inside and outside the Chinook like detectives. There had to be a clue somewhere that could give us a lead. Damned if I knew what it was, but it just had to be there. You develop an instinct for things like that, a feeling that there is an answer if we look long and hard enough.

"I didn't expect to find it, but had faith in the dirty knuckles guys who were constantly out there with the ships and loads. It was sort of a challenge match for them. Come up with something that'll work, and be a hero. Cobra was going to happen, one way or another—a light was going to turn on in someone's head as it had with Tim Devito."

Warrant Officer Wally Fox was a standardization pilot with 7-101, the Chinook battalion. 'SP's' principal duties focused on safety, ensuring that Chinook pilots followed the same procedures so that there was no confusion in the air. Now Fox had to undo procedures, alter and reshape the way things had been done for years, in order to squeeze in the loads needed for Cobra. He made himself miniature scale models of a howitzer and its prime mover HUMM-V. In a nervous outlet like whittling, Fox fiddled with his models, mating them in combinations as varied as the Kama Sutra.

In an idle moment, moving the models without looking at them, he felt his hands close. The models had come together side by side, a wheel of the howitzer nestled between those of the HUMM-V. The package was twice as wide but half the normal length. Fox put it down, stood up and stared at what his subconscious had produced. Craning his head to where a Chinook's altimeter would be, he could see it would have a clear sensing of the ground.

He pushed back his cap. Flight manuals, regulations and loading tables spun through his mind like a slot machine, all coming up lemons. This was bizarre—something had to be basically wrong with slinging a howitzer and HUMM-V side by side. They'd slip apart, or something obvious like that.

Frank Wilmoth was commander of the 101st's Chinooks (7-101). With so much at stake, he let Fox experiment.

A howitzer and a HUMM-V—old ones that could be best spared if there was disaster—were lashed together as Fox directed in a jury rigged sling. A Chinook came in to hover. The dust centrifuge blasted the men on the ground as expected, but they battled through it to snap the novel load to the hanging tether. The pilot studied his altimeter. It was registering actual height. The tether grew taut; the sling compressed, clamping the howitzer to its HUMM-V with a scraping sound, but only for a moment. The load lifted off the ground. The dust subsided as the Chinook made a cautious circle over the desert.

The external load held stable while the observers held their breaths. Now the acid test. The Chinook began a tentative approach. It paused at the height of the tether. The pilot could read his altitude. Wrapped in the sling, the howitzer and HUMM-V settled in the billowing dust, then stood embraced and defiantly on the sand. Fox looked at Wilmoth. Wilmoth looked at the departing Chinook, its load apparently undamaged on the ground.

"We need some pictures," he smiled. "They're not going to believe this back at Ft. Eustis."

Adams was able to scratch off a major problem from his list of impossibilities. There was one more for his Chinooks. HUMM-V's, the only vehicle that provided ground mobility for Cobra, and the prime mover for mounted TOW's as well as howitzers, were designed to be external loads slung under Chinooks. If the book were ignored, one could be stowed inside, thereby increasing the chopper's speed and reducing its gas consumption. High on Adams' wish list was a way to put two HUMM-V's inside a Chinook.

The internal space and tolerances were tantalizingly close to enough. Wilmoth's loading specialists backed in HUMM-V's, drove them in forward, backed one, drove the other forward— but all with the same result—they didn't quite fit, even with the Chinook's seats removed for a few extra lateral inches. No more room had been designed because the book said not even one HUMM-V should be carried internally.

Yet with four more inches of clearance, Wilmoth could have

245

two HUMM-V's inside his Chinooks. Through trial, error and by stripping door handles from the vehicles, three of those inches materialized.

As Fox had made the howitzer-HUMM-V lashup his personal Rubik's cube, Staff Sergeant Pelletier of 7-101 felt his to be the two-HUMM-V internal load. His inspiration came from a driver's complaint:

"Hey, Sarge, how am I gonna' get my door open without a handle?"

Obviously he couldn't, and that turned the light on for Pelletier. With no handles, what good were the doors? They came off, and Wilmoth had his last inch.

Tolerances were paper thin, and the drivers wore headsets loaned from the Chinook crew in order to be guided up the ramp. Maneuvering the vehicles was a twenty minute ordeal of minute adjustments; but then the ramp closed and the chopper took off with weight nicely balanced, and higher speed from the absent drag of an external load.

The solution seemed to be at hand, but yet incomplete: inside the Chinook, space was so tight there was no room for the HUMM-V's' drivers. When the ramp went down at Cobra, they couldn't get in their seats to drive the vehicles away. Pulling them out would take winches and additional vehicles which themselves required unavailable space and weight.

The only way a two-HUMM-V internal load would work was if the drivers remained in their vehicles during the flight, absolutely a no-no acccording to regulations, and for good reason because in a crash the drivers would be trapped behind their steering wheels. It was a call Wilmoth had to pass to Adams and finally to Peay, the buck's last stop.

Peay: "I didn't have the history of the 101st with me in the desert, but I remembered the 327th [today's First Brigade] were pretty much trapped in their gliders when they went into Normandy and Holland. I was asking the HUMM-V drivers to do the same—accept the fate of their aircraft without a chance of escaping it."

Many drivers were artillerymen. Rumor had it that the artillery would have to stay at TAA Campbell if the dangerous Chinook rig didn't work, so Cobra would have to rely solely on Apaches and Air Force support. Lt. Phil Jones explained the situation to the HUMM-V drivers in his battery. Their sentiment was that they'd worked so damn hard getting their vehicles into the Chinooks, they had to see if they could get them out at Cobra.

So courage to ride in a death trap was amply available. What was still needed was another step of logistical ingenuity to fill the gas station. The first of the fuel supply had to come in right behind the infantry with the initial flight of Chinooks. There were two standard fuel containers, both rubber, required for a FARP. The largest were 10,000-gallon 'gas bags' with attachments for pumps and hoses. They would be filled from 500 gallon bags called 'blivets.' Normally the gas bags were collapsed like accordions and sling-loaded under Chinooks.

Wilmoth: "That's the safe way to set up a FARP: unhook the gas bags, roll 'em out, bring in blivets and drain them into the gas bags, then open the station for business.

"That wasn't going to get the job done at Cobra. We had to have the gas bags pumping fuel into choppers within the first hour. Transferring fuel from the blivets took too long."

Blivets could be flown in almost full of gas, but not until the planning for Desert Rendezvous had anyone attempted to fly with a loaded gas bag. Filled with fuel, it lay on the ground like a pillow for Atlas. Wilmoth pumped 1500 gallons into one, then had a sling manhandled around the bag, curling its shortest edges. As gas sloshed into the center, the pillow took a globular shape about half the size of the Chinook from which it was slung. Arms went up—the signal to lift. Like a giant wrecking ball, the gas bag rose in the dust. Quickly the Chinook opened throttle so that air speed would overcome oscillation of the ball.

"We called it the red fireball express." Wilmoth recalled. "We did it because there was no other way, and I don't think it will be repeated in peacetime."

Though Wilmoth's Chinooks did their best and beyond, the logisticians' calculations still revealed decisive shortfalls. It was for Adams to see that despite all efforts, First Brigade could not get from here to there with enough gas for Third Brigade's returning Black Hawks. The air assault division could not do it all from the air.

Garrett: "The load carrying ships were maxed out beyond their ratings. It looked like there'd have to be a trade off between infantry and fuel, between tactics and logistics, but neither could give up any more space or weight. We had to start looking at a land lock spanning eighty miles of mean terrain in Iraq—the unexplored desert between TAA Campbell and Cobra."

Lt. Col. Jim McGarity, First Brigade's XO, had already taken a look—albeit only through his boyhood memories. He had lived in the Middle East when his father was a Turkish specialist in the US Army. While in Ankara, young McGarity had read of a 14th century Moslem explorer, Ibn Batuta, sometimes known as the Marco Polo of Islam, who had crisscrossed the antique world, and had the distinction of first noting the name Hindu Kush for the mountain range between Afghanistan and India that he traversed en route through the Mongol empire. Eventually twenty-eight years of travel took him as far as Java, Spain and even Timbuktu.

After his first pilgrimage to Mecca, Ibn Batuta decided to proceed to Baghdad though the blank on his map that was the Arabian desert. The great explorer named the route he discovered *Dub al Haj*—route of the pilgrim. An encyclopedia informed McGarity that the route had passed through Rafha, a town close by TAA Campbell, and wound north toward the ancient Mesopotamian city of Ur near the present day Iraqi air base of Tallil, a probable objective for Second Brigade. On McGarity's map, a faint and nameless trail with approximately the same orientation led out of TAA Campbell. He sent an Arabic linguist to visit a bedouin camp.

"Ask 'em if there's a name for that trail," McGarity ordered, "I think it may run right by Cobra."

The linguist visited one camp, obtained an answer, then asked at a second camp for confirmation. When he returned, McGarity was busy in the TOC tent, so the linguist waited, chatting with the staff. As soon as McGarity saw him he gestured for the linguist to come over.

"They got a name for it?"

"Yes, sir. A real old name. No one knew how old."

"What is it?"

"They call the trail, *Dub al Haj.* That means..."

"I know! I know!"

McGarity would have designated the trail MSR Batuta, but when he sketched the prospects of convoys to Cobra, Hill realized this would be a hard sell to Peay. Instead, the proposal was presented as MSR New Market, a 'land lock,' an umblical chord on the ground between TAA Campbell and Cobra. New Market is a town in the Shenandoah Valley where cadets of Virginia Military Institute (VMI) had valiantly held off the Yankees. Peay was a VMI graduate, and Hill a good salesman.

He needed to be, because a forgotten route of pilgrims was no main supply route for the most up-to-date army force in history; the through convoys would be motorized, not tracked, containing not only HUMM-V's that did well in loose sand, but also huge tankers without four-wheel drive. There would be several bulldozers to pull them out of sand traps and plow through escarpments, but the engineers estimated that as many as thirty percent of the HEMIT's, with their precious aviation fuel, could become stuck and might have to be abandoned.

But Hill had the most telling argument; namely, what other choice was there? Only if *Dub al Haj* was negotiable by wheeled vehicles, could a sufficient backup of fuel reach Cobra in case bad weather delayed Third Brigade's leap to the Euphrates. Roaring over the desert nonstop on G Day, the first convoy could be greeted by Hill late that night. What's more, many Chinooks would thereby be freed to haul ammunition in case he had to fight for Cobra. MSR New Market was the answer to many questions, even if it replaced them with one second in importance only to the site of the FARP. G minus 7 reconnaissance therefore focused on the two overriding questions: could gas tankers drive up *Dub al Haj,* and where could Hill put the gas station? The answers were for Aviation Brigade to obtain.

Garrett's pilots were intent to find out. At last they had permission. On G minus 7 they burst into Iraq like flocks of migratory birds following spring. They could not simply fly to the critical terrain, set down, and take notes; a deception plan had to hide their true interests. Therefore, 1-101 and 2-229 flew about three deception missions for every one that sought vital intelligence.

The Kiowas and Apaches sprayed into the AO, Cody and Bryan still respectively specializing in night and daylight reconnaissance. They went out in waves, each dashing farther over the Iraqi desert, reaching phase lines, returning with their videos, then the next wave moving closer toward Cobra. Usually, Kiowas and Apaches went together, the former protected by the latter.

At midnight of G minus 7 (February 17th), a pair of Gabram's Apaches took off for the first eyeball look at what was hoped to be MSR New Market. FLIR, which had been the eyes of TF Normandy, was of little use that night for rediscovering the filaments of *Dub al Haj* because they showed no heat contrast from the sand through which they meandered. However, there was a quarter moon, so NVG became the Apaches' telescope.

On the map, a twist of the trail indicated an escarpment, a crumbly ridge of sand that if guarded by Iraqis would stop McGarity's task force twenty miles en route to Cobra. He had named his expedition TF Citadel in honor of his university, and at the expense of the battalion XO's under his temporary command, three of whom were West Pointers.

"They didn't seem to mind," said McGarity. "There was a lot of doubt about the land tail [convoys], so those guys weren't anxious to have the name associated with their alma mater. Based on the first look at the route, it seemed they were probably right."

What pilots reported was movement and flashlights where the trail crested the escarpment. Somebody was out there, and they weren't pilgrims.

Next morning, 2-229 continued the investigation. Beginning in wide circles, two Apaches zoomed in their sights all around the trail crest, suspicious of a triple A ambush. They circled closer and tighter as their caution eased. At a hundred feet of altitude, they began to make out a few dark spots in knolls. Didn't look like much but maybe these could be entrances of some sort. Probably only target practice, but why not put a Hellfire into one?

Constraints, crosshairs on, laser return —fzzz —TOF zero— the missile enters something the size of a manhole. A knoll bulges and heaves up its earth.

Nearby, figures spurt like ants to the surface. The co-pilot switches to his chain gun, but just in time the figures throw down their weapons. The wingman circles down. These guys, ten of them, want to surrender. The two Apaches discuss what the hell to do. Bryan never briefed them about anything like this. How does an Apache take prisoners?

The radio sizzles with DMAIN. There's some confusion, as many organizations want to get in on the first real action of the war. Meanwhile, the two Apaches are to orbit and keep the Iraqis covered.

Roger, roger, the amused and bemused aviators reply—but we're not AWAC's with hours of fuel.

Garrett prevails: Aviation Brigade, rather than the infantry, should complete the capture. Pathfinders, normally used to open LZ's, are a platoon of very versatile men and immediately available for the job. They leaped into two 2-17 Cav Black Hawks and flew off to the initial skirmish of the ground war for the division. DMAIN was abuzz—the first of the bad guys were about to come out with their hands up. Except for the veterans of Vietnam and TF Normandy, 17,000 Screaming Eagles considered themselves cherries. Seeing the enemy would change that somewhat. A crowd of soldiers who had no business being there began to gather at the pathfinders' landing pad.

Lippard: "The ten EPW's came in just outside our perimeter. They were loaded into one of the double decker buses we'd been using to move our troops around. The MP's were in charge, and sort of acted like stars of the show. A lot of spectators were snapping pictures as if Elvis had just got off that Black Hawk.

"The interrogation was done in the EPW cage at D-Rear. The atmosphere was like an ARTEP [a peacetime test of a unit's proficiency, a make or break test by which the unit was judged]. I think the Iraqis were the calmest people in the cage.

"They were all border guards, commanded by a captain who'd learned English in Cairo. One was an NCO and the other eight privates. They were healthy, clean, wore serviceable uniforms, and well fed. Their only big complaint was no communication with battalion headquarters. They'd just been stuck out on that escarpment and told to watch it, and if anything happened to send a vehicle back to As Salman, sixty miles north.

"The last time they sent a courier was to get their pay. They hadn't been paid for two months. The courier never came back, so they didn't have any wheels. The interrogator asked why they wanted money way out in the middle of nowhere, and they said that was how they got resupplied—by buying food and wine and anything else they needed, including homosex. Bedouins would come by now and then with stuff for sale or barter. The border guards had swapped AK-47's for older rifles. Didn't matter to them—they weren't planning to fight anyone.

"Our interrogators expected to draw information out, but these border guards were real talkative and cooperative, like they'd figured out the international situation and realized Saddam was a bad bet. They only felt bad about their buddies in that bunker that got Hellfired. Those guys would have surrendered too.

"They knew a lot about their chain of command—where the important officers were, where to look for triple A, just about everything we wanted to know. The interrogatars cautioned that these were border guards, not regular soldiers, but we got the feeling that the Iraqis might just be overrated."

XVII

Where is the prince?

Peay was tempted to take a look at the first EPW's himself. In Vietnam they had been vital indications of the battle to come. Guerrillas, hard core Viet Cong, or North Vietnamese Army? What they were showed the way to fight them. How much food and ammunition did they carry; how was their health? Were they dejected or defiant? In Vietnam, EPW's in tiptop condition like these first ones would have aroused much apprehension.

The action on the escarpment was not over so Peay waited to see if some regular soldiers, not just border guards, might yet be captured. The Pathfinders became a small air-ground task force with 2-229's Apaches. Before long they uncovered more Iraqis, blasting them from their bunkers. Something significant seemed to be developing, so an infantry platoon from Second Brigade—already on alert in case there were downed choppers—joined the aviators. The platoon bagged 31 more prisoners, all grateful to surrender, and flew them directly to the EPW cage for interrogation. These were regulars, the kind Peay was looking for.

Even as the skirmish continued, flushing out an Iraqi truck that Apaches destroyed, it was reported to the world in a televised CENTCOM press briefing, also broadcast by Armed Forces Radio Network heard by the very troops involved. This was the ultimate real time coverage which amazed Lippard as much for its distorted content as currency. The CENTCOM briefer, a brigadier general who became familiar to stateside viewers, announced with a straight face that Apaches had "herded" scores of prisoners over the border into captivity! Lippard was not aware that the 101st was a party to this deception: Schwarzkopf had permitted aerial reconnaissance but no U.S. infantry in Iraq. Not wishing to indicate how his order had been bent, the Screaming Eagles, with tongue in cheek, fed CENTCOM the "herding" story.

When informed that the new EPW's were from the 45th Division, Peay rushed down for a look. Their impression molded all his decisions thereafter:

"It was what I didn't see that was very telling. These troops, in well prepared positions and adequately supplied, didn't show a will to fight. They were up against a frightening force, having never been hit by helicopters before, but they quit at the first opportunity.*

"That fact led to a hunch which strengthened during the rest of the war—that if we exploited surprise and shock, the Iraqis might fold faster than anyone expected.

"This wasn't the NVA in front of us. They'd plant a company on a trail and tell them to die in place so the rest of their regiment could get away. And that company would fight to the last man. We'd have had to kill them all.

"The Iraqis, you could say, were more sophisticated than the North Vietnamese. One of the EPW's said he owed more to Iraq than to Saddam. He knew the score, and could see this war might be a blowout. Gen. Powell said something about how Saddam had pulled on Superman's cape. These EPW's seemed to have learned that."

Peay's staff noticed how his shoulders, constricted by the tensions of preparation, began to rise out of a stoop. Lt. Col. Riccardelli, commander of the 311th Military Intelligence Battalion, interpreted the general's new carriage with personal satisfaction. It had been his interrogators who had translated the EPW's sentiments that Peay found so encouraging. For Riccardelli, this was the payoff for frustrating months of imaginative but futile efforts to provide the intelligence needed to

---

* Before meeting the 101st, these troops' combat experience had been in quelling Kurdish insurgencies. Quite possibly, they participated in a Babi Yar, the massacre and mass burial of a thousand captive Kurds near As Samawah.

transform Desert Rendezvous from a speculative to an informed plan.

His best Arabic linguists had been pulled out of Kentucky in early August to provide translators for corps. Not until G minus 7 did he get them back. All during Desert Shield he'd been embarrassed for providing little more than a rehash of intelligence passed down from higher headquarters. His battalion (with the highest educational level in the division) contained enormous analytical and interpretive talents, but they had lain fallow without the basic seeds of information. His electronic specialists had heard only hissing static while the 101st was corps covering force. The 311th's interrogators could do no more than practice on each other. Their photo interpreters had but outdated photos passed down by the Air Force. Riccardelli felt himself to be Peay's official portraitist of the enemy, but despite a full palette of colors and poised brushes, there was no picture to paint for want of an image.

Riccardelli had sublimated his frustration into physical exertion. An ambitious triathlete (swimming, running, cycling), he brought a racing bike to the Gulf, and though sand clogged gears and chain, he'd averaged some 25 miles per day training in the desert.

"There was plenty of time and space for running too. My swim stroke decayed to nothing, but by G minus 7 I was really in shape for a biathlon."

After that, Riccardelli's athletics suffered but there was compensating pleasure when scores, then hundreds of EPW's resulted from G minus 7, 6 and 5 reconnaissance raids. The last component of his battalion's skills engaged on the morning of G minus 4 when Kiowas came upon a bunker complex called Toad because it squatted midway up MSR New Market.

The 'toad in the road' was a most disturbing discovery. Several wells near a sharp bend in the *Dub al Haj* were shown on maps; McGarity's bedouin allies reported that the wells were a water source and resting place for pilgrims. Consequently, Toad was a natural outpost, probably a defensive position, for the 45th Division. 1-101 took a close look at it on the night of G minus 6. FLIR film came back with some new and troubling images—camouflaged buildings and vehicles.

A detailed daylight recon by 2-229 reported infantry dug-outs, then Kiowas from 2-17 Cav diagramed a bunker complex estimated to hold about a hundred troops. This information was correlated with some Air Force warnings of triple A in the vicinity. As a major obstacle on MSR New Market, Toad would have to be speared—but without a ground attack. Those were still the rules—no infantry formations to enter Iraq prior to G Day.

Peay permitted Garrett to attack Toad on G minus 3, reasoning that even if the Iraqis deduced the significance of MSR New Market, it would be too late for them to react effectively. Garrett decided to give the mission to 3-101, his Cobra battalion. Cobras were Vietnam era gunships, relics in a 'technological warp.' Compared to Apaches, Cobras were Sherman tanks beside state of the art Abrams. Nonetheless, 3-101's crews were as high speed and low drag as Cody's: they just drove jalopies instead of Corvettes. And 3-101, commanded by Mark Curran, had a vital security mission on G Day, so before then Garrett wanted to give them some playing time. Toad would be Curran's show, with Bryan's Apaches on standby in case there was more in and around the bunkers than had met the eye.

What Curran hoped to see, and soon, were a lot of white flags on the ground. The rules already had been stretched enough so that there was precedence to send Pathfinders into Iraq for the purpose of receiving surrenders and backhauling EPW's. But if the Iraqis put up a real fight, Peay could find himself red-faced in a dilemma: either accept the presence of Toad—a stronghold alerted by 3-101's attack—squarely blocking his MSR, or be in flagrant violation of the 'no infantry in Iraq' rule. It was for Aviation Brigade to obviate his embarrassment, but for the worst case an infantry battalion from Third Brigade stood ready at pickup zones (PZ's) to join the attack.

As the sun rose on G minus 3, so too did Aviation Brigade's Tac CP, a Black Hawk crammed with radios, generators, map boards and key people, who could set down almost anywhere and control a battle fifty miles away. This morning the Tac CP perched atop the high ridge that marked the international border. Flying there in his C&C ship, Garrett arrived in time to witness a flight from the past: Cobras, noses down and full throttle, heading north to do battle for Toad.

Whatever else they lacked as an army, the Iraqis' skill in cover and concealment was admirable. Curran's Cobras approached an escarpment, seeing little sign of defensive positions. Provocative dives drew no reaction, nor did strafing of suspicious terrain. Kiowas from previous recons pointed out hard-to-find bunkers; 3-101 attacked them with rockets, TOW's (substitutes for Hellfires), and 20 mm cannons. This fire moved a lot of sand, revealing a complex quite larger than suspected. A mortar was exposed, and a triple A gun. Their crews must have either vacated or excavated. Then a TOW set off a huge secondary explosion. If the Iraqis had left, they'd left everything behind.

But Curran was convinced they were still around, just deep underground. He felt like a boxer slugging an opponent on the ropes and at will, yet he still wouldn't go down. The morning wore on, and Curran began to worry that Toad might be saved by the bell. Toad was today's target; more helicopter missions were scheduled for the night and following days right up to H hour of G Day. He summoned Air Force A-10's with bombs and big rockets. Toad began to mushroom with deep-digging explosions. Curran now had his own dilemma: he had to scare these moles enough to force their surrender but not scare them so much that they burrowed deeper in their holes. He cursed as his Cobras expended all their ordnance. The A-10's had already departed, and now 3-101 would have to go as well. They swung wide into a departing orbit.

Apparently the Iraqis saw this as victory: the attackers were leaving, leaving the field to the defenders. They dribbled some fire into the sky, a parting gesture of defiance—and fatal folly. Now Curran, and soon Garrett, knew Toad was occupied and dangerous. 2-229 roared up from TAA Campbell to relieve 3-101 like a tag team. Bryan's Apaches beat up on Toad without resistance, but with no signs of surrender either.

Garrett: "Now and then a face would look out of an opening during lulls in the attack, but that was it. It was getting into the afternoon, and I was frustrated because we could run out of daylight. If division wanted Toad, they'd have to put in the infantry battalion. That's what I recommended on the radio but the word came back, 'negative—no troops on the ground until there were signs of surrender.'

"A second air strike only made the Toads hunker down some more. Then Division radioed that Riccardelli was running off some surrender leaflets, and a loudspeaker team would show up at my Tac CP shortly. They were to get out to Toad and convince the Iraqis to give up."

Riccardelli had been following the action on the radio. Anticipating such encounters, he printed leaflets for Iraqis to read while under bombardment. Psychological warfare had already been employed during the air campaign. Riccardelli did not know how Iraqi reaction was gauged, but evidently the most effective leaflets preyed on the sense of defenselessness on the ground and omniscience in the air; e.g., after B-52 strikes—the most obliterating attack short of nukes—thousands of leaflets fluttered down addressed specifically to the unit which had been bombed. The messages were like, "How did you like that, Hamurabi Division? If you have comrades in 3rd Regiment, assure the families their men were immediately buried." [Islam requires that corpses be buried before nightfall on the day of death.] "We'll be back for 2nd Regiment on Tuesday at 2:00 p.m.." And they were, with another earth opening B-52 strike.

Such leaflets were extremely demoralizing, but of no use to Iraqis because there were no allied troops nearby to accept their surrender. But now, on a small but significant scale, Riccardelli saw opportunity for his psychological operations (PSYOP) people. He would use a multi-media campaign to bring out the defenders of Toad.

Garrett: "That PSYOP effort was a case of rushing in where angels fear to tread. This Black Hawk shows up at my Tac CP with the loudspeaker [plus an Arabic linguist] and leaflet guys. I open the pilot's door and brief him on frequencies and call signs, then tell him to fly up and report to the Apache commander on station. I verified the coordinates where the Black Hawk was going, and told him to just look for the oribitting Apaches. There'd probably be plenty of fireworks going off too, so he couldn't miss Toad—it was the only show in the county.

"He blasted off, and I had this funny feeling. The attack

helicopters had been operating in Iraq for several days, but this young warrant had never seen Indian country. Here I'd just sent him, single ship, on his first mission. I felt something was going to go wrong.

"So I cranked up my Black Hawk and took off after him. By the time I reached Toad, he'd found it all right—flown low and slow right over the bunkers, dropping leaflets. The Apaches were holding their breaths. I think they were too amazed to tell him to get back up in the sky. Then I see him land right where the bunkers are thickest! I knew my premonition was about to come true—I'd just sent a plane load of fellow soldiers to their deaths.

"It was too late to call them off. I watched the loudspeaker team dismount and make their pitch. Apaches hovered over them menacingly, but this was still a very gutsy thing. And it seemed to be working! Some Iraqis rushed out of their holes like ground squirrels, grabbed leaflets, and ducked right back in. Pretty soon they're up again waving undershirts."

With white flags the vital sign DMAIN had been waiting for, no time was lost providing the infantry company Garrett had requested. Their arrival brought out the first fifty surrenderees. A thousand eyes watched from hiding as their comrades stumbled down the hill, then grouped with hands on head. A Black Hawk landed, provided them water, and this gesture lured out more Iraqis.

But there was a hard core who were going to fight, raising for the first time a question, as dangerous as it was ambiguous, that was to become the great dilemma of the ground war, especially at its climax—what to do when part of an enemy force waves white flags while the rest continue to resist? At Toad that day the Screaming Eagles kept shooting till there was no return fire. Iraqis who tried to surrender just had to wait for their belligerent comrades to join them or die.

Throughout the afternoon, 1-187 won over the defenders of Toad whom the PSYOP people couldn't convince. It was gritty, sweaty, basic infantry work: shoot and rush, cover me then I'll cover you, and talk a lot to the Apaches who cover everybody and respond to gun flashes from diehard Iraqis. They were a paradox for a platoon leader from 1-187 to whom they eventually surrendered:

"They had good fighting positions. I went back over the hill before we pulled out, and it looked like they were set up for interlocking fire and mutual support, a really professional defense. They used it too, and our guys were sucking sand.

"The Iraqis fired plenty, but it was high—like they didn't want to stay up long enough to aim and see where their rounds were hitting. One bunker would shoot, and we'd be pinned down, but another bunker wouldn't take up the fire when the Apaches hit the first one.

"It was like they were making a statement: 'We resent you Americans being in Iraq, but it's not worth getting killed trying to stop you.'"

Riccardelli sat in on their interrogation at DMAIN: "That second group was surly. They cursed us—and Arabic curses are long and eloquent—but they seemed most pissed at their officers who were living good somewhere way in the rear, and angry to a lesser degree, at the guys who had given up without a fight."

More than four hundred EPW's were flown out of Toad, nearly a battalion, including their commander and nine other officers. The enemy's best blocking position on MSR New Market now appeared to be removed, but the very presence of so many enemy astride what was thought to be a forgotten trail in the desert was disquieting. If so many unsuspected Iraqis had been discovered in the reconnaissance to date, what surprises might be in store at Cobra which had only been inspected from the air?

And it seemed the closer aerial reconnaissance drew to Cobra, the more Iraqis there were around it. EPW's indicated triple A between Toad and Cobra. This was verified by cav Kiowas scouting north of Toad. As morning fog broke up over the desert, a flash burst on the ground. This was not an immediate alarm for the pilot: the Air Force had continued their campaign overhead, streaking across the 101st's AO at high altitudes, sometimes jettisoning fuel tanks and occasionally bombs they didn't want to take home. Unidentified flashes on the desert happened every day.

But this flash became a glow, the unmistakable signature of a SAM igniting its propellant. The burn extinguished, but the long, slender missile turned toward the Kiowa. He went to ground like a falling stone. His partner sheared off in the opposite direction, both pulling high inertia turns as the SA-8 missile bisected the air between them, missing by 50 meters.

"Up till then," said the pilot, "we felt we owned the sky. That SAM was a reality check. The opposition had a lot of ordnance down there, and they must have at least a few guys willing to fire it."

The close call was as sobering for aviators as a torpedo attack is for sailors—one hit kills many men—but Peay was feeling relief, and rather than steeling his division for grim work ahead, he encouraged a surge of confidence based upon the preliminary exploration of MSR New Market.

"It was all coming together. The plan was looking better all the time, and the enemy didn't seem able or resolved to interfere. I felt that to a very important extent I'd already done my job. Things were in place. People knew what they had to do, and I had every confidence they'd do it. I just had to call the right plays, and they'd execute."

Peay could see roles and personalities meshing even while grating. By G minus 7, perhaps the central figure was Joe Bolt, Peay's chief of staff. During Desert Shield the division had been scattered by the covering force mission and the training cycle through the FOB's where Shelton usually hung out. Adams was in constant transit between King Fahd and the ports, while Peay moved about the division's many far-flung locations.

Thus during Desert Shield the center of the command centrifuge was division headquarters at King Fahd where Bolt had become the pivotal, permanent fixture; and now, because of the three generals' frequent absences, he was also the authority figure. The brigade commanders had not entirely adapted to that new relationship; they were better accustomed to dealing directly with the generals. But Bolt, the oldest colonel with the widest expertise, kept them on their toes and sometmes their teeth on edge. His encyclopedic familiarity with how the division worked, from finances to fuel to funerals, was rarely matched by even Adams or Shelton, and caused lower ranks to feel as if they were surveilled by a full-time inspector general. Hill's formidable seniority and experience required Bolt's deference, but the other brigade commanders had to catch javelins when they were targets of his attention.

Said one of them, "When you thought you were doing fine, Joe could explain how you weren't. Looking back, he was right 95 percent of the time, but that fact didn't show he was empathizing with your problems. That wasn't his job. He did it awfully well, but with everyone busting their butts already, he wasn't any help in finding you more time or resources to do better. Actually he was dunning stuff from corps all the time, but that wasn't something we knew much about. What we knew was that sparks could fly in a meeting with Joe, and you rarely left without getting singed."

Now with Desert Storm underway the entire division was coiled for 44 days in TAA Campbell, which for all its territory did not seem big enough for eight colonels. "Snow White and the seven dwarfs," one of them put it. In these close quarters, Bolt, the perfectionist, poked his antenna everywhere he did not put pressure. Peay was quite aware how his chief of staff could set people on edge, especially in the personnel and logistics sections whose work would climax before G Day. Bolt was a lightning rod, but even more important was his valence with Peay:

"Joe and I could glance at each other, or pass a word on the radio, and understand each other's intent. That's a priceless relationship. He wasn't making life easier for most people, but being a Screaming Eagle at any rank isn't easy. You have to work harder, stand taller, and do better. Joe was great at bringing that out. He had a tough love for his fellow Screaming Eagles, but a greater love for the division's reputation and history."

Standards again. The 101st Air Assault Division was up to their crew- cuts with them. Standards are not self-justified, but enablements for an extrinsic purpose. The purpose here was war fighting, and 17,000 soldiers waited, many sceptically, to see the relevance of the exalted standards so long imposed upon them.

Peay had little doubt that they would. To his ear the division at TAA Campbell was humming, a well tuned high reving engine waiting to move into gear and thunder north. A photo hangs beside his desk at the Pentagon. At the door of a Black Hawk, Schwarzkopf is gesticulating as if to emphasize a most serious point. Bareheaded, Peay listens with an incongruous grin.

"We were still ARCENT covering force. Gen. Schwarzkopf's message to me at that time was make sure your people can cut it. The time for mentoring is over. We'll be going over to attack early next year. Get the right people where they belong.

"I'm smiling because I've got all the right people. I got the best, and it was a pleasure to reassure him about the 101st."

Looking down the pyramid of his division, Peay saw no cause for misgivings or even second thoughts. Looking at the divisions on his flanks, he was confident they would not leave him exposed on the Euphrates. The French were an unknown quantity, but were followed and supported by the redoubtable 82nd Airborne; moreover, Iraqi forces in this far western corner of the theater were so scant their hands would be full if not in the air. On Peay's right was the most formidable mechanized division in the kingdom, Barry McCaffrey's 24th Mech, replete with the best tanks in the world, and spoiling to fight. Despite their grandiloquent names, no Republican Guards divisions were going to get through him; indeed, they would have all they could do to get away from McCaffrey who had been Peay's principal ally in pushing corps for a hell for leather charge to Highway 8.

The question marks in Peay's mind were about corps and higher headquarters. Gen. Luck was an air assault proponent, quite prepared to test its full potential, but his staff's eyes glazed over when looking beyond a hundred miles into Iraq. Which is to say, the corps battle plans were excellent but the campaign plan hazy. Now headquartered in Rafha, the corps staff crossed their fingers about Cobra, and crossed themselves for the fate of the Euphrates leapfrog. In their eyes these were such chancy missions that subsequent operations seemed not to have crossed their minds.

Whereas, beyond the hundred mile horizon was where Peay was focusing. When asked to name his most conspicuous virtue, those best acquainted with Peay cite farsightedness, his ability to envision a situation several stages in the future. Hardly had the Hail Mary strategy been unveiled than he began pondering its 'end state': where should his division be when the shooting stopped? His conclusion was that the 101st—no other force was capable—should be completing a reconnaissance in force near Baghdad.

Assuming success for Hail Mary (as everyone in CENTCOM did) perhaps as early as G plus 10, Peay foresaw Saddam's 40 divisions defeated and devastated south of the Euphrates, leaving the land between it and the Tigris strewn only with those remnants of Saddam's shattered army who could get out through Basra. As events proved, this indeed became the scenario, played out at fast forward.

Projecting his imagination, Peay saw Saddam damaged but not destroyed, still controling his subjects and most importantly their perception of the outcome of the war; to wit, that Iraq—in the name and for the glory of Islam—had stood up to infidel powers and Arab quislings, fought valiantly and withdrew before overpowering might, and only so far as prewar borders. He'd depict himself as having survived ruthless bombing, much like Churchill, to emerge equally defiant and undefeated. Such was the perception Saddam could impart to his subjects—if allied soldiers did not intrude into his heartland. It was that end state which Peay was convinced the 101st could forestall: namely, the domestic perception on which Saddam's postwar regime would depend.

Peay proposed to do so by carrying the war, and evidence of the end state, deep into Iraq. Saddam's invention of pseudo and moral victory could not stand in the eyes of his subjects who would witness Screaming Eagles landing at will throughout the Tigris-Euphrates peninsula, even to the suburbs of Baghdad, but short of the defensive ring of Republican Guard divisions Saddam prudently kept near the capital to prevent his overthrow. Though trained for urban combat at FOB Oasis, the air assault division was not designed for house to house fighting. It would not be necessary: four hundred helicopters circling and touching down around Baghdad would be proof positive that Saddam, like Hitler at the end of his war, ruled nothing more than his bunker.

Peay called his plan the Baghdad Sequel, duly logged by Mixon in January. To execute it at the conclusion of Hail Mary, Peay needed a well furnished division base near the Euphrates. Tallil air base was such a site. Almost the size of King Fahd, the 101st could come out of the sand to land on hardstand, then occupy protected buildings for headquarters, maintenance and billets.

Corps passed on the Baghdad Sequel, kicking it up to higher headquarters without a recommendation. They also passed Tallil (beyond the 100 mile horizon) back and forth between Peay and McCaffrey, as an objective for one or the other on G plus something. As a 'hard' objective, more like a fortified city than an airfield, it could be taken at less cost by a mechanized than an air assault force. But Tallil was a little off the 24th's axis of attack, aimed at closing the noose at Basra. McCaffrey could do without the possible delay, and Peay preferred for Screaming Eagles to seize their own roost. Both generals were ready to throw down their Kevlars if they had to cross their logistic tails. It would be like a high speed merge from intersecting freeways in the fog of war—convoys jumbled, horns honking, radio frequencies overlapping, quarrels for space—and worst of all, the possibility of fratricide. Peay and McCaffrey looked to corps to prevent collisions and gridlock. The simplest way was to keep the 101st north of the 24th throughout the war. That meant Tallil should be the 101st's objective.

But Luck saw the campaign developing where either division could go for Tallil. He accommodated their respective interests almost to a fault, with the result that both developed plans to seize the airbase; but betting was that the mission would fall to the 24th because Luck, as much as Schwarzkopf, leaned toward any plan that minimized casualties.

The Baghdad Sequel could be launched from an alternate site due north of Cobra in the Euphrates valley, barely 100 miles from Baghdad, so Peay had an option independent of who did what with Tallil. If he could obtain endorsement from Schwarzkopf, the Baghdad Sequel, an order of magnitude more important than Tallil, could be Saddam's *coup de grace*.

From previous assignments, Peay and Schwarzkopf were acquainted by more than reputation. While both were working at the Pentagon, their sons played together at Ft. Myer, VA. Because of Schwarzkopf's late marriage, their wives were the same age and knew each other as Brenda and Pam. The 101st's first briefing for Schwarzkopf was in September when he took Cody aside, telling him to stay away from reporters.

Peay: "We had only Aviation Task Force at that time, and a skeleton staff. I was just learning my way around. So the briefing certainly wasn't very sophisticated. In fact, I'm afraid it was pitched at a company grade level. Gen. Schwarzkopf was gracious enough not to ask questions we couldn't answer.

"The next time I saw him was at the major commanders' conference in Dhahran. That was in early October, I believe. The flag officers from all services were there at the Air Force Officers Club [an installation that predated the Gulf War]. 7th Corps hadn't yet arrived.

"Gen. Schwarzkopf brought us together for two purposes. The meeting lasted four or five hours. The first part, which I thought he conducted masterfully, was sensitivity training in cultural relations. He was uneasy about how we Americans were barging into Saudi Arabia as if the kingdom was Grafenwohr [an isolated, insulated training site in Germany]. He had some familiarity with the Middle East, and wanted us to get smart about how very different things were here.

"To do so he read passages from an excellent book that I later studied.* The passages he read were really startling, concerning the perception of women, the meaning of personal deportment, the relation of man to man and man to God—non-military subjects from which an entirely different political and philosophical ethos flowed.

"The purpose of his readings wasn't just to improve relations with the host nation, Saudi Arabia. What we were hearing him address was the very viability of the coalition. We were too busy at the time to contemplate how improbable this coalition was, but this meeting gave us an appreciation of its fragile

---

* *The Arabs* by David Lamb

nature. A rape or some drunk driving could have disastrous repercussions.

"At Dhahran he wasn't the 'Stormin' Norman' people have heard about. We were listening to a deep and broad gauged officer speak more as a diplomat than a warrior. I was really impressed at how he addressed the different services. If this had been an all army conference, I think he would have been more blunt and forceful—the Schwarzkopf we in the army knew. But each service is a different sub-culture, different mentalities. He was getting his message across in four military languages, all at one time and with the same words. Quite a remarkable, versatile performance.

"In the second part of the meeting he got into the prospects of a ground offensive. There was nothing about Hail Mary, only an assurance that before we attacked there would be one helluva air campaign, and sufficient intelligence for planning.

"In late November, we all got together again in the same O' Club. This time 7th Corps' advance people were there, and the subject was Hail Mary in its early formulation. We [the 101st] knew from that point that we'd end up on the Euphrates, and I began thinking about the Baghdad Sequel. I wasn't ready to propose it to Gen. Schwarzkopf, but I expected to see him again and intended to push the sequel as an option worthy of serious consideration."

Hess remembered briefing Schwarzkopf on the sequel in November: "He said, 'That would be a conclusive ending, Binnie. Keep working on it.' So I kept Mixon on it. Personally I thought if we continue educating Schwarzkopf on what the 101st could do, he'd keep us in mind. We were able to pitch the sequel on two more occasions. Each time I thought his reaction grew more favorable."

But December whirred with activity throughout the JOA, and Schwarzkopf could not be maneuvered into suitable surroundings to elicit a decisive endorsement. CINCENT's next visit to the 101st was in the field during the covering force mission where he was shuttled around by helicopter with the press in tow. He never sat down long enough to hear another pitch.

Peay: "In Riyadh he was surrounded by generals all the time.

When he visited the 101st he wanted to see troops, mingle with them, gain confidence from them, exchange a boost of morale. I wasn't about to interrupt what he enjoyed most, so the Baghdad Sequel was shelved for another day."

But there were other influential visitors who heard Peay's plan. On two of their trips to the JOA, Cheney and Powell looked in on the 101st. The first occasion was a happenstance. The VIP's were scheduled to visit elsewhere, but weather delayed them at King Fahd. Hastily ordering up a brunch, Peay also tried to get a nibble on the Baghdad Sequel.

The reaction from Cheney and Powell was polite, theoretical interest. The presidential purpose for Desert Storm seemed to be a box beyond which they'd not allowed their thoughts to project. The liberation of Kuwait was the mission, no less but no more either. Apparently they did not feel it necessary to cite the obvious for Peay.

But he was ready if they had. Liberation of Kuwait meant more than expelling Iraqis. It meant removing the threat of invasion as much as the occupying army. Indeed the worst case contemplated in Washington at that time was for Saddam to withdraw his forces to hover across the border till the Americans went home and the coalition dissolved.

Maybe we'll consider this later, was the subliminal message Peay perceived from his guests at brunch.

"I felt that the sooner, rather than later, we got an order turning Hail Mary north, the more effective we'd be beyond the Euphrates. I guess I didn't have much company in believing that Saddam, more so than his army, was the real objective of this war. He would be within reach of the 101st. From the banks of the Euphrates we could turn his country, his army, against him in a few weeks. That wouldn't be an open ended quagmire; it was a quick fix."

Thus Peay kept thinking ahead, betting somewhat on the outcome. The present was already under control, with only one remaining uncertainty, the same one that had haunted Desert Rendezvous from the start: were there suitable LZ's at Cobra? Whether to Baghdad or to grief, everything would start from there.

XVIII

MU 705725

Videos were a memory from King Fahd, but Garrett nevertheless became a couch potato on G minus 7.* The film was
silent, black and white, but he reran it at every speed. O'Neal
was the camera man, Tom ("party in ten") Drew the star, with
cinematography by FLIR—yet the action was tame compared
with TF Normandy films:

At a steep angle, Drew's Apache approached a *sabkha*. When
he reached a height of thirty feet, what looked like fog began
to spiral from the surface. Drew settled quickly to minimize a
building dust cloud, then Garrett studied the next frames in
slow motion till the Apache was once more aloft. What O'Neal,
in another Apache, had recorded was the first landing in Cobra.

Garrett: "From the map and experiments, we had an idea of
what to look for. On our side of the border we'd hopped
around, landing on a variety of sites. Generally, *sabkhas* proved
to have the least dust; they were shown as gray areas on the
map, so we focused first on gray areas within Cobra. Trouble
was, up in Iraq sand drifted a lot and filled *sabkhas* like silt.
What I saw in O'Neal's film were brownout conditions, marginal for an Apache, impossible for a Chinook. If Cobra was
going to work, we had to land a whole lot of Chinooks."

The problem, daily growing more imminent, brought back a
humiliating experience. Fresh from Vietnam, Garrett had com-

---

* Throughout the JOA, the countdown for G Day was put on a two day hold as
the Soviets made a last chance appeal to Saddam. Thus there is much chance
for historical confusion, whether recollections refer to an announced or actual
G minus X.

manded an air cavalry troop (company) at Ft. Lewis, maneuvering it through its annual proficiency test. He was doing fine, dispatching helicopters left and right, using the map to determine their destinations.

"Then I got a call from the chief umpire: meet him at certain coordinates. I hopped up there, and he tells me I just lost a flight when they landed in an enemy kill zone. On the spot, he flunked me on that phase of the test. I never again neglected to make a personal recon."

In the daily briefings for Peay during the preceding week, Garrett had hinted that he should make a personal reconnaissance and set down himself in Cobra. Otherwise, his recommendaton would be qualified regarding this question of the FARP site on which everything depended. Now, on G minus 7, Garrett no longer hinted but announced his intention to fully investigate Drew's *sabkha*. Peay realized the import. If the Iraqis could choose one officer to take prisoner, he would be Garrett, the master-mind of the division's aerial plans.

"Are you sure you have to go yourself, Tom?" asked Peay.

"I've done the homework—and really need to read the dust signature myself, sir."

"Well..." Time paused for a moment as the CG mused. "... OK." Garrett exhaled audibly. "But take some friends."

"Yes, sir."

His friends were Bryan, and three other Apaches from 2-229. Garrett loaded his hard points to capacity, not to fight but to add enough weight that would require full power from his turbines, thus raising about as much dust as a Chinook. His recon was to be by day so he could best see the signature.

Garrett sanitized: the images and statements of American POW's Iraq had shown on TV were proof enough that inevitably torture followed capture. It crossed his mind that as the most senior POW in Iraqi hands he would have to make policy decisions for all the inmates in a prison —decisions like how much torture to endure before compromising the Code of Conduct. He knew there was nothing like FLIR with which to see into the darkest fate that can befall a soldier.

But Garrett had written some premonitory thoughts to his

children, even before he realized his counsel might apply to himself:

I want to talk to you three kids about personal discipline, and mental and physical toughness. A lot of my young soldiers (mostly Tracy and Megin's age) have been thrust into a very hard situation. Daily, they concern themselves with the basics of survival; absolutely no comfort, break, or respite.

The vast majority are toughing it out in style, with grace and a sense of humor. Are you made of that kind of stuff? If not, do a little contemplating about your ability to function when the chips are down. Examine what's really important and what's 'nice to have.' Don't wish for more and more all the time. Take care, careful care, of what you do have. Use it wisely and efficiently, and enjoy it fully.

Test yourself once in a while. Stretch and harden yourself. It will make you stronger, more independent, better able to handle crisis and hard times, and it will give you inner strength and self-assurance.

Bottom line: challenge yourself—stretch—grow. Become all you can become. Grow strong and tough—not mean—tough.

Garrett's flight swung far out to the west, as if they were choppers snooping for the 82nd. Some bombing was scheduled in the vicinity of As Salman, and he hoped five more aircraft in the sky would go unnoticed. There would also be a diversionary reconnaissance over MSR New Market. Hopefully, reports from the Iraqi outposts would be so numerous that their headquarters could find nothing significant in what appeared to be just another Apache patrol.

The rocky desert was too flat to provide concealment, even for Apaches flying nape of the earth. Hills were no higher than ten meters from the table top surface, and miles apart. Lower mounds of natural rubble were the only other elevations. Garrett could not detect the contours of great basins, but southwest of Cobra there was one twenty-five miles across, revealed by the cluster of *sabkhas* at its center. For deception and for practice, he set down on one, raising not a trace of dust. Damn! These were perfect conditions for Cobra—but Cobra had to be another twenty miles away.

They approached from the southwest, scurrying over the last miles of New Market as if it interested them not at all. Drew had not used GPS on his earlier touchdown, so Garrett had only approximate coordinates of its location. But from Drew's description, the site ahead looked familiar: two huge *sabkhas*, side by side, one of them the shape of a footprint, the other a tadpole, both crossed by a shallow wadi.

Garrett was in the front seat, holding a newly fielded GPS called a slugger, about the size of a small VCR. He told Erik Pacheko, his pilot, to descend on the center of footprint.

"Landing," he announced to the four protecting Apaches. They took up overwatching orbits.

Ten feet above footprint, dust erupted in a maelstrom. The heavy Apache pressed down toward the surface as if Pacheko were landing only because Garrett had ordered it.

"Pull up!" Garrett countermanded.

Instantly and gratefully, Pacheko complied as Garrett imprecated the fickle desert. This was where Drew had landed—according to his doppler coordinates which were less accurate than a slugger's—but a hundred meters, even fifty, was enough for the surface of a *sabkha* to frustrate those who presumed its constancy.

Garrett's Apache rose out of its dust cloud. His four escorts assumed he'd confirmed what he came for. Nothing passed over the radio, but on intercom Garrett told Pacheko they'd come back later to footprint.

On Garrett's large scale map, the two *sabkhas* were enclosed by a rectangle overprinted by the Air Force before the war: "WARNING: flying outside airspace controlled by Iraq is PROHIBITED." He felt Iraq also controlled the surface space, and that the conditions for Cobra—if there was to be a Cobra—might be quite unpredictable.

But first to check out tadpole. The Apaches looped away beyond Cobra's horizon, weaving over distant desert as if in search for targets of opportunity. They were back in a half hour, flying a random criss-cross. The deception produced serendipity, for other features of the AO caught Garrett's eye: a trail, more traveled than New Market, running east-west from As Salman. This would be the 82nd's MSR , called Virginia, if corps swung them east as Hail Mary progressed. For long stretches, the Iraqis had paved Virginia, unwittingly paving the way for Iraq's invaders.

Peay did not want MSR Virginia to cut through Cobra, mixing the 82nd's vehicles with the 101st's. Thus the road/trail marked the northern limit for Hill's defensive 'goose egg.' Garrett swept low over the bend that would be this boundary, and saw a problem for Hill. The highest ground in the area (though not high enough to show on the map) stood just outside the goose egg, yet would have to be controlled by First Brigade. That meant Hill needed to stretch his thin line of infantry, or artillery and air strikes must provide some slack by dominating the high ground. More and more, Cobra seemed to require a snake charmer, some magic to fit the serpent into a bag of the right size.

Garrett took another turn around the troublesome high ground. His escort dipped lower. To some of them who had attacked Toad, this ridged escarpment seemed just the sort of place where Iraqis liked to dig in. One more turn, and the flight had to move on, but Toad veterans thought they saw some bunker features.

They also noticed another *sabkha*, a narrow one in front of the escarpment, right at the edge of Black Hawk range from TAA Campbell. The *sabkha* was also on the map, and thus an LZ candidate for First Brigade. Garrett made a mental note to advise Hill he might consider landing a battalion south of this *sabkha* but not on it because it was dominated by the escarpment not shown on the map.

Then the Apaches closed in on tadpole, different only in shape from the footprint, receiving the same rainfall, enclosed by identical beaches. The tail of tadpole tapered south. Within a sometime-swamp like this would be the world's largest helicopter gas station, or the 101st Air Assault Division would run out of gas.

The first swoop swirled up dust before Pacheko could set down. He darted laterally a half mile and descended again. The windshield browned out for a moment, then cleared. Garrett felt the Apache's weight supported by the surface. He opened the door. The landing gear had indented six inches of silt. He swiveled in his seat, stuck the slugger out the door to get open access to the satellite somewhere in space. Ten digit coordinates came up on the display. Garrett recorded them with a parenthesis ('maybe'). Black Hawks could go in here, and maybe lightly loaded Chinooks. Heavier stuff would have to land elsewhere.

Working south over tadpole, Pacheko set down again. New coordinates, same conditions; Garrett jotted them down. This wasn't going to do it. The problem absorbed him so much that time passed unheeded, but Pacheko felt they were lingering too long. The four escorts had begun to weave repetitive patterns as if their talent for deception was approaching exhaustion. After his fourth discouraging landing, Garrett glanced to the west, and from ground level saw the lay of the land a bit differently. It seemed to tilt down slightly to the north. Impulsed by a combination of impatience and imagination, he ordered Pacheko to hop back over to footprint. Its basin might be a meter higher at its south end, reason to hope, however faintly, for less silt and hence less dust.

Garrett felt an unexplainable mirth as his flight covered the short distance between the adjoining *sabkhas*. Here he was 45 years old and a full colonel, father of three, bobbing across the desert from nowhere to nowhere, searching for a combination of silt and dust like a toddler mixing mud pies. At the moment his mission seemed as ridiculous as serious, and a task that a year before he could not have imagined unless he'd had LSD instead of GPS.

"An old image of the army is a predictable life of routine. I was laughing to myself about that."

From the direction at which Garrett now approached it, footprint looked different, most noticeably because of a prominent mound, almost a hill, at the south end of the *sabkha*. It seemed like a beacon. Without a word from Garrett, Pacheko landed a quarter mile north of the hill.

Garrett: "We bumped—it was that hard. I was looking at the hill, expecting it to disappear in the usual brownout. But there it was—clear as before, behind a thin veil that dispersed quickly. We'd landed on hard crust, not much silt, and dust we could live with. I saw cracks radiating on the surface from where we landed, and the *sabkha* seemed to be made up of big dried plates. This sure wasn't tarmac, but it should support Chinooks. I stuck out the slugger, and wrote down the coordinates. This would have to be the FARP, for better or worse. Things got worse real quick."

Bryan had widened the Apaches' orbits so as not to draw attention to Garrett's landing. Nearing the 'surprise' escarpment, he spied a figure moving, an unarmed soldier apparently, transfixed by sight of choppers rearing over the skyline. He was on the edge of footprint, maybe a mile from Garrett, and Bryan believed he saw the Iraqi pull up his pants as if he had been using the *sabkha* for his toilet. Before the Apaches got close, he waved his arms, then disappeared like a ground squirrel.

Pulling up to swing south, the flight overflew the escarpment.

Bryan: "I guess they didn't think we'd come back. Damned if they weren't out there sunbathing, and I think it was on top of bunkers."

Cross hairs. Constraints. Lasers on. Weapons switch to 30 mm... Gunners await Bryan's order to attack, but there's none. In the pre-mission briefing, Garrett had said not to fire unless fired upon. Let sleeping Cobra lie. Bryan rejoined Garrett hovering over 'Hill's hill,' as the elevation at the south end of footprint would be called, then the flight streaked home with the information they'd come for: the Cobra FARP would be at coordinates MU 705725.

Hill could now tack down his template. Corps, who'd been exhorting Bolt for hard coordinates, could finally post their maps and ARCENT's. Peay's last tactical question was answered, and commanders walked to their long sought G Day LZ's at many sand tables. Attached with Garrett's caveats and misgivings, the FARP was on paper and new players strode to center stage.

For a high risk tactical air assault, the largest in history, Lt. Col. John Broderick now became a figure as central as he was unlikely. Broderick, a Quartermaster officer, commanded 426th Supply and Transportation (S&T) Battalion in DISCOM, the division's logistical and administrative component, whose job it was to keep gas flowing and guns firing in support of the combat components. S&T, naturally, were functions performed from the rear.

But Desert Rendezvous put the supply cart before the war horse: fuel, 200,000 gallons of it plus transfer and pumping equipment, had to fly 90 miles forward into Cobra before the bulk of the division's combat strength left the ground. Basically, Hill's brigade was to guard the gas station. Broderick would manage it, make it work or Desert Rendezvous couldn't work. Garrett had found him the best site available, but from then on the FARP had Broderick's name on it.

Peay: "From my experience in two wars, I know of no similar unit with such vital responsibilities to be carried out in this unique and dangerous situation. If a combat battalion failed, another would step up—but if S&T failed at Cobra, there was no one else to do the job. It was that simple, and responsibility for that job was John Broderick's."

Adams: "You can compare this to D Day in Normandy. Imagine all the tanks coming ashore out of gas. Broderick had to get on the beach ahead of them, set up a gas station, fill 'em up and send them on their way—all the while subject to enemy fire and counterattack. They don't train S&T guys to do things like that. Though we rehearsed what had to be done, no one was certain it was possible. A lot of people put their faith in Broderick."

His hair a tapestry of black and white, his physique rounded to the countour of army chairs, indicated that Broderick was accustomed to march at the rear of the parade. But now thrust into prominence, he stood tall within his province. The tacticians had to have this or that no later than G plus so many hours or even minutes. All right, general; all right, colonel; all right, sir—now here's what we're planning to do... Tacticians blanched as he related lift intervals, pumping rates, blivet and gas bag replenishment, with their technical details attached like magnetic filings. Tacticians browbeat logisticians, but are actually afraid of them. Logisticians control tacticians like the mafia controls politicians.

But Broderick was prepared to share the tactician's fate. He convinced Hill to bring in the first S&T elements (including Broderick) only two minutes after the first infantrymen set foot on Cobra. That would be none too soon. Sixteen refuel points for Black Hawks and Chinooks, plus eight more for Apaches, were to be pumping within two hours. That was what Broderickdule. was planning to do.

Previously divided between Aviation Brigade and DISCOM, the entire FARP capabilities of the division were assembled under Broderick for rehearsal of what had never been attempted before—something like pooling all the fueling and maintenance facilities of various airlines at a major airport to handle a week's volume of traffic compressed into a day. Compatibility of equipment and procedures was Pandora's Box. Broderick lifted the lid, trying to examine the problems one at a time; but mutual effects reverberated, jarring all into a jumble with the only integrated product being the pain of Broderick's headaches:

"You could start anywhere. Flow rates for example. Aviation Brigade could put up FARP's really fast, and had plenty of people to pump fuel from small capacity blivets. Back in DIS-COM, we had much bigger fuel capacity and flow rates from gas bags, but many fewer refueling personnel. Our normal FARP was semi-permanent—didn't have to come up or down in a half hour. For Cobra, we had to think like gas retailers instead of wholesalers.

"Same thing with maintenance. Aviation Brigade had what was like roadside service, mobile facilities that got vehicles back on the road—back in the air—using stuff in a tool kit. They'd bring you a few gallons of gas too, enough to get you back to a full service station which was in DISCOM. We were the only ones who had pump mechanics. They were critical to keep flow rates going. I had two Black Hawks in the first lift, and I took Sgt. Strobel, my top pump mechanic, and maybe the most important man in Cobra.

"The integrated Aviation Brigade-DISCOM FARP had to refuel so many birds, so fast, that it was like driving your roadside service to the filling station, then setting them up together for maximum efficiency. That's what everything came down to—efficiency. If we didn't get the very maximum volume of gas from pumps into ships, we couldn't meet the tactical schedule.

"Very early in our planning we realized we'd have to refuel 'hot,' meaning we'd pump while the ships kept running, blades spinning, turbines heating. That's dangerous. That's the reason every gas station has a sign, 'Turn off engine before starting the pump.' A huge explosion and fire is very likely when you have hot engines next to gas fumes. The pumps and choppers were engineered to contain escaping fumes, but we never stopped thinking, 'what if?'

"What if the mating connectors didn't quite hook up? There wouldn't be any warning, no time for prevention or damage control. We'd hear that big puff of sound from a fireball, followed by other blivets, pumps and choppers blowing up.

"There was no way this division could be defeated, but we sure could destroy ourselves.

"Spark and gas fumes—that was disaster scenario number one. Brownout and crash was number two, and even worse.* With the space we had, the ships would be landing very near the pumps. Then they'd line up on the ground, nose to tail, like the O'Hare runway during peak hours. The situation at Desert One was multiplied a hundred times: aircraft landing, taking off, every few seconds.

"Everyone had to do exactly what the plan required. No slack. No interpretations. Get in the pattern. Drop your load. Land in a near brownout, stand in line, refuel hot, and take off back into the pattern.

"You're putting yourself in other people's hands. Maybe that's the hardest part of it—you'd do it with Joe, with Bob if you had to, and while you went through the rosary, do it with Jim—but this time you had to do it with guys you probably never even met—low ranking guys, like the pump operator, who signals you forward, jams a nozzle in your tank (almost without looking) and gets ready for the next chopper. Your life's in his hands for some long minutes.

"Then a voice you never heard tells you to take off through brownout on a certain heading. He'd better be right, because the sky is full of ships listening to him—taking his orders. And he's a corporal!

* Number three was enemy intervention: 'indirect fire' from the Iraqis, Hill's job to prevent.

"This isn't combat where you feel alone against the enemy. This is a test of trust in how well other guys can do their jobs. We had to develop that trust in rehearsals."

The plan Broderick rehearsed was guided by Garrett's concept to keep the FARP as simple and safe as inevitable chaos would allow. First off, the Apaches, Cobras and Kiowas would FARP up at the northern end of tadpole, the maximum distance they could be from the main FARP servicing cargo choppers. Tadpole was feasible because the gunships raised less dust, and so could land on more silt. There was both a plus and minus for the gunship FARP. On the positive side, the Apaches would not need to refuel on G Day, thanks to the aux pod they'd carry from TAA Campbell. On the down side, ammunition would have to be flown into their FARP because they would probably be attacking Iraqis all day. Fuel and ammunition, side by side, were tinder for accidental explosions, all the more likely as refueling and rearming would go on at the same time.

Broderick: "People remember how hairy it was landing to refuel at Cobra, but there was plenty to worry about too at TAA Campbell where everything started. The PZ's were much more bunched up there. Power failure on take off—just one Chinook crashing—could set off a chain reaction like a string of firecrackers. At the PZ's, there was simultaneous liftoff, and the mother of all brownouts. We spread as much aluminum matting as we could get, and oiled the sand to hold down dust.

"We had one secret weapon for the whole refueling operation, called 'Super FARE' (Forward Area Refueling Equipment). These were complicated devices for working blivets in series so there was no downtime in pumping. We'd asked Gen. Peay to let us spend about $30,000 on equipment available in the petrochemical industry around Dhahran—adapters and fittings mostly. He said OK, but don't arouse attention with these purchases.

"So we'd spread out purchases of key items over several months. About half my career has been with military pipelines, so I was able to get the stuff we needed for Super FARE from the oil company suppliers, though we had to scrounge all over the kingdom [a scavenger hunt Peay—a man not given to exagerration—considers a logistical miracle]. The oil men kind of looked at me funny—thought maybe I was going into the petroleum business after the war—but no questions were asked.

"Two innovations had to work if Cobra was to succeed—sling loaded gas bags and Super FARE—but if an earlier decision hadn't gone the way it did, I think Cobra might have failed. This was the decision to use a single fuel called Jet A throughout the division. In Desert Shield, ground vehicles burned diesel, and aircraft Jet A which is a dual purpose kerosene. When we started planning Cobra, we saw enormous efficiency if everything ran on Jet A—we could use standard drums eliminating the possibility of pumping the wrong fuel in a dust storm. Now the HUMM-V is designed to run on either fuel, but ground vehicle people said conversion to Jet A would foul the lubrication of the injector pump, so they didn't want to do it. The call went all the way up to Gen. Peay. It won't appear on any citation he receives, but going to one fuel might have been his most important decision."

Like Garrett, Broderick felt a personal recon of Cobra was essential but he was denied. As G Day drew closer, choppers were to stay away from Cobra completely. Peay approved each day's reconnaisance plan, and proved as unyielding to his colonels as Schwarzkopf had been to his generals. Confined to TAA Campbell, what the division planners could do was establish traffic patterns—draw cloverleaves above the dust conditions they would have so dearly loved to check out.

The traffic pattern for the gunship FARP was steered away from footprint, which needed all available sky for the square dance of 300 Black Hawks and Chinooks coming, gassing, going, and passing. The dance would be called by Corporal Alcus Davis.

"I'd been with FCC [flight coordination center] over a year. Thought I'd get some experience in the army, then be a civilian air traffic controller. But I got to like working with helicopters, so I re-enlisted and got too old for the FAA.

"The most traffic I ever handled was maybe fifty ships at a time. Back at King Fahd they told me to get ready for something big. What they didn't say was we wouldn't have our regular rigs—two trucks and a tent, plus our little fold-up tower.

"When we got ready for the rehearsal at TAA Campbell, they tell me, 'no trucks, no tent, no tower—just me and my radio.' The rest of the stuff was too heavy to take up there in the first lift. Well, I guess I could deal with that: the rest would be coming up the next day or so. How many aircraft would I have to control before then? My sergeant smiles, and says, 'All of 'em.' I'm wondering if he means all the Chinooks or Black Hawks—either one of 'em is a load. Good thing I didn't know that I'd be turning around all the lift choppers a couple of times. I wouldn't have slept too good—but I'd gotten some lozenges for my throat."

XIX

Cry havoc...

He either fears his fate too much,
Else his desserts are small,
Who dares not put it to the touch,
To win or lose it all.

On the eve of D Day, 1944, Field Marshal Montgomery recited these lines by the Duke of Montrose to the Allied corps and division commanders, including the 101st's, assembled to invade Normandy. On the eve of G Day, 1991, the 101st's commanders searched futilely for such emotive words in minds crowded with unrelenting details. Time for private thoughts was scant, and they were directed homeward with memories shockingly vague: six months in the sand seemed to have worn down the features of those who waited and wrote back in America.

The size and scope of the impending offensive occupied whatever mental space remained, with little left over for reflecting on its meaning.

Said a colonel, "To look out over TAA Campbell boggled us, and we understood what it contained. Of course back home the entire division sometimes had marched in mass, and that's a grand sight, but you don't see much of the equipment in a parade. Now it was right out there on the desert, men and materiel in dispersed camouflaged clusters—trails in between like long spider webs, and choppers droning around like bees. We were immense. We were everything warfare is about. I think it was Chaplain Kitchens who compared us to the biblical hosts.

"Then to think that the 101st was about the smallest division in ARCENT—not to mention the Marines—just pushed your imagination off the chart. Stupendous, colossal—all the Hollywood words couldn't begin to describe it. This wasn't just big screen, panoramic and Dolby. This was real, in every dimension, in all directions."

Clark: "It was mega-awesome. Groups of troops would stand and just look, like this was some great sunset. To me TAA Campbell was a number of things. First, its business purpose which was a launching pad for a division attack. The 101st hadn't attacked as a division since World War II! That was enough to make you gulp. But I also saw us as an organization chart come to life. There's this cascading pyramid of boxes on page after page. You could imagine Indians [staffers] in little offices in the Pentagon who had worked up these charts with lots of notes, dotted lines, tables, footnotes and appendices: that was the air assault division on paper.

"The desert is unique because you can lay out that organization chart and see it right there, come to life. You need a helicopter to comprehend it all, but the scene really hits you from any level. I wished those Indians could see this too. An awful lot of people worked to make this division a reality. I wish they all could have seen it while we revved up on G minus 1. For me it was the first time I understood what we were as a totality, understood as an eye witness. While we were the covering force, the division was too spread around to see it all.

"Before we were sort of abstract, with some familiar components, but most you'd hardly ever seen and only knew about by their mention on a troop list. Now you could drive or fly around, and say, 'Hey, that's the 20th Engineer Battalion—they do the welding.'

"The other thing I wished was that the American tax payers could see what they'd bought. Defense spending has a reputation for waste, but here were end items well worth what they cost. Things worked. It took a lot of learning to adapt to the desert, but in TAA Campbell we were the best operators of the best equipment in the world."

Adams: "By G Day we were state of the art, and that impressed even me who had watched us evolve since September.

Take the TACSAT net for example. The division was flashing encrypted messages and faxing stuff around off lap tops like some TV commercial for AT&T."

Hill: "We were beyond ready. I think I was more nervous about the press joining us than us joining battle with the Iraqis."

Heretofore shepherding journalists like a girls school outing, CENTCOM now sent down media when commanders consented to receive them. Peay decided that for the 101st, selected journalists could join the division on G minus 3. His press officer had sought those who showed general military perceptiveness and apparent trustworthiness. Few made the cut by the first criterion. If none had, Peay was content to fight his campaign unreported.

So selection was remarkably easy. In Riyadh, full fledged 'war' correspondents were as scarce as bars:

"Anyone who was not confused by the difference between an F-16 and an M-16," Peay's press officer noted, "was a candidate. Most of the guys with track records had already gone to other units because of their connections. There was a Johnny come lately who promised a cover story in a major weekly, but Gen. Peay wasn't going for his kind of publicity. We wanted reporters who would tell our story and weren't just looking for one. Didn't matter who accredited them."

Peay was looking for character, but didn't want characters. With only the possessions they could stuff in a rucksack, about a dozen media bounced into TAA Campbell in HUMM-V's after dark. All males, they had been yanked on short notice from 'the JIB,' CENTCOM's media pool in Riyadh.

They debarked in bewildering surroundings, with no briefings on the 101st's organization, which is like none other in the army, much less on Desert Rendezvous. Said one, "In Riyadh, the Screaming Eagles had a new nickname, 'The Stealth Division,' because we couldn't see it—we just knew it was out there somewhere. I knew more about the Medina Division than the 101st."

Since his days in Vietnam, Peay had felt that no press was better than faulty press, and had consented to only one TV interview himself during Desert Shield (with Peter Jennings).

Now, on the eve of war, Peay modified his attitude, denying media no information that might preclude faulty reporting. He had Hess fully brief the Desert Rendezvous plan, its purpose and objectives, so that reporters could see for themselves how well (or poorly) it came off.

So small were their number, the media could accompany only a few units. They were not given a choice, but assigned to the infantry brigades where the most combat was expected. The NBC crew sat tall at the briefing when they learned they were headed for the Euphrates with Clark. John Kinford of New York Times , who drew First Brigade, knew little about the Screaming Eagles' present identity, but had read up on their past. Musing aloud after studying the Desert Rendezvous maps, he pointed out a remarkable historical coincidence: the flying times for D Day, 1944, and G Day, 1991, were both about 53 minutes. Peay's staff looked at each other—Kinford was OK. Hill decided to take him into Cobra on an early flight.

With so few hours until the ground war, the reporters scattered to hear what commanders were telling their troops. In 3-502, a first sergeant did most of the talking. The reporter was puzzled: it seemed that anger against the Iraqis needed to be worked up. He heard the sergeant blame Saddam for the present cold, previous heat, vipers, scorpions, MRE's, slow mail, alcoholic and sexual deprivation.

Hill dashed around the desert in his HUMM-V, squeezing time to address each of his 18 companies. His message was principally informative. He began with the strategic picture, descrbing the marines' mission of deception and frontal pressure in Kuwait, moving over to 7th Corps' main attack in Schwarzkopf's strategy, then the vital role of 18th ABC to cut Saddam's MSR and how the Screaming Eagles would do it. Of course Third Brigade couldn't do it unless First Brigade did Cobra. Hill proceeded through each battalion's mission at Cobra, reaching the point where companies already knew what to do. Kinford was impressed that by capturing a private in First Brigade, the Iraqis would have Schwarzkopf's battle plan.

Hill sniffed: what the Iraqis learned they could discuss in the 101st's EPW cages.

In Aviation Brigade, Garrett was talking to pilots rather than troops. His exhortation was to consider the upcoming ground war to be the graduation exercise for previous training; i.e., new rules, or modifications of old ones, would appear as an executive summary of 'the book.' With fresh memories of Desert Shield safety purges, the IG, and Luck's 'crawl, walk, run' dicta, Garrett's pilots felt they were almost listening to heresy as he demanded they insert a new disc in their mental computers:

"We always operated well within the envelope before. Now we'd push over the boundaries, and fly on the red line. Even if everything worked as planned, fuel warning lights would be glowing a lot of the time.

"Same thing with maintenance. We'd already changed out 'time parts' like bearings if they were approaching their lifespan, so on G Day regular maintenance schedules could be suspended. Come down for maintenance whenever you can, but don't panic because you're way over in hours. For example, we'd been carefully preserving our leading edges, repainting or taping them constantly, but now was the time to fly blades till they shook. Then pull 'em off and put on new ones. We had the stocks now, and now we'd use 'em.

"That's what I tried to get across—maintenance was what we did to reach this point when we'd go to the wall. Previous maintenance was like credit we'd built up—we called it 'banked time.' Now we'd draw on it till we were broke. Let me worry about our operational rate on G plus 5 or 6. On G Day fly like there's no tomorrow."

Human maintenance was another problem Garrett had similarly and analytically anticipated. The upcoming exhaustion and sleep deprivation would produce altered states of consciousness. Quite reasonably, the flight surgeons sought to restore normal consciousness with drugs, so for weeks Garrett had his men experiment with uppers and downers to become familiar with individual reactions. The purpose of the downers was to rest up aviators whenever there were time-outs; the uppers were for fly or die emergencies.

Nevertheless, the official reversal from abomination to endorsement of drug use was altogether too sudden and upsetting. Though Garrett required his pilots to have appropriate pills on hand, only a few were popped.

"Even though drugs were a carefully calculated factor in risk management, it didn't surprise me that pilots weren't ready to take them. Hell, maybe they thought they'd become instant addicts. What did surprise me was the feedback—what they wanted in these last days. It wasn't uppers and downers: it was more training! They'd been skimming the dunes, landing in brownouts for six months, but they wanted to rehearse their skills a little more.

"Coming up to G Day, we hadn't been flying much in order to build up the maintenance credits I'd been talking about. My guys felt they might be a little rusty. I told 'em, forget it—they were the best trained pilots ever to go into combat, and had shown it over and over in training. If I was satisfied with their proficiency, they didn't have to worry.

"I think that message was effective. They knew this division wouldn't short change its standards for any reason. If they didn't think they were peaked for the war, they could believe it because I said they were.

"One reason I wanted to make that point was my recollection of Cody approaching me, back when he was planning Normandy. He'd been working in a vacuum and needed feedback. I'd been too distracted to give it to him, to notice that he needed it—to tell him, yeah, your plan's great and you'll do just fine. So on G minus 1, I wanted to make sure everyone knew he had my confidence. Peay was also exuding that sort of confidence. It gave me one less fear, and I wanted to pass the same feeling down the line."

There was a last 'what if' item, however, Peay reviewed with the command group which showed the limits of confidence. Like TF Normandy's sanitization before takeoff, the daunting subject of casualties had to be dealt with by the possible victims. Even generals could go down, so Peay plotted with Shelton and Adams where each of them would be during G Day and how the succession of command would devolve if they never saw each other again.

Garrett: "Fear was the last and most important subject in my talk to the pilots. Very few of them were Vietnam veterans. The others felt—though they would never say so—that veterans had experienced a sort of epiphany that immunized them from fear forever after.

"The truth is that fear, or lack of it, is very situational. In 'Nam I'd flown into hot LZ's whistling the tune of the day, watched tracers reaching up, and somehow was convinced they weren't for me. Being young has a lot to do with that but not everything. Other times, on some zone recon, 1500 feet over quiet jungle, I felt the NVA had me in their sights the whole way, and I was scared shitless till we landed at An Khe.

"I couldn't explain this to a group of 1991 pilots on G minus 1. Maybe I didn't want to deflate the image they held of veterans! What I told them was that fear was really nothing new for them. They'd experienced plenty of it already in the desert. Our training here wasn't just tough and realistic, it had been a genuine fear generator, a real pee bringer, and they'd already been as scared as they'd probably ever would be in the war.

"They'd already met the challenge of the most dangerous enemy they'd face—the nape of the desert.

"I wasn't bullshitting them either. I've never been more tired, exhausted, spent and worn out in combat than I was in Ranger training. Desert Shield was the Ranger School for pilots. They'd graduated, and were more than ready for the secondary enemy, the Iraqis.

"I told them to fly as they had trained, not try to invent new maneuvers or get down lower on the deck. Just execute their skills as they already had—and go for the gold, not a DFC."

With Schwarzkopf's avengers locked and loaded, primed and peaked, G Day was postponed as the coalition felt out Baghdad for indications that the war need not proceed from air to ground. Compromise, accomodation, and face saving proved to be wishful thinking. In Arabic, Saddam means 'he who confronts.' He didn't know what he was confronting, but Secretary Baker hoped a glimpse of reality would get through to Saddam by cultural intermediaries like King Hussein. However, though slipped by three days, G Day rolled up as inevitably as every other date on the calendar. In the 101st, all was prepared for the worst. Next door in the 24th Mech, troops had donned MOPP 4. The Screaming Eagles would only carry their chemical protection.

Peay: "Our mobility was our principal protection. Moreover, there was no indication that the enemy in our AO had the means to deliver chemical munitions—no long range artillery, and we already knew how inaccurate their Scuds were. Up at Tallil we knew they had a lot of chemical agents stored in bunkers, but we still weren't sure if Tallil would be our objective, and if it were that wouldn't be till G plus 3 at the earliest. On G Day we'd go into Cobra bare."

If the Iraqis' chemicals were a secondary concern, their air force, though bashful, was still a major threat; so much so that triple A (Vulcans) were scheduled for early deliver into Cobra. A few Iraqi kamikazes crashing into the FARPS could undo the air assault division.

Lippard: "We got more uncomfortable now when the sound of bomb blasts rolled across the TAA. Were our fast movers working over New Market, or had the Iraqi Air Force finally decided to get in the war?

"There were more Scud alerts. Our ADA sounded sirens, and tracked the Scud south till it was gone, then they'd broadcast an all clear. The closest one hit Hafer Al Batin, but the bombs and sirens were like fanfare for G Day.

"There was time for one more peace rumor. We heard on AFRN that the Russians were trying to get Saddam to back down. This time we knew it was his last chance. All we had to do was flip the switches and go!"

Peay himself quenched this last rumor. Over the TACSAT net came a short message from DMAIN, racing across computer screens, then spitting out hard copy, torn from the printer and rushed to the commander addressed:

SUBJECT: MESSAGE TO ALL SCREAMING EAGLES

1. DIVISION OPORD 91-1 IS EFFECTIVE FOR EXECUTION UPON RECEIPT OF THIS MESSAGE. G-DAY H-HOUR IS 240600C FEB 91.

2. THE DIVISION'S NEXT RENDEZVOUS WITH DESTINY IS NORTH TO THE EUPHRATES RIVER. GOD SPEED AND GOOD LUCK!

3. AIR ASSAULT. SIGNED MG PEAY

In TAA Campbell day temperatures were pleasant 60's, but nights became quickly chilly. Peay's message announced that First Brigade would lift off at six in the morning, just when cold and warmth were mingling—producing fog.

This weather pattern had Cody more nervous than he'd been before Normandy. 1-101 had a great deal of work to do in the earliest hours. Preceding First Brigade's armada, Apaches would overwatch the placement of radio beacons along the route, beacons Hill's Black Hawks would follow like ships guided by buoys. Fog made the beacons all the more important, but fog could also delay their placement by the admirable Pathfinders whom Cody would protect as they touched down and set up the beacons.

There was no slack in the schedule to allow for such delay; none at all, because of the micro-thin fuel margin once the Black Hawks took off. When they started flying north for Cobra, they had to maintain a constant 90 mph air speed. Any slower or faster could mean disaster.

Faster meant higher fuel consumption just as with a car. Slower meant more time in flight, too much time for troop filled Black Hawks that would be running on empty even if they reached Cobra on schedule.

Garrett looked up at the starry sky, but in his mind he also saw next morning's fog. He'd been reviewing plans for the aviation task force that would explore from Cobra to the Euphrates in preparation for Third Brigade's leap. From TAA Campbell the desert rose into a plateau around Cobra, then descended again into the Euphrates Valley. Satellite photography had shown him three distinct weather bands: constant clear air over Cobra but morning fog at TAA Campbell and AO Eagle. He felt he was becoming obsessed with fickle fog. To clear his head, Garrett decided to visit Hill, see if he seemed as worried about H Hour weather.

Leaving DMAIN, Garrett heard the familiar 'chunk' of entrenching tools as a company from 2-502 took up guard. Calvin Greer was becoming the best informed corporal in the division. As he dug a foxhole for his wife, she briefed him on what to expect for Second Brigade. They would move up to assume First and Third Brigades' sectors in TAA Campbell; indeed, Second Brigade (minus 1-502 which was going with Hill) would soon be all the infantry left for protection of DMAIN where she worked. No problem, Calvin assured her, 2-502 had scared off an Iraqi corps at Hafer Al Batin.

"Good, I won't worry, Honey." she replied, "Anyway, G2 says there aren't too many Iraqis around here."

Hess had made that same point to his counterpart, Col. Frank Akers, G3 of corps. They had been Rangers together in Grenada (Rangers are another army network and fraternal order), a relationship that was expected to work to the 101st's advantage. But instead, much to Hess's disgust, Akers had required Calvin's battalion to be corps reserve rather than take one from the 82nd whose G Day mission was secondary to the 101st's.

Across the concertina that separated DMAIN from Calvin's company, he could see comrades looking his way and joking. One gestured for him to get in the foxhole with Dessie, then another cupped his hands and half shouted, "We'll cover for you!"

"Hey, why am I doing this?" Calvin grumbled. "DMAIN's suppose to dig their own positions."

"Cause you love me, Honey. Can't you make it a little wider? I want Andrea in here with me if there's shooting."

"I never thought I'd married a REMF. Now you get some coffee out to us in about an hour."

Garrett could hear HEMIT's and HUMM-V's converging on First Brigade's sector as stockpiles moved up and Hill's battalions contracted their perimeters toward the aluminum pads Broderick had laid down for the fleet of Black Hawks already perched and silent for the night. Generators hummed, tents flapped open and shut for visitors, so that it seemed few of First Brigade were resting for the morrow—certainly none of the headquarters. Those sleeping did so right beside the Black Hawk that would fly them the next day to Cobra.

"Always first, sir!" the sentry saluted, admitting Garrett within the concertina enclosing Hill's TOC.

"How's it going, Tom?" Garrett asked, pleased by Hill's relaxed confidence.

Hill came around his field desk, soon to be dismantled, extending his hand. "What can I do for you, Tom?"

"Just dropping by—to wish you all the best."

Looking at each other, their thoughts rewound to Vietnam. They'd not been acquainted there, serving in different eras, but both felt a similar and sentimental deja vu. Decades before, helicopter assaults were every day occurrences. None this big, very few in which the enemy was so well located, but many in number—so many they were hard for memory to separate. For one Viet vet to talk with another always brought glances and cocked ears from desert cherries. Here were two colonels, brigade commanders, beginning to talk, more casually than the way they must be feeling on a very significant evening. The TOC grew quiet.

Garrett glanced at Hill's map. Suddenly the present blew out memories of the other war: the LZ symbol for 1-327 was squarely on the *sabkha* under Iraqi guns on the surprise escarpment.

"What the HELL!"

Hill looked at him blankly. "Somethin' wrong, Tom? Tom... Tom, where's my G minus 7 report?"

A glitch, an untraceable glitch. A lapse, a gremlin between headquarters, a slip between lip and cup—whatever had happened, Hill had never been informed; and instead planned a battalion LZ on the suicide *sabkha*. Thoughts returned to Vietnam again, to times when the results of inexcusable miscommunication like this were later recorded on The Wall in Washington.

1-327, commanded by Frank Hancock, was the infantry battalion most affected. Hill reminded his cherries that in war last minute changes were the norm and nothing to get upset about. Hancock's LZ was slipped south about five miles, and concomittant changes implemented by all concerned, a large number, but most importantly by Broderick who erased and redrew 'goose eggs' on his map throughout most of the night.

Goose eggs were ellipses enclosing the planned locations for units and installations like refuelers, ordnance teams, maintenance areas, and artillery emplacements. Goose eggs on the map would have to be checked out on the ground for suitability. Broderick knew he would spend G Day rushing from goose egg to goose egg, landing or diverting flights depending on how well nature cooperated with the newly revised plans.

"It was a crap shoot. I felt many goose eggs would be OK, and others wouldn't. You win some and lose some in life—that's a constant. It's just that the military hates uncertainty more than most professions. We're very rational and methodical. We're most comfortable dealing with quantities, hard numbers. Unknowns bother us a lot, and all our planning is to bring them down to the irreducible minimum.

"We reluctantly accept that we can never know in advance all we want to about the enemy, but even then we analyze everything he is capable of doing, then identify what's most probable. Very rational, very methodical. I knew I'd be dealing with probabilities on G Day. Probabilities are the next best thing to hard numbers. What I was praying for was that probability wouldn't come up snake eyes at some vital point."

Peay: "Yes, but like our pilots, we had trained for years in dealing with fluid situations. That's the nature of air assault—fast moving, rapidly changing situations, and horseback decisions. We maximized our probabilities by training, planning and rehearsals. Moving Hancock's LZ did not worry me at all. We could do things like that routinely—even if the doers had misgivings.

"Maybe that's the greatest benefit of being a veteran. You've experienced similar situations, so you recognize by peoples' reactions that they are prepared, or not prepared, to handle whatever hand probabilty deals them. My gosh, in the desert I heard briefings from captains that showed far better understanding of reality than many colonels professed in Vietnam. Move an LZ at the eleventh hour? No big deal at all, not for my guys, because I knew how capable they were.

"Sure, the LZ switch must have made a lot of people apprehensive. You think if something this basic and important slipped through the cracks, what else is out there that can go very wrong?

"Well, it's probabilities again. Diligent people, checking, cross checking, rechecking—realizing the importance of their dilligence—well, it's most improbable that anything vital will get through a sieve so fine.

"And it didn't, did it? Tom Garrett felt he just happened to visit Tom Hill, and the 'suicide *sabkha*' came up. I think that was the 1% inspiration that follows 99% perspiration. You can't explain rationally how the error was discovered, but that's part of the metaphysical component of the Screaming Eagles.

"I could understand the nervousness around DMAIN better than they could understand my confidence. I slept better on the night of G minus 1 than I had the previous week."

Hill was ready to bed down once he felt Hancock understood the ramifications of the LZ switch. Garrett and Broderick, Hill was sure, had performed similar adjustments. Like Peay's confidence in the divisions on his flanks, Hill easily relied on the competence of his colleagues.

Twilight in the Arabian desert is often splendid. Late February is not the best sunset season, but on February 23rd Hill saw the departing sun as a fuzzy period, the final punctuation mark of the preparatory ordeal begun at King Fahd in broiling August. 'Payback time' was probably the prevailing thought arising from the expanses of TAA Campbell: we have waited dutifully for our nation, the coalition, the UN, to do their best. Now we'll take the job, and we know how to do it. Saddam, you asked for it, you could have begged off, now you're going to get it. This was like Lou Hall's sentiment when he pronounced, "this one's for you, Saddam," now chorused by 17,000 inner voices.

Kinford was by his side as Hill watched sixty parked Black Hawks lose their features into shadow, each with twelve infantrymen sprawled around it, a few cigarettes flaring then glowing. Hill felt the sureness, rather than the loneliness of command. Kinford perceived it and asked for his thoughts.

"Frank Dietrich," was the answer, a name that meant nothing to Kinford. Hill is not one to preface his remarks, so Kinford had to ask, and heard emotion in the answer: "Colonel Dietrich was the finest brigade commander to serve in Vietnam. I was a lieutenant, a platoon leader, in that brigade, and now I command it. There it is right out there."

"What was...?" Kinford did not catch the name to scribble in the fading light.

"Frank D-I-E-T-R-I-C-H. What a master. Just an absolute master of the toughest warfare there is. Operation Geronimo. Never heard of it have you? No one remembers it except the NVA.

"Dietrich took the Oh-deuce into this valley up north from Tuy Hoa, pretended he was interested in this particular mountain, but slipped around to the other one where this NVA battalion had their base camp, and...

"Well, this is another war, but if if I capture Saddam in Baghdad, that won't mean as much to me as beating the boondocks for Frank Dietrich. He never got a star. Do you know how many turkeys did? All he could do was win. Did it in three wars. Those are big boots to fill, Frank Dietrich's, but you can bet your press badge First Brigade will do him proud tomorrow! This one's for you Saddam?—unh unh—this one's for Frank Dietrich—and for a lot of guys who were spit on or ended up on the Wall."

Kinford's silence was appropriate for the settling of twilight.

"It's a grand sight, isn't it, John?" Hill continued. "Payback time. Oh, yeah. These troopies are going to stick to Saddam. I'm going to do it for Frank, and hope I'll do it as well as he would. Cry havoc, let slip the dogs of war."

HIll's TOC tent came down, leaving the brigade commander under a poncho and the stars. He fell asleep with a faint tapping in his ears—Kinford was typing his first report from the staging area. To him, Hill seemed not to be asleep but rather thinking with his eyes closed. Kinford stopped typing to ask a question:

"Where did you get, 'Cry havoc,' Tom?"

Hill reluctantly came awake, and grumbled: "Isn't that from one of the Henrys?"

"I thought maybe a Richard."*

"Let your editors look it up. I'm going to get some z's."

---

* Understandably under the circumstances, both gentlemen's memories were faulty. "Cry havoc..." is Mark Antony's line in Edward DeVere's *Julius Caesar*.

XX

O' beautiful for purple sky

In Vietnam they were called 'lurps,' long range recon patrols; now they were known as LRSD—rhyming with thirsty—long range surveillance detachments. Four six-man LRSD teams flew stealthily into Iraq during the night of G Day eve. Essentially they were spies. With radios, they would keep Cobra and its approaches under surveillance, requiring a reptilian talent to move nothing but their eyes for hours on end.

Burrowing into the sand at sites picked from aerial photos, they spent the night making themselves indistinguishable from the desert. From then on their job was to wait, watch and report. If Iraqis began moving into or around Cobra, DMAIN had to know it. LRSD would also advise of any weather changes at the planned LZ's. As dawn oozed over their hiding places, they were happy to have nothing to report: the Cobra weather couldn't be better.

The weather at TAA Campbell couldn't be worse. A fog bank had settled on the border like an Iraqi gas attack, and was nearly as daunting. Gabram's company (the Bearcats) found less than a mile of visibility when they lifted off at 0238, precisely the same time TF Normandy had opened the air war on 17 January. Now, a month and a week later, the coincidence went unnoticed as the Bearcats were preoccupied with a big job and bigger problems. They were to insert the beacon teams, Pathfinders dropping off unmanned radios that would guide First Brigade's Black Hawks to Cobra. The beacon teams were in three Black Hawks themselves, trailing the Bearcats navigating with sluggers.

To avoid Iraqi radar, Gabram's flight flew at thirty feet of altitude, but here the fog was thickest. He tightened his formation till pilots could hear each other's turbines above the roar of their own. Even this close they lost sight of their wingmen. Only the Apaches had FLIR. The other choppers were flying on NVG, their blades whirling scant feet apart.

Suddenly they saw a flash below like a light bulb turned on in a tub of dishwater. A shrill explosion followed the flash—in the fog a Kiowa had struck a dune at a speed of 90 knots. There seemed no chance of survivors. Bearcats tensed in vicarious agony, imagining the death and disaster below.

Gabram ordered a turn, bending the flight to orbit the grisly torch of burning fuel, its black smoke merging with the gray fog. Cody was aloft, following the Bearcats' progress and reporting weather updates to DMAIN. He told Gabram to continue with his mission: the radio beacons for Hill had to go in. With FLIR, Cody was able to locate the crash.

He saw three figures beside a flaming wreck; these were probably the crew. All looked to be alive, certainly a miracle. He scanned the surrounding terrain. Soldiers were advancing toward the fire. Switch on the chin gun—cross hairs, constraints... Now Cody glanced at his slugger and checked his map. He was in Iraq all right, but quite close to the 101st's outposts. Gilman was his pilot. Buzz 'em, Cody ordered. Gilman swooped down at the advancing soldiers. They neither raised their weapons nor went to ground.

Calvin Greer felt out of it, as did his battalion, 2-502. Dessie had told him they were now corps reserve. The 1-502 would fly into Cobra today, the rest of Second Brigade tomorrow, but 2-502 ('Strike Force'—the author's outfit in Vietnam) was staying behind like some rear detachment. Calvin was resigned to follow the war on AFRN. Transistor radios could be heard all along his company's outpost line that was submerged in fog and darkness at 3:30 on G Day morning.

The explosion sounded different from the familiar karumpf of artillery or rumble of Air Force bombs, and had been preceded by the drone of some low-flying choppers. When the explosion flashed north of Greer's position, the first cry was "Incoming!"

Hey, he realized, we may be getting some war after all. Automatically, everyone went on 100% alert, but it took some minutes for the officers to decide what to do. Radio messages shot back and forth with DMAIN. Soon Greer's sergeant told the squad to saddle up. They were going out on a little patrol. A friendly aircraft may have crashed, but take no chances. Greer locked, loaded, and moved out. This was excitement, and it felt good to have an Apache covering the patrol.

Cody switched off his chin gun. Closer study convinced him that the advancing troops were wearing Kevlars. Gilman came in for a shallow landing; he touched down and saw sand from his rotor wash was blasting the three men staggering away from the wreck. Two of them supported the other. Cody leaped out with a first aid kit. They recognized him, and one saluted. They all looked shamefaced but uninjured; Cody couldn't see that one had third degree burns on his back.

Cody shook their hands, then his head. By all odds, that Kiowa should have been their coffin. His open relief alleviated their guilt at having crashed. Not their fault, Cody counseled— no one should be flying in these conditions—except that this was war. Rather than an ill omen, Cody interpreted the accident as a sign of good fortune: the Kiowa couldn't have crashed at a better place, right in front of 2-502 who was about to evacuate the survivors. A few more minutes of flight and they would have been in real Indian country. This is still going to work, Cody decided, but when he went up again, fog was about to clamp the Screaming Eagles on the ground.

Gabram had throttled back, feeling ahead in the soup with utmost caution. Not a single accident in 1-101 after seven months in the desert; now a Kiowa down in the opening hour of Desert Rendezvous. Garrett had prepared them to fly till they die, but at this rate Aviation Brigade would be decimated before the shooting started.

Gabram was further disadvantaged in the fog: he could not talk to his flight to determine if they were all still with him. Though the radios were 'secure'—the signals scrambled so Iraqis could not understand what the aviators were saying— new radio traffic could alert them that something in the air was coming at them. So the Bearcats groped ahead slowly and silently, as if reading the terrain by braille. Only the first beacon team was inserted before Cody determined that this wasn't going to work after all.

The Bearcats could creep forward, dropping off their beacons, but to no end if First Brigade's Black Hawks, scheduled for lift off at 5:00 a.m., could fly no faster than Gabram. Not even that fast, for they had no FLIR. The Black Hawks' fuel consumption remained the critical factor: the slower they flew, the more gas they'd burn because of longer flight time. The plan was to sprint to the Cobra LZ's at 100 knots. No way they could do more than 30 in this confounding fog.

Cody sighed before pressing the transmit button. 18,000 soldiers were poised to go, now he was about to tell them they shouldn't. He flicked to First Brigade's frequency—better to tell Hill himself, have him hear the dreaded recommendation in Cody's words, and besides DMAIN would be monitoring.

Postponement of Hill's H Hour would be Peay's, not Cody's decision, but he hardly expected to be overruled.

Fog was as thick at Hill's PZ, so he had no reason to second guess Cody whom he knew would fly NVG through the rings of hell if he thought Black Hawks could follow. Concerned but not yet alarmed, Hill passed the word to his battalion CO's: Indefinite weather delay. Start thinking about how we can make up time at Cobra.

Peay would not let his division start using a word like indefinite. Slip Hill's H hour to 0700, he told Hess, then turned his attention to reports from the Kuwaiti front of the ground war just begun. At 0530, in a drizzle that became a cold rain, the Marines had plowed open their sand berms and advanced on the first line of the Iraqis' vaunted defenses. This was power against power, and the Marines appeared to be making good progress, good enough that Luck alerted the 24th Mech to move up their H Hour to 3:30 in the afternoon. The opening bell had rung, with the 101st still in their corner; the starting gun had fired but they remained in a sprinter's stance. Corps' main effort, and thus most of their assets, would shift to Schwarzkopf's favorite division. To be left behind was the most uncomfortable feeling that ever pervaded DMAIN.

Garrett had no time for funk. His and Broderick's plans were the most upset by the delay. Aviation Brigade had to roll things back rather than just hold in place. First the Bearcats with the beacon teams were told to set down and prepare for another try at 0600. The night flights had to be refueled, other aircraft recovered, crews rotated. And every quart of gas preserved: Broderick fidgeted till he heard Black Hawks that were warming up shut down. They had to go out topped off, but his pumping people were all packed up for Cobra.

Sixty-seven Black Hawks were about to carry the ball, with everyone else running interference. The way must be cleared for them and the Chinooks or Desert Rendezvous would not be kept. For the launch of Third Brigade to the Euphrates, the Black Hawks would be handed off to Lt. Col. Bob Johnson, a man familiar with pressure and who could play with pain, but also with a disquieting fatalism that sometimes made Garrett nervous.

Johnson had come from Special Forces, where he led a Black Hawk attack on the Governor General's mansion, one of the hairiest actions in Grenada. A heavy caliber round blew through his fuselage, obliterating a vast amount of bone and tissue in the thigh. He almost died from shock and loss of blood, but stayed alive to hear how lucky he was—he'd only lose one leg. That was the beginning of Johnson's fatalism.

But fate granted him his leg, a mercy offset by welling pain that returned with tidal regularity; a reminder to others watching his heavy limp that big bullets do not just make big holes: they destroy—they blow away, and what is gone never returns, leaving the wounded man incomplete.

Only intervention by influential people restored Johnson to flying status, and he came back with an acute appreciation for people: his own Black Hawk people in particular. Comrades, fate had shown him, were what the world was worth. If you don't love your fellow soldiers, who can you love? He loved them to the point of uncritical judgement, and they him. Garrett had to watch that trait. He had other battalion commanders who were more characteristic of the 101st ethic, who were "all over every detail, Murphy proofing every possibility." Love is unconditional acceptance, but Murphy proofing accepts nothing at face value.

Along with love for his people was another up side to Johnson's fatalism, a savor for the small pleasures of life, since life itself had come so short a distance from ending for him. Illustrative was his amazing capacity for popping corn no matter the time, setting or circumstances. So when Garrett came around to discuss the weather delay, he was not surprised to find Johnson munching fistfuls of popcorn.

There were others whom Garrett would have preferred to readjust the planning, but watching Johnson's jaws bulge like a chipmunk's brought to mind the old army saw that a plan never survives the first enemy bullet. When that bullet cracked by, there was no one better to be flying, for Johnson would then be at the right place at the right time, leading his battalion whose first stop is Cobra.

0630. The fog is lifting but slowly. Cody's up again as if he could beat back the fog with his rotor blades. In fact it has receded to the north, like a matador's cape dragged along the ground. But not nearly fast enough. The old man's not going to like this, but Cody has to tell him straight: the Black Hawks can't go at 0700.

Garrett is consulted and agrees. All right, Peay concedes, but this is the last postponement. H Hour is firm for 0800. Garrett salutes. Cody does a rosary. They both think the world of Peay, but he is not Canute to whom nature does his bidding.

Peay: "They [his weather advisers] didn't seem to recall these same conditions all the time we'd been in TAA Campbell. Every morning there had been pretty heavy ground fog. G Day it was heavier than usual, but all month it had rolled back by sunup. I wasn't taking much of a chance, I was taking the odds."

Odds or not, the operation is to be severely telescoped. With an 0800 lift off for First Brigade, Gabram is out in front by mere minutes. The Bearcats would be dropping off beacons almost as they heard Black Hawks thunder over the horizon. No slack, no margin of error. Gabram is rolling out a carpet only a few feet ahead of the parade.

Now the sky shows mere whisps of fog at the PZ. Hill is disturbed by Cody's report that up north it is not clearing fast enough for Black Hawks to maintain 100 knots. "Let's go, God," Hill urges.

Around him the 101st contemplates itself before his brigade takes to the air for the largest helicopter assault in history, the first time the division has launched so much of its strength since World War II. The eyes of an eagle flash in many faces.

Wrists turn again and again as watches are watched as never before. The minutes are spinning down. Troops load as rotors rev. Sarge feels this is the pulse of the Screaming Eagle beginning to race, supercharging with adrenalin. Shouts are exchanged between Black Hawks but are lost in the din.

The second flight has their cameras out and clicking. This is an hour to remember, to record. Circles of handshakes: "Go get 'em..." "Air assault" "See you in Cobra." Caught up by the event, John Pomfret of Associated Press scribbles impressions. He describes the dust and exhaust fumes of liftoff "turning the sky purple." It is a spectacle of military majesty.

At a remote corner of TAA Campbell, Yancey is unloading his truck when what looks like a dense flock of quail takes wing miles away. He is so far away, the delayed sound of throbbing rotors seem to be an unconnected phenomenon, but so many in number they set up a deep harmonic no one has ever heard before. His thoughts are, there they go, and how much work by so many people finally got them in the air. Sweeping north, they cast fleeting shadows on the sand, almost a continuous shadow, which Peay imagines to be that of a giant eagle. Caged since Vietnam, it soars off toward new prey.

Broderick looks back from the door of his Black Hawk, into a dust cloud that seems a volcanic eruption. He prays that the ships below him have not browned out.

We've hurled the spear, thinks Garrett, let's see if it's on target. The target is 90 miles away, a *sabkha* deep in the desert of Iraq. The spearhead is the first lift, 500 soldiers of First Brigade. Until they're on the ground, they're as defenseless as passengers in an airliner.

Gabram's first touchdown is clear. Pathfinders spill from a Black Hawk that climbs again almost before their feet hit the ground. He hears their radio beacon come up on a previously silent frequency. So far so good, but up ahead the fog bank looks like an old marshmallow. He closes up the formation, and it becomes an arrowhead shooting into the mist.

A few miles behind, the Black Hawks (Lt. Col. Russ Adams leading) can also see the fog like a thunderhead sweeping toward them. Should they throttle back? No, Adams decides. They've got to get through it, so damn the fog and full speed ahead. It's on him, a gray blanket thrown over the windshield. Pilots' eyes are on the instruments now. Just keep altimeters at 30 feet, boys, Adams telepathically tells them, and pick up the beacons. Follow the beam. "On the beam": an expression as old as instrument flying.

They are twenty miles deep into Iraq. Garrett watches them on radar, but it does not show him the fog bank that will reveal its effect only if the flight of Black Hawks hesitates. It doesn't. Garrett closes his eyes, imagining how eyelid range is about as far as the pilots can see. He also revisualizes the bow of Iraq's desert, low at the Saudi border, low at the Euphrates, but high at Cobra. The fog's only at the low ends. Keep the faith, Russ—you'll break out in twenty minutes, *inshallah*.

Cody's aloft, dealing out his Apaches after reshuffling the deck. Davis takes off from TAA Campbell to provide him C&C midway to Cobra. Shufflebarger's A Company (the Spectres) get their new mission—blast through the fog all the way to Cobra to make sure the Iraqis' heads are down. Start the shooting, in other words, and report the situation back to Davis. Garcia (C Company—the Paladins) will come up a half hour later with four of his Apaches plus two of Gabram's, soon to be joined by Cody who has now flung his entire battalion out in front of the Black Hawks like destroyers searching for submarines ahead of a convoy.

This wasn't the plan, to expend Apache flying hours so utterly and early in the game, but the fog delay requires some changes. Bryan is to launch his Apaches all the way to the Euphrates. Garrett alerts Curran (3-101) to get his Cobras ready to back up Cody and cover MSR New Market as TF Citadel roars and bucks through the sand with 5000 soldiers and 600 vehicles, the largest caravan in 300 years on the *Dub al Haj*. They will snake through the desert in a column so long that it takes all day before it crosses the border, and the first vehicle

DESERT RENDEZVOUS

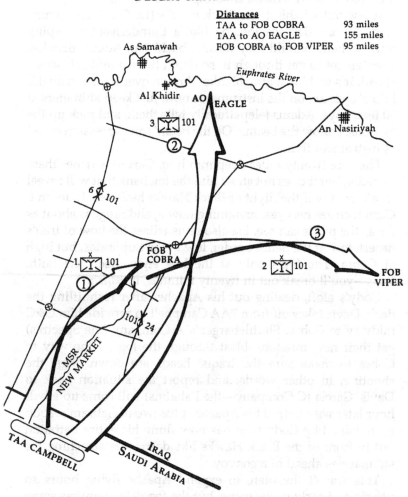

Distances

TAA to FOB COBRA	93 miles
TAA to AO EAGLE	155 miles
FOB COBRA to FOB VIPER	95 miles

As Samawah

Euphrates River

Al Khidir   AO EAGLE

3 ⊠ 101

An Nasiriyah

②

6 ⚔ 101

③

FOB COBRA

1 ⊠ 101   2 ⊠ 101   FOB VIPER

①

101   24

MSR
NEW MARKET

TAA CAMPBELL

IRAQ
SAUDI ARABIA

is scheduled to reach Cobra before the last leaves TAA Campbell, a span of over a hundred trail miles. They of course must drive on all the next night, like some military Baja race, to reach Cobra on time.

Time, even more than before, is the very essence of Desert Rendezvous. The first flight of Black Hawks can not make up the lost three hours even if they slice through the fog bank at 100 knots. Behind them now are thirty Chinooks, carrying artillery, HUMM-V's and ammunition. Chinooks, like the Black Hawks, must complete three round trips this day.

So that Cobra is secure to receive TF Citadel.

So that Citadel's HEMITs can deliver their 200,000 gallons of fuel.

So that Black Hawks can refuel after flying Third Brigade 155 miles from TAA Campbell to the Euphrates on G plus 1.

This is the syllogistic sequence for Desert Rendezvous, followed by all elements of the 101st now separated by scores of miles, soon to be hundreds. The major premise is for Hill to validate, for his infantry to confirm.

Hill's first company on the sand at Cobra is from 1-327, a renowned battalion in Vietnam, also an element of First Brigade there.* John Russell commands A Company in 1991. He is a man who feels his ultimate mission to be the same as Cody's: "You look around at your soldiers, and you're responsible for them. You have to bring them all back." The face of a widow at Ft. Campbell, of a fatherless child, causes more trepidation for Russell than the aperture of any Iraqi bunker. A/1-327 spews into the sand steeled to fight; Russell is prepared, then fittingly relieved: "I thought the LZ would be hot, but it wasn't."

Yet there is fighting, and plenty of it, to the north where Cody and Curran have exposed a major problem first discovered by Garrrett when he found the FARP site for Cobra: the 'surprise' escarpment is peppering droves of swooping Cobras, Apaches, and A-10's. U.S. tracers are red, the Iraqis' green; they crisscross the sky like a Christmas celebration.

Russell turns his company toward the air-ground battle. That

---

* 1-327 had been commanded at a critical time in Vietnam by David Hackworth, in Desert Storm a correspondent with Newsweek. Unmoved by sentimentality, the JIB barred him from joining his old outfit.

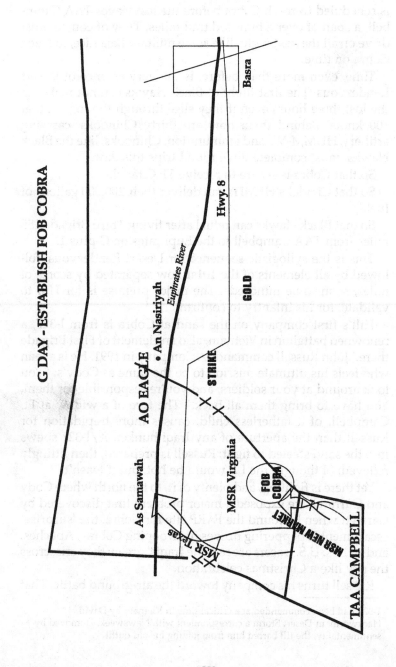

G DAY - ESTABLISH FOB COBRA

Basra

Hwy. 8

An Nasiriyah

Euphrates River

GOLD

STRIKE

AO EAGLE

• As Samawah

MSR Virginia

FOB
COBRA

MSR Texas

MSR NEW MARKET

TAA CAMPBELL

escarpment has to be cleared before Cobra can be secure. From 'Hill's hill,' where he could see for miles, Hill reflected on Garrett's serendipitous visit on G minus l: "Had we not shifted l-327's LZ [from the 'suicide *sabkha*'], we'd have been in a major fight involving the first Black Hawks going in."

Instead, Frank Hancock, commanding l-327, has room to deploy his companies and maneuver against the escarpment. Opposing him is a battalion of the 45th Iraqi Division, commanded by an Egyptian-educated lieutenant colonel, Hassam Takriti—who has relatives in Detroit as well as Saddam's hometown of Takrit. He had been fighting the attacking aircraft to a stand off. The scales tipped somewhat when Chinooks dropped off their sling-loaded howitzers. The artillerymen are exultant. They are finally to fire off some rounds in anger.

But artillery imperils attack aviation. Helicopters must avoid the 'gun-target line' when howitzers fire, for these friendly rounds are anti-aircraft projectiles till they hit the ground. In Vietnam, Hill had had a choice, howitzer volleys or strafing aircraft, one but not the other at the same time. In the desert he watches them choreograph, hears their coordination on the radio, melody and counterpoint, sweet music to his ears. Iraqi heads are down, their guns fully engaged with the attack from above. Hill tells Hancock to get going while the enemy is so distracted. LRSD reports no Iraqi positions between him and the escarpment, so as soon as they pile off their Black Hawks, l-327 deploys to take the high ground. Company objectives are pointed out on the march and marked by artillery.

There's only one battery, six howitzers, on the ground so far, and they didn't bring much ammunition. Consequently, puffs along the escarpment become fewer, forcing Cobras and Apaches to take up the slack. They soon will have more missions for Hill's other battalions that are touching down and scattering to take up an elliptical perimeter ten miles long and eight wide. Hancock must get on the escarpment while l-327 still has all the fire support. Despite loads as heavy as a hundred pounds, his troops lunge forward over three miles of rocky, rising ground.

Capt. Allen Gill commands Delta Company, containing l-327's TOW's. With artillery support and the Cobras' ammunition diminishing, he must get his ground fired missiles into action before the infantry can assault. His TOW's are mounted on HUMM-V's; with five of them and scouts on motorcycles he drives out in front of the infantry.

The attack has to be coordinated, and he begins to do so over the air with Russell and the Cobras—but then Gill's radio goes out! He switches HUMM-V's with a platoon leader, and jolts across the sand to join Russell a mile from the escarpment. There Gill hears good news. Some white flags have appeared under the Cobras' pummeling.

He studies the ridge through binoculars. He can hear Iraqi small arms but is uncertain from where it's coming. It doesn't seem to be coming his way, so he orders his little motorized task force to move out. But first Gill picks up a linguist with a bullhorn.

Gill takes the point with only fifteen soldiers behind him, and heads for the nearest white flag. This could be a trick, but the gods favor the bold. Other TOW's overwatch his advance, trying to stare down any Iraqi gunners. The Cobras fly daisy chains over Gill's venture to induce surrender. He asks them to cease fire temporarily, a carrot for the Iraqis that they know can quickly become a stick again.

Are they beaten? As Gill draws closer he sees dark lips of well-designed trenches backed up by bunkers. Closer still and he realizes that trench lines terrace all the way up the escarpment. All white flags except the one in front of him have been retracted. A single volley from the escarpment could turn his task force into a junkyard. He'd read how the Japanese and Viet Cong had suckered in Americans like this.

Cocking his Kevlar to shadow the pallor of fear, Gill dismounts, and draws his pistol like a cop about to arrest a dangerous speeder. He gestures the linguist up beside him, and winces at the trembling Arabic announcement on the bullhorn. The words set off a reaction on the escarpment. The situation is about to change, not to the liking of many Iraqis dug in and pumped up to fight. The Cobras don't hesitate: rockets once more sprout along the ridge.

This flushes out five, ten, then fifteen Iraqis in front of Gill. He waves them to his rear, takes the linguist's arm and begins to climb the escarpment. The first EPW's looked scruffy; now one better dressed and tidy climbs out of a trench. The linguist determines he is a captain, commander of the company defending the lowest terrace. Gill hands him the bullhorn—tell the rest of your men to come out. They do like flooded rats. Gill calls off the Cobras. The Iraqis, all veterans of the Iran war, have had enough. The escarpment disgorges 339 EPW's in stages of shock, plus a score of dead and more wounded, with enough supplies, anti-aircraft and anti-tank weapons, as well as ammunition to fight on for days.

They had expected to fight in a few days, but not now. Takriti's battalion is the reserve, the counterattack force for 45th Division whose mission was to stop the French at As Salman airfield. The French had jumped off in the morning. Takriti thought he had plenty of time to prepare.

Surrender of the escarpment came not a moment too soon, for the buildup of supplies could not pause, waiting for Hill to declare Cobra secure. Slow-flying Chinooks, lugging their sling loads, were the most vulnerable aircraft in the sky train, and they lumbered in while the fight for the escarpment was still very much in doubt. Cody paid special attention to their protection:

"As long as they stayed south and scooted right into their LZ's they were out of effective range of triple A on the escarpment. Just the same, when a flight of Chinooks arrived our gunships redoubled suppressive fire. Curran was doing a helluva job.

"I got distracted for a minute. When I looked up, three Chinooks were already over the main FARP, chugging north toward the escarpment. They must have been disoriented and mistook MSR Virginia for MSR New Market."

Cody headed for them full throttle like a cowboy cutting off strays.

"I scream on the air command net, 'Three 'hooks, northbound over EA—turn around!' They must have known who I was because they banked into a 180 just about the time some tracers start reaching for 'em.

"I'm about to piss in my pants. Gilman starts to go in for the AA guns so the Chinooks can get away. Trouble is we don't notice that we're also targets. But O'Neal and Jones are my wingman. They blast under my tail and take out an AA gun. They pull out and tell me I was taking fire. Sort of smirking, like, 'It's OK, Commander, we gottcha covered.' Did they ever! I had one of those after action fear rushes that's worse than anything while you're in action. From the time I sighted the three Chinooks till O'Neal and Jones saved my ass was probably less than a minute, but for me it was scarier than the rest of the war, including Normandy."

Broderick too was having his scariest moments. On the ground only two minutes after Russell, he scurried from one goose egg to another, checking which would work and which were too dusty. His couriers were military motorcyclists, perhaps the most popular jobs in the division. Move a landing panel here, a sign there, wave off a flight, bring another in. Roar away on a Kawasaki 250 to another LZ and tell the sergeant to roll out his hoses another 50 meters apart. Colonels obey corporals from Broderick; battalions do the bidding of bikers.

In fact, the entire layout of Cobra is supervised by Hill's sergeant major, Bob Nichols. He is a New Age NCO, sort of First Brigade's deputy commander for matters Hill has entrusted to him:

"There were too many moving parts for the normal chain of command, so I made Bob the mayor of Cobra. Think of Cobra as the state capital. He ran the city while Broderick had jurisdiction of the capital building which was the main FARP. They had to coordinate of course, and did magnificently. From the hill it looked like chaos, but I could see the FARP going up as Hancock was taking the escarpment down."

Corporal Alcus Davis had the best view of all the chaos, on the sand but also in the air where he was focused to the point of neck strain. He and his radio had privileged space on Hill's hill, for Alcus was the air traffic controller. All sorts of interesting happenings were going on around him at this focal point for Cobra:

A LSRD surfaced as Alcus landed. Peay arrived at mid-morning, climbed the hill to be greeted by Hill. They were both grinning and joking about the absence of amenities. EPW's from the escarpment were guarded at the foot of the hill by

MP's who had cut their hair into Mohawks (drawing growls from Weiss) to better intimidate the Iraqis, who were surprisingly obedient, even jubilant. Many spoke English, and before G Day was over the MP's had them singing, "We have a rendezvous with destiny..."

"The MP's would give 'em pushups if they got the words wrong," Alcus recalled, but he had his own oral performance, broadcast continuously throughout the sky: "Every flight from TAA Campbell reported in. I'd give it heading, wind and LZ conditions. That's just out of my mouth, then another flight leader checks in. I look up his LZ, and tell him the same sort of stuff. Down there [at the FARP] I see the first flight landing and disappear in the dust. He keeps the ground taxi short as possible. The next flight's right behind him.

"Somehow it's all working. Pumps go up and get connected just fast enough so flights aren't on the ground long. Then I've got to vector them out. Things get a litle confused at times, but my job's not to sort things out in the air. It's all just comin' and goin' like trains you can't slow down.

"Once and a while an Apache came in and jumped the gas line. They're supposed to FARP over on another side of Cobra, but I'm not about to tell 'em that. Guess they figured they had priority 'cause they had to go out and shoot."

Alcus transmits instructions at an auctioneer's speed. He will control more than 300 sorties before a flight arrives with his control tower and relief. Before then, Cobra's perimeter will spread out all around him, as well as depots, supply dumps, ammo points, medical stations, equipment pools, blivets, gas bags, Vulcans, HUMM-V's, TOW's, trucks, radios and radar. A vast base, centered on a sixteen-pump gas station, springs up out of the sand like sprouting dragon's teeth.

Peay pinches himself. There have been mishaps, malfunctions, damage, and close calls—but no American deaths. Seven choppers, among the hundreds in the air, crashed or experienced 'hard landings,' the aviation euphemism for an accident in which no one is killed. An Apache was stitched over the escarpment but wobbled into its FARP with a shredded tail rotor and severed hydraulic lines. This was the only damage inflicted by the Iraqis, and not as serious as three Chinooks which had to cut their sling loads. Lost when they plummeted into the desert were a comunications van, and First Brigade's computer equipment, causing a grave and unique shortage in this high tech war. Before Hill could leapfrog north from Cobra, perhaps as part of the Baghdad Sequel, Adams would have to find a way to reconnect him to the division's sophisticated network of lap tops.

Huber with a little pop-up tent and two men arrived to be the assault command post (ACP) for DMAIN. Shelton the master tactician soon joined him, consulting with Peay about what to do next. Again weather is the obdurate obstacle, Saddam's first, last, and best line of defense. Where fog had protected him on the morning of G Day, rain was his ally by evening. Cold dry winds swept the high plateau at Cobra, but in the Euphrates valley the wind delivered a deluge from blanketing clouds. What was the state of Third Brigade's LZ's? Peay's brain trust expected tolerable conditions, a major assumption based on unpredictable rains.

XXI

Sand is mud

Though secure by mid-morning, Cobra would not fulfill its purpose until TF Citadel's gas tankers rolled in late on the night of G Day. Betting that they would make it, Garrett launched aerial reconnaissance of the Euphrates valley on schedule. The fog delay had been made up, and the Desert Rendezvous game plan was back on the right page.

Third Brigade's long pass on G plus 1 had always represented the highest risk in the play book because Highway 8, Saddam's MSR, was tantalizingly 'a road too far.' Black Hawks could just reach it from TAA Campbell but Chinooks could not; they were short of range by about thirty miles. Only Chinooks were big enough to carry HUMM-V's and artillery, the power Third Brigade needed to hold a grip on the highway.

On G Day there was not yet enough gas at Cobra to refuel the Chinooks; but by noon on G plus 1 there should be, at which time they were to fly up from TAA Campbell into a tentative LZ called Sand. There they would debark TF Rakkasan, comprising half of 3-187, the mounted TOW's, and towed artillery, all under command of Greco. He would start them north to link up with the balance of Third Brigade scheduled to arrive on Black Hawks that night where they would set ambushes on Highway 8 in a huge goose egg called AO Eagle. That was the plan and had been all along. The high risk was that if linkup was prevented by either weather or enemy intervention, both Greco and Clark, each unable to support the other, faced 'defeat in detail,' a euphemism for the fate of commanders who separate their forces before an enemy superior in numbers.

The first question for Peay and Shelton was to determine how superior were the Iraqi forces that could be concentrated against Clark and Greco. Corps ascribed to the worst scenario. Not only were the mobile brigades at As Samawah and An Nasiriyah available to counterattack a threat to Highway 8, but the very success of 7th Corps flushing the Republican Guards out of Kuwait, might create a huge force desperate to escape. Peay could recall that the heaviest fighting at Bastogne, Belgium, was not while the 101st was encircled there but when Von Rundstedt pulled out of the Bulge. If Third Brigade was to withstand such a destructive backwash, they had to have all their combat assets together and quickly. So finding the precise location for LZ Sand became as important for Garrett as had been his search for a FARP site in Cobra, but this time there were hours rather than days to find it.

Searching and finding was the job of 1-17 Cav, the division's reconnaissance squadron (battalion), commanded by Lt. Col. John Hamlin. As Third Brigade's tenuous prospects developed on the Euphrates, he became part of a small working reunion of the West Point class of 1972. Flying beside him was Cody, on the ground at LZ Sand would be Greco, and Hank Kinnison (commanding 1-187) in AO Eagle. The 20-year acquaintanceship of these four lieutenant colonels—they'd also served together in the 101st during several periods—contributed to battlefield telepathy.

However no one was clairvoyant in locating LZ Sand. On G Day Aviation Brigade set up its CP at Cobra even as Hancock, also a classmate of the four, was taking down the escarpment, and sent Hamlin on his way with Pathfinders under 1st. Lt. Jerry Biller of 3-187, a brave little band called Team Jerry. Orienting on MSR Virginia, Hamlin's Kiowas and Black Hawks scouted northeast as the farthest flung elements of Schwarzkopf's army. 2-229 was also in the air G Day afternoon, the Apaches splitting off from Hamlin at the junction with MSR Texas, the road to As Samawah. Crossing the regional watershed, they beheld an emerald contrast to the drab monochrome of the desert.

There it was, finally, the Euphrates, the objective and goal. The river was churning chocolate as if angered that yet another war would be fought on its banks. The valley seemed to sulk under scudding clouds as if it did not wish to be exposed.

Neither did Garrett wish to show Peay's hand. The valley had to be reconned from the air but in such a way that the Iraqis were given no clues to a major landing. Plunging through the overcast, 2-229 picked off several military vehicles with FLIR; then the Apaches aerially invested As Samawah itself, with the hope that its garrison would stay put if they felt under attack. Turning east, Bryan's ships then worked over Highway 8. This was all as Garrett had desired: deception and intimidation, feints and false alarms.

2-229's aggressive activities were principally a screen for Hamlin searching to site LZ Sand. The terrain over which he scouted was unlike any previously encountered: greening, rolling hills splashed by wadis and *sabkhas* now bulging with water. The map suggested a suitably flat valley amid hills too low to interfere with landing Chinooks. After a series of deceptive touch downs, Biller pointed to the center of the valley. His Black Hawk pushed down, its blades vacuuming the surface, and with great relief for all, generating no dust.

The chopper settled—as if in curing concrete. It sank a full foot in undetected mud. The pilot had to pull full pitch to take off. This wasn't going to do it, not at all. If a Black Hawk nearly got stuck, 60 Chinooks would submerge. What's more, LZ Sand was not just a site from where TF Rakkasan would march off to the Euphrates; a small FARP had to go in here too, semi-permanently.

Some hundred miles south, in blowing sand rather than sucking mud, Lt. Col. Bob Vanantwerp—also West Point '72—struggled to get up with his classmates. He commanded 326 Engineer Battalion, much of which was now TF Grader, the road crew for TF Citadel. His engineers had the formidable mission of converting the *Dub al Haj* into MSR New Market, trafficable for old stiff-axled trucks and tankers as well as HUMM-V's and HEMIT's with cross-desert mobility. TF Rakkasan's Chinooks were to refuel, not at TAA Campbell where they started, but at Cobra from TF Citadel's tankers, and it was Vanantwerp's job to clear the way for them to Cobra.

Though his life was a success story, Vanantwerp had something to prove as an engineer. He'd been the First Captain at West Point, marked from his graduation with great promise, fulfilling it with accomplishment and a personality that graciously ascribed credit to his subordinates, a trait particularly endearing to Peay who is easily revolted by self-aggrandizement. Their relationship, unusually close for their gap in rank, is evidenced in a facetious memorial to a Vanantwerp failure. There on a plaque in Peay's Pentagon office is a faucet—a faucet from which nothing flowed but frustration.

As planner and chief engineer of tent city, Vanantwerp had assured Peay that the Screaming Eagles would have full pipes within a reasonable time. That time never came, and neither did any running water till after the war. Though pipes and faucets were widely installed, Vanantwerp could never tap into King Fahd's hydro system, as its development was suspended while the Saudis' engineering efforts were diverted by the war. The 101st's faucets remained dry, and Vanantwerp twitted daily at staff meetings.

He could console himself that basically he was a combat, not a civil engineer; that TF Grader would bury his—and 18,000 sweaty soldiers'—disappointment at tent city. His task force of dozers and road graders roared and pitched behind the scouts leading the way. On the *Dub al Haj*, his major challenges were natural sand berms and mammoth holes gouged by wind and rain.

The route became a serpentine as TF Grader angled up the berms to cut through their ridges, and shoved heaps of sand into the gouges. The HEMIT's were the test vehicles. If they could traverse the ridges and wallow around the holes, TF Citadel could deliver the payloads. If HEMIT's broke down, repair teams would scramble over them like pit crews in the Indianapolis 500; but if they got stuck, Vantantwerp had to get them rolling again.

Choppers from 2-17 Cav scouted ahead. The head of the endless column came upon Toad, grateful to find it gutted, unoccupied, and littered with abandoned Iraqi materiel. At Toad the escarpment required switchbacks. Vantantwerp's earth movers blew out clouds of exhaust while clanking into the crumbled sandstone. When a dozer broke through the final overhang, the convoy stacked up below tooted encouragement. Toad would probably be the worst patch of MSR New Market, and now it was conquered.

Overheated engines took on water at nearby wells, then McGarity looked forward to making up time. But up ahead the scouts halted as if enemy were in sight.

"What's the delay? Over."

The answer was puzzling: they'd come upon a sophisticated electronic device, something that looked like a bomb embedded in the ground. It had U.S. markings but the scouts suspected in was some kind of Iraqi proximity mine. Well blow it up and get going, came McGarity's order.

A liberal quantity of C4 was packed around the object and ignited electrically—destroying one of the Pathfinders' radio beacons that had guided Hill into Cobra! The loss proved more amusing than disabling, as by now Black Hawks were roundtripping into Cobra on familiar patterns through clear skies. Flight rules were the simplest: see and be seen.

TF Citadel's convoys had started at staggered times, so large gaps opened between them. MP's dropped off to keep later serials on course and the MSR secure from Iraqi stragglers.

Beyond Toad, the Cav spotted an unidentified squad moving toward intersection with TF Citadel. The figures went to ground, the scouts orbitted them, calling up two Black Hawks of infantry that landed and surrounded the Iraqis who sullenly were captured. MP's arrived to fly them back to TAA Campbell and one of the most interesting interrogations of the war.

The Iraqis had been armed but in bedouin garb, the first time that combination had been found with EPW's. They expressed none of the commonplace relief to be out of the war, were uncooperative and taciturn. Their leader was versed in the international protocol for treatment of prisoners of war, insisting that his band was required to provide only name, rank and serial number; furthermore, Iraqi soldiers did not have what the West considered to be serial numbers.

Quite right, the interrogator admitted, but prisoners of war must be in uniform, or openly wear some identification if they were guerrillas. Otherwise they could be regarded simply as armed men, presumably bandits or smugglers. The interrogator hinted that they might be turned over to the Saudis in that status where Koranic, rather than international law, would apply. Bandits were thieves in the eyes of Islam, and the punishment for thieves included manual amputation—as the mysterious Iraqis were well aware.

They were separated, each to mull his imminent future, then re-interrogated individually. The leader upheld his previous stance, but the others relented to say something about themselves. They were conscripts. OK. Only the leader was a professional, not in the army but the secret police. Oh? What were secret police doing way out in the boondocks?

They were 'loyalty enforcers.' This squad patrolled between As Salman and Toad, tracking down deserters. A Kiowa had strafed and knocked out their truck while they were staking out a well. Impersonating bedouins, their practice was to drift through the area, loiter at wells, where deserters came out asking for help. First the 'bedouins' demanded money; once it was provided they executed the deserter, reporting his name and home town to their headquarters in As Samawah, so that retribution also would be exacted on his family. These EPW's, in other words, had been a roving death squad.

How did they report to As Samawah? Radio. Where was it? Destroyed with the truck. 311th MI asked Aviation Brigade for a chopper to find the truck but none was available. Did the death squad remember the frequency used? One of them did. This was passed on to corps which began to monitor the loyalty enforcer radio traffic.

"These teams had quotas," said a linguist involved. "Every night they'd come up [on the air] and report to As Samawah the names and home towns of some deserters they'd executed. To make sure the right families were fingered, they'd tortured the deserters to get the addresses of relatives."

Well done, As Samawah would answer after checking the army's roster; now keep close watch around Ash Shaykhiyah— our reconnaissance force there has dwindled from so many AWOL's. Thus for corps, the enforcer net became a source of information about Iraqi morale as well as locations for their units. "One time they tortured a guy right on the radio. It made me sick. He's screaming the maiden name of his mother because As Samawah wanted to locate her."

Glitches began to appear in the enforcer system. A deserter was reported who turned out to be the former lover of a general. Regrets, but the death squad had already buried him. That caused a change in procedures. Henceforth, execution of deserters was to await authorization from As Samawah. Roger, but the squads in the field also had complaints. Their victims were increasingly destitute, so the enforcers' funds were running low, which made business with real bedouins very difficult; indeed the death squads were resorting to murder and plunder of real bedouins who consequently were abandoning the Iraqi desert. The upshot was that the death squads themselves were experiencing desertions.

"Of course the enforcers were smart enough not to give their real names and home towns when they joined the death squads. For them it was just a matter of making some money—they weren't any more loyal to Saddam than the guys we captured from 45th Division. If the war kept going against Iraq, the death squad we captured said they planned to kill their leader, then head north and rip off civilians in the Euphrates valley. They were disgusting. I wish we'd left 'em in the desert with nothing."

Though a valuable source of intelligence, corps began to view the enforcer net as something to exterminate for ethical reasons.

"By G plus 2, we had most of the teams DFed [located by radio intercepts]. Nobody asked me, but I said we ought to strike 'em. The officer above me agreed—he said we should be helping deserters—they were the people most likely to revolt against Saddam when the war was over. I think that idea went over to SOCCENT and they did something about it. They might have hit the hit men. But I don't know. Plenty of them were still reporting after the ceasefire. In fact they didn't seem to notice the war was over. Desertions went way up when it was over, so business was better then ever."

As TF Citadel reduced the distance to Cobra, Sgt. Maj. Nichols prepared a reception committee. His would be a performance that Peay often cites in lectures on new uses of sergeant majors. 1,900 vehicles were headed toward Nichols:

"Our job was to 'herring bone' each unit off McGarity's column and guide 'em into their assembly areas. Priority was for the HEMIT's. I remembered Gen. Luck's comment when we back briefed the plan. He said 45 HEMIT's had to get into the FARP that night. Colonel Hill was looking at me to make it happen."

As recently as the previous year, the crucial handoff of TF Citadel to Cobra would have been an important assignment for a full colonel if not one of the division's two brigadier generals. But the experience of advance parties coming into Dhahran in August and into TAA Campbell in January had shown Shelton and Peay that sergeants were the people who made rubber move on the road. Sergeants could swear at each other without hurt feelings, exchange blunt comments without arousing inter-unit hostility. Officers had their place, but face to sand-blasted face at night, was not the best place. There may have been majors and lieutenant colonels who resented pre-emption of their traditional responsibilities, but sergeants were most adept at getting things done in the inevitable confusion of the Citadel-Cobra merger. Nichols was like the flagman controlling landings on old aircraft carriers: pilots followed his signals without question or hesitation.

And such flagmen picked up the fighters as far out as possible. Likewise, Nichols had his bikes twenty miles south of Cobra. First they made contact with TF Citadel's choppers in the afternoon. Soon McGarity's vehicular spearhead was in radio range, about the same time the southeastern skyline flashed with pyrotechnics from the 24th Mech's opening barrages.

Nichols had done a week's work since his Black Hawk landed that morning, scant minutes behind 1-327. He had Hill's CP up in thirty minutes, had linked up with a LRSD, planted dozens of signs for arriving units, exchanged updates with Broderick as they passed on the fly, purged himself with gallons of sweat, and eaten a peck of dust. But his longest day was just beginning. Though 8,000 men of First and Second Brigade

were in the airhead, it was the 5,000 on the road that mattered
now.

"We could see Citadel's dust plume a long time before we
picked out any vehicles. I was with my HUMM-V on this ridge
watching for 'em and listening to their radio. It seemed just a
few hours ago I'd lifted out of TAA Campbell myself, so it was
hard to believe they'd come all this way cross country. But I
looked at my watch—they'd been on the trail 12 hours, a
hundred miles, and reported all 45 HEMIT's rolling. That made
me feel real good because I remembered what Gen. Luck had
said.

"But they weren't at the FARP yet, and till they were, my
team's job was just beginning. I made sure my HUMM-V was
standing out where the Citadel scouts could see it. We started
talking to 'em on the radio, and had a big orange panel to make
positive identification. I heard the leader say, 'We got you in
sight.'

"When their first vehicle came up the ridge, he looked like
he'd been in a blizzard, he was so covered with dust. I went
over, gave him some water, and shook his hand—wish someone
had got a picture of that—and told him where to go from here.
Then the serials came on hot and heavy. We peeled each one
off, assigned him to a bike guide and they roared off to where
they were going.

"The late afternoon was easy, but nothing could slow down
when it got dark. MP's were great in sorting things out, and my
guides were perfect. [Most guides had rehearsed their routes
while awaiting TF Citadel.] Everything was cooperation plus.
Egos were parked back at TAA Campbell. I didn't get any
bitching about how this or that assembly area was no good—
and some of 'em sure were. Units would say they'd like to do
some adjusting in the morning, and I said, 'Fine. Just settle in
for now.' "Not much bitching at all. When the battalion XO's
[commanding the TF Citadel serials] saw someone from their
unit who had air assaulted in, they knew they'd linked up and
were pretty happy. I was too. It was almost like the reunions
when we got home—you're so glad to see someone, you don't
care much about anything else.

"After the last serial closed, I reported in to Colonel Hill. He looks at me like a cop after I just failed a sobriety test. I guess I looked pretty punchy. He gave me a direct order to go down—he didn't want to see me anywhere except under my poncho for the next four hours."

Team Jerry's touch down and sink in showed at once that the LZ planned for Sand wouldn't work—no way. What now? It was Biller's call, and he had to make it fast. Though flying low enough to whip grass on the hills, he could not determine landing conditions from the air. Neither was there time to land and lift, land and lift, hopscotch all over the countryside. He began to think like the artillerymen whose rule is 'make a bold correction'—don't nibble with small distances. Biller decided to head higher into the hills, reasoning that the steeper ground might mean less water because of more runoff. Five kilometers from his first try, he told the pilot to try again. The Black Hawk's nose flared, the grass whipped, and the chopper's skids cautiously settled—and disappeared. "Shit!" Biller and his pilot cursed in unison. Once more they'd landed in shit.

Another five 'k's' west and no change in the terrain. This was like panhandling for gold. It was instinctive, nonrational, and probably luck if they found what they were looking for. Skids down again—they're gone in the ooze—but this time the crew feels the chopper stop, not sink. Worth a look. The mud's just ankle deep. Biller works for Greco and can imagine his boss's expression when he steps into this muck. But he should have seen the other sites. Biller gulps, climbs back into his seat, and radios new coordidnates for LZ Sand—NV 400080. There might be a better place somewhere around, but Biller feels that tomorrow Greco will have more to worry about than dry boots.

"Unass the bikes," Biller orders, and they splash down, as Hamlin takes up watch from the air. The coordinates are relayed back to DMAIN 125 miles from the new LZ Sand. Peay has returned from Cobra to DMAIN because he needs to see Clark: Hamlin's description of conditions in the valley may require a major change of tomorrow's plans.

The reason once more is weather. While Peay's window is blasted by sand when he lands at TAA Campbell, Biller's bikes are slewing through sheets of rain. Saddam's secret weapon has been fired again, and this time not in the form of ephemeral fog. The downpour in the Euphrates valley will not only delay Desert Rendezvous, it can prevent link up of Clark and Greco, and points toward their defeat in detail. As Peay and Clark get together, a radio relay is set on Biller's frequency to monitor his progress.

As Team Jerry goes, so will TF Rakkasan tomorrow (G plus l). At the moment it looks like a no go.

Down one side of Ft. Campbell, KY, extending into Clarksville, TN, is Route 41-A. Around the main gate to the sprawling base, 41-A is a strip of fast food and other soldier-oriented businesses. In many ways the strip represents home. Sentimentally, 41-A is the name Third Brigade gave the route between LZ Sand and AO Eagle. Biller leaves Pathfinders to guide and a LRSD to provide eary warning for Greco, then Team Jerry starts exploring 41-A, Hamlin overhead but invisible in the clouds so not much help if they run into anything more than more rain.

That's quite enough of an enemy. Biller has a slugger, but a 'satellite shadow' is approaching, a time when the infallible orbiter in space is obstructed by the planet itself, a period when the slugger goes blank.

And the Kawasakis are underpowered for the mud, often stuck when not slipping. The 101st's leap for the Euphrates is starting with a stumble.

At least 41-A is mostly downhill and Biller is off to an early start. Hamlin advises him of the change in plans back at TAA Campbell. Because of closing weather, everything's been moved up: Greco's first four Chinooks are expected to touch down around noon the next day. After that, it will be six hours before all of TF Rakkasan is on the ground, just about when dark settles in. Till then, Team Jerry—forty stout hearted men—are the only friendly troops near the Euphrates Valley. In the rain, Biller smiles to think how he is driving as fast as possible right toward two Iraqi brigades. The mouse has set out for the elephant, but elephants are said to run from mice.

Revising an earlier forecast, the weathermen predicted the worst rain storm of the year would hit the Euphrates valley by nightfall on G plus 1. Third Brigade's air assault into AO Eagle was originally scheduled for nightfall, the best time to elude Iraqi visually guided triple A. Recognizing a tradeoff, Peay had asked Clark's thoughts about going in during daylight.

The two went back a long way, first in Vietnam with the 1st Cav, then working together for Gen. Wickham in the Pentagon where pressure was constant, mistakes maximally conspicuous, reliability and proficiency remembered. So they knew each other almost telepathically, yet as they discussed the new weather forecast for AO Eagle, they knew this was not a council of war: if Peay said go early, Third Brigade went. Nevertheless if he perceived by voice inflection, intimation, body language, or otherwise that Clark preferred the original or a delayed schedule, Peay would do some serious re-thinking.

The most important determinant for their respective opinions was the tempo of progress so far. Cobra had made up the time from the fog delay. The 24th Mech had jumped off early, as had 7th Corps, and both were up to full throttle, picking up steam. The heavy Republican Guards divisions had not yet been brought to bay, but 7th Corps was bearing down on them. In short, the end sweep of Hail Mary had a clear field and was headed toward the end zone. To hesitate now would break the momentum. Clark recommended that Third Brigade go early, just what Peay wanted to hear and really expected.

So Team Jerry drove on into the rain and darkness, a platoon against Iraq; Biller's nearest allies on the ground a hundred miles away in Cobra. He lost his way in the elements, and with it the hope that 41-A was passable. Nonetheless, TF Rakkasan was coming in the morning, with the rest of Third Brigade close behind. Peay's gamble to go early looked as wild as the night through which Biller lurched.

Back at Cobra that night there were signs of an Iraqi counterattack. 3-101's gunships were screening the western half of the perimeter. Through NVG they could make out six tanks not of American design. The tanks moved tentatively east as if feeling for First Brigade's front lines. Radioing the information back to Huber and units on the ground, the gunships awaited permission to attack. They had no Hellfires but their rockets might persuade the Iraqis to back off. 2-327's TOW gunners focused on the direction the gunships said the tanks were coming. Lasers flicked on. The gunners confirmed that these were not U.S. tanks—which was no surprise to Hill who knew the nearest Abrams were over with 24th Mech on his other flank. The only friendly armor west of him were with the French. If they had strayed this far into the 101st's sector, they were lost indeed. Hill gave permission to engage the unknown force, but reminded 2-327 to first flash the allied recognition signal. This was done, and a radio switched over to the French frequency. 2-327 broadcast a warning: "Six tanks headed east, halt! You are approaching an American position."

The message was not answered, and the tanks came on. Each one of them was now in a lasered cross hair. The gunners had trained in desert firing for months, cleaned, protected and manhandled their TOW's in heat, cold, dust and rain. Approaching them now in the night was the payoff for the most eager crews in the division, for they had not yet fired a single missile. The tanks weaved professionally from dune to dune, driving closer into TOW range. The Americans were silently intent, holding their breaths while holding the triggers.

The recognition signal was repeated, somewhat compromising 2-327's position, but this was a sacrifice to prevent fratricide. The lead tank stopped. Lights flashed at him all along the U.S. line. He retreated into defilade and a gunship flew low across his bow. The tank commander climbed out, apparently to look at his compass away from the magnetic distortion caused by the huge metal mass of his tank. There were no sluggers in the French Army, and their maps were primitive. The tanks seemed embarrassed as they backed up and clanked away to the west.

They had been ten miles out of their sector, bound for sure destruction. Hill pondered whether to report the incident to corps but decided against it. There had been times he'd been lost as a lieutenant in Vietnam and could empathize with a young officer who now surely realized how close he'd come to leading his command to their deaths. And there was a very bright side of the incident for Hill: his own young troops had held their fire like veterans, probably better than veterans.

Hill took stock:

He was feeling even more like a veteran, a veteran of one war too many. These young guys could stay awake forever, or thought they could, but he knew the familiar feel of creeping fatigue. Now it was time to check everyone out, listen closely for halts in speech and watch for eyes momentarily out of focus. Now the peril of bad accidents rose as work, especially around the howling FARP, became routinely trying. Yet Broderick's guys were on their toes and doing superhuman feats. With luck, and it would take some, fuel and fire could be kept apart with adrenalin.

Peay looked all right. He'd round tripped from TAA Campbell already, talked with Clark there, and Hill had just seen him on a folding chair that leaned against Huber's ACP Black Hawk. Peay was in his normal, reflective mood, probably thinking two days ahead. Huber looked like he could use some help—Hess should send him some more people. Shelton looked tireless; he had a natural late night countenance. He was also at the ACP monitoring Aviation Brigade's night operations to the north. Huber has just got to get some Indians from DMAIN if the chiefs continue camping out in his pop-up tent. Hill is grateful the ACP hasn't asked him for support, a courtesy not often observed when a higher headquarters is the tenant of a lower.

Purdom is over on another side of Cobra, probably updating his plan (Desert Squall) to take Tallil if corps doesn't change their minds again. Hill has more than a professional interest in Desert Squall: if it comes off, one of his battalions will be attached to Purdom for the attack. Hill hasn't seen Garrett who set up his CP up at the gunship FARP. Clark is back at TAA Campbell getting ready. G Day had been First Brigade's day; tomorrow would be Third's.

Not much had gone wrong, and plenty could have. A dozen choppers damaged to various extents, and some valuable loads like First Brigade's computers lost, but there was only one real cloud on the horizon—a cloud of dust. Ron Adams had seen it even at 1500 feet altitude at night when his rotors produced so much static electricity from the dust that his ship seemed to carry a halo of sheet lightning.

The dust had risen on the same wind that was blowing rain in Biller's face. One flight of Chinooks with gas bags could not land with only 200 meters of visibility, meaning there was not quite enough fuel for a generous margin tomorrow, but HEMIT's from TF Citadel should soon take up the slack.

So the Screaming Eagles had landed a hundred miles behind enemy lines with danger all around them, but Hill would not exchange this position with that of any Iraqi colonel tonight. The latter's day would come tomorrow when he could regroup and retaliate with protection from 'Allah's war stopper.'

XXII

Sentences in history

Compared to the previous morning when dragon's teeth had sprouted so suddenly, dawn at Cobra on G plus 1 was calm—a calm before the *schmall*. When the tail of TF Citadel closed, the 101st had in 24 hours transplanted itself a hundred miles into enemy territory. Much remained at TAA Campbell where Third Brigade prepared to launch, but the division's base was now essentially deep in Iraq.

Where he wanted to be, Peay looked in two directions. North to the Euphrates was his primary objective, but in the east, Tallil filled his screen. Aerial photos revealed it to be a hundred acre fortress cast in concrete, pimpled with bunkers, bristling with radar, triple A and well protected SAM's. Along the perimeter were rows of tanks dug in behind revetments. If Second Brigade had to do it, their air assault would be like breaking into a huge penitentiary, complete with barb wire fences and watch towers. Purdom was a congenital worrier, and with Tallil to worry about he was gravely apprehensive. A Murphy proofer, his Desert Squall plan was thick with details. It was for such meticulous thoroughness that Peay had given Purdom command of Second Brigade.

If Tallil remained an objective for the 101st, then they would go at it with every weapon in the sky, plus artillery in World War proportions. The Air Force was alerted to provide utmost support, including B-52's on a scale reminiscent of Vietnam.*

---

* B-52 strikes were not contemplated to strike within Tallil in order to preserve the runways for the 101st's subsequent use; i.e., the Baghdad Sequel lived in Peay's mind, if only as a hope.

Additionally, Garrett would throw both Bryan and Cody at the fortress with their full battalions: 38 Apaches, a force larger than ever before concentrated on a single objective. In hours, more Hellfires would strike than in all previous combat combined. The feeling around Cobra was that we don't want to go after Tallil, but if we have to, this is going to be the greatest show on earth—and in the sky. Nevertheless, without yet a single death in the division, Peay was being briefed to expect hundreds.

Third Brigade's northerly mission was as appealing as Second Brigade's to the east was appalling: air assault was designed to 'hit 'em where they ain't,' not where the enemy was strongest. Tallil would be the hottest LZ in history; however, aerial reconnaissance indicated that Clark's LZ's in AO Eagle would be cold. Cold, but no one yet knew how wet.

By early morning of G plus 1, Biller was able to provide some information. Team Jerry had sloshed, slid and slipped in a looping advance, northeast toward a bend in an oil pipeline which was to be Third Brigade's CP. The hills were buttery slopes, the shallow valleys morasses. Though the rain abated, trafficability on 41-A had hardly improved. Greco and Clark discussed Biller's report and decided there wouldn't be much improvement, especially with greater storms predicted for the evening of G plus 1. Clark went with Greco's first lift to make a personal reconnaissance. It would take more than Hell and high water to convince Clark to postpone Third Brigade's air assault, but he had to see for himself if the linkup between TF Rakkasan and AO Eagle looked feasible.

Without a linkup Third Brigade would have no anti-tank defenses except from the air. Without some cloud clearage, the only air support would be from whatever number of A-10's the Air Force could spare, and the 101st's all-weather Apaches. The Apaches were busy on recons, and the next day most were reserved for the all-out effort against Tallil.

As Clark lifted off with Greco from TAA Campbell, the chorus of warnings from corps seemed to rise with them. The developing situation was one that had had Luck's staffers shaking their heads since Desert Rendezvous hit their desks: Peay would get a light brigade hung out in the valley during

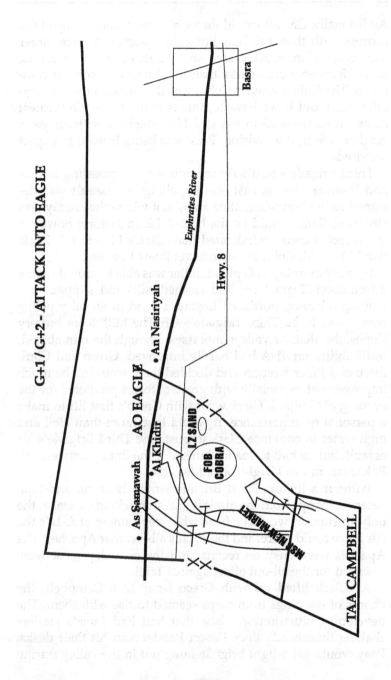

G+1 / G+2 - ATTACK INTO EAGLE

Basra

Euphrates River

Hwy. 8

An Nasiriyah

AO EAGLE

As Samawah

Al Khidir

LZ SAND

FOB COBRA

MSR NEW MARKET

TAA CAMPBELL

bad weather. Someone would have to go up and help them against Iraqi armor. That someone would have to be the 24th Mech, and they had other very important things to do, like go for Basra to slam the door on all those Republican Guards divisions. Third Brigade's predicament could throw off the intricate timing of Hail Mary and even extend the war.

Passing over the eastern edge of Cobra, Clark saw how it was now a vast oval sprawl of nearly 100,000 acres with artillery emplaced and pointed in all directions. The FARP's were gassing everything that came up to the pumps, though at a slower tempo than yesterday, and prepared to go into overdrive again to refuel Greco's Chinooks when they returned throughout the afternoon. Kiowas and Cobras flew wide circles outside Hill's perimeter, diving occasionally on MSR Virginia, guns stuttering, searching out Iraqis who straggled away from the French advance that had carried As Salman airfield. The French armor would now halt and begin screening the west flank of Schwarzkopf's offensive. The 82nd Airborne passed through them headed east —in five-ton trucks!—an amusing sight for the 101st's aviators as they protected the roadbound convoys of erstwhile paratroopers.

This was more than a chuckle because Clark's air assault would be a never-before-in-history side-step of one division over another. Virginia was the 82nd's MSR, a land corridor boring through the 101st's territory. Third Brigade was not to be connected to Cobra by land; instead, Peay's choppers would be a logistical overpass, demonstrating the unique three dimensional mobility of the air assault division.[*]

Clark had served with the 1st Cav in Vietnam, a forerunner of the air assault division, and knew the difference between strategic and tactical mobility. No matter how readily choppers flitted his troops across the map, once they were on the ground their mobility was in 'black leather personnel carriers.' The HUMM-V's were great, but most of his troops would move in boots alone. If the weather didn't clear, Third Brigade would be basically foot-slogging infantry.

LZ Sand hove in the distance. To Clark and Greco it didn't

---

[*] As the war careened toward its gridlocked climax, the 101st would continue to skip around at will.

look too bad from the air. The Pathfinder's arms were raised in a V. As the first Chinook approached he tried to step back, but his boots wouldn't move. His pratfall seemed ominous to the landing troops: it didn't look like mud down there, it was patchy with grass, grass growing in the sand. Must be like quicksand, the men of TF Rakkasan concluded.

They leaped from the Chinooks, scrambling to unload the internally loaded HUMM-V's. Their scramble became a tableau. Feet that hit the ground running, stuck and stayed, to be pulled out one at a time. Sixty-pound rucksacks drove legs deep like a piledriver. The Chinook blades whirled for take off, the pilots accustomed to short minutes for unloading. They craned around in their cockpits—what the hell was taking so long?

Clark plodded to the edge of the LZ. Biller had not exagerrated. 41-A was going to be forty miles of no road. Obviously it would take Greco some time before he could even get under way. Clark returned to his Black Hawk as sling loaded howitzers sank like cement sacks into LZ Sand's quagmire. Maybe it was better up ahead. Pulling full torque from the rotors, Clark's Black Hawk rose from the muck and headed for Team Jerry. In daylight, Biller might be making better progress.

He wasn't. Team Jerry had taken small arms fire from some buildings along the way but ignored it, pressing on with four-wheel drive and mud-filled motorcycle chains till they reached an irrigation ditch not shown on his map, twenty miles from the pipeline. Clark checked in with him, then scouted on to the pipeline. Damn, there was another such wide ditch, after Biller crossed the first one, if he could. Clark banked, flying by LZ Sand on his way back to TAA Campbell where Third Brigade was waiting at the PZ's for his last minute instructions. He radioed Greco to get small dozers up front to push causeways across those irrigation ditches. For the troops back at the PZ's, Clark could only advise them to take some extra socks because feet were going to be soaked for a long time.

With a 250-mile round trip, it took six hours for Wilmoth's Chinooks to deliver TF Rakkasan. For the return flight they refueled at Cobra, topped off at TAA Campbell, then took a shortcut back to LZ Sand by crossing a slice of the 24th Mech's AO. Greco couldn't wait for all of TF Rakkasan to assemble at LZ Sand. He sent out each lift as it arrived. This split the task force into five convoys, with the attendant possibility that some would get lost. During daylight, that shouldn't be too much of a worry: the twisting ganglion of Biller's tracks through the mud was sufficient guide.

At night—they'd surely be plowing north all night—there would be more of a problem because NVG foreshortened distance and flattened dimensions. Greco had too few men to drop off guides. He had to get going because Third Brigade was coming. They'd be landing about forty miles north of him. Forty miles of no man's land that had to be traversed before link up between Clark's light infantry and Greco's heavy supporting arms. Failure to link up could indeed make Highway 8 'a road too far.'

1-502, manning the southeast quadrant of Cobra, first heard it—a distant, lambent tone above the desert, deepening into what sounded like a single engine, its pistons pumping rhythmically. 1-502 radioed Huber's ACP: "Here comes Third Brigade."

The first lift came in 65 Black Hawks, V's in trail, like a slow moving barrage of arrowheads. They'd taken off after the morning fog lifted, a cloudless voyage of 155 miles until they reached the Euphrates valley. They soared right along Cobra's eastern perimeter, a sort of pass in review for their comrades on the ground, and that's how Peay on Hill's hill, saw it. There would be no AO Eagle were it not for FOB Cobra. The ball had been lateraled from Hill to Clark, with Peay the quarterback watching the exchange. He'd been a second string quarterback at VMI, noted more for his sense of the game and field position than physical skill, and he now watched the play unfold:

"They were so low I could see soldiers in the doors of Black Hawks grinning and pointing at us. Some people on the ground waved back like shipwrecked sailors. Everyone realized what was happening, and I think most of us remember it as the high point of the war. Those dusty, worn out guys at Cobra gave thumbs up to the Black Hawks. Third Brigade signalled back with V's for victory."

For two hours the Black Hawks flew, Garcia's Apaches weaving between their formations, scanning the route for triple A.* Cody's other companies were attempting to recon Tallil, because Second Brigade was still scheduled to attack the next night. For its radar alone, to say nothing of its triple A, Tallil was frighteningly more difficult for TF Normandy's veterans. They had to come at the air base 'downhill' over flat desert where Iraqi radar could pick them up; whereas in the Normandy raid, Apaches had sneaked up through wadis. This was one of two increased dangers accepted for moving up landing times into daylight. The night-fighting 101st was contradicting its doctrine, but Peay would gamble—as he'd shown on H Hour—when the odds were with him. His worth was in perceiving when they were.

His bet looked good when not a shot was directed at the passage of Clark's sky train. But the second forecast risk was soon verified by radio intercepts: 65 Black Hawks had been spotted by Iraqi outposts, and the garrisons at As Samawah and An Nasiriyah alerted. Peay had to assume that Baghdad was now aware of the threat to the lifeline of the embattled Iraqi army in Kuwait. Simply by counting Black Hawks and multiplying by twelve, Saddam's generals knew how many American troops were descending on their MSR. This display of strength was a possibly decisive drawback to landing in daylight. Clark and Peay would learn if they'd won the gamble by how soon and seriously the Iraqis reacted. Too soon would be before linkup with TF Rakkasan; too serious if the brigades at As Samawah and An Nasiriyah coordinated their counterattack in a rainstorm.

The Iraqis reacted, but at the highest levels. Foreign Minister

---

* Cody's other companies were attempting to recon Tallil, because Second Brigade was still scheduled to attack the next night. For its radar alone, to say nothing of its triple A, Tallil was frighteningly more difficult for TF Normandy's veterans. They had to come at the air base 'downhill' over flat desert where Iraqi radar could pick them up; whereas in the Normandy raid, Apaches had sneaked up through wadis.

Tariq Aziz protested to the UN that for troops to be introduced along the Euphrates was outside the Security Council mandate. No fair! Then he went on the air, describing the outrage to his nation: "The forces of aggression have barbarically deployed in these areas with a show of muscle by dropping troops from helicopters."

By the time Third Brigade was dropping troops from helicopters, the 45th Iraqi Division had reported the creation of Cobra in their rear. So it was unmistakably certain to Saddam how far the "barbarians in helicopters" had traveled in 36 hours: at least 90 miles from the Saudi border to Cobra, now another 60 to AO Eagle. That put the 101st closer to Baghdad than to where they'd started.*

If the Iraqi high command still held hope to supply their beleaguered army in Kuwait, every force near the Euphrates would be thrown against Third Brigade. Peay saw this as his threat as much as Saddam saw it as his. Peay had to know what trustworthy Clark thought about the situation once he was on

---

* At the time of this writing, there is virtually no material available from the Iraqi army concerning their conduct of the war. However, all evidence is that they did not know where the 101st was at the start of G Day. EPW interrogation indicated the Iraqis believed TAA Campbell was a Syrian position. Though there were some close calls with LRSD's, no Screaming Eagles were taken prisoner, the usual means for locating opposing forces. Three soldiers attached to the division were captured in the last hours of the war (see Chapter XXV), but divulged no intelligence. So the question of whether or not Saddam understood the threat of the air assault division to his capital—and consequently to his regime— must await research not currently possible. However, two strong inferences indicate that he did.

The first is Baghdad's simple mathematical calculation of distances: if 3,000 heliborne soldiers landed ninety miles deep in Iraq were followed by another 3,000 sixty miles deeper, it would take only one more such leap to put thousands around Baghdad and suddenly.

The other inference indicates that Saddam did his math because he began pulling his Republican Guards out through Basra the moment he realized Third Brigade had lodged on the Euphrates. He could have withdrawn other equally formidable divisions, but Republican Guards represented his personal security, and they force marched straight for Baghdad. So it's clear he felt he needed them there.

It's equally clear that the 101st, though he probably did not know their identity, were the cause of his need (Kurdish and Shiite uprisings were elsewhere). In this sense the Baghdad Sequel, though never executed, was a psychological accomplishment, unnerving Saddam and perhaps was the most convincing proof for him that the jig was up.

the ground. Mucking through the bottomlands of the Euphrates, his radioman struggling to keep up, Clark was handed the handset with a stammered exclamation that "Genp" was calling.

Though scrambled to prevent Iraqi interpretation, Peay's question was itself a cryptic shorthand:

"Bob, have you got it?"

There was a second's pause, but years of overlay, in Clark's answer: "Yes, sir." That was a prediction, a hunch, a feeling, a conviction, and enough.

Locations for Third Brigade's LZ's had been well calculated, then confirmed by Hamlin's scouts. The green fields below were lush contrast to the Screaming Eagles' desert habitat, and contained a new, troubling element—people. The valley was populated by farmers and herders, not scattered and itinerant bedouins.

The LZ's were dotted with huts. Peasants cowered inside them as flocks of goats scattered under the frightening beat of helicopter blades.

One of the criteria in selecting LZ's Crockett, Festus and Chester was civilian presence on them, and Clark preferred no contact with civilians at all until his ambushes were firmly emplaced on Highway 8. His troops splashed into the mud and slogged toward their positions. Each hut was checked out en route, but few weapons were found and only two words spoken to occupants: *Salam Alakham* —a wish for the peace of God.

This was about the only Arabic the infantry had been taught, an excellent all-purpose phrase that quieted fearful civilians and even prevented outbreak of firing at night when a vehicle approached an ambush. Halted and surrounded by many caliber weapons, the driver—be he a Jordanian trucker, Shiite chicken farmer, or deserter—had every instinct to flee. He'd be killed if he tried; but upon hearing *Salam*, even drawled or with a Yankee twang, the driver calmed long enough till an Arabic linguist (there was at least one per battalion) came up to question him.

Staggering through the mire, Third Brigade must set up before dark, a period of three hours for the first flight, increasingly less for the following waves of Black Hawks. Just south-east of the town of Al Khidir (population approximately 15,000) that sprawled on both sides of the Euphrates, Highway 8, paralleled by a double tracked railroad, dog legs 45 degrees in an 'm'-shaped loop of the river. On the shank nearest Al Khidir, a company of 3-187 (the other two infantry companies were with Greco in TF Rakkasan) moved into a flanking position off the highway. Three miles east, 2-187 (Lt. Col. Andy Berdy) was to flank the dog leg. 1-187 was in reserve along the pipeline, having seized a small airstrip and a pumping station five miles east of Clark's CP, the terminus of 41-A, TF Rakkasan's hard sought destination.

Since Clark's assumption of command in November, Third had become known as the Lone Star Brigade, a nickname justified by considering how he designated his various positions. His was Waco (where his staff has ensconsed in a one-room building called The Alamo), Greco's Austin, Kinnison's Abilene—though he was from Lubbock—and the road north to As Samawah labeled MSR Texas.

As planned, Third Brigade was taking the shape of a two-pronged fork, battalions deployed on the tips, connected with a third battalion near Waco with the handle (41-A) leading down to LZ Sand. From Waco, 3-320 Artillery could support both TF Rakkasan and the fork tips. The FARP for Third Brigade's choppers was out of enemy artillery range back at LZ Sand. Thus Clark, with a thousand troops in AO Eagle by dark and till TF Rakkasan joined them, was expected to ambush the enemy's supply line while his own, 41-A, was secure if not yet trafficable. He was a spider that had spun a hasty, fragile web that now awaited the arrival of flies.

"They came in 'one-sies and two-sies,'" Clark recalled of the first encounters. "The Iraqi Army didn't seem to understand what we'd done, even though they must have seen us do it when all our Black Hawks landed."

The Iraqis learned from a series of small skirmishes, which, as in every war, are the sentences in its history. The officers' plans were working; now it was time for the enlisted men to go to work.

Sergeant Gary Rister, Specialists Fred Kranz and Dave

Wyrick of 2-17 Cav were Pathfinders for TF Rakkasan. They're a beacon team, dropped off at 9:30 a.m. on G plus 1 about midway between Cobra and LZ Sand. The beacon had to be precisely located, and Hamlin had done so with a slugger, but the best place for the beacon to transmit was about the worst for the team's concealment. They got the beacon working, then slinked off to watch it from a 'hide.'

It's broad daylight, and there's not a friendly sight or sound in twenty miles. The wind whistles across dry uplands like the high plains of Montana, and as much exposed. They fan out, searching for a fast hide under some outcropping or in the walls of a wadi.

Wadis don't work: there have been recent rains so the sand is too soft. Rister signals this opinion, heads toward Kranz who is approaching a knoll that looks like it has a good view of the beacon. The knoll is a pile of gray sand and slate, with shadows where the men could lie down with some concealment. In a freeze-frame moment, flashes erupt in the shadows with the heavy thump of AK-47's.

The team dives as the fire echoes between hills. The Americans no longer feel lonely, but doubly exposed. Rister has to decide whether to crawl away, try to reassemble his team and watch the beacon from a mile away or...

Well, the Iraqis must have seen them insert the beacon. They'll go out and get it and then get after us. They're not going to get that beacon. Rister will fall back and destroy it first. He's between the bunker and the beacon, so might as well fight it out here. What we need are a couple of Apaches. He crawls around where he can see Wyrick about fifty meters away—good man—Rister can see he's already on the radio.

But after a few minutes, while the Iraqis continue to fire at where the team went to ground, Wyrick looks over at Rister and raises his hands palm up. Wyrick either didn't make radio contact or the gunships are tied up at LZ Sand. OK, Rister decides, we'll play infantry. Pathfinders only fight when they have to, but here they're cornered, forced into a shootout.

Something about the sound and aim of the AK-47's emboldens Rister. The smart thing obviously is to get the Iraqis to attack, try to pick 'em off as they come out of the bunkers (where there's one bunker like the one which fired at him, there are always more). But instead Rister signals for his buddies to move on the bunker. Fire and movement: you cover me then I'll cover you. This could confuse the Iraqis. They've never been very aggressive, so this little surprise attack might distract them from the beacon. Better to do this now while there's plenty of daylight. At night they could slip around us.

Using much practiced fire and movement, the three men leapfrog toward the bunker—then other bunkers open up on them. Ricochets whine off rocks like some western movie. With fire coming from three sides, Rister has to keep his team moving, while he does some thinking. To pull back will probably be more dangerous than advancing, and he must keep his only advantage, which is psychological.

He remembers the G minus 7 actions, especially at Toad, where the Iraqis seemed awed by what came at them from the air and ground: short, sharp actions decided early by heavy firepower and rapid movment. Rister's team is heavily armed, dripping with grenades and extra magazines for their M-16's. He signals to increase the rate of fire, focused on the first bunker, though the others are equally threatening. He's following a hunch.

Iraqis don't have much initiative, so it was probably the guy in charge who ordered his men to open fire. That fire came from the first bunker. Knock it out, knock out the man in command, and his men may back off. That was as much as Rister could hope for, a stalemate or standoff. Shooting, scooting, crawling and covering, the three come abreast thirty meters from the bunker where Rister sends his pair around to the sides. The three will close in concentrically. They can't cover each other's backs—they'd be exposed to the other bunkers—so the assault will have to be quick, very quick.

From the bunker, muzzle flashes of two AK-47's spurt from the main aperture. Rister unclips his grenades and lines them up in the sand so he can throw them fast. Then he experiences one of those sudden, odd, irrelevant thoughts that sometimes break into all-engrossing combat: he's impressed at how white hot are the muzzle flashes, a novelty because he's never seen one aimed at him.

They're shooting high. Wyrick and Kranz have crawled out of his view. Rister has to guess when they'll be ready. Can't wait too long or the other bunkers will pick them off. Can't start too soon, or the bunker won't be flanked. Another hunch. When he's down to four grenades, he'll go for the bunker, his buddies will see him and also attack.

"AIR ASSAULT! AIRBORNE!"

Rister remembers screaming other words at the bunker as he comes off the sand. The rapid poppity-pop from three charging M-16's suppresses the AK-47's into a timid reply. Three grenades bounce on the bunker, roll down and detonate, causing no damage to its thick shell but apparently stunning the occupants. Kranz spins inside ready to kill, but his finger releases the trigger from his last burst. The split second pause preserves the lives of three wide-eyed Iraqis. One already has a white rag in the air.

Rister and Wyrick pile in right behind Kranz. Now protected by the bunker, they are as relieved as its original occupants. The Americans are gasping from hyperventilation, the Iraqis from terror—terrified expressions that even startle their captors.

Rister: "We must have looked awful wild. I couldn't believe none of us had been hit, and the Iraqis couldn't believe they'd live another heartbeat."

Rister's hunch was right: one of his captives is the lieutenant in charge of the outpost. Wyrick pushes him out of the bunker with the white rag. The other bunkers cease fire. Inside their bunker, the team debates what to do next. They don't want to push their luck and assault again, but the other bunkers shouldn't be left occupied either. The Americans need to catch their breath; this pause solves their problem by allowing the remaining Iraqis to slip away, probably to the road to As Samawah and desertion.

The bunker was a good place to stay. The Pathfinders could watch their beacon and search the abandoned bunkers. The Iraqis had fled, leaving piles of maps, documents, some weapons, and gas masks that didn't work. The Pathfinders had learned a major reason why chemical warfare was not employed against coalition forces—Iraqi troops were ill-prepared to resist a chemical counterattack.

The afternoon sun turned turned tan with wind-blown dust, then squalls mixed in causing a weather phenomenon unexperienced before by the Americans—a mud storm. Rister's team was scheduled for extraction at dusk. They were feeling good about themsleves, and felt better when radio contact was restored with gunships.* But communications were sporadic. Wyrick was the RTO (radio operator), and had never heard such strange goings on in the ether. He was picking up traffic from far away divisions in 7th Corps loud and clear, then roaring static, then tomb-like silence. Seemed a *schmall* was building:

"I knew then commo was going to be a big problem."

One message they received meant another big problem. Deteriorating weather and a LRSD in trouble had cancelled their extraction. Be prepared to protect the beacon for another 24 hours. The Pathfinders groaned. A Black Hawk had swooped down to extract the EPW's and documents, but no other choppers were scheduled to visit. Rister's team was short of ammo and rations. They went back through the bunkers picking up a couple of AK-47's, but the Iraqis had left no food.

The LRSD in trouble was the farthest from Cobra. They'd been watching the road to As Samawah since early on G Day, from a plateau above the edge of the Euphrates valley. Below them, as in AO Eagle, the flood plain was well populated. Goatherds and shepherds sauntered into the greening hills to graze their flocks, much as their Mesopotamian ancestors had for millenia. The tinkle of bells passed by and around the LRSD. They were on terrain that was family pastures, as familiar to the herders as their huts.

The LRSD became concerned when, unlike the afternoon before, the morning pattern of grazing on G plus 1 seemed to avoid their plateau. The LRSD had been inserted into a valley out of sight; thereafter Apaches from 2-229 had crisscrossed MSR Texas, but the LRSD was nervous that its landing had been spotted—there were just too many herders in these hills. Since the air war began, Saddam had put out bounties for downed

---

* All three were awarded Bronze Stars for valor.

fliers. Discovery of this LRSD would surely make some civilians very rich.

Almost from the time they went into their hide, the LRSD had plenty to report as they watched the junction of MSR Texas and Highway 8. They were able to tip off 2-229 where military trucks were concealed. In time, the Iraqis began to feel their traffic was being observed from the ground. Naturally they would have inquired among the local populace, asking if they'd noticed anything unusual in the vicinity. By the afternoon of G plus 1, suspicion must have focused on the LRSD's plateau.

Three trucks loaded with troops sped down MSR Texas. The LRSD commander instinctively perceived their mission was to comb the plateau. He had a good defensive position and six tough men, but LRSD's, like Pathfinders', job is not to fight. He radioed for an emergency extraction. Two Black Hawks and two Apaches from Cobra were on alert for just such a mission. The race to the plateau was on, bad weather favoring the Iraqis in their trucks.

Rescuers and pursuers arrived almost simultaneously, the Black Hawks first. As the LRSD loaded on, they could hear gears down-shifting to climb the plateau. With rockets the Apaches stopped them a half mile away, destroying two trucks, the third escaping under a concrete bridge.

The LRSD was all too glad to get away, but now Peay had no permanent observation on Iraqi movements out of As Samawah, nor from An Nasiriyah. Night was closing, winds were rising and clouds falling. The worst scenario was set for Third Brigade. If the Iraqi army was to attack, it would be from As Samawah and An Nasiriyah, and it would be tonight.

1-187 was racing with the night. Three hours of overcast daylight remained when their Black Hawks settled in the goo of LZ Crockett, and they had much to do: seize the Darraji air strip, the pumping station, then set up a defense around them against anything coming down the pipeline, the eastern-most and most isolated position in AO Eagle. C Company, commanded by Capt. Tim Fahy, led the battalion off the LZ. His task was to reduce the pumping station so A Company could pass through to capture the air strip.

Pre-attack intelligence reports didn't describe half of what C Company would run into. 2nd Lt. Dave Priatko's platoon was in front with Sgt. Sean O'Brian's squad on point. The spearhead of Peay's 160-mile, 10,000-man aerial lance tipped at this point. The plans were the best they could be, but another old army adage still applied: a poor plan well executed is far better than a good plan poorly executed. Execution is the report card, hopefully the payoff, for training. Considering how long, how hard, C Company had trained in the desert over the past six months, no one was surprised at how fast they came out of the box and off their LZ, mud and wind notwithstanding.

The pumping station turned out to be much more than a building, it was the hub of concrete clusters built for the rigors of petroleum engineering, and equally significant as a military stronghold. Aerial photos had shown an enclosing fence and berm but revealed too little of significance inside. The job for O'Brian's squad was to breach the fence (like that around a prison) and berm, opening the way for his platoon to go for the pump house. A flat morass of a hundred meters stretched between him and the fence. Two companies set up to support his squad, in a larger scale version of Rister's fire and maneuver.

The climb to Calvary for an infantryman is to cross an open field, a field that in a flashing instant could become a field of enemy fire, exposed and essentially helpless. This ordeal for O'Brian was foretold by reports from B as well as C Company: they saw movement behind the fence. The breach point is covered by Iraqi soldiers. Call it courage, call it scaffold psychology—Priatko called it an absence of options—O'Brian has to lead his men across that open field.

As they approach the fence its every barb and strand becomes hallucinatorily vivid and distinct. A time warp for O'Brian's squad, elongated minutes when they hear nothing except their deep breathing and the suck of their boots. Then the sound of ripping paper overhead. They wince, then quickly realize this is artillery from 3-320. The air bursts over the Iraqis' stronghold may keep their heads down.

O'Brian's at the fence at last. Gratefully his men flop down in the mud to start snipping at the wire with bolt cutters, and feel around for land mines. The Iraqis hadn't shown much as soldiers but with mines they didn't even have to. Mines require no courage by those who use them, only inadequate caution by those against whom they are used. Mines never sleep, flee, nor surrender; they're a hundred percent accurate, for they don't explode until their target detonates them. O'Brian strokes the surface of the mud as he would a woman's breast. The prickle of a mine's prongs could be his last sensation.

One man wriggles through the breach in the fence. He's on the other side, prone and pointing his M-16 at anything that might move in front of him. The breach is widened till his squad can join him, fanned out on the ground, looking over to O'Brian for instructions. He feels this is the essence of leadership—eyes focusing on his, men willing, waiting to obey his commands—stunning when first experienced.

From back across the field, Priatko witnesses their success. He radios the report that O'Brian has made it. He's in the stronghold, so lift the artillery. Silence returns over the pumping station. Priatko sees O'Brian's men flitting into the buildings, checking them out just as they had trained at FOB Oasis. Priatko takes the lead and hurries his platoon across the field and through the breach. Inside the stronghold he sees how much there is to it: interior berms, bunkers, triple A revetments, reinforced wire fences, plus a dozen concrete structures. Clearing this place is far too big a job for just his platoon. Priatko looks up and sees Fahy beside him. C Company has poured through the breach.

Warm food, items scattered in haste, the long ash on a burning cigarette, indicate that at least a platoon of Iraqis recently vacated the pumping station. They were probably a triple A unit. For whatever reasons, maybe the low clouds and the intimidating din of scores of helicopter engines, they hadn't fired on the Black Hawk flock. But where did that Iraqi platoon go? Fahy rushes the search, worried less about overlooking something than in reaching the eastern gate where C Company is to support A Company's attack on the air strip. It's dark enough now that the elusive Iraqi platoon could reach the air strip and join whoever's already there.

Fahy feels that's where they have gone. But why? Why not at least fire from behind the fence where they could have wiped out O'Brian's squad with a machinegun burst? Or if this platoon were REMF's, why didn't they just give up? They had the perfect opportunity to surrender. Fahy begins to believe the worst: the Iraqis at the pumping station stronghold felt there is safety over at the air strip. For some reason they became convinced they would neither have to fight nor surrender. Fahy radios his forebodings to A Company's commander and Kinnison: 1-187 has been lucky so far, but there's a fight coming.

Descending darkness preys on Clark's thoughts. Even more than the mud and treacherous weather, the night will hamper, delay his plan. Blond, some say bland, Clark remains unproven as a brigade commander. He has handled himself astutely so far, profiting from his predecessor's (McDonald) exacting standards for staff work, and benefitting from the opportunity to give the battalion commanders looser reins than McDonald permitted. They like working for Clark. He will let them fight their battalions without looking over their shoulders. Kinnison and Berdy—Greco is still struggling up 41-A—in turn will similarly put trust in their company commanders' judgement as darkness becomes the ultimate fog of war. The same is true within the companies, a cascading devolution of execution to the ultimate war-decider, the trigger-puller.

In the first week of basic training, the trigger-pullers were talked through a ridiculously simple exercise. They were handed large cardboard rectangles with a ball above it, both black on white background. The rectangle represented the front sight blade of their weapons, the ball the target.

"Center the ball over the rectangle," they were instructed with all seriousness by a beribboned sergeant. He gravely came around to see that the ball was indeed centered, a rudiment any six-year-old could do in a moment. "This is your sight picture," the Purple Hearted sergeant announced, then went on to instruct skills more difficult but secondary.

As the night of G plus 1 enveloped Third Brigade, the most important function at any level was getting a sight picture.

B/2-187 was the main ambush on Highway 8. 3-187 was closer to Al Khidir, but it was a skeleton force until joined by TF Rakkasan. If the Iraqi counterattack came from the west, 3-187 would provide warning but not much protection; if it came from the east, 2-187 on the dog leg would be the first to know. B company was western-most, commanded by Capt. Mike McBride. His men, most of all, had to have good sight pictures.

At first, night vision goggles helped a lot. Civilian vehicles came down Highway 8 cautiously, were stopped by B Company and turned around. Shortly the Americans posted a sign in Arabic on the road: 'US forces. Stay out.'

Weiss guffawed when he heard about the sign: "Could you imagine an ambush warning like that in Vietnam? These guys [Third Brigade] were ready to kill—they'd been ready since Desert Shield started—but they didn't want to hurt anybody who didn't shoot at them." Weiss shook his head. "Different war, different warriors..."

McBride was less concerned about tipping off his ambushes than the clouding of his company's NVG. They could see in darkness but not in sand. In a rising tempest, the elements were pre-empting the battlefield. Ferocious wind drove rain, then stinging dust, in B Company's face. Nothing could move but sand and air. Someone checked the direction: the storm came at them from about 330 degrees, nearly due north. *Schmall* means north in Arabic, the equivalent of a New England Nor'easter. Clark reported to Cobra that he was hunkering down to withstand the *schmall*. Cobra couldn't hear him because they were in it. Cobra was being swept by a dry, war-stopping hurricane.

XXIII

The schmall from hell

"**B**efore the second lift of Third Brigade's Black Hawks could thrust north, the window of flyable weather slammed shut. At Colonel Clark's request, this lift of 800 troops dismounted at FOB Cobra where they remained overnight."

So read Lippard's official journal as a gritty curtain rang down on the weather window, grounding all aircraft. At TAA Campbell and AO Eagle, the *schmall* blew in gusts of rain; but at FOB Cobra, atop the arch of Iraq's desert, it was a pure sandstorm. Cobra submerged into a communications black hole as cyclonic winds seemed to suck radio signals out of the sky.

Working for Weiss at DMAIN was a soldier he knew only as 'Sam,' probably the most improbable Screaming Eagle in the desert. He was a Saudi, and Sam was an acronym of his Arabic names too difficult for Americans to pronounce. Sponsored by the kingdom, Sam had completed junior college in Wisconsin and was reluctant to go home after falling in love with a co-ed, then marrying her without the knowledge of his family in Dhahran. In the spring of 1990, Sam enlisted in the US Army Reserve to ensure his citizenship as his student visa had expired.

"He was supposed to go into the Saudi Army to pay back his student loan," Weiss chuckled, "so when he joined up in the States, Sam thought he had it made. 'I want to serve in the Midwest, not the Middle East,' he told me, but guess where the army sent him in August?"

As a liaison with the Saudis, Sam served well at King Fahd

though in constant fear that his family, even more than his government, would discover that he had returned and was so close to home. If he had to go into Dhahran, he wore an oversize Kevlar with driving goggles. He was permitted to wear a name tag that read simply SAM—though this drew stares from aviators.

As tents luffed and lost their pegs at TAA Campbell, Weiss called for Sam. The Screaming Eagles did not want to appear intimidated by this sandstorm, but the looks around DMAIN implied that this was much worse than bad. In forecasting the evening of G plus 1, the always restrained official language of Air Force weathermen contained unusual adjectives like 'severe,''powerful,' and even 'dangerous'—but Weiss was beginning to think this might be the mother of all *schmalls*.

"Sam, you've seen plenty of these, haven't you?"

"Yes, sergeant major."

"How bad is this one?"

"Sir, this a *schmall* from hell."

At Cobra, it sandblasted paint from metal. Latrines blew across the desert like tumbleweed. Helicopters strained against guy lines while their exhaust ports packed with sand. Engines would have to be thoroughly flushed with chemicals before anything flew again.

Tents flapped, billowed, then blew away, some never to be recovered. Men lay prone, drifts of sand piling on one side, scoured cavities on the other. Any loose cloth popped like a runaway machinegun.

In the early stages of the *schmall*, 1-101 made brave to support Third Brigade according to plan. This was more than a tough mission for Cody: his longtime and closest friend, Tom Greco, was lunging head down northward on 41-A, and 1-101 were Greco's eyes and guns overhead. Cody had stationed Mike Davis in a C&C ship above TF Rakkasan, with inflexible orders to remain there even if all Saddam's MIG's, SAM's, Grails and triple-A gathered to destroy him.

But Davis's windshield turned opaque from sandblasting. It became certain he would be a liability rather than an asset if he remained in the sky over 41-A. 1-101's journal related his reluctant withdrawal:

G plus 1, 5:00 p.m.:
In marginal weather, 5 Paladin guns and 4 Stingrays depart to holding area vicinity LZ Sand. [Davis] also displaces to LZ Sand to establish Attack Command Post.

7:00 p.m.:
A and B Company mission [Tallil recon] again put on hold, this time for extremely poor visibility and FLIR picture coupled with no illumination due to sandstorm.

7:45 p.m.:
As weather deteriorates, [Davis] decides not to launch Stingrays, just Paladin guns.

8:00 p.m.:
Only two Paladins can launch for mission in this weather. FLIR penetrates only one-eighth mile but Paladins press on.

9:45-10:00 p.m.:
Paladins destroy two enemy cargo vehicles and towed triple A on Hwy. 8. Estimate 3 enemy KIA. Returning to Cobra. Remainder of Paladins and Stingrays socked in at LZ Sand. Will try to return to Cobra in the morning.

11:50 p.m.:
1-101 to ground all aircraft except for emergency call from Third Bde.

Third Brigade had now become split into thirds about fifty miles apart: Clark's first lift on the Euphrates, the aborted second lift grounded by the *schmall* at Cobra, and TF Rakkasan still ploughing north on 41-A. Clark and Greco were on their own till the skies cleared. This was to be Peay's longest night, the night of the infantry, the time for only close range sight pictures.

2-187 would see most of them, because Clark had designated Berdy's ambush postion at Abilene the brigade's 'main effort' to block Highway 8. Berdy is 42-years-old, and exhausted by his trudge through the tar-like mud. He wheezes with relief as he receives his companies' reports that they have set up and tied in their positions. Berdy's now convinced that war is for young men, hoping only that his are less tired than he and that the Iraqis are having a bad night too.

Tension overrides his fatigue as he hears small arms announce the first contacts on Highway 8. Everyone will have to do double duty because 2-187 is half strength due to weather cancellation of Third Brigade's second lift. Berdy's no longer worried whether he can stay awake. He's only a hundred meters from the highway himself, dangerously close but with the advantage that he can hear and sense the battle without intervening reports from his companies. He's also a cherry— only a very few battalion commanders are Vietnam veterans— but he feels he can gauge the situation as it develops at Abilene.

Strategically, Abilene is an ambush but tactically it is a defense. Classic ambushers hit then run. They determine the location for the action while the enemy determines the time. Abilene is where Clark wants Berdy to be, but 2-187 can not pull off the highway after hitting the first Iraqi force to enter the kill zone. He must stay and fight the second and all comers, even after they've been alerted by the first. Like Purdom at Hafer Al Batin, Berdy must 'retain' Abilene, a delicate term for die in place unless Clark authorizes retreat.

Berdy is not thinking retreat. What he hears of small arms fire and from his radio is a mixed and perplexing situation. The Iraqis have been in a ground war for 48 hours, but up here on the Euphrates many seem unaware that the war has arrived.

For Berdy's men, the long-sought highway is a strip of gray in whirling darkness. Squad-size patrols slither down to examine vehicles abandoned on the asphalt. There's a Toyota on the shoulder, motor running, its radio blaring like a boom box. Where did the driver go? Scared off by the sound of Third Brigade's helicopters? The squad leader is puzzled. He just turns off the grating Arabic yodel from the radio (sung by a woman obsessed with 'Ali') so he can better listen for approaching vehicles.

Another civilian vehicle stops on the highway. A woman gets out and looks at the surrounding embankment where men of 2-187 feel themselves to be concealed. She knows different, and opens her blouse to expose a breast, indicating that she needs food for her baby in the vehicle. A sergeant emerges from the darkness and gives her MRE's collected from his squad, then returns to the shadows and his ambush.

Later, a military truck screeches to a halt before it reaches the roadblock. Now some action for which 2-187 has so long prepared. Tracers streak through the night, shredding the truck. But the Iraqi soldiers are already gone before one of Berdy's patrols check it out. It becomes clear to him, and his company commanders, that the ambush is comromised but also avoided pretty much by Iraqi forces. Each engagement seems offbeat and off the track of conventional warfare. Shooting is as complex a matter for the troops as it is for police in the United States.

The hard-bitten infantrymen are soft hearted. If, through NVG, they see a civilian vehicle, they stop it like an MP rather than with a machinegun. Military trucks are another matter: put a fountain of fire on the hood and windshield, then sees what comes out. From one such truck, a squad of Iraqis erupt like popcorn and shoot back. Fair game! Capt. McBride's men advance on them like like leeches to heat. All are captured or killed. Hand slaps between the Screaming Eagles. This is more like it—a job for which they'd trained.

But nothing has trained them to handle civilians and soldiers coming down Highway 8, alternately and intertwined. This typifies Iraq at present: the populace doesn't know what's going on because their government tells them nothing or lies. The military is centralized like their government. If the chain of command hasn't told the troops that their MSR is being strangled, they don't know and assume it's still open.

To be on top of such ambiguous situations, McBride moves from one to another, determining how to do the right thing. His company's biggest fight is protecting wounded Iraqi soldiers from the fire of their comrades. US Army annals reveal no other instance where soldiers are cited for heroism in saving the lives of enemy troops.

This was Sgt. Steve Edwards' action at a roadblock he created with two abandoned Hondas. Outposts reported a military truck speeding toward him. It tried to ram through; his squad blasted it, killing 13 inside and wounding two Iraqi soldiers in the cab. Edwards could see them writhing and moaning. The right thing to do is get them out and back to U.S. medics. Through stinging sand of the *schmall*, Edwards leads his squad across the flat ground between the ambush and the highway. A second Iraqi Army truck had seen the first start to burn. Seventeen Iraqi soldiers deployed from the second truck and were soon joined by a squad from a third. Edwards' squad is eager for the challenge, no matter that the objective is to save two Iraqis from immolation.

NVG is not much good in the sandstorm. The combatants can do little more than fire at each other's muzzle flashes. From the widening arc of flashes, Edwards determines that his squad is being flanked. These Iraqis are pretty good. Maybe they're the point for the main effort to reopen Highway 8.

McBride is wondering the same thing. We ought to get some EPW's from this group and find out if they belong to the brigade in An

Nasiriyah. He tries to pass that word down to Edwards but the sergeant's too busy as his engagement has come to close quarters—too close now for help from 3-320 Artillery.

Outnumbered in a vigorous fire fight, Edwards begins to reflect on the objective here. Why are we risking our asses to medevac Iraqis from the middle of other Iraqis who are shooting at us to prevent the rescue?

Too late now, there's no backing out. Besides, his men are fully engaged to the front, and Edwards has to worry about the flank. Can't see anything lying in the mud. He rises to a squat, then stands up to check if the Iraqis have gotten around him. A small back blast from that direction. It's a rocket-propelled grenade (RPG), a little off target but aimed his way; its explosion is muffled by mud.*

Edwards' squad increases its fire to protect him. They also move around, and apparently impress the Iraqis to be a larger force. Head to head at twenty meters range in the darkness, the Iraqis fire with abandon and anger, but as Edwards' squad shift positions the Iraqis grow concerned about their own flank. Out in the field where they have less cover, Iraqi fire dwindles. They seem to fear Edwards may be getting around them; but at the road embankment they fight on, encouraged by the chatter of their light machinegun.

---

* An old joke about Vietnam Lurps attending a first aid class:
  Lurp: How do you treat a casualty who's been hit by an RPG?
  Medic: You try to keep him from going to pieces.

Then flames reach the first truck's fuel line. The gas tank blows, and the burning truck begins to illuminate the embankment, revealing Iraqi positions around their machinegun. Without a word from Edwards, his squad centers it in a cone of bursts. A scream, the barrel points up, convulsing figures roll off the embankment. B Company's machineguns supporting Edwards rule the night. Soon there's no answering fire. It's white flag time.

The Americans rush for the truck as if in a bayonet charge. Surrendering Iraqis scream for mercy, but they're not the target. Two of Edwards' men leap onto the running boards and pull the originally wounded Iraqis from the cab. Others throw down their weapons and help. This is mercy in action, and prompts EPW's to call for other comrades to come in and give up.

"Shrewd battlefield psychology?" Edwards is asked later, but he shrugs off the inference. His men just didn't like to see wounded men burn up in a truck. The Americans had not experienced the heart chill, the dehumanizing hatred, engendered by seeing their buddies die that way—or at all. They'd not felt the blood lust, the omnipotent passion for *revenge*.

This emotional lacuna would be the great differentiator from Vietnam. Shelton was a Vietnam vet of several tours, had seen severed ears as souvenirs; and though in no way a blood lusty man, he appreciated the satisfaction of killing an armed enemy. Not long after Edwards' battle to save Iraqi wounded, Shelton reviewed FLIR film of 1-101's night interdiction elsewhere on Highway 8. The pilot stood behind him to explain the action. As the screen fuzzed into light, the highway was empty, but soon a truck rolled into the picture, causing Shelton to remark, "Boy, I wish I could be an Apache pilot."

"I was identifying the truck, sir."

"Roger." Shelton smiled as the truck traveled on obliviously. It seemed not even to hear the Apache trailing it. It was a five-tonner, unmarked but the type often used by the Iraqi army. The truck bed was covered by canvas. Shelton didn't doubt it was a troop carrier. Constraints flicked on. "Yeah," he murmured approvingly, noting the laser return. Shelton leaned forward. But the truck and film rolled on. "Shoot," he urged.

And on. "Shoot!" And on. "SHOOT, dammit!" The laser and constraints went off. The embarrassed pilot stopped the film.

"I wasn't positive, sir."

"Positive?" Shelton exclaimed more in amazement than anger.

"Sir, I couldn't tell if those were soldiers in the cab." Shelton gasped and collected himself. This was a different war, a new generation.

The night ticks on at Clark's CP, punctuated by fire flurries from actions like Edward's. One a.m., two a.m.—it doesn't sound as if the Iraqis are making best use of their opportunity in the *schmall* to break through Third Brigade's ambushes. This will be welcome news to transmit through division to the worriers at corps, but the sandstorm breaks up communication to Cobra. TF Rakkasan has reported in sporadically: they have some vehicles lost and have taken some EPW's. Team Jerry is still trying to find a way for Greco, and Kinnison will send a patrol down to guide Greco as soon as he seizes Darraji air strip, Peay's launching pad for the Baghdad Sequel. Darraji is Clark's main tactical concern tonight. The Iraqis may have regrouped there; if so their expulsion will require the most devilish of infantry maneuvers, a night attack.

Fahy has C Company deployed to cover A Company's attack. He's around the eastern gate of the pumping station, with a stretch of two hundred meters to the air strip. 'Lead from the front' is a motto for Screaming Eagle officers, and Fahy joins his most exposed squad who now must do what O'Brian's squad did previously—cross a field of fire.

They're caught in the open. Iraqis fire plentifully but wildly as A Company dives into the mud like otters. Priatko sees they're getting flanking fire from bunkers. The best way to support A Company's attack is to go for those bunkers, at least keep them busy and their fire off A company. Priatko dispatches a squad on that mission, then sees that he's sent a boy to do a man's job. He goes out with his second squad to build up necessary counterfire. No cover—this is up close combat on a soggy football field. If the Iraqis ever lowered their muzzles they'd graze on the Americans.

But the Iraqis are still in shock. They decide to melt away into the storm before A Company can storm the air strip. They leave enough behind to have held out for another day: 60mm mortars, heavy machineguns, RPG's, as well as their triple A that could have scoured the battlefield.

By 3:00 a.m., Third Brigade, despite their half strength, are holding all their objectives. Daylight, if the *schmall* abates, should bring linkup with TF Rakkasan. Then the longest night will be over for Clark, a supreme relief for Peay who is prepared to conquer anything except the weather.

Meanwhile, Cobra is as isolated as a polar expedition in a blizzard. Except over land line, Peay can talk to no one outside the tiny tent of the Assault CP where he, Shelton, Huber and an RTO are the paralyzed nerve center of the division. The generals have slumped in folding chairs through the night, awakening instinctively when a message gets through from Third Brigade. The key man for the time is back at DMAIN, Joe Bolt, who has gone another round with corps over Tallil.

Is it on or is it off? Corps is not saying yet—seems to depend on the 24th Mech's progress that has been slowed by the *schmall*. As soon as the weather clears, Peay wants to fly over and see McCaffrey to get this thing settled. Meanwhile, Hill has done some coordination of his own and tidied the AO. On the corps operations map is a circle with an X in it, a point on the ground where the 101st and 24th Mech are to tie in. Remembering the drift of lost French tanks toward Cobra, Hill wants no similar encroachment by either American division, an increasingly probable accident in this blinding *schmall*. He sends an officer with a slugger to the circled X; the officer is not to consider his mission accomplished until he shakes hands with a counterpart from the 24th Mech.

On the 101st's western boundary, a tie in with the 82nd is delayed as they untangle themselves from a backlog of French traffic. Behind them, corps supply trains are groping forward toward MSR Virginia. All of Luck's commanders are advancing persistently (for Peay, the advance is TF Rakkasan's struggle toward Waco), but the *schmall* has geared down the war from fast forward to slow motion.

Until this *schmall* returns to hell, all that can significantly progress is planning: 2-502 is released from corps reserve and scheduled to rejoin Second Brigade, an indication that Luck's plan is for Purdom to draw the Tallil mission after all. But the *schmall* prevents 2-502 from taking off for Cobra. Without four battalions for Second Brigade, the betting changes back to the 24th Mech. Purdom is a man scheduled for execution, but receiving eleventh hour reprieves from the governor. Purdom wants all concerned to stop speculating and put on their game faces—he schedules a sand table exercise to go over every phase of the Tallil air assault.

By now TF Citadel has been dissolved. However MSR New Market still crawls with vehicles hauling supplies for the logistical buildup of Cobra—Cobra, the gathering place, the coiling of the spring for further leaps, whether toward Baghdad or Basra. But migration toward Cobra virtually halts as windshields seem to be looking into a spinning mix master. It's too easy to drift off the track as trail signs have been blown back into Saudi Arabia, and guides are hunkering under ponchos.

Garrett's battalion commanders, stretching his 'emergency flights only' rule required by the *schmall*, are overflying MSR New Market in an effort to reposition aircraft between Cobra and TAA Campbell. Some choppers must be south and others north when operations resume. Some try to get in the right restarting position despite the sandstorm. The beacons on New Market help. Traveling south, Black Hawks set wind assisted speed records. Battling north, they must often set down, clear windshields, then take off again between gusts. Fuel lights are on when they reach Cobra after hours of up and down fluttering flight.

Between Cobra and LZ Sand, Rister's beacon team has forgotten about extraction but not their mission. The beacon's signal is weakening. Wyrick leaves the bunker to change batteries. At first he thinks he hears the wind cracking, but sand begins to spurt about him as AK-47's again echo through the hills. He dashes back to the bunker, tries to raise Cobra on his radio, but the pathfinders realize they're still on their own.

At LZ Sand, Hamlin has not given up on flying recon for his

classmate, Greco. Officially, aircraft are grounded but there is always the emergency escape clause. 2-17 Cav uses it liberally to take off whenever visibility opens to an eighth of a mile. There's a fork on the road to the pipeline that has yet to be checked out. When wind 'subsides' to 25 knots, Hamlin launches a Black Hawk loaded with pathfinders, covered by two gunships from 3-101. No one expects to see much, but simply to be in and on the air near TF Rakkasan will be moral support for Greco.

Flying slow and low, the scouts find the fork. The branch to be reconned runs due north, straight into the vector of the *schmall*. They quickly set down, then prepare to take off again realizing the wind will not lessen. The pathfinders are signalled in from their perimeter defense of this tiny, impromptu LZ. Wait a minute, they radio back, there're some Iraqis out here. Blades feather as the choppers wait.

Five, ten minutes they wait. Fifteen. What's going on out in the sandstorm? There's been no firing, but Curran's men feel uncomfortably vulnerable. They'd be sitting ducks if a squad of Iraqis stumbled onto them. Finally, after twenty minutes, the pathfinders race back to their ship and signal thumbs up. The next two hours are a bobbing battle with the elements as the Black Hawks try to rediscover LZ Sand, an effort as futile as skin divers finding the Titanic.

The twenty-minute touchdown is forgotten until the flight gives up and instead lands at Cobra. Then Curran has time to ask—what were the pathfinders doing out there that took so long? Who were the Iraqis they found?

All right, the pathfinders would relate the incident, and swore in advance everything they said was true:

Fifty meters or so from the touchdown, they literally tripped on some bunkers covered with drifted sand. They saw a light inside one, shoved an M-16 in the aperture, with a *Salam Alakham* greeting. A female shrieked from within. The pathfinders pointed their weapons at the door as it shoved sand; then they dug from the outside, realizing the woman couldn't get out by herself.

She emerged, dressed in an ankle-length black *chadri*, the coverall of Saudi women that during Desert Shield had inspired the nickname BMO—black moving objects. She would have to be frisked, and this could be awkward. The senior NCO moved toward her hesitantly. She seemed to understand his intention. First she gesticulated toward the bunker, the cascade of Arabic consonants imploring the Americans to be merciful. Yes, he understood: the NCO would frisk her in the privacy of the bunker. He followed her—but leaped out when he saw many wide eyeballs, white in the darkness. He spun away from the entrance, as his pathfinders leveled their weapons to cover him.

But the woman clung to his back, almost bringing him to the ground. She released him, reached for her skirt and flung it overhead, leaving her quite naked in the needling sand storm.

Most of the twenty-minute delay had been in determining the purpose of her exposure. Without an interpreter, the pathfinders nonetheless were able to perceive a complicated situation and its history. The men in the bunkers were unarmed deserters, one of them her husband. Briefly they'd been captured on G Day—by the French who agreed to trade prisoners for favors from the wife. She was prepared to barter herself again if the Americans would only spare her husband. Touched—and short of time—the pathfinders trudged away, disappearing into the sandstorm without exacting a quid pro quo from this Iraqi Isabella.

The pathfinders' encounter typified how the *schmall* transformed the war into combat between the blind. Until the air cleared for sight pictures, reflex was the substitute. Every man seemed to be a point man.

At the point for Clark's entire operation was Capt. Rick Carlson, commanding C/3-187 at Austin, an ambush very short handed until TF Rakkasan arrived. Mortars and artillery would have to take up the slack for the absence of enough direct fire weapons, but he had a good man on a light machinegun, PFC Charles Woody. C Company's kill zone covered the approaches from Al Khidir where a concrete bridge stood over the Euphrates. Whenever TF Rakkasan joined C Company, destruction of that bridge would be the battalion's objective, but on the morning of G plus 2 Carlson could only watch it, hoping the bridge was not Saddam's funnel to pour reinforcements and armor into AO Eagle. It was the only bridge still standing within twenty miles.

The first Iraqis to approach it were local Shiites, quite grateful for C Company's presence. Al Khidir would be a stronghold for later uprisings against the regime, and its inhabitants provided useful information about the hated Saddamite garrison. Like the current municipal government: a local guerrilla drove up in a Mercedes riddled with a bullet holes on the passenger side. The Mercedes had lately been the official car of Al Khidir's mayor. Deposed and beheaded, he needed it no longer.

Would the garrison try to break out? Carlson wanted to know. *Inshallah* —the Shiites were making life difficult for them in Al Khidir. Should the guerrillas flush the garrison into the ambush? Thanks very much, but hold up for a while, Carlson answered, worried that C Company's forces were too skimpy.

During the night, nearly till dawn, Al Khidir crackled with small arms fire that could be heard even over the howling *schmall*. The Shiites were settling old scores, the garrison was fighting back, and the situation could only be guessed. His eyes silting with dust, Woody watched to the east, the opposite direction from Al Khidir. Without warning, a sedan sped through the *schmall* toward Woody's position. His platoon was turned the other way, toward the town. Iraqis opened up from the car, trying to blast through with heavy fire and high speed. Blindsided, Woody's platoon was pinned down by the surprise attack. He cut loose a magazine but the car came on; apparently it was armor plated. Dodging bullets, Woody raced to intercept it, scrambled to a closer position, and blew out the windshields. All six Iraqis in the car then turned their weapons on him. It was an uneven fire fight till his platoon regrouped and forced the car back. No more surprises, *schmall* or no *schmall*, the men muttered; and no Iraqi is going to get close to the bridge again till Greco arrives and tells us what to do with it.

With that resolve, Carlson judged that Woody's small scale action would be the first of many. Carlson roamed through his company's positions, sensing their excitement of first combat. This was also his first experience of war, and for him it focused on getting support from his mortars and artillery. Whatever it took, that car had better be the last to escape his kill zone. 3-187 had a tradition to uphold: their last big action was in Vietnam on Hamburger Hill. That battle must have been tough; however, it wasn't fought in a *schmall*.

At TAA Campbell, Cobra, LZ Sand, on 41-A and in AO Eagle, Screaming Eagles began wearing gas masks. The filters soon clogged with *schmall* dust, but that was better than sand papering the throat with each breath. The weather defeated most military radios, but the 101st was able to keep up on the war by listening to short wave broadcasts from London. At 4:00 a.m. on G plus 2 (26 Feb.), BBC reported that Saddam had ordered his army out of Kuwait. This drew cheers from soldiers huddled by transistors, and promises to expedite his order.

But the next newscast contained a term that so far had been gratefully forgotten: mass casualties. A Scud had fallen on a building in Dhahran. Initial estimates of casualties were 12 dead, 30 wounded and 42 missing National Guardsmen from Pennsylvania. Something close to a revenge motive crept into conversations. Three days earlier, the division would have been delighted to hear Saddam was pulling out. Now developments were about to orient on preventing him from doing so. The next development was certainly marked 'Tallil.' The accelerating situation forced corps to finally decide the issue of who and when.

From Lippard's history:

> "As the divison prepared for future operations, the choice between an assault into [Tallil or an ammo dump nearby] hung in the balance. Early indications had suggested Second Brigade would be going into [Tallil], but messages from corps on the night of the 25th indicated assault into [the ammo dump]. Colonel Bolt now informed us that the objective would be the latter after the 24th Mech seized the former."

For the G5 section of the division staff, the likelihood of either mission raised the neck hairs. G5's province is all matters civilian: refugees, sustenance of war victims, restoration of basic municipal services in war-ravaged cities, martial law and order—and also an obscure sub-department labled 'culture and archeology.' Unbeknownst to Peay or Purdom (as well as Cody whose scouts had flown the area), there were stunning cultural and archeological artifacts between Second Brigade's two possible objectives.

Within G5 a whisper started: "It's on to Ur!" It was passed to Dave Wood, Purdom's XO, but the whisper was lost in the clamor of changing plans.

Thousands of years before, the Euphrates ran some six miles north of its modern bed and there joined with the Tigris. Near this junction was the original metropolis of western civilization, the city of Ur, legendary home of Abraham, he the pater familias of three great religions, Judaism, Christianity and Islam. Iraq was known as Mesopotamia at that time, and since, 'the cradle of civilization.'

Encyclopedia Britannica would have been as pertinent for Purdom as the writings of Ibn Batuta had been for McGarity. Ur's location, just northeast of Tallil and south of An Nasiriyah, is described in Britannica:

> Although most of the ruins of Ur as seen today—and the ziggurat is one of the best preserved in Mesopotamia—belong in their present form to the Neobabylonian period, recent excavations have shown that the site has been occupied from extreme antiquity... Graves are dated provisionally to 3500 B.C.
>
> The great temple area at Ur is both striking and has had many archeological results. The sacred enclosure as it exists today is the work of Nebuchadrezzar. The outer wall appears to have been pierced by six great gateways. The southerly was restored by Cyrus the Great.
>
> The ziggurat stands in the northwest corner of the sacred area. It consists of three stories. The lowest measures 210x140x20 feet. A small building crowns the third stage. This was the bedchamber of the god and goddess, not a temple as Herodotus supposed. The actual temple laid in ruins between the time of Hammurabi and the Kassite dynasty.

How an enormously solid, three-story structure like the ziggurat eluded detection in aerial photos and reconnaissance can not be explained by Peay, even after the war. Certainly the *schmall* obscured any features of ancient Ur as H Hour approached for the assault on Tallil, but Second Brigade's OPLAN, in preparation for longer than a month, made no mention of Ur or any archeological sites whatever.

Elsewhere in the theater Air Force pilots had complained of Iraqi vehicles snuggled against another zigurrat where they were spared from allied bombing for historical considerations. Around Tallil-An Nasiriyah, the zigurrat of Ur was the highest structure in the battle area. If it were used for observation or triple A—for which it was eminently suitable—it would have drawn Hellfires until its destruction or Iraqi evacuation eliminated its military significance.

The militarily justifiable obliteration of the abbey of Monte Cassino in World War II besmirched the allied crusade against fascism, the occupation of Angkor Vat by the Khmer Rouge further blackened their reputation, the shelling of Dubrovnik by the Serbian army in 1992 horrified the civilized world—but if the 101st were to wreak but a small portion of their horrific firepower on a principal artifact of original civilization, the reason could not outlive the result. Normandy, Holland, Bastogne, Ashau, and Cobra would be forgotten—as would the sobriquet, Screaming Eagles. Only 'The Destroyers of Ur' would attach to every mention of the division thereafter—for as long thereafter as Ur had existed theretofore.

G5 is traditionally a rather slighted staff section. In previous wars, war fighters judged G5's value by how well it could keep refugees off the MSR. Whatever Peay's G5 knew about the significance of Ur, it never reached him. Blithely, Purdom's OPLAN was approved, all the way through corps. Luckily it was never executed.

Ur was saved by the *schmall*. Over history, ten thousand *schmalls* must have blasted its walls, its temples and zigurrat, while Ur was inhabited, then when it fell to ruin. Ur was saved by Luck, by luck, and the *schmall* of 26 February 1991.

With weather precluding Purdom, Luck finally gave approval to a plan whereby a brigade (197th) of the 24th Mech would drive north off the pipeline to seize Tallil. Eager to be first into Basra, Tallil was a digression for McCaffrey, causing him to vent anger which bulged the walls of his tent when he learned that the air base—after all the debate and palaver— would be his objective, not Peay's. The 197th attacked from due south, away from Ur, attacked with armor on the ground rather than helicopters over the zigurrat. After hours of delay to refuel 197th's tracks, it was a quick, clean attack—the defenders better prepared against an air assault than the tanks that burst through Tallil's front gates.

Inside they destroyed six MIG's on the ground, two Soviet T-55 tanks, and innumerable triple-A weapons. In a hurry to catch up with the rest of 24th Mech, the 197th was gone in three hours. When weather cleared, Garrett flew into the desolate, smoking hulk of the airbase. He was delighted to see a Hind, the latest model Soviet attack helicopter, parked undamaged on a runway. Though the *schmall* had blown over, still no one noticed the zigurrat in the distance.

XXIV

The Audible

As the *schmall* raged all during G plus 2, Peay had plenty of time to plan his next moves. If corps told the 101st to seize Tallil, fine: Purdom had that plan all wrapped up and rehearsed. But if Tallil went to the 24th Mech—as indeed it would—what then? Schwarzkopf had abundant armor forces charging east to cork the bottleneck at Basra. Was there a chance he'd release his air assault division for operations north of the Euphrates? With everything else on his mind, would he remember the Baghdad Sequel?

Peay was still hoping, so he had to be in a fly pattern if Schwarzkopf passed for the end zone. Upfield was where Peay wanted to go, and had Bolt check with corps to sense if anything like a Baghdad Sequel was being contemplated. If it was, Peay needed a base, an FOB like Cobra but farther north, for a launching pad to hit Saddam where he lived. At the moment, AO Eagle best filled the bill. Tallil was too far east, though it would be valuable for its hard stand and hangars—a sort of King Fahd to Eagle as TAA Campbell had been to Cobra. The Darraji air strip in Eagle would be crammed with helicopters, but even overcrowded it had much better physical facilities than Cobra and was significantly closer to Baghdad...

Though the *schmall* provided a pause for Peay to plan, the situation at AO Eagle required some immediate decisions. Like the bridge at Al Khidir where Woody had shot up the armored car, and Carlson awaited Greco. If the 101st were to spring into the Baghdad Sequel they'd need that bridge intact, perhaps to run an MSR up into the Tigris-Euphrates peninsula. Third

Brigade's original mission included destruction of the bridge to forestall counterattack, but from Clark's reports it did not appear that Iraqi reinforcements would try to cross it. Leave it up or knock it down? Unless Peay changed Clark's orders, 3-187 would begin efforts to destroy the bridge.

They were now filling out their strength, and more capable to do the job because the crucial link up had finally been accomplished. TF Rakkasan at last lurched into Waco, then Greco set off for Austin to beef up Carlson's ambush. Clark now had his full complement of TOW's and towed artillery, plenty of force to back up his infantry, including engineers who cratered Highway 8, stopping all traffic more authoritatively than Honda roadblocks like McBride's.

The linkup had happened because skies had cleared, and the *schmall* from Hell left a heavenly surprise in its wake: the hot winds had largely dried up the LZ's for Third Brigade's long-delayed second lift. The fickle gods of weather had abandoned Saddam as earlier they had jilted Peay; so now supply trucks on 41-A bumped along through drying mud, wondering why the route had been so much trouble for TF Rakkasan. The weather too was fine for flying. Rister's beacon team was finally extracted, 48 hours late and famished.

Only the bridge at Al Khidir was spoiling Clark's G plus 2 day. The engineers studied it from afar, did some calculations, then advised that they had too few demolitions for the job even if 3-187 attacked and seized the abutments at both ends. Al Khidir, from the sounds of insurrection and anarchy during the night, was not where Greco wanted to send his infantry unless there was no other way to take down the bridge. Yet unless there was an nth hour reprieve from Luck, Peay felt he had to destroy it. In that state of mind he was less than unhappy about the difficulties Clark was encountering in finding a way to do it.

What about the Air Force? The request went back to Cobra, thence to TAA Campbell, thence to corps in Rafha where the reply came back—sure, right on—there'd be some A-10's on station at daybreak of G plus 3. How about Greco lasing the bridge for them? They had smart bombs, and some practice with Special Forces in laser ground guidance, so let's do this bridge with high tech in high style.

Fine, Third Brigade responded: the A-10's should come up on 3-187's frequency, then together the Army and Air Force would drop the bridge. An NBC TV crew was with Clark at Waco; they'd be delighted to record the joint accomplishment.

All is in readiness at Austin, lasers focused, and civilians told (through the guerrillas) to stay away from the bridge. But as the early morning wears on, word comes up that the A-10's have been diverted to support the 24th Mech, now corps' main effort. Does division want this bridge knocked out or not? Third Brigade begins to wonder. Yes and no. Peay has not quite given up on the Baghdad Sequel. Garrett is advised to try Hellfires on the bridge, a temporizing measure that is hoped will drop a span but not destroy the abutments for subsequent use by the Screaming Eagles.

Paladins draw the mission, and take off from Cobra to arrive over the bridge at 7:15 a.m. Iraqi soldiers hate Apaches more than anything else in the sky. The *schmall* is gone, and the Apaches are back—greeted by vengeful ground fire that causes Third Brigade to re-estimate the size of Al Khidir's garrison. Do Paladins want artillery to suppress the ground fire? Clark hopes not—artillery would tear up the town. No problem, Ken Brown, Palladin lead, replies—we'll just stand off a bit over Austin.

From a hover, constraints go on, lasers bounce back from the center span. Fzzzz... TOF four seconds, three, two, one... Apache engineers ... Concrete puffs in a white cloud from the arch of the bridge. The dust settles and Brown assesses the work. The guard rail is down and the span cratered. Three more Hellfires saw half-way through. The Iraqis cease fire as if to see whether their solid brdge can hold up.

Paladins realize they are being watched from all sides, so the last two Hellfires must be precise like the final blows of an axe that topples a tree. They blast away the remaining chunks of concrete that splash toweringly into the muddy Euphrates, leaving twisted rebars groping in a gap of air.

The severed bridge at Al Khidir symbolizes Peay's hopes cut off for a Baghdad Sequel. Before the Apaches were over the bridge, he received the division's new mission. It would not be north. Instead corps says veer east, set up a hasty FOB in an area already overrun by the 3rd Cav. From there Aviation Brigade is to interdict the Iraqi retreat toward Basra. The new FOB is called Viper, a hundred miles from Cobra. Be prepared, Peay is told, to launch a brigade from Viper another hundred miles farther east into a marshy region hard on the Shatt Al Arab and the Iranian border, some thirty miles above Basra.

This last landing is named EA (engagement area) Thomas, surname of 2-327's CO, the battalion to lead the assault for First Brigade. Second Brigade tosses aside their Tallil plans and saddles up for Viper, a last-second change known as The Audible—quarterback Peay barking out oral instructions that will shift 5,000 men, hundreds of choppers and vehicles, from one objective to another.

Schwarzkopf's purpose for Viper and Thomas is clear: trap and annihilate as much of the retreating enemy as possible. Viper will be like an aircraft carrier in the sea of sand, a place from where to launch Apache strikes, cutting the threads to which Iraqi forces in Kuwait still cling. EA Thomas, in turn, will be a seal on the cork if the 24th Mech gets to Basra.

The Audible starts with a quick huddle at the undermanned ACP in Cobra. Peay, Shelton, Hill and Purdom have their heads together, with Huber listening in to take notes. Cross-eyed from lack of sleep, his hands sweat as he realizes there can be absolutely no stenographic errors. The brains of the division are tossing out thoughts, batting around concepts, formulating then changing tentative plans in a four-branched stream of consciousness. Huber has got to get the outcome right. Hard copy, even though only handwritten, of Peay's orders must follow the huddle within minutes. Everyone has got to know what's to be done, and there will be no time for corrections.

Get it right the first time, Huber exhorts himself. Changes of plans caused by original misinterpretations are extremely demoralizing for units that must make the actual adjustment—they sense that the higher headquarters don't know what they're doing. The two generals and two colonels know, but only Huber's notes can record and send their intended message. He listens intently...

Peay's concept—Second Brigade to Viper, half of First Brigade to EA Thomas—is clear enough. We've got to get 2-502 up from TAA Campbell ASAP, Shelton comments. Nods all around. This may not be the most significant shuffling of units but it sets Hill beaming. He's to turn over 3-327 to Purdom, but in exchange Hill picks up the battalion he served with in Vietnam. What First Brigade will be, temporarily, is the First Brigade that was the 101st's original force in Vietnam and fought there separately till the rest of the division arrived two years later. Hill's new First Brigade was his old outfit.

The conferees are happy for him, but have much more on their minds than historical coincidences. No one has seen Viper, not even from the air—it was seized only an hour before. Huber scribbles that Aviation Brigade is to get 2-17 Cav out there fast. Garrett must also be alerted to get a FARP rolling toward Viper. Shelton fears EA Thomas will be overrun with refugees. And what about Iran? What do we do if a chopper goes down in Iran, less than twenty miles away? One war is enough for the moment. EA Thomas is on order. Viper is tomorrow morning.

Morning? Huber hears the question raised, but answered by consensus. Yes, the division's doctrine is to air assault at night, but the Iraqis have already been kicked out of Viper. It's safer to see where we're landing if, rather than tonight, we go in tomorrow morning. We'll be operating out of Viper in the afternoon, plenty of time to influence the armor battle closing in on Basra. Go for it, Purdom.

The huddle lasts less than half an hour. The principals scatter to give warning orders to subordinates. Huber begins his transcription, hoping that word of mouth does not distort what he is writing by hand. No one has had a longer, more tiring war than Huber. He was the first Screaming Eagle to arrive in Saudi Arabia and is reputed to have said, stepping onto the tarmac, "One small step for an Oh-five [lieutenant colonel], but a giant leap for the One-oh-one."

No one is kidding him now. He's got to put a lot in motion pretty much by himself. Huber faxes his handwritten minutes of the huddle to TAA Campbell, but by the time the order is formally printed there it will be an historical document.

Viper is now on everyone's front burner, EA Thomas right

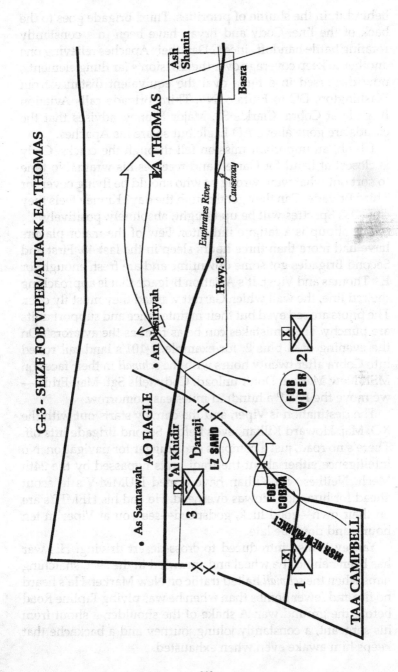

G+3 - SEIZE FOB VIPER/ATTACK EA THOMAS

EA THOMAS

AO EAGLE

Ash Shanin

Basra

Causeway

Euphrates River

Hwy. 8

• An Nasiriyah

• As Samawah

• 'Al Khidir

Darraji

LZ SAND

FOB VIPER

FOB COBRA

MSR NEW MARKET

TAA CAMPBELL

X 2

X 3

X 1

behind it. In the shuffle of priorities, Third Brigade goes to the back of the line. Cody and Bryan have been in a constantly rotating battle handoff since G Day, their Apaches relieving one another to keep coverage over the division's far flung elements, now dispersed in a huge oval the equivalent distance from Washington, DC to Buffalo, NY. Third Brigade calls Aviation Brigade at Cobra. Clark's S3, Major Kinney, advises that the clouds are gone above AO Eagle but so are his Apaches.

Uh-oh, an important mission fell through the cracks. Cody is closest at hand for Garrett and receives his wrath. No time to sort out what went wrong or who should be flying cover for Third Brigade. Can they get through the day? Kinney feels they can. OK, Spectres will be up tonight, absolutely, positively.

The slipup is a fatigue indicator. Few of the major players have had more than three hours sleep in the last 48. First and Second Brigades got some downtime and are fresh enough for EA Thomas and Viper. It's Aviation Brigade that is approaching the red line, the wall which Garrett warned they must fly over. The pilots are red eyed but their maintenance and support units are punchy. Their mistakes can be as fatal as the aviators'. On the evening of G plus 2, for example, 1-101's land tail rolled into Cobra after twenty hours with the *schmall* in their faces on MSR New Market. Don't unload, Cody tells Sgt. Maj. Erhke—we move the FARP a hundred miles east tomorrow.

The destination is Viper, and the convoy starts out with the XO, Maj. Howard Killian, even before Second Brigade lifts off. There's no road, just a compass and slugger for navigation. No intelligence either about the Iraqi units bypassed by the 24th Mech. Neither will Killian have armed HUMM-V's to scout ahead for him, nor Kiowas overhead. He and his HEMIT's are on their own—good luck, godspeed—see you at Viper in ten hours, and don't be late.

Yancey is also introduced to cross-desert driving. His war has been behind the wheel and sprawled in the seat, snatching naps when the *schmall* halted traffic on New Market. He's heard no fire and fewer bombs than when he was plying Tapline Road before the ground war. A shake of the shoulder, a shout from his sergeant, a constantly jolting journey and a backache that keeps him awake even when exhausted.

There was the night of G plus 1 when the driver ahead of him fell asleep at the wheel, not awakening even when his truck stalled. Just another stop for terrain, Yancey assumed, and keeled over asleep on the empty passenger seat, engine idling. Not enough people for shotguns any more. No one to keep the driver awake. No orders except "drive on," and no one to say where they are going.

Sarge couldn't tell where he was within fifty miles. First his squad had investigated Toad for TF Citadel. His men had unearthed an RPG launcher, two pistols, and other enemy equipment. They wanted to keep them. Sarge felt they deserved the souvenirs and turned in only the RPG. Now his squad is somewhere between Cobra and Viper, or maybe it was LZ Sand—they hadn't received any useful maps—with the mission to guard a trail junction till someone relieved them. He puts fifty percent on alert, shifting every three hours. The early sleepers won the second shift by a coin toss. The situation is changing so fast, the first shift would probably get no sleep before a new mission comes down and they're on the road again.

With the first shift are squad members who had picked up the souvenirs at Toad. Sarge asks to see the stuff; he'd not had a chance to examine it closely. Canvas webbing and packs, tatty equipment of Soviet origin. His eyes widen when he reads the label of an ammo box: "Jordanian Armed Forces."

Would this be valuable intelligence for G2? Sarge is torn, whether to report his find—and why he retained it—or say nothing. He tries to remember who's in the coalition. Foggy with fatigue, Sarge asks around. One of his sharp soldiers can reel off the countries alphabetically: Abu Dhabi, Afghanistan, Bahrain, Dubai, Egypt, France, Kuwait...

"No Jordan?"

"No Jordan, Sarge. They're with Iraq."

Well if a PFC knows that, Sarge decides, it won't be news for the G2.

Up on Highway 8, Third Brigade is also noticing an international flavor in the war. A man dressed in flowing Kurdish garb tries to slip around the Abilene position. When accosted, he pretends not to speak Arabic. When patted down, an Uzi is found strapped to the thigh. His interrogation gets serious. Who is he and where's he going? He shakes his head. Maybe he's a Shiite guerrilla; let's turn him over to them. The man finds his tongue in English, quickly producing a military ID that had ingeniously been double imaged into innocuous travel papers, a professional bit of fieldcraft that causes the MI people to whistle. The ID is from Amman and states the bearer is a member of Jordan's special forces.

"OK, sir, what are you doing down here?"

"Am I a prisoner of war?"

"That depends on your story."

First he's a third country national on leave, attempting to visit a girl friend in As Samawah. Does he usually go on leave with a concealed sub-machinegun? Yes, that's his unit's policy. What about the Kurdish costume? His girl friend is Kurdish. Come on—we know the Kurds around As Samawah are like the Jews at Dachau: they're not inhabitants of the town, they're prisoners outside.

The man comes clean. He'd been sent to find and kill a certain Kurdish escapee believed to be at large and troublesome on an island north of As Samawah. This story seems improbable, that the efficient Iraqi secret police needed to call on a Jordanian to track down a fugitive. But he sticks to his story, stating that he had learned Kurdish from Syrian Kurds, and headquarters had offered his services to Iraq as a courtesy.

Didn't he know he was traveling through a war zone? He shakes his head: an air war, yes, but no one in An Nasiriyah (where he had gone to be briefed by the Iraqis) believed that American troops could get up here so far and so fast. When he first came upon Abilene, he thought it to be a Shiite road block.

Like the mysterious Jordanian, most of the traffic is flowing west in a sidewash from what Sec. Cheney called "the mother of all retreats." Overwhelmed by sudden defeat, Saddam never mounted a serious attempt to reopen his MSR to Kuwait. Though slow to react, he was quick to perceive his army there was lost. The Republican Guards he had pulled out earlier through Basra fled for Baghdad where he needed them most, doubtless to block an air assault like Third Brigade's. If his prime worry had been about Schwarzkopf's armor advancing north, Saddam would have halted his Republican Guards along the Tigris where the marshlands would have been ideal tank traps against 7th Corps. Saddam and Peay seemed to be the only commanders who appreciated the preeminent threat, which was from helicopters.*

So Peay has to turn to the new, less appetizing item on his plate, Viper. The goose egg was selected hastily, around the auxiliary strip of an airbase known as Jalibah Southeast.** The desert around the strip had been a bombing range for the Iraqi Air Force. Viper was extensively cratered, and no doubt littered with unexploded munitions. Its only appealing features are the strip and a location ninety miles from EA Thomas.

With sixty Black Hawks, Purdom can quickly catch up with the 24th Mech. He is to launch around 8:00 a.m. on G plus 3 (27 Feb.). The first difficulty arises in command and control: Purdom's C&C ship breaks down, and he asks Cody for use of his Black Hawk (piloted by Terry Seanor, he who eluded the phantom MIG on the night of Normandy). Cody is covering the air assault, but requests from brigade commanders are rarely refused.

Monitoring radios like a bank of TV screens, Cody flies over to Viper in a Kiowa. In this scout ship it will be easier for him to set down to confer with people on the ground. In his Apache, he might be tempted to do some shooting, and today he realizes must be devoted full time to Garrett's instructions.

Once more a great stir of dust, the launch of a heliborne brigade. First and Third had lifted from the oiled-down pads of TAA Campbell, but Second Brigade takes off from raw sand at Cobra. For an hour it seems the *schmall* has returned: Cobra

---

* Immediately after the ceasefire, Schwarzkopf had this to say in a press conference: "The 101st Airborne Division was within 150 miles of Baghdad, and there was nothing between them and Baghdad. If it had been our intention to take Iraq, we could have done it unopposed. But that was not our intention. We never said it was our intention. Our intention was purely to eject the Iraqis out of Kuwait and destroy the military power that had come in there."

** Jalibah was Schwarzkopf's original choice as the place to receive the Iraqis' surrender.

is enveloped by billowing clouds as lift after lift pokes through brownout to clear sky.

Already loaded with a hundred pounds of weaponry and equipment, an RTO tries to sling his radio atop his mountainous rucksack. The additional weight tips his narrow equilibrium. He topples over, helpless as a turned turtle. It takes three other overburdened comrades to pull him to his feet. He staggers toward his Black Hawk.

Under such monstrous loads, the soldiers of Second Brigade can only waddle off the LZ's at Viper, but they're not expected to have to fight upon landing because the 24th Mech is pushing the line of battle east like an outrushing tide. Second Brigade's pathfinders leap to the ground, expecting their easiest assignment.

The ground is crumbly and ruddy like TAA Campbell, but it's speckled with unnaturally bright spots. Pathfinders investigate the objects glinting in the sun—and shout with alarm. The ground is strewn with what look like Christmas bulbs—deadly Soviet bomblets, duds on the Iraqi practice range. The bulbs are latent land mines. They should have exploded in the air, so are hypersensitive, easily detonated by touch. The pathfinders radio a recommendation to change LZ locations. In the brownout of landing, troops—their heads bent from the weight of their loads—won't even be able to see the bomblets, much less avoid them.

The warning hits the airwaves like cold bacon on a hot griddle. Shelton, Purdom and Garrett all monitor the report. The command net goes silent as coordinates are checked and alternatives considered. Pathfinders are the ultimate in credibility. The apprehensions and interpretations of officers—officers of any rank—are challengeable and essentially speculative. But when a pathfinder—looking at what's real on the ground—sounds an alarm, everyone listens. Listens, but not necessarily accepts.

Silence can be ominous, especially when it breaks a rapid tempo of radio traffic. That means the main men are reconsidering in the light of new realities. The reality here is that the pathfinders' coordinates are precisely where the ACP is to be located. Going out for a piss in the dark, Gen. Shelton could easily kick a bomblet tonight. A true blue infantryman, he's well liked, and no one wants to be in the honor guard for his funeral. The airwaves are like a party line: many people monitor what is not their business. RTO's tap their officers. Better listen in, sir, sounds like there are going to be some changes.

But it's too late to change what is already a horseback plan. The lifts are warned, but heightened caution is to substitute for a change of LZ's. The Screaming Eagles are pushing their luck—no one killed in the war so far—but speed is of the essence, bomblet minefields notwithstanding—and minefields are an occupational hazard. Luck is as long as you have it. Like Sherpas, like coolies bent by their loads, Second Brigade's infantry plod from the LZ's watching for Christmas bulbs.

Everything to do with Viper screams haste. Viper is there for future purposes, like the islands seized in World War II for subsequent operations. Get in so the Apaches can get out! Second Brigade wends their way through the bomblets, marking off dense areas, but for the most part leaving safety an individual concern. Miraculously, no one loses a foot, and Viper's perimeter is created much like Cobra's though with a tighter perimeter. When 7-101 lifts in a hasty Apache FARP, it will be time for 1-101 and 2-229 to do their thing to the Republican Guards, a celebrated foe they have yet to meet.

Garrett has his CP at Cobra pack up and follow him to Viper where he's already orbitting, overwatching 7-101's arrival. With slim instructions, a lot can go wrong in the execution of The Audible. Goose eggs quickly circled on maps have been moved on the ground because of the bomblet threat. Garrett is aware of the natural tendency of his Chinook pilots to land where others have landed, but they must split off once they reach Viper to destinations depending upon their loads. On the radio he is guiding some uncertain pilots when Shelton asks him to come down to Jalibah's control tower. This will be Garrett's improvised CP. For closer coordination and joint use of a generator, he has 1-101 co-locate by the control tower.

Shelton is brief and blunt: sizeable Iraqi forces are reported seeping out along a causeway that parallels Highway 8 southwest of Basra. They may make it to An Nasiriyah, and the Air Force is too busy elsewhere to stop them. Furthermore, oil field fires are so dense the bombers are having a helluva time getting low enough to interdict the causeway. Except for the smoke, the causeway should be a happy hunting ground for Apaches: it is a narrow six-foot high embankment for a railroad track and service road. For much of its length the causeway falls off into marshes, so there's nowhere for Saddam's armor to go. Go get it. Consider the area between Highway 8 and hundred-mile lake (Har Al Hammar) a free fire zone. Who and how soon can you launch?

Garrett flips through Aviation Brigade's timetable, and advises Shelton that the first Apaches into Viper were Bearcats leading Second Brigade. Four should be available, if they can refuel promptly, for the causeway mission before noon. Shelton's order is an audible within The Audible and definitely top priority. Garrett hands over the aviation aspects of Second Brigade's insertion to Cody and appropriates 1-101's attack CP as it sets up. Now Cody has lost his C&C ship to Purdom and his key staff to Garrett!

No complaints. The war is rushing toward denouement, and everyone wants to get in their licks. Gazing at the smoke clouds to the east, Second Brigade already feels the end is near. TOW gunners grouse that this will soon be over without their ever having fired at Iraqi armor. Well, there may still be a chance at EA Thomas.

That plan is still so sketchy as to be ethereal. Oil fire smoke grows denser by the hour, so an aerial recon is impossible. The two-battalion task force has only photos of their LZ's and objective, which is about four square miles of flat terrain sprinkled with buildings just southwest of Ash Shanin, a town crammed into a peninsula where the Tigris and Euphrates form the Shatt Al Arab.

Because of other allied forces converging on Basra, the Thomas task force will have to fly up a narrow corridor, crowding the sky like a shooting gallery for triple A. When they land, they will be fifty miles from the nearest friendly units with a hundred thousand Iraqi troops in between. EA Thomas is to be the wax seal on the Basra cork, but the pressure of retreating forces already north of Basra is building carbonation of immeasurable pressure that the task force will have to withstand.

The Basra-Ash Shanin highway is known to be jammed by refugees as well as retreat. The two hysterically mixed would be a horror for the task force. The EA is a box bounded by levees—good protection, but the fields of fire and sight pictures will be full of peasants and their families.

Huber had been shaken by the prospects of Tallil, but EA Thomas bodes to be much worse. Even if it means putrefying piles of civilian bodies in front of the levee, the task force must be defended from the air as much as from the ground, and that means Apaches. At the moment the 101st's Apaches are scattered over several area codes from Cobra to Eagle to Viper.

2-229 is in the best shape. Flying armed recons on MSR Texas and displacing toward Viper, Bryan still has his C&C in order and ready to support EA Thomas if the task force is to air assault. Rhonda Cornum, 2-229's flight surgeon, is vaguely connected with the tactical situation. All she knows is that the war is going well; that none of her warrior colleagues whom she holds dear but at professional distance, have become her patients, and she quietly rejoices that she's met the test by setting standards for herself and army women yet unborn.

Near the Apache FARP she sets up 2-229's medical station. In maybe just a couple of more days combat casualties could be but a memory of fear, and the medics will turn their care to Iraqi civilians. Around the FARP people are looking at each other as if to say this is the last act and everyone's still on stage. A lot of pictures are snapped. Windborne cold whips the photographers. Parkas are the uniform now, highlighting the climatic contrast with the first snapshots of the war that began, it seems so long ago, in the suffocating August heat.

In and out of the FARP, Cody trades Kiowa pilots like a pony express rider changing mounts. Amid all the turmoil of Second Brigade's air assault, he has a distant but distinct worry—Killian's cross country expedition from Cobra to Viper. It had departed in the morning and with luck it will arrive a few hours after dark. Early in the afternoon, Cody sends Paladins back to look for Killian. If the convoy gets bushwhacked out in the desert, the Viper FARP soon will be out of fuel and ammo.

Turmoil at Cobra, changes of mission, and broken Saudi trucks had delayed Killian for seven hours. Shooting an azimuth to Viper with his pocket compass, he led 35 HUMM-V's and HEMIT's protected by only two machineguns. His destination is a hundred miles away across open desert and in the wake of Desert Storm. Thin plumes of smoke mark burning Iraqi vehicles. At first he investigated abandoned bunkers, but examining the horde of junk and refuse took too much time. He is to take no prisoners, just point them back down his tracks toward Cobra where they could surrender and receive food and water he cannot spare.

But only bedouins, who had dispersed in the slipstream of onrushing armor, arise on the path of the convoy. They peep out from lean-tos to safeguard small camels and donkeys that bolt at the noisy appearance of Killian's giant HEMIT's coming on like dolphins on the waves of dunes. Bedouin dogs bark and snarl at the roar of bucking vehicles, but soon there is only more sand, more scrub sprouting from the recent rains, more wind, cold, and pastel sky.

Killian is as worried about the sky as the Iraqis had been. His route traverses a vast and unfrequented wasteland that it is still essentially Iraqi territory, the 24th Mech's sweep through it notwithstanding. During the air campaign, this region has been Scud country, and the Air Force still searched for them. From the air, Killian's HEMIT's look very much like mobile Scud launchers. Periodically, he stops the convoy for the crews to wipe dust off the inverted V's that identify all coalition vehicles. Once or twice contrails appear in the sky, and a single A-10 makes a low pass, turning out the Americans who show their desert uniforms, much lighter in color than the Iraqis. The A-10 wags its wings, and heads east.

Killian's slugger is his lodestar. As long as it shows a progression of numbers approaching those of Viper's coordinates, Killian is not lost. Around noon, the slugger screen goes blank—and so does his face. Halt, stop, wait...what do we do now? To go in any direction is foolish. Killian knows the approximate azimuth to Viper, but he's a motor officer, not an explorer. If he misses Viper, the Republican Guards won't miss his convoy. Tracers into his HEMIT's, and the convoy will look like the oil fields of Kuwait.

Does anyone have a satellite schedule? To Killian's great

relief, someone does, and it reveals that the convoy is indeed in a satellite shadow which will last for about half an hour. They stretch and piss, wait out the minutes, then numbers reappear on the slugger display, and the convoy sets off again.

In mid-afternoon, Paladins appear over the eastern horizon. Killian's radio crackles with friendly, familiar voices. Five more hours in the jarring desert, then the Viper FARP will have its fuel and ammo for sure.

Darkness has closed in for two hours, and over the last miles Killian uses his headlights. They pick up white engineer tape, marking off areas dangerous with bomblets. The long snake of vehicles winds through the final hazard. He pulls off his Kevlar and enters Cody's CP, expecting congratulations and beaming faces.

Davis shakes his hand appreciatively, but the tent is subdued. What's wrong? The situation map shows bold arrows probing toward Basra and Saddam's coup de grace. All seems in readiness for the launch into EA Thomas, but no one's excited and the air is heavy with remorse. What happened? 2-229 has taken casualties, Davis says somberly—KIA's and MIA's.

The division's first.

XXV

Bengal balls

An hour after Paladins set out in search of Killian's convoy, four Bearcat Apaches with two Kiowas for radio relay, departed to interdict the causeway, Gabram in command. They were flying from one war to another.

The 101st had been the wide out in Hail Mary, sprinting down field on the open flank. Inside them was the 24th Mech, the tight end bumping the linebacker before releasing into a pass pattern. Inside McCaffrey, 7th Corps was battering through the line on a power sweep. Now the wide out was circling back in toward the broken field where tacklers and blockers were colliding.

Scooting northeast, Gabram did not hear the sounds on the line of scrimmage as much as he saw their consequence. What he saw was the Wagnerian immolation of Kuwait's oilfields, pouring forth in stygian smoke that formed like a bank of thunderheads clouding a thousand square miles, smoke that filmed windshields with grime and blotted out the sun. Launched in haste, his four Apaches were but a penlight to probe this darkness at noon. The rest of 1-101 was gathering at Viper while 2-229 readied to follow the Bearcats. Where the subsequent raids would be directed on the causeway largely depended on what Gabram reported after he did a battle handoff to Drew.

'Turbo' is flying Gabram whose call sign is Zero-six. TF Normandy crews Jones-O'Neal, Rodrigues-Lee Miller are alongside, with Pointer-Long the other seasoned pair. Gabram is out front, but his main concern is for those behind him. The long wafts of oily smoke obscure vision much more than natural clouds. He frequently looks around, asking where the others are if he can't see them, which is often.

But they can see him and, with amused detachment, pass on observations like, "You're taking ground fire, Zero-six."

From being locked and shocked in combat for three days, these Iraqis near the causeway have learned something: Don't fire on an approaching helicopter, especially an Apache—wait till it flies over, then shoot it in the back. Gabram's is the first Apache they see. He can't see their fire from his rear, but his buddies can.

This situation where the CO is a lightning rod produces the gallows humor: Doug's uncovering a lot of targets for his team, while they hear him become more and more nervous in the role of bait, but a role which he will not relinquish.

There's an equally important component to his nervousness. For every tracer he hears is directed toward his ship, Gabram sees a white flag fluttering on the ground. The Republican Guards in retreat are a horrific mixture of defeat and defiance. Precisely locating the source of ground fire is nigh impossible when acres of armor sprawl between narrow, smoke-choked horizons. This isn't like Normandy, Toad, Cobra, AO Eagle, or anywhere else in the war. Ft. Rucker didn't teach Gabram, and Cody didn't brief him about combat in chaos.

The frantic waves of surrender are poignant but do not override the compulsion of survival and dominance. To catch his breath and reappraise the situation, Gabram swoops his flight out over the hundred-mile lake and its vast surrounding marshes. In back of him is roiling smoke, symbol of one man's destructive psychosis. Ahead of the Bearcats rise a thousand marsh birds, symbols of nature in helpless alarm. Turning back toward the causeway is crossing the boundary and blurs it. Saddam's firing of Kuwait's oil fields is as much war against nature as against nations.

The flight returns to its purpose. Those are Republican Guards down there, Saddam's gang of thousands. Whether they're waving white flags or pointing triple A, they deserve killing for what they have wrought. Kill and kill some more: that's the fastest way to end the war and the killing.

A hodgepodge of hatred below, but in military terms a target-rich environment, so rich that Bearcats can be selective. Ah, a towed SA-6, the most formidable counter-weapon to Apaches, pulled off the road. Give it Hellfire. Gilman attacks. The launch, the strike. He pulls up, surprised how the missile trailer erupts in pyrotechnics he must fly through.

Elsewhere Iraqis cross the desert in formation as if to counterattack. What could be their objective? Are there American forces so close by? There shouldn't be, but it's also a confused situation for Americans down there. Switch to 30 millimeter. Approach from the flank.

The gun cameras record a scene from World War I: intent, preoccupied ripples of infantry rushing over open ground, 'mowed down' as that term must first have been used in war. Who's dead and who's not after the Bearcats strafe? Who cares? The prone infantry are all bundles on the ground.

Now to the causeway. There it is. Nothing moving. Someone struck it, the Air Force no doubt, and did a good job. Trucks, tanks, BMP's, vehicular flotsam and jetsam, tracked and wheeled, many shattered, all immobile. But the Iraqis are experienced enough to freeze with Apaches overhead. Target selection problems again. Many vehicles appear undamaged. Are they abandoned or are the drivers playing possum? Switch on FLIR. It detects heat from vehicle engines. If it's still warm, blast it.

From patrols over Highway 8 for Third Brigade, Bearcats remember how concrete culverts and bridges are favorite shelters against air attack. You've got to get your nose in the sand to see what's in there but these dark corners are high reward targets. Ranking officers appropriate such shelters for their cars. Jones Hellfires a culvert. From the explosion the target seemed thin skinned, and a pair of sedan wheels blow out the other side. They bounce, roll and curve, finally splashing into the marsh.

He takes a closer look at the marsh. Lines of bent and broken reeds appear like capillaries. Sure, that's where a lot of troops must have run away. Along the bank is a rash of tiny objects. Boots! For some reason these guys threw away their boots! A sweep of chin guns would surely find plenty of troops in the marsh grass, but why bother shooting up a barefoot cowering rabble.

Turbo is eager to take out more armored vehicles, but Gabram is preoccupied with controlling his flight and listening to other action on the causeway. East of the Bearcats, 2-229 reports an enviable kill—an Iraqi helicopter in flight.

Some small chopper like a Kiowa darted up hell's highway, skimming over destroyed and derelict vehicles, apparently in search of a particular one. The Apache initially mistook it for an allied chopper, maybe Saudi, because Iraq had not put a plane over the front since the ground war began. Searching the radio frequencies for friendly aircraft, the Apache determined there was none in the vicinity matching his description. He also deduced the chopper's mission: some general was stuck in the deadly traffic jam and had ordered his own extraction.

Wisely the Apache trailed the chopper from afar, waiting till it set down beside the teeming road. A figure sprinted from a BMP to the chopper. He jumped in quick as a pathfinder; the door was still open and the chopper beginning to climb when a Hellfire joined him. Still spinning, the tail rotor flew another half mile, returning like a boomerang in search for the vanished chopper of which it was once a part.

"Four more and you're an ace!" someone kids the victor.

Gabram is also relaying battle reports back to Viper, and his radio crackles with other distractions. Miller's mad. Some Iraqis are pointing AK-47's in the air with white rags attached to the barrel. He's sure he was fired upon by these ambiguities. Gabram must let each gunner make private decisions. His own is to spray the ground and keep the Iraqis' heads down.

The smoke, this goddam smoke, is the ultimate distraction and danger. Bearcat One-zero is flying tail cover for the flight, and Gabram can never see him for the smoke. He calls him every minute or so—Where are you..? What do you see on the ground..? We're crossing the lake again on 320... One-four, are you engaging? Affirmative. One-four just keys his mike so Gabram can hear the background rattle of 30 millimeters. "OK," he orders. "Everyone up and stack left."

Gabram wants to take a head count visually, so he calls his flight to 75 feet of altitude, echeloned to his left where he can see them. Reluctantly, the Apaches surface like spear fishermen from their individual hunts, but smoke continues to sweep between them. Impatiently they report in and look around. No one can see everyone else but everyone is seen by at least one other, including even One-zero. They want to get back to work, and their tone on the radio implies that Gabram is being a bit too up tight about formation flying.

He *is* up tight. His Bearcats can gorge on the causeway cornucopia, concerned only about target selection; but he has to make sure they all come home from the feast. If he saw Saddam Hussein himself, riding away in a convertible, Gabram wouldn't let a Bearcat at him if it meant risking a crew. The end is too close, home is too near. He's sure of it after seeing and strafing that ghastly causeway.

Gabram can't believe his watch. It shows he's been riding the causeway for an hour, but it seems like three. Nope, the fuel gauge confirms. Drew won't be up for thirty minutes, another thirty minutes before Gabram can get out of this smoke from hell. My God...the flight just swept by a power line twice our altitude! His map shows numerous towers but not that one. There goes Pointer after a BMP. Does everyone want to stay up here except me?

No: Turbo has now become concerned. "We're in too deep," he opines on intercom. The flight has drifted east down the causeway where traffic is fused in an endless junkyard. Tanks push burning wrecks out of the way, Iraqis fight each other for operating vehicles, and the air above is a maelstrom of tracers coming and going. Apparently an Air Force strike just pulled off, maybe regathering to roll in for another pass, because an SA-6 missile erupts and streaks into the overcast. Perhaps the Apaches have strayed from their AO. Boundaries in the air were vague to begin with and are now surely confused as the air-land battle overlaps in both dimensions.

Time to salvo rockets and get out of the tracers. Gabram's voice takes on the hard edge of a commander. No more mother hen, no more mister nice guy or flying buddy. Break off and get back in formation *now*.

Roger. Roger. Roger. The Bearcats respond obediently. That is a mess down there and good riddance.

Gabram aligns on an azimuth back to Viper, and turns up volume on the 1-101 net. Where the hell is Drew? Gabram shouldn't leave till he's done a battle handoff which includes a fast brief for Drew on the causeway situation. Wait till he hears about those power lines and the mad mess on the ground. Gabram would recommend that Drew abort, but that probably won't go down with Cody.

From monitoring relays, Cody obtains a sketchy idea of what Gabram has encountered. Cody would love to get into the action himself but bringing in Second Brigade's lifts to Viper is a full time job and more. Enviously he hears Bryan launch for the causeway. The two are the highest ranking trigger pullers in the division; indeed attack helicopter battalion commanders are the army's only officers above the grade of captain who are expected to personally engage the enemy. It is their most highly valued perk, and Cody can sense his last chance slipping away in the waning hours of the war while Bryan gets in some last shots.

A clipped conversation betwen Bearcats as they watch for Drew's three Apaches. The Kiowa relay has finally raised him. He'll soon be within radio range and Gabram has a lot to tell him.

"I'M OVER A FACTORY!" There is terror in the unfamiliar voice. Someone answers indistinctly.

"That's Guard," Turbo tells Gabram. The Guard frequency is for May-days, monitored by all aircraft in the sky.

"I SEE A EAST-WEST ROAD. THEY'RE SHOOTING AT ME... IN MY HARNESS!"

"Some guy's coming down in a 'chute!" Gabram gulps.

"Roger," Turbo clenches his teeth.

Somewhere to the southeast, Capt. Bill Andrews has ejected from his F-16, hit by a SAM. He's disoriented, trying to describe to an AWAC where he is floating down. Taking a guess at the coordinates, the AWAC broadcasts to any aircraft in the vicinity. The coordinates are way out of Gabram's AO but he responds and offers to fly there. Thanks from the AWAC. He'll get back to Gabram. Stand by. But the Guard frequency goes silent.

The AWAC's call was monitored at Viper. Drew has more fuel and ammo. He diverts toward Andrews' coordinates. That's why he's late for his handoff with Gabram. Drew scanns the sky for a descending parachute, but sees none or any sign of it on the ground.

The Air Force has special teams, SAR's like those which accompanied TF Normandy, to rescue downed pilots, but the nearest SAR team is an hour more distant from the scene than Viper. Bypassing channels, the AWAC asks if the 101st will take the mission. Sure, Garrett replies: an American is an American and an aviator an aviator, no matter what color his uniform.

2-229 has two Apaches and a Black Hawk available and fueled. Moreover, Doc Cornum has just reached Viper, where she hears that Andrews reported a broken leg from ejection as well as being shot at, and probably hit, in his parachute. Obviously a medic should accompany the rescue, but better still a doctor in these circumstances. That would be ideal; however, Cornum at the moment is one of but two flight surgeons at Viper. In the event Apaches on the causeway take casualties, she should be available to treat them.

Cornum could raise that point, but ultimately it's not her call. She's more concerned that someone will bring up the rule about no women in combat. As it relates to herself, she despises the restriction.

"All my energy was focused on one thing: keep the pilots healthy enough to fly and destroy the enemy. Fly and fight. I loved it." She would express the same sentiment in congressional testimony the next year.

At Viper she wonders if Bryan is being consulted about the rule, but he's up on the causeway and time is critical. 2-229's assistant S3 inquires if Cornum has her medical bag handy. She does. Unless she demurrs, she's going. She goes before someone changes his mind.

If Andrews is where the AWAC says he is, the rescue shouldn't take long. To be successful, it can't take long, since his coordinates are squarely in a cauldron of Republican Guards. Two pathfinders pile into the Black Hawk beside Cornum; essentially they are her bodyguards. They will sprint out into the desert to prevent Andrews' capture. Once they have him covered, Cornum will quickly prepare him to lift out in the Black Hawk, then administer first aid on the flight back. Two Apaches will overwatch and protect the extraction.

A woman's work? Well, Bryan could have had any flight surgeon in the army, and he asked Cornum to leave her position in aeromedical research at Ft. Rucker. 2-229 took only the best; its role was too important to do otherwise, and its history too impressive.

For the battalion's call sign is Bengal, a reference to their military pedigree begotten from the Flying Tigers of World War II fame. The original Flying Tigers were hired guns for Chiang Kai Shek before America entered the war against Japan. Then they were incorporated into the Army Air Corps, receiving an official number. When the Air Force became a separate service in 1947, they took the number with them but not the orphaned nickname. Flying Tiger veterans used it to start a freight airline, and several years before the Gulf war they adopted 2-229 who proudly showed the orange and black colors of their step-parents, and on the air called themselves Bengals.

No FLIR-finding, Hellfiring Apache warrior in the battalion better represented the Flying Tiger against-all-odds tradition than did Rhonda Cornum—even her lingerie that day was orange and black. Her call sign was Bengal 00, which on the radio and for irony became Bengal balls.

For the Andrews rescue, Cornum feels she is in the best of company. Lance McElhiney, her closest friend in 2-229, is flying the lead Apache. In Vietnam, his gunships received more stitches than Cornum sewed in med school. Flying her Black Hawk is another Viet vet warrant officer, Bob Godfrey. He was an IP at Ft. Rucker as was his co-pilot, Phil Garvey. Ft. Rucker, AL is the Army's Aviation School where 2-229 originated before its attachment to the 101st. Godfrey and Garvey were instructors in the school, but both volunteered to go over with 2-229. Bryan had been grateful to add them to his stable of top notch aviators.

As Godfrey and Garvey run up the engine, an argument breaks out over a pathfinder who wants to join sergeants Patbouvier Ortiz and Roger Brilinski who were already aboard. He's Sgt. Troy Dunlap, not normally assigned to this Black Hawk, but gesticulating in the roar of rotors for permission to come along. No, too late—we're about to take off—but Ortiz waves for Dunlap who dives in.

This is not a medevac chopper painted with a red cross. Crew chiefs Dan Stamaris and Bill Butts man machineguns at the doors. The pathfinders are loaded for bear with grenades and extra magazines for their M-16's. If they get on the ground and come under fire, the Black Hawk will take off without them till the Apaches suppress. All this Cornum understands and her stomach churns, though from excitement more than fear.

Impatiently, the Black Hawk roars its power then springs into the air. On the vibrating metal deck, Cornum rearranges the contents of her medical bag. Get the IV fluid on top—Andrews has probably been bleeding heavily. Have the Hare traction splint in easy reach—we might set his leg before extraction. Maybe I'll have to resuscitate him, so...

So sudden. Minutes before she'd been sipping black coffee, reflecting on the war about to end. Godfrey had enveloped her with a bear hug; he'd never done that before, so the hug seemed to say, 'It's over, Rhonda. We made it. We did it. Were going home!'

That's the way it looked on the ground. At 100 mph and 20 feet of altitude, Godfrey flashed over advancing columns of the 24th Mech. Cornum waved to the troops riding bundled in parkas. They waved back. This is a victory procession.

But sooty, choking smoke rolls like a weather front toward the three helicopters that cleave it like darts. Godfrey and Garvey are debating whether to don NVG even though it's still afternoon. U.S. vehicles are only minutes behind them when green tracers search the smoke, firing at the sound of the flight. Cornum remembers running over a hornet's nest while mowing the lawn on her farm in the Florida panhandle. That's what this is—the hornets are pissed and out to sting. Stamaris and Butts return fire with long bursts.

The pathfinders knock her sprawling on the deck. Then draping themselves on her, they try to shield Cornum with their bodies, but the fire is coming from below, so she's actually shielding them! Stamaris' ammo belt is jumping, the barrel chattering, and fills the cabin with pale caustic smoke. Brass shell casings hop all over the deck; one burns Cornum's cheek. All this and the mission is only minutes old.

She looks up, noticing how the crew chiefs are talking rapidly with the pilot. Cornum jams on her headset, to hear Garvey shout, "We're taking fire!" This transmission must be to the AWAC because everyone in this Black Hawk sure knows it already.

This is abort time. As Turbo had remarked, "We're in too deep." Too deep into unconquered Iraq, too close to their still potent fury, too far from Andrews to do him any good. Better he a wounded POW than eight charred bodies lost in vain attempting his rescue.

Godfrey breaks left, starts a twisting climb, but it puts him in a patch of clear sky. Triple A discovers him, follows him as he tries to dodge back into the smoke, finds his tail boom, rips open the fuselage, gouges through the deck, and kills Butts crouched at his machinegun, still firing. A last burst of bullets from the dead man's hand, then the barrel twists vertical. Butts is doubled over his safety belt, gushing blood swept away in the airstream.

Both pilots are shot through the body but still they bank the shuddering, yawing chopper away from a persistent spray of ground fire. The engine's damaged, screaming as if in agony, shaking the ship apart.

"We're going in!" Garvey yells. Nearly unconscious, he remains to the end, yanking severed controls. The ground and muzzle flashes rush up inescapably. Eight Americans tense in paralysis for impact and certain death.

Inescapable? Certain? Cornum's mind is honed with the analyticality of her profession, causing her to notice how adrenalin supercharges, engraves the moment—indeed creates a time warp in which thought acceleration expands the span of 'real' time. Real time, in retrospect, was probably less than thirty seconds from Butts' death till the others.

It comes in the blow of impact, the killer of senses, delivered as if by the fist of God. Irresistible, deafening. Objectively, ten tons of shrieking metal, exploded gears and spun-off rotors churns and flings through the sand. The Black Hawk disintegrates in a quarter mile swath, the fuel so dispersed there is no petroleum fire. Subjectively, Cornum observes the crash from above the helicopter, seeing what sight could not reveal before the instant of black oblivion.

Why's everyone on such a downer? Killian wants to know, after he arrives at Viper, exhausted but triumphant, with his convoy. Davis hands him the log. The entry at 271730 Feb 91 reads,

2-229 CSAR UH-60 crashed vic PU860880. Apache wingman reports that his flight was engaged by heavy AAA. Both aircraft took multiple hits and UH-60's tail boom separated, then aircraft hit the ground at 130 knots, cartwheeled and totally destroyed. All 8 POB's believed KIA, including MAJ Rhonda Cornum.

Garrett: "The crash report knotted my stomach. No one wanted to believe it, but McElhiney saw Godfrey go in, and from his description there was no possibility of survivors. They'd flown into an enormous bunker complex, the headquarters of a Republican Guard division, and more triple A than any of us had seen in the war.

"Bryan was the most devastated. He asked to fly in with the 24th Mech who were coming up on the crash site. That night they had quite a tank battle and overran the bunker complex. I hope they got the guys who got Godfrey, and I think they did."

Among the many coincidences that swarmed around the crash, one of the tank drivers who churned through the bunkers was the son of a school bus driver for Rhonda Cornum's daughter, Regan, in North Dakota. Kory, her husband was an Air Force flight surgeon stationed in western Saudi Arabia. Bill Andrews had been his classmate at the Air Force Academy.

Kory had visited 2-229 at TAA Campbell, and Bryan knew him. For the seven families in the states, the somber notification procedure was already in motion. All eight would be reported as MIA until their bodies were recovered. Kory Cornum was an exception, who could be advised through CENTCOM channels, but neither Bryan nor Garrett felt up to calling him. It seemed a cruelty to raise Kory's hope in the slightest by classifying his wife as MIA when inevitably she would be found dead. Through back channels with AFCENT, Garrett began quiet arrangements for Kory to accompany Rhonda's body home. Garrett was deeply depressed, assuming that her corpse would be too mutilated, probably too fragmentary, for Kory even to view.

Aviation Brigade's CP at Viper was under stress as well as a pall. The EA Thomas mission was still on. The Bearcats' causeway recon had flown half the route, and what they had to say shook the planners. Gabram was shaken himself in a way Garrett hadn't seen since the aerial perils at the siege of An Loc in the spring of 1972. The fatigue of fear was in Gabram's face, his description of the causeway chaos and carnage came out hesitant and disjointed. His appearance and demeanor told Garrett more than any detailed report crisply delivered. The message, though not the messenger, could not be more clear: the air corridor crossing the causeway would be a nightmare, and the situation up at Ash Shanin undoubtedly worse. Godfrey's Black Hawk seemed an omen of more crashes and casualties.

Life as a crap shoot is epitomized by war. With the perspective a veteran of Vietnam's indiscriminately bloody war could bring to this philosophy, Garret recognized that the division's roll was probably over. Poker now became the master metaphor. Play the percentages. Hedge bets, and fold a bad hand. The casino lights were dimming. The gambles had been shrewd and exciting, but let's get out of here with what we brought in.

Now Peay's up at Viper to make his own estimations. Shelton, Cody and Broderick all drive Corvettes at home, a coincidental common emblem of hell for leather aggressiveness. But now their faces are long and not from fatigue. None can feign enthusiasm for EA Thomas. Garrett adds another unfavorable factor to his counsel for Peay: the Hellfires are becoming erratic. There is so much particulate matter in the smoke, laser beams are diffusing. Weather changes, but this fouling smoke is predicted to hang in heavily, perhaps for months.

Peay knows somewhat more than his officers. At corps, cease-fire has been bruited as more than a rumor. Luck may have been consulted—though Peay was not—about ending offensive operations the next morning. Peay directs that EA

Thomas planning continue, but feels himself that now it will never be executed.

He wants to know the details of Godfrey's shoot down. Garrett takes responsibility for authorizing the mission, but that's not Peay's point. Why weren't the coordinates verified and superimposed on the map of enemy positions? Didn't anyone see Andrews' parachute on the ground? If not, Godfrey should have been told to abort. No excuse, sir. An AWAC vectored us—we took his word for it. When can we get into the crash site? The 24th Mech has secured it ,sir; Bryan is going in personally tomorrow.

The wind picks up for the rest of the afternoon. Apaches continue to mug the causeway, but sand in the air mixes with soot, effectively defeating FLIR and lasers. The Screaming Eagles are cocked to land the knockout punch, but also look around for the referee to declare a TKO. By late afternoon, rumors of 'end-X'—end of exercise—flash across many radio nets. Kuwait City has been liberated. During the night corps passes down two advisory messages, and the 101st's units are told to stand by for a cease-fire announcement. It comes from the lips of President Bush himself in a radio broadcast the next morning (G plus 4, 28 Feb). Starting at 5:00 a.m., coalition forces would halt their offensive.

The hot line between Washington and Riyadh had been ringing all during the 27th. Egypt and Saudi Arabia were leaning on Bush to let up before Iraq's command structure disintegrated in desertion and even mutiny, resulting in anarchy with unpredictable consequences. Schwarzkopf could have all the time he requested, but Powell made clear to him that it seemed only a few more hours were necessary. CINCCENT acquiesced. A lot of forces would get away, but he never expected to have to fight them again. The terms of the cease-fire would be dictated to an Iraqi lieutenant general in a few days.

Cornum has made a stupendous discovery: the rational mind survives death. This is so because, though she was killed by the crash, she can yet observe and analyse. She considers it might be an out of body experience—she is certainly detached from her body because it communicates no pain—but her rational mind rejects the possibility: what she's experiencing is no body. Neither could this be what medical literature describes as a near death experience. No, that would be accompanied by a white light and an ascension toward it. Instead, there is dim darkness, and from her memory of the physical world she knows the crash had occurred in late afternoon.

Where she was, what she is—temperal references like 'now' seem irrelevant—absorbs her awareness. Yet it's hard to discard memories of her recent physical life. There are posthumous sensations—that floating, weightless feeling—immunity from the law of gravity.

Consider the huge mass of wreckage pressing her body into the sand like so much concrete. Insensate, she regards it as she would her tombstone. Cornum also perceives cold but does not experience it. Senses and perceptors have separated. This is a twilight zone, in a pleasant way. In other ways not because emotions remain with her: like vicarious grief with Kory when he is notified of her death, his impossible explanation to Regan that her mother is dead.

Rhonda wonders if it is possible to hover earth indefinitely—is that what ghosts do?—to enter minds of the living, not to haunt but instead impart comfort from the other side. But could there too be a down side to the afterlife, and worries continue after life?

Like a gentle correction, her body intrudes. She becomes aware of its alignment. Head to the side, torso compressed but comfortable; only the arms have not reported in. Stillness and peace, surely the environment of the hereafter. Maybe some facsimile of the body accompanies her.

Why am I lingering here if I must be bound for the beyond? My eyes see flame nearby. I connect them with the oil fields or maybe my Black Hawk. Incongruous that I begin to feel fear, fear of burning when I'm already dead.

Dead or alive, I want no part of that fire.

Before I was killed, I could move my limbs... I still can! What's there to fear once you're dead? But I'm afraid.

"I wasn't convinced that I was alive, but if I was, there was no way I was going to die in a post-crash fire. That was the only thing that motivated me to try to move; otherwise I could have stayed there forever."

Cornum squirms under the crushing wreckage. Fear is her most persuasive sign of life. Like a camera coming into focus, her rational mind quickens, and recognizes soldiers in dark uniforms gathering around her. They look sharp for Iraqis. She perceives them to be Republican Guards. One leans over to yank her to her feet. Her arm comes alive, flapping like wings of a decapitated chicken, sounding like a chicken wing ground in the jaws of a mastiff. The sound, and that of her hair-whitening scream, returns life as a pain-filled sensorium.

27: Iraq agrees to all U.N. resolutions.

XXVI

Cease fire!..

In the night of G plus 3, artillery flashes were puckish winks taunting those who believe there will be a cease-fire in the morning. Too much war is still going on. Too many gaps in the encirclement. Heavy U.S. divisions are sliding brigades around, and the EA Thomas task force is set to go. Aviation Brigade is talking about what to do if a chopper goes down in Iran. The consensus is just pretend it's still Iraq.

The other consensus is about auxiliary power units (APU). The *schmall* from Hell drove sand into critical machinery deeper than anyone believed sand could go. APU's are the starters for all helicopters. Without them (not many run well any longer) the division's air fleet will have to slave one chopper off another like a truck convoy in Alaskan winter. This will take much longer than the warm-up for Cobra or AO Eagle. It will have to start very early in the morning. So before midnight, an hour after the cease-fire warning, Cody lay down in his tiny TOC tent, instantly falling into a sleep of exhaustion.

His next recollection is a shake of the shoulder. It's 5:00 a.m., and Garrett wants to see him. Groggy, Cody asks Davis how many APU's are up, who just smiles and opens the tent flap. My God, Davis looks like a zombie from outer space. He may be losing the bubble. Cody wonders if Davis got any sleep that night. The Audible disintegrated TOC staff rotation, and Garrett probably wants to admonish 'eyeball maintenance.'

Or maybe Garrett wants an attitude correction after Gabram's disenthusiasm about the causeway. Cody is prepared to defend his company commander. Gabram was only exhibiting the truth, and the gun videos substantiate his opinion. Cody wonders if Shelton and Peay saw them. The videos speak for themselves. It's not that the causeway and the EA Thomas corridor are too tough, it's that they're war in anarchy. Cody searches for words to make the point to Garrett. No one should have to face his boss without a first cup of coffee.

Bemused, Cody opens the door to Garrett's CP, to find his boss beaming.

"Expect no mercy!"

"No, sir, I won't."

Garrett's staffers are grinning at Cody. If he's to get an ass chewing, Garrett should have the courtesy to do it in private. Instead, he comes around his desk and hugs Cody like a French mayor.

"The battalion was magnificent, Dick. I'm so damn proud of you guys!"

Garrett's ready to cry, but whatever for? End-X...? That's it! Cody's been on enough FTX's to recognize the relief, to perceive the generalized gratitude of a job completed. For the first time that morning he remembers the rumor: a cease-fire was scheduled to go into effect at 0800.

Schedules in this war have been like five-year plans in Cuba—statements of intent. Could the last one be different from all those before? Could be. Everyone had heard Bush himself announce it at 0500. Sure enough, Cody no longer hears artillery. An occasional chopper lifts off into the dawn but the sound is unwarlike and reassuring.

At the ACP nearby, Huber is like a ticket agent reassuring passengers that flights have not been cancelled. His field phone jangles incessantly; everyone wants to verify the cease-fire with G3 Ops—Bush's announcement does not suffice. Huber wishes he had a recording: "Yes, there is a cease-fire. Please shoot no more Iraqis unless they shoot at you. Hold if you want other information." Then recorded music.

Around Viper there are many but wary handshakes. Anyone who believes Saddam, shouldn't. But just in case this is for real, cameras are passed around for keepsake snapshots.

At Cobra, Phil Jones has just begun a long walk from the lead vehicle in a convoy of towed howitzers. He must shake each driver awake and get ready to roll for Viper. Now the 0500 radio message obviates the movement. Let the drivers sleep. Jones crawls back in his cab and nods off himself.

Back at DMAIN, Dessie Greer is delighted when rumor comes down that soft hats may now replace Kevlars at TAA Campbell. For the rest of the day, her head feels lighter than she can remember. She's still worried for her husband because 2-502's plans were changed so often in the last 24 hours, it's shown at several places on the situation map. Actually, Calvin at the moment is guarding a broken truck somewhere between Cobra and Viper where he will be among the last to learn of the cease-fire. There's no water to heat MRE's, and his squad is running low of even these unpalatable rations. If a vehicle ever comes along, the driver will share his rations even if his generosity is forced.

With the push of tactical supplies suspended, Broderick turns to the plight of isolated elements like Greer's. He stumbles into DISCOM and begins to outline his intentions to the commander, but Col. Gerald can not follow what Broderick's saying. That's because Broderick can't keep his thoughts connected. Gerald tells him we'll talk about this later, now get to bed. Broderick rises to leave, but Gerald suspects he'll go off to other business.

"Go to bed," he orders, "here." and points to his own cot. Embarrassed to soil it with dirt, sand and dust, Broderick nevertheless does what he's told—and falls asleep as soon as his eyes close. Ringing phones and loud discussions do not awaken him, as Gerald himself assures that his S&T commander gets four hours rest.

Gerald's DISCOM, spread 600 miles from King Fahd to Viper, cannot rest, even after the victory to which it so greatly contributed. It was probably Saddam's foremost strategic miscalculation to disbelieve that CENTCOM could move so much materiel, supporting so many soldiers, in such a sparse and roadless environment. Never in history had huge U.S. forces moved over larger distances in less time. It was people like Gerald who made it happen.

Even under the cease-fire, they keep moving, a logistical

momentum catching up with the headlong offensive of the previous three days. Peay has now jumped his CP to Viper. Like worker bees following the migrating queen, DISCOM comes in trail, laden with supplies.

From Lippard's log:

I flew into Iraq today with BG Adams in his Black Hawk. I don't know why I was surprised but Iraq looked just like Saudi Arabia! We went up MSR New Market but didn't see much traffic, just a few small convoys of HUMM-V's and 5-tons. There were MP outposts scattered many miles apart. Each was a hard top HUMM-V with an M-60 machinegun inside a plastic MRE bag to keep the dust out. These MP's were reservists from North Carolina. It was easy to identify their accent on the radio. We'd wave, they'd wave and ask when they'd be going home. That was the question everyone was asking, and the cease-fire had just started!

There was a lot of debris on New Market, dropped by convoys. A lot of lumber, wire and a few water trailers. You could tell how much of a rush there had been because a UH-21 chopper was still on its back where it crashed landed a few days ago. A flat bed truck had just reached the scene to haul it out. Gen. Adams said something about how there was going to be a helluva police call [clean up] before the division left Iraq.

It took us an hour to reach Cobra where we refueled. The FOB was a huge gypsy camp of supply trucks, shelter halves [pup tents], tankers, bladders, blivets, Black Hawks and Chinooks. Pumps were lined up like the biggest gas station in the world.

We took off again, heading east on MSR Virginia. It was asphalt for a while, then a dirt road along a berm 3 to 6 feet higher than the surrounding desert. Traffic was bumper to bumper. Corps and the 82nd were both using it. Most of our vehicles had to go cross country to Viper, but I bet they got there quicker than they would have in this traffic jam. It was moving slow but it was also colorful. A lot of vehicles were flying state flags. I recognized Illinois, Texas, Tennessee, and the Confederate 'Stars and Bars.' The 82nd also flew some guidons. We'd wave and they'd honk, sort of like a wedding convoy.

There was only one place where it looked like there had been much fighting between Cobra and Viper. Now and then there was a burnt out Iraqi tank and charred chassis. When their trucks burned, they burned to the ground. Nothing but the frame and rims left. Around an old ruined fort, about two-thirds of the way to

Viper, there were numerous fighting positions, trenches and revetments. I had to admire the Iraqis for their field fortifications, but not the way they abandoned them! In this area the real evidence of fighting was on the face of the desert. We could see it well from the air. Horizon to horizon, the desert was crisscrossed with tire and tank tread trails. It was a giant maze that was the history of a battle.

We arrived at Viper around noon. It looked a lot like Cobra on a smaller scale. They were even having a small *schmall* when we arrived. The ACP was located near the airfield control tower. SFC Chapman gave me a tour of the main tent. It was a miniature version of the DMAIN TOC—four GP tents lashed together into a square structure, with all staff elements represented. We were here because MG Peay wanted a conference with BG Adams and Shelton. LTG Luck was also scheduled to arrive at 1300 but we didn't wait around that long.

On the flight back, I was impressed how diverse the desert is. Viper was pretty green by desert standards. It had a lot of the short shrubs we'd seen before, but also little clumps of grass. We cut across a different area on the way back with sand as white as snow. What a great beach! All it needs is an ocean. I knew we were getting close to TAA Campbell when the sand turned red again. Another clue we were back in Saudi Arabia was that the Arabs were driving Toyotas instead of camels and burros. When we landed, it was raining again, off and on.

The 'small *schmall*' at Viper prevented Bryan from visiting the crash site. Lt. Gen. Luck also cancelled his visit. 18th ABC seemed to be catching its breath like a sprinter leaning on his knees after the 100 meter dash.

Up at AO Eagle, things had lightened up. Berdy's troops were constantly escorting civilian vehicles around the craters in Highway 8. Inhabitants of Al Khidir emerged to beg for food at Austin, and it was provided even though 3-187 went on short rations. Gratitude poured on Third Brigade like the rains of G plus 2. They were regarded as liberators rather than invaders as their activities began to resemble disaster relief more than interdiction. They were the farthest north of all coalition forces, and closest to the Iraqi population.

Peay would reflect on Third Brigade's reception by Iraqis when U.S. politicians used terms like quagmire in describing the perils of an advance on Baghdad. From the experience of

Third Brigade, Iraqis were more likely to receive the Americans as most Germans did when Hitler's regime was destroyed. When world-shaking aggression erupts from a dictatorship, the world soon ignores the fact that the first, and in significant ways, the worst fated victims are compatriots of the dictator. A higher percentage of Germans, for example, were consigned to concentration camps than other more publicized nationalities. Bush had declared that the Iraqi people were not his enemy, only Saddam. Bush could have gone further, and considered that he and the Iraqi people had a mutual enemy in Saddam.

To Clark's surprise many Kuwaitis, a hundred miles from their homes, approached his positions. They were victims of Saddam's 'Iraqi-ization' of Kuwait, the execution of his prewar plan to expunge the emirate from history by expatriating its population.* Most had been stripped of identification and proved their nationality through marks of abuse: welts, bruises, burns and broken bones. The torture had been accomplished in Kuwait to extract information about valuables hidden in their homes. Then they were trucked away at night, up Highway 8. The lucky ones had been transported after the ground war started, when U.S. warplanes strafed the trucks (most were military troop carriers), causing the drivers and guards to flee into the marshes. By G plus 4, nearly two hundred Kuwaitis found their way to Third Brigade's roadblocks.

Fifty more EPW's were taken in AO Eagle, and with the cease-fire hundreds more tried to give up—apparently to escape the wrath of the Shiite Iraqis. But there was a Catch 22 in the cease fire terms: with the war over, technically there could be no more prisoners of war. Iraqi soldiers then could no longer surrender, only approach the Americans as refugees. Naturally, genuine refugees recoiled to have their recent oppressors join them in camps; this was a matter the 101st was grateful to turn over to corps.

There was a matter, however, that Clark was delighted to settle at Waco. Outside the pump house where he located his

---

* Among the terms of the cease-fire, formalized on March 3, was the requirement that Iraq return or account for the thousands of Kuwaiti civilians it herded out of their country. Iraq's refusal to do so was its first, and a continuing act of defiance toward the UN.

CP, was a large stone monument on which a bust portrait of Saddam had been attached. The Americans' first instinct was to destroy it but Clark stayed their hands, realizing that visitors would enjoy this example of big brother art. Clark called for one of his talented amateurs to faux paint a new background for the dictator —Third Brigade's Rakkasan patch.

Ironically, pictures of Saddam were gaining value. For U.S. soldiers, possession of war souvenirs like captured equipment, weapons in particular, were so controlled as to be virtually prohibited. CENTCOM's purposes were safety—items like Soviet grenades were unquestionably and highly dangerous—and to prevent introduction of high caliber weaponry into the civilian communities when U.S. divisions came home. The troops were convincingly advised that those caught with contraband weapons faced court martial—but worse than that—venue would be in the JOA, a pre-trial sentence because of the delay in returning home. By reason of this built-in penalty, CENTCOM's no souvenirs policy proved effective.

So what was there to take home to show the family and remember the whirlwind war? What better than an authentic picture of its cause, Saddam Hussein. Souvenir economics started with a curious incomprehension between suppliers and buyers. Shiites of the Euphrates valley delighted in destroying, or at least defacing, every image of Saddam. This gladdened their hearts but did not fill their stomachs. MRE's did that and, to the amazement of the Iraqis, their benefactors inquired about the availability of Saddam pictures. There are no shrewder business men in the Middle East, which is to say the world, than Iraqis. A Saddamite painter, who'd made a career of governmental portraits, was hauled from a fetid prison cell in Al Khidir and put back to work at what he did best. Third Brigade was as happy with their souvenirs as he was for his furlough.

Casualties in war are inevitable, and the inevitable happened again, but again to 2-229 and only ten minutes before the cease-fire was announced. Sgt. Batista did not see the Christmas bulb alternately buried and uncovered by surface wind that weaved the loose sand in smokey wisps. The explosion blew away his foot. He had to wait two hours for a medevac. If only Doc Cornum were here.

Cornum and her companions in the ill-fated Black Hawk are an obsession for Bryan. *Schmall* or not, he will personally search the crash site, and get there in a HUMM-V if necessary. The wreck is about forty miles from Viper in the 24th Mech's AO, on the friendly side of the cease-fire line.

Next day, the sandstorms subside as if out of respect for a funeral party, but Bryan's mission is more grim than memorial. In his Black Hawk are Eric Pacheco (Garrett's pilot during his search for the Cobra FARP location), and Mike Pandol, a demolitions expert to check the bodies for booby traps and blow up anything left of the wreck that might be valuable to the Iraqis. The other passenger is one of Cornum's medics, Sgt. Homan, who will be the field mortician, preparing the bodies for delivery to graves registration at Viper. Eight black rubber bags are on board for this purpose.

Bryan feels he will be lucky if all eight bodies are found, even luckier if they are relatively intact. The crash coordinates are in his slugger. Slowly, almost reverently, his Black Hawk circles at thirty feet. Most noticeable are smashed bunkers and the metallic litter of a battle lost by the Iraqis. The only sign of life are waves from two guards posted by the 24th Mech to secure the wreck. But where is it?

There is no wreck, only wreckage. Bryan's practiced eye identifies the tail boom, apparently shot off before the crash. The angle of the tail boom sugggested the direction of flight, but with the tail rotor gone, Godfrey would have twisted violently before hitting the ground. It was all too easy imagining the final moments.

Away from the bunkers are three segments, in graduated sizes, that look to contain aircraft parts. They are partially buried, and Pacheco lands so as not to blow any more sand over them. The three Bengals trudge toward their duty.

From the largest fragment of wreckage, about the size of a jeep, protrudes a jagged sheet of plexiglass. In their minds the aviators try to reconstruct the cockpit. It's time to dig. Godfrey's, then Garvey's backs are first uncovered. They're facing into densely compacted sand; their shoulders, still restrained by harnesses, are gently pulled back as if from a mold. There's little else, for the legs were amputated. Pale as the thin clouds overhead, Homan scribbles on official forms. Cause of death? He hesitates. Multiple from impact. Though not required, he adds "instantaneous," though no one could know. The insertion into body bags is not as revolting as feared: sand has dryly clotted blood and caked viscera, packing the abyss where once was a lower torso. Bryan checks himself. This is an experience endured many and many a time in Vietnam—58,000 times. It is a closing ceremony to the initiation of war, and the last to be heard of the Nintendo metaphor.

Six more bodies must be found. Bryan will not leave till they are. Widening their search, his men separate, for the rest of the wreckage is scattered as if by a hurricane. After twenty minutes, Brilinski is uncovered, his waist harness attached to a piece of fuselage. That leaves the flight surgeon and four pathfinders undiscovered, and the searchers reduced to gloom. The pathfinders may have survived the wreck—God knows how—and would have fought to the last man. If they died in ground combat, the Iraqis might have buried them in mass graves as was their practice with their own dead.

The searchers return to spread sand at the main crash crater. A foot is unearthed, then two more. Butts and Ortiz are accounted for. They had not been in ground combat. Bare headed, the aviators assist Homan with his melancholy task.

"Hey!" A few yards from the crater, Pacheco pulls up a flight helmet filled with sand. The name on it is Cornum. But little else is found in the next half hour. Then, near a shattered bunker, is more personal equipment: Cornum's flak vest and medical bag, ransacked by Iraqis. For the rest of the afternoon, nothing more turns up.

This futility now becomes source for a certain optimism. The Iraqis had left the bodies where they died, and no mass graves are discovered. Dunlap, Stamaris and Cornum, from all indications, are possibly alive—unless they were executed or died of injuries after the Republican Guards took them away. There is hope enough to list them as MIA.

Garrett: "The shoot down was like a 2x4 between the eyes. Things had been going so unbelievably well for us as we swept across Iraq that the elixir of a costless victory flowed freely. Then the shoot down revealed the reality of war and dropped it in our laps. To make it worse, Rhonda was on board. That didn't surprise anyone who knew her, but it added to the already severe blow—not because she was a woman, but because she was immensely popular throughout the brigade, not just 2-229th.

"With Bill Bryan, I went in to see Gen. Peay and reviewed the conditions over the marsh and along the causeway and its approaches. Yesterday had been a hairy afternoon, and I wanted the CG to have a good picture of how dangerous and ill defined the situation was where we left it. A pursuit is like that—the enemy's organization and control break down— some units are trying to surrender while others are shooting at you. But if you get timid, if you don't press home the attack, you lose the opportunity to make victory decisive.

"Gen. Peay wanted to know about Rhonda's mission in some detail. I told him how it unfolded from my perspective. A radio call came in to the C&C ship which was functioning as my CP on the ground at Viper. The message was from division and said an F-16 pilot had been shot down at coordinates that plotted out close to where Bryan was shooting up the causeway. I called 2-229's TOC and asked if they could respond, thinking they would contact Bryan and he would use aircraft he already had on station up there. Instead, 2-229's TOC launched Godfrey's flight and notified me that it was en route. I acknowledged, and asked if Godfrey had Apache escorts in case he couldn't link up with Bryan. The answer was affirmative. Next thing I heard was that the Black Hawk was down and an Apache shot up.

"It took a while to sort out how this misguided mission occurred. The basic reason was that the coordinates relayed to us were grossly erroneous. Andrews was not over the marsh [he indicated he was over dry land in his statements overheard by Gabram on the Guard frequency], but rather over a very hot battle area well to the south, a good twenty miles out of division's AO.

"But a pilot on a rescue mission has other things on his mind than unit boundaries. Godfrey, using good initiative, contacted an AWAC who unintentionally vectored him into disaster. An AWAC 'sees' air targets and other transponders. It can't discern ground targets, much less determine what's friendly or hostile down there. Godfrey and McElhiney figured the AWAC understood the situation pretty well, not an assumption anyone can criticize but it led to tragedy."

With no record of the AWAC's conversation with Godfrey, Bryan replayed McElhiney's video tapes over and over, correlating the pictures with a map, in order to determine the doomed Black Hawk's actual flight path. Where the pictures cut off was the grid square where the 24th Mech was asked to look for wreckage. They found it, guarded it, and that's where Bryan began to comb the sand.

At Tabuk airbase in extreme northwest Saudi Arabia, Kory Cornum was nearly as happy as every other member of the 58th Tactical Fighter Squadron for whom he was flight surgeon. The announced cease-fire had gone into effect, and rumor had it that the squadron would start home in three weeks. Kory's elation was dampened only by Schwarzkopf's televised briefing to the media on 27 February, the last full day of the ground war, at which time CINCCENT cautioned:

"Even as we speak right now there are incredible acts of bravery going on. This afternoon we had an F-16 pilot shot down. We had contact with him; he'd broken his leg and was on the ground. Two helicopters from the 101st—they didn't have to do it—but they went in to try to pull the pilot out. One of them was shot down, and we're still in the process of working through that. But that's the kind of thing that's going on out on the battlefield right now. There are great heroes out there, and we ought to be very, very proud of them."

Kory certainly was, whoever those heroes were, but he felt queasy because that rescue mission sounded like something for which Rhonda would volunteer. With the 101st scattered throughout southern Iraq, he decided against trying to invalidate his fears; and after all, the Screaming Eagles had hundreds of helicopters and many brave men flying in them.

Yet his comrades silently empathized with him, and as if to banish his apprehension, chose Kory's room for a celebratory party. Assuming Rhonda was similarly carousing somewhere out in the desert—though without contraband alcohol available to the airmen—Kory stayed up late, lifting many drinks to a forthcoming reunion. In spite of a hangover, he woke early the next morning and took a shower while his roommate slept in.

When Kory emerged from the steamy bathroom, both his wing and squadron commander stood by his bed—with a chaplain. They brought the staggering news, read from a printout. The colonels offered every facility to get through to Bryan for an update. Kory thanked them manfully, then when the door closed, he turned to his roommate. Exchanging no words, they both sobbed.

Across the miles between Tabuk and Viper, hope still flickered. The men in her professional as well as private life—Kory, McElhiney, Bryan, Garrett and many others—found most hope in Rhonda herself. A licensed steeplechase jockey, a sport parachutist and outdoorswoman, she was tough and resilient like top grade leather. And as the beginning and middle of this war had been nothing like Vietnam, neither would it end in a pall of uncertainty. Gen. Powell said as much soon after the ceasefire: the war would not be over till every POW and MIA was either released or accounted for.

Five from the ill-fated crew had settled all accounts on this earth. They were the first from the division to return home, their memorial service performed at Ft. Rucker before their comrades could attend, though Becky Garrett flew down from Ft. Campbell, representing Aviation Brigade and all the division's support groups. Said one wife,

"Thinking of the five who were killed caused really conflicting emotions. First, there were so few. We had been so fearful there would be many, many more. We had to be grateful, and we were. But it was a guilty gratitude. Whether there were five or five thousand, it didn't matter to the widow and children, so we grieved for them with all our hearts. I thought of what they were going through, like stepping to the edge of an abyss and imagining what it would be for me to fall off. You don't want to think about it very long, yet you feel you ought to because the awful emotions should be shared. Does that do any good for the survivors? I don't know. But it's an obligation—

that's the way it seemed to me—so I tried to do it, even when I felt guilty and grateful at the same time.

"I felt that God was telling us we were lucky this time. No one should push their luck. When I talked about this later with my husband, I got upset and urged him to leave the army, especially with the incentives the army was offering [during the downsizing after the war]. He wasn't thinking that way. He said that casualties were practically nothing because everyone was very good at their jobs. He's very rational, and that's why we stayed in."

Garrett felt the remains were returned home too quickly, as if there had been insufficient time for the right sort of farewell from their comrades. As substitute, they were saluted and memorialized in absentia out in the desert, the classic army tribute from the living to the fallen. It was a frequent picture from Vietnam but virtually unrecorded photographically in the Gulf: the rifles of the dead stuck in the ground on bayonets, topped with their helmets. And before the rifles the highly polished boots, burnished to a brilliance never achieved by their owners in life, for the hands of the survivors erased faults and rubbed in memories with the polish, imparting a perfection, a mirror of the best.

Because Roger Brilinski, William Butts, Philip Garvey, Robert Godfrey, and Patbouvier Ortiz were members of 2-229, Apaches flew over in formation at the conclusion of the service, the last chopper peeling off as the missing man. The gusty wind at Viper was welcome for once, drying tears of colonels and corporals.

March 1991

3: At Safwan in Iraq, CENTCOM dictates terms of cease-fire to the Iraqi army.

4-6: Iraq releases all 25 U.S. POW's.

7: Republican Guard formations that had been saved by the cease-fire attack rebels in southern Iraq and Kurdistan.

XXVII

...and start waiting.

If corps' horseback plan had been followed—a plan that assumed another twelve hours of war—the EA Thomas air assault would have gone off precisely at the minute that instead the cease-fire began. So Bush's announcement was the referee's whistle, halting play, stopping all action. With its Apaches off the causeway, the 101st was the only ARCENT division not in contact with Iraqi forces when the cease-fire was imposed. Immediately commanders looked around, dredging from memories fallible from fatigue, matters and details lost in the eleventh-hour scramble to close the noose at Basra. Never had a war ended so precipitously.

The halt left skid marks on the road, and Peay would make the most of what might be only a pit stop. First Brigade, ensconsed and isolated for a couple of days now at Cobra, was certainly ready to go again. Third Brigade, well settled in AO Eagle, stood fresh enough to jump elsewhere with few hours' notice. Second Brigade had rushed about considerably in the last hours, so Peay would have held them in reserve. Aviation Brigade was leaning in the harness. They needed rest the most, and so were grounded for maintenance unless unquestionably essential missions arose.

This was Peay's intent but his lieutenants, from force of habit and really inculcated from Peay's example, had much to do before their units reached the state of tidiness they knew he expected. Moreover, and even more importantly, they realized that Bolt's influence would soon be felt, with scarcely less impact than had been Saddam's. The division began to revert from go to show, the first indication being the return of clean-shaven faces after the aberrant facial shadows tolerated during the hundred hours. Peay noticed the change, but it was less than a concern, hardly even a curiosity. The automatic return to standards was exactly what standards were for.

He was more interested in how, in why, the Screaming Eagles could have performed so nearly without flaw, surpassing even his high expectations. It was more of a surprise to his subordinates that he needed to inquire.

"The old man," one of them related, "was dead right on several points—that support from home was awesome and a major, if intangible, combat factor. We really didn't have to call on that factor—the fighting never got that tough—but it was there like reserve horsepower in an engine. We never really had to go into passing gear. But believe me, if something... something like Hafer Al Batin had required high heroism, you'd have seen it in spades. You could just know that by the look in guys' eyes. It was a look they got from home.

"And all that great equipment came from home too, of course. A lot of newspeople who trashed our tanks and helicopters had been silenced. Our stuff is the best in the world, and the whole world now knows it. We always did.

"Peay certainly appreciated how our training had been very applicable for desert war. That's not just our training in Desert Shield either, but the basic stuff and SOP's developed over the years. That was like football training camp, and Desert Shield was like the week of preparation before the opening game.

"What seemed to surprise him a bit about our performance was the importance of having worked together for so long, and I don't mean just in the previous year. Many officers and NCO's were on their third or even fourth tour with the 101st. That made a lot of difference, to know how guys thought and reacted by knowing them from way back. When things were moving fast forward because of The Audible, I could just monitor the TAC net and recognize players from their voices without even hearing their call signs. I'd served in the division with this major or that light colonel I was hearing on the radio, knew them when they were lieutenants and captains in the 101st. Key players were known quantities is what I'm saying. That was hard to put a value on, but it was a tremendous value.

"The army tries to diversify assignments to broaden experience, but when a division assignment comes up in the career pattern, Department of the Army is usually sympathetic about getting you to the division you request. People want to come back to the 101st or they wouldn't ask to. The big reason, I think, is Ft. Campbell and the surrounding community. It really is a community, the best relationship I've ever seen or heard of in the military. We mutually appreciate each other. We're like a big family, half in uniform and half out."

Quite by coincidence, Mrs. Peay had scheduled a pot luck for the wives' support group leaders at an hour that turned out to coincide with the cease-fire. The entire support framework, called the 'chain of concern,' mirrored the men's chain of command and paralleled the hierarchy of the rear detachments. In Peay's absence, the garrison at Ft. Campbell was commanded by Col. John Seymour, lately with 5th Special Forces there, who had an immense task in training thousands of replacements as well as heading the rear detachments and coordinating the home front with the Gulf front. His organization did not always mesh with the women's but neither diverged from their common purpose. The two chains, as they were linked together, were indeed a strong bond. Pamela Peay had held several such pot lucks, occasions when the frictions from brittle relationships were put out of mind, and diversion enjoyed with casseroles and wine; occasions when incongruous problems on the home front were recounted more for amusement than solution. Home front war stories often related to the scarcest resource for the chain of concern—men.

Mrs. Peay had helped recruit men from Clarksville and Hopkinsville to replace boy scout leaders gone to the Gulf. Garages from these towns were asked to provide instruction in basic auto maintenance to waiting wives. More civilian mechanics volunteered than needed. Maintenance of the vast grounds at Ft. Campbell also suffered from the scarcity of men.

There was one plot in particular that began to show neglect—
the grove of Canadian maples—and the women wanted it kept
up like Arlington Cemetery, no matter who tended it. That
situation presented a typical problem for Seymour: maintenance of the grove was contracted exclusively to a civilian
landscaper, but Desert Storm priorities at Ft. Campbell prevented payment to the contractor. Mrs. Shelton was serving as
surrogate support leader for Second Brigade as Mrs. Purdom
was an army nurse in the JOA. Second Brigade support groups
decided to just leave Seymour out of the loop, and clip and trim
around the maple grove themselves.

Mrs. Dan Lynn was at the nexus of the two chains because
her husband commanded the 101st's rear detachment. She
knew all the home front war stories: like the one about the wife
who asked her congressman to return her husband because her
vagina was sealing with scar tissue. "Congressionals" were no
laughing matter, so Lt. Col. Lynn duly had the complainant
examined by a gynecologist who determined that the problem,
though real enough, could be remedied by masturbation.

Even before news of the cease-fire terms reached home, Mrs.
Peay's last pot luck was a light-hearted affair. Mass casualties
were now but an imaginary fear as if from last week's nightmare. The intricate sensitivities of notification were now
largely moot, all the more a relief because the procedure had
been a friction point between army regulations and the chain
of concern. The regulations clearly prescribed that next of kin
would be first notified by an officer accompanied by a chaplain.
A horror keenly recalled from 1965 was the practice of tele-
grams from the Secretary of the Army, delivered to new wid-
ows by taxi drivers. As if in atonement, the army of the '90's
rigidly required the officer and a chaplain procedure. But
support groups were new since Vietnam. The 101st's chain of
concern convinced Lynn that, in most cases, a widow would
benefit if the support group leader was notified first, then
accompanied the officer and chaplain.

Lynn stuck his neck out considerably to offer the support
groups a back channel compromise: if, in advance, wives indicated they would prefer that their support group leader be first
notified, she would be. Now the difficulty shifted from Lynn to

the leaders to present the contingency to each wife. Many recoiled in contemplation of the question. There was a widespread form of denial—"Don't even *talk* to me about notification!"—and the support leaders backed off. So the decision settled with them, based upon an estimate of each woman's temperament and reaction.

Now at Pamela Peay's last pot luck the question of bending notificaton regulations was like the memory of a car accident that almost happened. Talk was animated with anticipation, especially about the three week leave promised after the soldiers came home. The ubiquitous question was when would they get back. Phone contacts had been rare since the ground war began. The senior wives cautioned, sometimes scolded, that rumored dates were utterly unreliable. Everyone would just have to wait a bit longer, and their waiting skills were well developed.

At the Peay pot luck, only Becky Garrett's wives were troubled and subdued. The reason was Schwarzkopf's announcement that had rocked Kory Cornum. Follow-up reports were that it was an Apache shot down, erroneous news that similarly devastated 1-101's wives. Then the helicopter was identified as a Black Hawk, widening the anguish to all Aviation Brigade's battalions, especially 5, 6 and 7-101. The final and official version of the tragedy sent Mrs. Garrett to Ft. Rucker to honor the return of the five dead, leaving wives at Ft. Campbell in the uneasy state of guilty gratitude.

Through the pain of two broken arms dangling uselessly, a bullet wound, a smashed finger and knee, Rhonda Cornum was feeling similar sentiments. Except for Dunlap, bound and blindfolded beside her, she grieved for all others on the Black Hawk, assuming they were killed.[*] For several days she was relayed back through Iraqi military channels, thoroughly raped in the process, but philosophical throughout. She resolved that if what she underwent was not life threatening, excruciating or likely to protract imprisonment, she would endure it by virtually ignoring it. For her, rape by the enemy—like bullets from

---

[*] Cornum's experiences of captivity, release and homecoming is described in her book, *She Went to War* (Presidio Press: 1992)

the enemy—was a risk of war assumed by soldiers of both sexes. With hardly an exception, all male POW's captured by the North Vietnamese had been routinely raped; and as Cornum later told Cody later, she could deal with her rape better than any men she knew.

En route to Baghdad, she was transported with another POW, sprawled on the bus seat with a cast on his leg but still in his flight suit. Cornum was able to peek under her blindfold to read his name tape: Capt. Bill Andrews—the man she had gone to rescue. Stamaris was also on the bus with a badly shattered leg, for which Cornum would later serve as consulting physician to the Iraqis. With Dunlap, Stamaris and Andrews accounted for, Cornum was on a relative high:

"I was fortunate to have had other experiences that prepared me to live with that kind of failure [Shoot down and capture]. I considered Andrews my patient from the second we got the order to get him. I had done everything I could for him, which wasn't much, but I'd tried. If I felt guilty every time one of my patients did badly, I couldn't be a doctor. Most doctors have that attitude, and it gave me an advantage as a POW...

"I had a detached view of myself from the moment I realized I was pinned under the fuselage of the helicopter. It was as if I were the doctor and my body was the patient. I remained free, but my body was a prisoner."

Dunlap, Cornum and Andrews were interrogated successively but unprofessionally because they could hear what the others answered. Dunlap, perhaps to set the example, was defiant. For all three, the first question was why were you in Iraq? His answer was to kill Saddam. This drew several blows. When Cornum was ushered into the interrogation room, Dunlap was bent over in a chair, his head roped to his boots.

She temporized in her answers, providing those she knew her captors already knew like her unit—the tiger patch of 2-229 was sewn on her flight suit. And she lied, conservatively, to tactical questions, invoking plausible ignorance appropriate for a doctor. She also occupied herself by gleaning information from the interrogator's questions. But these misled her, causing her to think that fighting continued whereas the cease- fire had been in effect for several days.

Talkative by temperament, Cornum felt she needed to keep talking—talking about anything—for until she stopped, she would not be beaten. If she were, she felt that her medical knowledge would inform her when blows reached the point of permanent disablement. She was afraid she'd surrender at that point, almost sure that she would, a humiliation of greater degree than her rapes, with only the solace that she couldn't tell much even if it was all she knew. The pain wall loomed but she tried not to see it. After all, Scheherazade had told tales for 1001 nights not far from here, resulting in her salvation.

Unbeknownst to Cornum, the war was over, and so her tactical interrogation was pro forma. Espoused by a career torturer, Saddam's methods surely would have broken her at once had they been applied with rigor. Andrews, next to be questioned, seemed aware of the war's end and turned away every probe by invoking the Geneva Convention that required a prisoner to disclose only name, rank and serial number. Cornum could hear his interrogation and felt she had fallen short of professional standards.

The 101st, indeed the entire desert army, was troubled by the absence of another standard: how to conduct themselves in a state of no war, no peace. They were to be ready to resume the fight on a moment's notice, but all eyes looked to the rear, not the front. A plan to retire the division to King Fahd had to be developed, a plan almost as elaborate as Hail Mary. Meanwhile, "When are we going home?" rumors struck hearts and minds like an irresistible epidemic.

The contagion spread mostly from home. Under growing grass roots pressure from a nation impatient for the return of their victorious forces, Bush had to make good on his promise that they would not stay in the Gulf a moment longer than necessary. He repeated his promise, but when was that moment? For Third Brigade, it seemed indeterminate as Shiite uprisings broke out like grass fires along the north bank of the Euphrates.

For the rest of the division, even scary rumors could not displace those of homegoing. Orders from corps came down to destroy Iraqi war materiel and bunkers. Soon Cobra, Viper and Eagle boomed with engineers' charges. Division G2, however, was still interrogating EPW's. One of them, an officer, related that Saddam would launch a sneak chemical attack on the night of 2 March. Deadly gas would be delivered by long-range artillery. The Iraqis hoped, said the EPW report, that impacting rounds would be mistaken for engineers' demolitions. The diabolical threat—a rumor that would have put everyone into MOPP before the war—drew no serious reaction from the impatient Screaming Eagles, only the observation that this was another reason to get out of here.

Leaning forward like a ski jumper in flight was Second Brigade. With the Aviation Task Force, they had been first to reach Saudi Arabia, and so had been promised to be the first to leave for home. Bush was making good. On 4 March 900 riflemen were scheduled to fly from Rafha, near TAA Campbell, for King Fahd and hence, it was hoped, directly back to the States. Bye bye sand, sweat, scorpions, Saddam, slit trenches and Saudiland—Second Brigade was on its way!

Hello delay and disappointment. The movement was a presidential decision made without preliminary planning or time for coordination of the sky train needed to drive the desert army in reverse. The lucky 900 huddled in the rain for two days and a night on the tarmac at Rafha. Sand storms, like a parting blast from Iraq, further delayed their C-130's, but Peay sensed that a bad plan was more to blame for a personal anathema called harassing the troops.

He knew another general who felt the same way when it came to troop harassment. For the first time ever, Peay got on the phone and asked to speak with Schwarzkopf. CINCCENT heard him out, probably with silent nods of agreement, but his reply was two Spanish words, *El Presidente*. Good intentions from the White House were translating into bad moves in the Gulf. Put up with it. Things will smooth out. Peay walked and talked among the 900 as if in personal apology. No big deal, general—we're going home!

So was Cornum. After the interrogation, but more importantly after the sign off on cease-fire terms that required prompt return of allied POW's, she was hospitalized in Baghdad. Consulted by her Iraqi doctor, she examined her own X-rays, agreed to limited surgery on her arms, but declined a blood transfusion preparatory to the operation.

"I was still weak, but not so weak that I wanted to risk tapping into the Iraqi blood supply. Hepatitis and the AIDS virus would have worried me anywhere. I figured that if I had needed blood after the wreck, I already would have died. I knew I was no longer bleeding, so I didn't want any blood."

Consulting for herself right up until the anesthetic took effect, Cornum suggested that the IV be inserted into her jugular as her arms were unavailable. After two days in the hospital, tormented more by mosquitoes than her injuries, she was ushered from her ward, and with Stamaris on a stretcher, bused across town at three in the morning to a prison. Allowed permission to use the water closet, she walked down the cell block which she determined was being used exclusively for POW's. That the Iraqis had collected them seemed a good sign, though she also suspected that the POW's might have been gathered for the purpose of some propaganda video.

At dawn she was trussed in yellow prison garb marked PW, hosed with a cheap cologne, and with the rest of the cell block marched to a bus that delivered them to a hotel lobby where they were permitted to mill around without blindfolds. With this liberty, the POW's convinced each other that their status had changed. This was quickly confirmed when Swiss came up and introduced themselves as representatives of the International Red Cross. They had taken custody of the POW's.

Surprise, relief, gratitude came over them in waves, then prisoner stories exchanged. The earlier the captivity, the more brutal had been the treatment. An Air Force major related how the Iraqis had attached his ears and jaw to a car battery. He refused to talk till one of the jolts blew out a tooth filling. Navy lieutenant Jeffrey Zahn was advised by later POW's that his battered face had appeared on the cover of *Newsweek*.

The man Cornum wanted to meet was Andrews. That done, she felt her mission, begun when her Black Hawk took off, was complete. But the episode was not complete for Andrews nor his squadron. When they learned of the fatalities from the attempted rescue they set up an educational fund for children of the dead.

From the Baghdad airport, the POW's (which included Britons and an Italian) watched a Saudia 727 land and debark its load of Iraqi EPW's. The cease-fire called for a prisoner exchange, and the Iraqis got much the better of it in numbers. They debarked sullenly without cheers and no one kissing the ground, or anyone to meet them except guards who marched them away to waiting buses.

The allied POW's boarded the same 727. Even after takeoff they were silently contemplative till the pilot announced that he had entered Saudi air space; then joy exploded as a British Tornado, followed by a U.S. F-15, waggled their wings in welcome and escorted them on to Riyadh. There Schwarzkopf stood on the tarmac to greet them. Cornum's salute was stopped by her cast, but a gesture he nonetheless appreciated. En route to a bus, the press called to her, asking how she felt. In reply she shouted a Screaming Eagle battle cry—"Airborne!"—misinterpreted by the reporters as, "There are more!," setting them in a tizzy, as this was to be the only flight of returned POW's.

On the hospital ship *Mercy*, moored off Bahrain, Rhonda and Kory reunited:

"He came to me and wrapped his big arms around, trying to figure out where he could hold me without hurting. It was hard.., with casts and slings holding me together, but he touched my face and kissed me gently. I looked at his face, and looked again."

Kory told how he had learned she was safe. At Tabuk on 5 March he was hovering around the Air Force intelligence office when a call came through from ARCENT Casualty Center. They wasted no time to tell him that Rhonda was safe with the Red Cross in Baghdad. He leaped and whooped to the delight of his comrades who converged on his room to help pack his bags, then sent him off with champagne and tears.

Dan Grant of 2-229 was also on the *Mercy* to bring greetings from everyone in Aviation Brigade. Cornum was soon to depart for the States. She asked Grant when the rest of her battalion would follow. He had no idea. Neither did anyone else in the 101st. Peay, as always, was thinking ahead: on 8 March he required a briefing to sketch the first 180 days of training once the division got home. His staff sighed: the briefing seemed incredibly academic, for the first step in the homeward direction would not be taken till the 101st was relieved by units from 7th Corps. From all indications, that seemed anything but imminent. From Lippard's log:

8 March: Nothing seems to be happening. We still have no word of any formal signing of the cease fire. 3rd ACR is already starting to move back south of the LD [border]. The 24th will soon do the same. We just sit. There is a feeling amongst the staff that the 24th has been politicing corps and may get out before us.

9 March: Morale is starting to sag a bit. All we hear on the radio is "The troops are coming home!" but we haven't moved, other than the lucky 900 from Second Brigade.

Something stinks at corps. We are now last priority for ammo turn-in. How long will it be till we are last priority for everything in the redeployment? The 24th has aced us.

I think if ARCENT would state that no 18th ABC soldier was to leave Saudi until the divisions flew, this redeployment would go a lot smoother.

10 March: The 900 are home! We're told the first 101st soldiers arrived at Ft. Campbell yesterday. They came in on three flights, 747's I believe, after a delay from a snow storm in Massachusetts. The division received permission to move the rest of Second Bde back to King Fahd, and all of Third Bde from AO Eagle to Cobra. Progress! But we're not out of here till the cease fire is formalized. No one can figure out why it hasn't been.

11 March: After 69 Black Hawk sorties and a ground convoy, Third Bde is back at Cobra. Aviation Bde was tagged to screen AO Eagle from the air. There's nothing up there now except a FARP and a platoon of infantry. Second Bde has started to move by air (C-130's) and road to King Fahd.

12 March: Of all the silly stunts! Third Bde has to move back up to AO Eagle. Seems corps jumped the gun in telling us to move them south yesterday. A damn shame, and actions like this are not morale builders.

The temperature got up to 84 degrees today, not uncomfortable, but the sand was bad. We had a 'speed max' which is sort of a large dust devil covering about a square mile. Winds were light, so the dust kind of hung in the air all day.

The "silly stunt" resulted somewhat from confusion in terminology. In the air assault division, an area can be screened from the air, but elsewhere in the army screen means to have patrols and outposts on the ground. After Third Brigade's brief departure, Aviation Brigade was screening AO Eagle, as they understood the term, but when CENTCOM learned there was but one platoon on Highway 8, Clark was ordered back.

Schwarzkopf also wanted more muscle up on the Euphrates because the Iraqis had begun their habit of cheating on cease-fire terms. Thus, as Desert Shield had started, so Desert Storm would end: with a show of force to forestall further Iraqi transgressions.

Clark had been gone less than 24 hours. When he returned with two battalions, the scene, indeed the scenery, had much changed. He assumed he could re-establish his CP at the pumping station but the building had been trashed in his absence—and Saddam's monument irreparably defaced by local Iraqis. They had also made off with plywood floors, windows and their sidings, everything not embedded in concrete.

13 March: The days are getting slow and boring. Still no word on a formal cease fire or 7th Corps relieving us.

Second Bde's movement to CE II [King Fahd] appears to have been less than orderly. Convoy serials did not arrive in the same sequence they departed the TAA. A 31-man trail party was left behind. MAJ Sheppard of the G3 shop took control of the abandoned soldiers. COL Bolt requested to see the Second Bde XO reference the move.

The division is preparing for the Secretary of the Army's visit tomorrow.

14 March: He blew us off. Division was notified this morning that he would not visit the 101st. No matter, Schwarzkopf visits tomorrow.

15 March: We must be on someone's very black list or very much out of the way. Yesterday SECAR stood us up and today CINC-CENT cancelled out. He must not have any answer for our inevitable question, "When do we move out of here?" Corps says for sure that Elvis will visit tomorrow.

16 March: Our tentative CRAF [Civilian Reserve Air Fleet] dates are 3-15 April. How can we wait that long? We'll just have to.

Locals have been flocking back into the TAA. A big increase in civilian traffic the last week. A lot of Mercedes. The bedouins are also back, herding their camels. They're supposed to stay 50 k's south of Tapline Road, but that's being ignored and we let them scavenge our used engineer equipment.

A soldier from 2-320 Arty swallowed some Jet-A fuel while trying to syphon from one container to another. He was evaced in serious condition.

17 March: St. Patrick's Day. Well at least our LBE is green. 9-101's trail party arrived at King Fahd at 3:00 in the morning. Funny thing—it wasn't supposed to leave the TAA till 6:00. Oops! You'd get the idea that some people are anxious to get out of here.

18 March: Schwarzkopf was a no show again. But there are good rumors in the air. Word is 7th Corps units will begin relieving us in place on 21 March. If true, we can meet our air flow dates. We want to believe it.

19 March: It's going to happen! We got the FRAGO from corps. Everyone's excited. The move home is about to begin.

20 March: There was a powerful purple tint on the northeast horizon at sunset. I don't know if it was the oil field smoke or what, but it was magnificent. DMAIN will break down day after tomorrow. On to King Fahd.

23 March: Heavy rain all day. Tents were coming down for movement, and we were flooded. We'll manage. What matters is that the rain didn't affect the air flow.

24 March: At stand-to a soldier from 1-187 was discovered dead from an apparently self-inflicted wound. Two suicide notes were found near the scene.

25 March: The locals continue to make off with a lot of stuff we'll leave behind. One group with a Nissan pick-up loaded the lumber from BG Adam's bunker and drove off. No problem—the general's staff helped them load it. But now the locals are going after the helicopter matting [aluminum sheets], and that's a no-no. Our guards are armed to discourage such theft.

19 May—Clarksville, Tennessee:

During the interim period I neglected my log and will now try to bring it up to date while events are still fresh in my mind.

I departed the TAA on the morning of 27 March. At Rafha there was quite a crowd of 82nd soldiers also waiting for flights. Saudis were selling ice cream, lamb sandwiches, chicken, and Iraqi money for souvenirs. They were making out. A 2 Dinar note (I don't think it was worth the paper it was printed on) with Saddam's face on it was going for ten U.S. dollars. It was a two-hour flight from Rafha to CE II. I slept most of the way.

King Fahd was incredible. Transports, jet fighters, and army choppers everywhere. A short bus ride and we were at CE II, the division's hometown during Desert Shield. The division finance officer had been acting mayor while we did Desert Storm. All the tents in tent city were back up, and we looked like the Army of the Potomac. Row after row of tents. Now at last we had all the facilities the engineers had worked on so long—showers, hot chow, and even a place to wash our laundry.

We got very busy preparing our equipment for the return to the U.S.. We spent two days just cleaning the CP tents for inspection, then loading them into a milvan for sea shipment. I've never seen such chicken shit inspectors.

The inspections were required by the U.S. Department of Agriculture, for the purpose of preventing alien microbes from contaminating American soil. Secretary Madigan was able to turn back the desert army from their objective in a way Saddam had only dreamed. Over and over vehicles were rejected if even a granule of sand was found. Inspectors scraped the blunt end of toothpicks under the rubber moldings of windshields. A speck of sand, and a five-ton truck went to the back of the line. A Vietnam veteran expected the inspectors' tents would soon be fragged.

No, that might delay the grenadier's departure. Peay purchased flood lights so that wash racks ran nonstop. The spit and polish of these inspections meant troop harassment to the nth degree; but grimly the troops cleaned and scrubbed, in final preparations using their toothbrushes which soon became short items in the field PX. The 101st could consider itself lucky for having fewer vehicles. In the inspections lines of the 24th Mech, mighty Abrams tanks by the hundreds lined up meekly, their crews praying not to be rejected. Agriculture's ridiculous rigor even drew protests from Gen. Powell but no relief.

Lippard:

I attended sunrise services Easter morning. The Division Chaplain placed a large cross on top of a dune. There we were, singing hymns in the heart of Islam. I'll never forget it, and I can't remember another Easter.

I was supposed to leave Saudi on 4 April but by a stroke of luck I turned up on a manifest for the 3rd. We had manifest call at 1:00 in the morning. After a quick customs inspection (no one searched my bags), we lounged in a huge waiting room with TV's and a bank of telephones. I called my wife and told her my arrival time, then watched a very approriate movie, "Field of Dreams." We were already dreaming of the hours ahead!

We were loaded on two buses, one for smokers and non-smokers, then taken to the runway where we waited two hours. Eventually we loaded in a Tower Air 747. We were wheels up at 10:20 local time. That 747 shook with cheers.

There was a 4-hour layover in Brussels, Belgium, but no one could get off the plane. We picked up a new flight crew. They were super friendly and fed us good meals. We kidded them about "Where's the wine?"

We landed in New York at night. It was twinkling and glamorous. Many of us had only seen it in pictures. That's all we'd see because we weren't allowed off the plane.

We started our descent over Ft. Campbell at 11:30 at night. Not many lights were on and I couldn't make out any land marks. But a huge hangar was lit up like Christmas. We landed and rolled up to it, where we could see crowds of people waving flags. Col. Seymour greeted us as we came down the ramp. I think we were all very nervous. He led us into the hangar and told us to stay in a group for a few more minutes. We were pretty awed by what we saw. Huge flags and banners, a military band and volunteers waiting with refreshments. No speeches, thank God. Grouped on the other side of the hangar were our loved ones. The band started to play and we rushed toward each other. From then on it was all hugging, kissing and crying.

The only thing we had to do was turn in our weapons and pick up our bags at HHC. That night I signed out on 18 days leave. My adventure in the Persian Gulf was over. God bless the USA!

April 1991

3: Iraq supresses revolts.

16. Kurdish refugee camps created by Operation Provide Comfort.

XXVIII

Hangar of joy

Lippard's homecoming, with hundreds of thousands like it (at a rate of 5,000 per day), merged the Gulf and home fronts like waves curling onto a soft beach. Perhaps the lighthouse was Bangor, Maine, the closest U.S. refuel point for the homeward bound. Bangor is not a military town like Clarksville or Hopkinsville—hasn't been since a nearby SAC base closed in 1968—and war came by to visit only with the happy face of its ending. However, Bangor's American Legion and VFW were quick to recognize the airport's significance as the Desert Stormers' port of entry into the relief and pride of the nation that awaited them.

The local newspaper, in no way anticipating what would result, published schedules for arriving troop carriers which soon reached eight per day. Bangorians reacted spontaneously, initially with cookies and teddy bears, but most impressively with people. Elderly people at first, who had time to spend at the airport, then teenagers seeking autographs from anyone in uniform.

From appearances they seemed not to be greeters, but a rather normal crowd for the terminal—though the Bangor airport in early spring is normally uncrowded—just average civilian travelers like those the debarking troops remembered from holiday weekends. But suddenly the crowd began to applaud, an ambush of appreciation. The effect was startling, unnerving, almost embarrassing till perceptive soldiers went over to shake hands, then gratitude flowed from both sides. Beginning with these early encounters, Bangor's communal activity was to sound America's joyous fanfare and flutter its flags in welcome. It became common for townspeople to attend over a hundred refueling stops.

It never grew stale because the troops' reaction as they trudged jet-lagged into the terminal was spiritual elixir for both greeters and greeted, starting first with the moment of cautious curiosity as soldiers and civilians sized each other up. Here were the crew-cut youth, tautly lean and deeply tanned, striding down the concourse in those desert uniforms seen only on TV. They glanced up nervously at the watching civilians who looked so much like families awaiting the troops all across the country west of Maine. Then a band would strike up, often with "God Bless America," and the terminal burst with applause.

The soldiers halt, surprised, as hands reach out to shake theirs. They're not expecting this but it's wonderful. Some cheer, some dance—all reboard their plane wiping their eyes. For Screaming Eagles, Chattanooga had been their outbound supercharge, Bangor was the same sensation in reverse.

A Viet vet met 150 planes with a yellow ribbon for every passenger, and upon one of many posters to go up on the terminal wall was a large hand written poem:

Freddy McHugh was airborne, proud of the 101st.
But in 68, in Vietnam, the VC did their worst.
Freddy came home under a flag, to stay in Maine's cold ground.
Others came back, time after time—but no one was around.
Thank you, troops of Desert Storm, for bringing us back home.
Home at last, from a war long past—home from Vietnam.

The poet added this inscription, "Freddy, now you finally got the welcome you deserved. Love from your comrade-in-arms, Dan Cowdrey, 101st Airborne."

Garrett: "Of course Viet vets compared our two homecomings. They were both too extreme, one for being so cold and callous, the other for what we felt was excessive gratitude. I know it's a cliche now, but in the desert we did our jobs—did it very well, for which we deserved a pat on the back, and that would have sufficed. Not that we weren't overwhelmed by the way we were received; there wasn't a heart left untouched on my airplane. And that was just the beginning.

"Maybe the two homecomings were a way of evening things out. Maybe two wrongs, in our case, made a right. I felt I was representing so many guys from Vietnam who didn't get the second, the compensating homecoming. It made me wonder about the spitters and airport harassers who called us baby killers back then. I wonder if the Desert Storm homecoming finally turned their self-righteousness into shame."

Hill: "We sort of snuck in from Vietnam. First thing everyone did was get out of uniform. I didn't. I was proud of what I'd done, the people I'd served with, and the cause we'd fought for. It took years and the tales of boat people and re-education camps before the world was convinced about the enemy we fought over there. They were every bit as horrible as anything Saddam ever did. We were heroes for whipping him. We were baby killers for whipping the NVA. It's all in how things were perceived. In successive wars the army has had the worst of it and the best of it. I guess that's made me philosophical."

Abandoned and scorned by much of the public after Vietnam, the army was left to recuperate, but also to incubate the seeds of victory that sprouted through care, then eventually flowered in the desert. For Viet vets who stayed in the army, the years '73-'77 was the period of bottoming out. The end of the draft and building down in the aftermath of Vietnam distilled the army to a hard core of people whose most notable characteristic was job satisfaction. They saw the rationale for the military—even beyond the threat of international communism—and were intent to re-prove that American forces are the best in the world. They liked the people around them who felt and worked with the same attitude.

Men like Cody, a lieutenant during the bottoming out period, saw mentors in senior officers whom they could emulate in dedication, while feeling good about it.

Job satisfaction. In time junior officers' search for excellence was rewarded. It didn't matter that few outside the military cared. Between the two world wars, no one had much cared either; yet from the hard core of professionals emerged the likes of Eisenhower and Bradley, representing a host of admirable commanders who catapulted to seniority, and in four years vaulted the United States into super power.

They had come off a win in World War I. In contrast, senior commanders in the desert seemed to follow a checklist of bitter lessons from Vietnam, mistakes in Southeast Asia that would not be repeated in Southwest Asia. One of these was rampant careerism, corrosive of morale and costly in lives, as commanders were rotated in a heedless rhythm before their jungle experience produced benefits for the troops. Careerism—the slang term is 'ticket punching'—could not be expunged but at least minimized, and the right people kept long enough in the right jobs.

Consequently, command tours were stabilized in the late '70's, and candidate commanders examined as if they were nominees for the Supreme Court. To appear on a 'command list' was the equivalent of advancing to an exalted stage of freemasonary.

With no draft, the army recruited. With a far smaller force to be filled, they recruited with increasing selectivity. Educational standards went up from junior to high school graduates. By 1990, some college credits were all but required. Judges no longer considered a hitch in the military as an alternative sentence. The army became an institution that a young person got into rather than out of.

Commanders were vested with full authority of their title, enabled to punish and reward without much interference from above. With the draft went the most severe problems of the early '70's, racial strife and drug abuse. Sensitivity training and addiction-breaking faded in concern as the army's population changed. Those problems had been flushed out of the system like cleansing the Augean stables. Those problems were moved 'out there' where the army vowed they would never intrude again.

This selectivity watershed was marked most noticeably by the change in recruiting slogans. During Vietnam it was "The army wants to join you," a plaintive expression that Weiss still cannot repeat without grabbing the arms of his chair. It was Gen. Maxwell Thurman (later to command all U.S. forces in the invasion of Panama) who changed the recruiting message to "Be all that you can be."*

The pith of that message was conditional truth. You had to accept the entire value system of the military which, by its self-containment was perforce a limitation, but not a great deal more so than other professional universes like the ministry and medicine, much less so than law. What was preeminently true was that in the army of the '80's your development would not be held back by too few opportunities for accomplishment. There was no lack of challenges, and those met would be suitably rewarded by added responsibilities. You could be all that you made of your job. Elsewhere you might have had to wear the right skin, go to the right schools or marry the boss's daughter.

Parodoxically, great opportunity imposed a requirement for like mindedness: be all that you can be, but while you're doing it, stay within weight and physical fitness standards, don't get a speeding ticket and no more than one divorce; keep your dog in the yard, your kids' hair relatively short, and your pecker in your pants; don't take a drug without a prescription and watch the alcohol—prop blasts and happy hour are no longer army traditions. Drive under the influence and you might as well keep going out the gate.

Such requirements were part initiating, part procrustean, part value imposition, part enlightened direction, part posing; but all together they produced mutual, communal knowledge and awareness, the kind that resulted in telepathic understanding during The Audible. Everyone adequately knew where everyone else was coming from, a unique circumstance in other professions.

In time, starting around 1978, like mindedness became more a form of acceptance—even embrace—than acquiescence. Chapel attendance in the '60's had been sparse unless imposed by command suasion. In the '80's church going at Ft. Campbell underwent spontaneous revival. Whether because of closer rapport between chaplains and families, or by apocalyptic signs in what could be perceived as degeneracy in the nation,

* Thurman actually approved that message which was proposed by a major ad agency.

or the simple urge to worship in fellowship with like minded families, the reasons stand as a subject for study. What is clear is that the nuclear family remained the nucleus of the military community. Except in the lower enlisted ranks, two working parents were unusual, so much so that special support groups were created for them. Such socio-economic situations were identified and dealt with according to their seriousness for a military rather than altruistic purpose—to keep the soldiers' minds on their jobs. The Vietnam era had been characterized by its distractions; the army of the 80's was like minded because it was single minded. In the late '70's born-againess never swept the military as it did the nation, perhaps because its basis, though not its fervor, was already rooted there. Religion was not to be worn on the sleeve of a field jacket but was approved close under the shoulder patch. The army didn't mind being different if the difference corresponded with that of traditional values versus those of the New Age lurching from its crib.

It is curious that as America went through a period of challenged values, the value system of the military experienced solidification and validation. Perhaps it was the outward gaze at the culture of which the military was a subculture that convinced the army it had something their compatriots did not and longed for. Soul searching at Ft. Campbell was an archive from Vietnam. The search had found, and what was right was known and practiced.

This theory explains why certain steadfast soldiers remained with the army, though all had their misgivings, their times of doubt and temptation. The national economy in the '70's, as compared to the early '90's, was relatively prosperous though inflation devalued salaries, like those of service members, and caused civilian vocation to be all the more alluring.

Hill had seen the army at its worst, in the latter years of Vietnam and those immediately thereafter. In the early '70's he was ready to get out though he had an enviable and unique assignment for a captain. He was with the 1st Cav at Ft. Hood in his home state. For recruiting purposes, the division sent a platoon of horse cavalry around the region in 19th century uniforms, the boots and saddles (even handlebar mustaches) of the frontier. Hill was the platoon leader, his high profile job something of an emblem of what the army felt it should mean to the nation.

He mulled his prospects as he groomed his horse one day, when Mrs. Shoemaker, wife of the commanding general, stopped by the stable. They chatted. The future King Cobra contemplated quite different ambitions at the time—to buy and manage a string of motels. Still impressionable, he asked Mrs. Shoemaker for her opinion.

She deliberated, then answered, "You won't be happy, Tom." Hill thought enough of Mrs. Shoemaker to realize that her answer was not pat—that to another officer she might have endorsed leaving the army.

"You won't be happy." The honest sincerity of her answer rang true enough. Yet he also knew himself well enough to realize that happiness was a spinoff of job satisfaction. Even boots and saddles did not provide it in his current army. But Mrs. Shoemaker was right—neither would motels. Something more had to shape his decision. What kept the frontier army in the period uniform he now wore? Their job satisfaction was not in the brutal and isolated life or the hardscrabble hardships their families had to endure. It certainly wasn't the pay. All they had in plenitude was adventure, but not all could have been adventurers.

What kept *them* in? Hill continued to wonder. Like them, he felt confident (in contrast to enthusiastic) that he could make it on the outside: the frontier cavalry had been self reliant and so was he. Self reliance would get him through in civilian life. It wouldn't be fun, it wouldn't be satisfying, but it was possible even if unsuitable for his temperament. However, the possible is the essential; suitabilty is a luxury.

There was little to give up personally in this demoralized, undisciplined army of the early 1970's; that's why he considered motels. What Hill could not let go, and what settled his ultimate decision, was the continuity of the army. It could take the direction that he now deplored and discouraged him, or continue with the doggedness of the Indian-fighting cavalry.

Job satisfaction, the ultimate reward, he did not see in the army of the day, only and maybe its potential. The certain reward had to be in something else. That would in the effort, in doing right, in doing his best for that sake alone. Future reward was problematic, much depending on luck. Frank Dietrich never got the star he deserved more than any colonel in Vietnam. He stayed in. He stuck it out. He'd be remembered long after the careerist generals' obituaries. Remembered by men like Hill anyway, who decided to follow Dietrich's footsteps even if they led to a personal dead end. Somehow, someday, men like Dietrich would be vindicated.

As chief of staff of the 101st (succeeeding Bolt in 1991), Hill summed up his deliberations in the stable: "I wasn't going to leave the army to the ass holes."

He stayed. Peay, Adams, Shelton, Bolt, Weiss, Gile, Purdom, McDonald, Clark and Garrett stayed—not for job security, for there was little in the post-Vietnam downsizing. Job satisfaction would be in making the army all it can be with no guarantee except for the effort. Do this with like minded people and that was enough, that was all there could be for sure.

Acceptance of discipline, endorsement of standards. The period between the jungle and the desert was not for individualists or military homesteaders. It was a trial of commitment with intermittent squalls of doubt, also with valid remonstrations from outside that the army was not worth the costly burden of its upkeep. There is no doubt that the Reagan subscription to defense produced the dreadnought that struck down Saddam. But it was a close thing in time. With the cold war clattering to a close, the Gulf war gave Reagan's legacy a curtain call that brought down the house with world approval. But it was a very close thing, and something of a swan song, a finale.

Within two months of his homecoming, Peay was reassigned to the Pentagon, there to totally immerse in the stark problems of "keeping the army alive" with a defense budget scheduled for surgery on the jugular. The nation was broke and deeply in debt, discouraged and disgruntled with a flat, faltering economy. This created a situation exactly the reverse of Hill's in the stable: the best prospects, the security and job satisfaction were in uniform, the opposites outside. There would be many dedicated soldiers who would be turned out of the uniforms to which they had so recently brought such great credit.

In the Indian summer after Desert Storm, Clark came as close as anyone to developing a balanced view toward involuntary departures:

"They are a loss to the nation as soldiers, but a benefit for the habits and ethics they take into the civilian world. What they've learned in the army they won't forget. Reliability. Loyalty. Honesty. I think military service is now a great lead item on a resume. These people are going to do well because they know how to do well. They've done it already."

But what of the army they leave? Peay can reluctantly accept the metaphor of a skeleton army but not a hollow one. Gen. Gordon Sullivan, the Army Chief of Staff, addressed the difference with a slogan: "No more Task Force Smiths."

TF Smith was a tatterdemalion, battalion-size hodgepodge thrown onto the Korean peninsula in the early days of that war. TF Smith was wiped out by human tidal waves, but also by reason of its untrained soldiers, unreliable equipment and general unpreparedness. What Sullivan said was that if and when the army goes to war again, the force may be small—most surely it will be—but it will be poised and powerful.

The desert army was dismantled with the speed that brought the boys home after World War II. The mightiest of Schwarzkopf's formations, 7th Corps, furled its colors in Germany and went into deactivation for the first time since 1943, two of its divisions also retired from active roles. Army posts the size of Ft. Campbell (Ft. Ord, CA, for example) scheduled their closures. Congress prevented involuntary discharges till after elections, and demanded that commensurate cuts not be made on hometown reserve units. This was but costly delay and political prevarication. Military shrinkage was inevitable and inexorable. It struck the army like the Black Death in Europe, removing a quarter of the population.

But like London before the plague, hearts were light in April of 1991, and Ft. Campbell almost light headed. Lynn's office at headquarters was more a control tower than command post. Phones rang continuously like church bells on Christmas morning. When would this company of that battalion be arriving?—

a question that meant a special person for the caller. The schedules were put out through the chain of concern, but those who waited insisted on confirmation. Families were traveling long distances to meet particular planes. In Colorado, the co-workers of a Screaming Eagle's parents took up a collection for airfare. It was vital to know which commercial flight would reach Nashville in time for the parents to meet the military flight at Ft. Campbell, so the military schedules had to be right. Communications danced between Kentucky and King Fahd more than in any period during the war.

King Fahd confirmed manifests only after a plane departed. That provided some fifteen hours for families to assemble. Weather delays were updated through Lynn's office and the chain of concern. As the Gulf and home fronts began to merge, information became increasingly reliable. Yet now there was a final, indeed critical, question to be resolved between the two fronts: what should be the nature of homecoming?

Bangor had already provided the answer but it was not known in the Gulf. Independently, Mrs. Peay decided on the sort of reception already demonstrated by the Bangorians. All she saw, all she heard, insisted that would be the way—public, unceremonious and spontaneous.

Gen. Peay: "I didn't have a feel for the mood of the country. I requested that Seymour keep homecomings low key. Just get our fine soldiers off the planes and with their families. That's the guidance I gave him. I believed that's all anyone wanted."

Mrs. Peay knew better. Seymour and Lynn felt identically, and even if the CG's guidance was subverted by the triumvirate, the welcome home would be a party like nothing Ft. Campbell had ever experienced.

Defense Department policy for homecomings was intentionally vague, and summarized by a statement by an anonymous spokesman that the military would "step aside." The Pentagon was right that this last action of the war would be better executed by the home front.

But the military cannot accept free form events, even when condoned; so at Ft. Campbell a general homecoming scenario was planned and rehearsed. Each arriving plane would roll up to a huge hangar dedicated for receptions and no other purpose. Without clearance from the FAA, pilots opened a hatch over the cockpit where an arriving soldier raised the colors of the units aboard. Noses pressed and steamed up windows as passengers searched for special faces in the crowd. The plane slowly taxied toward the hangar where greeters had gathered on the apron to wave and cheer. Then they were ushered into the hangar, so as not to be seen from the plane—disappeared, as it were, like guests for a surprise party.

Under wintery sunshine or floodlights, the troops—usually about 400 of them—debarked stiffly. Seymour or Lynn shook hands with the senior officer aboard and described to him the simple program. Form up, march into the hangar; please don't break ranks till the music starts. Then let things happen as they may.

Where did the crowd go? the bemused troops wonder as they obey the last order they will receive for several weeks. "Hut... hut" their unsentimental sergeants bark, "Get in step. Look air assault.", for flashbulbs pop, news cameras whirr, as the march of the final formation is televised for viewers who will never get too much of these pictures, no matter that they're all about the same.

Veteran viewers know what's coming, and anticipate the tingle from the scene about to be repeated. Anticipation crackles from the screen. Anticipation hums from the families like high tension wires. Anticipation is latent lightning with the troops. The army is about to let it go.

Into the cavernous building. Stack arms. Sergeants have trouble now keeping attention—for the hangar looks as it never has before, festooned with banners, kinetic with emotion. Some soldiers remember this hangar, a desolate outboarding site nine lonely months ago before Desert Shield. Now there is a raised bandstand centered in front of the empty space between soldiers and civilians. The band is Tennessee National Guardsmen. The conductor's hand sweeps down and music booms, soon merged with echoing cheers and shrill cries.

The civilians rush for the soldiers who are confused for a moment, a moment before *the* moment when one experience ends and another begins. It's find your partner, find your family, find that person, lock her lips and body to yours for however long. Camouflage and colorful clothes swirl and mingle. Feet sweep off the floor and toddlers lift high on shoulders. No one remains detached, not spectators, bandsmen, volunteers at refreshment stands, TV or print reporters, least of all the crews of CRAF planes who brought the soldiers home. In uniform, from many airlines, they hurry ahead of the marching troops to watch them disintegrate into the whirlpool of love.

Anywhere the eye alights is a living snapshot, touching as a bridal couple's kiss, radiant as parents viewing their newborn together, as proud as families at college graduation, unabashed as salutes on the 4th of July to the stars and stripes on parade going by, hilarious as hitting the jackpot.

A reporter cannot make notes; they must wait till later when he recalls how his mouth ached from a continuous grin, how the last note of the "Star Spangled Banner" was followed by a thunderous cheer louder than he had heard in any stadium, how when this happened he thought his heart would explode in a critical mass with those around him, how he had never been in one place so filled with hybrid pride and gratitude, how tears ran so long they dripped from chins and ran unnoticed because the hangar was shimmering with tears. How God had blessed America.

Two, sometimes three flights per day or night, nonetheless reviving for Lynn who felt an ever ascending high when he thought he could get no higher. Indeed there were homecoming junkies, like T.C. Freeman, wife of a Clarksville banker, who met hundreds of planes because each arrival was a new beauty made of the same components like the succeeding panes of a kaleidoscope. And there was novelty to be seen by experienced eyes:

Lynn, the ultimate homecoming veteran, became an afficiando of signs. There were support group signs, elaborately done; professionally stirring signs from local merchants, touching signs from schools; but what said it best was the family signs emblazoned with first names. For Support Command's arrival, Lynn noticed three signs waving in praise of 'Jose.' Each was held by a comely woman unnoticed by, and apparently unacquainted with the other two. What a predicament,

Lynn silently observed, if they were all here to meet the same Jose.

In fact they were. One leaped upon Jose, her sign obscuring his view of the others. They found him already in a skin tight embrace. Most amazing to Lynn was that Jose managed to extricate and explain himself in staccato Spanish. The miracle intrigued Lynn so much that during the summer he, through considerable research (there were 14 Specialist Jose's in Suppport Command), located the man's commanders to learn his story:

One of the women was his estranged wife who decided to surprise him in hopes of patching up the marriage. Another was an old girlfriend from his hometown in New Mexico. The third was an "any soldier" correspondent from Rhode Island. The latter two ladies Jose had urged to meet him, and at first each had demurred because she had to come long distances. Caught up by the gratitude and excitement of the nation, both had relented at the last minute, but too late to inform Jose.

In contrast to Jose, there were soldiers who had no one to meet them. These were those transiting Ft. Campbell en route to bases farther west. Yet they were included in the hangar celebrations, identified by their shoulder patches, and embraced by local civilians. Phones were set aside for them, beer shoved into their hands.

The hangar glowed and rang for over 500 flights and two months. Back in Saudi Arabia, Adams was supervising the police call he had predicted in his flight over MSR New Market. An enormous amount of work was left to be done. It wasn't completed till May. As the redployment wound down, Screaming Eagles dribbled back where before they had poured. Planes brought fewer and fewer to Ft. Campbell until the manifest showed there was but one soldier left to arrive.

Seymour and Lynn consulted. The obvious thing to do was treat the man as a VIP—sort of like the millionth car to cross the Golden Gate Bridge—give flowers to his family and maybe a sedan for the day, but dispense with the band, and go ahead with conversion of the hangar back to its original purposes as an airplane garage. It was sorely needed, for hundreds of Aviation Brigade's aircraft were returning by sea.

Each colonel thought that a modified reception was the others inclination, but as they talked about it longer they decided—no, the man was a returning Screaming Eagle, entitled as all the others had been to identical treatment.

The man debarked, proceeding into utter disbelief. Seymour and Lynn were there to greet him, as was the band playing in the hangar, empty except for his family and homecoming junkies. It was an occasion enjoyed as much as all the others. When it was over the junkies went into weeks of withdrawal. It was as hard to describe as it was impossible to repeat. The chronic symptom was not emotional hangover but afterglow.

The chain of concern had thought through homecoming even into its aftereffects. With the cease-fire, family psychologists addressed the support groups, advising what to expect, what changes to anticipate when reunited with Desert Stormers. The state of a marriage, for example, would not be so much altered by the separation as accentuated: where an aspect of it had been good it would be better, where it had been bad it would be worse. Expect a euphoric period but don't be disappointed if it doesn't seem to last as long as other families'. Though three weeks leave was granted to everyone immediately, take the first few days around home to let the returnee feel reacquainted with familiar surroundings. Let him spend some time alone if he wants to, though parents and siblings may clamor to visit. For the first week, when you find the toilet seat up just lower it without comment.

It's OK if he seeks the company of his fellow veterans—they can't loosen bonds right away that they've developed in war. And don't be jealous that if for some subjects he seems to confide in buddies more than with you. The fact is that these buddies have been a substitute for you. Be glad that he's now closer to other people: that doesn't mean he's less close to you.

Unfortunately the returnees did not receive this professional counsel, so it was up to their spouses to get across a crucial and inevitable change in the relationship, one that could be for better or worse. The waiting family had become self reliant, had made decisions in the soldier's absence, and done rather well at it, sometimes better than he had before the war. Subtle, then perhaps stronger, power struggles could result until reworked relationships were settled. Some men might resent a familial co-chairmanship where there had previously been an acknowledged head, while others would welcome consensual authority. It can all be worked out if you know your guy, your *new* guy. The whole desert experience can be an opportunity to know him and yourself better.

Another issue was that of a payoff for the home front veterans. Acclaim and thanksgiving abounded for the returning desert warriors. Newspapers were bold with full page tributes from businesses, local and national, professions of admiration and gratitude to the liberators of Kuwait. These, of course, pleased the families, but where were the cheers for what they had gone through? Peay sounded them loud in his speech when his plane landed with the division colors, but otherwise appreciation for families was drowned out by adulation for soldiers.

For the families it began to irk. This combined with a fast growing possessiveness: the public had had their loved ones long enough. Wives wanted their soldiers out of the limelight and back in living rooms. Not even the Peays were immune. After his runway speech, the CG fielded long media questions with thoughtful patience, but his son, Ryan, grew restless for a homecoming hug. Finally a friend of the family whispered, "Go get daddy," and he did, touchingly tugging the general, ordering him in effect, to where his heart had been all during the interviews. Peay's wave to the reporters, and his bashful smile, said "see you later." Much later if his family had their way.

Hill didn't stick around for interviews. A list of requested speaking engagements crowded his desk, enough to cause him to disregard the support group psychologist's advice and instead get out of town. Still knocked out by jet lag, the Hills motored 16 hours nonstop to Texas for his wife's high school reunion.

Vicki Cody had been impressed by the psychologist, enough so that she'd planned three days at home before an ideal get-away-from-it-all escape to the Rockies and skiing. But Dick, for TF Normandy's exploit, was much in demand by the media, and found himself a movie projectionist of the FLIR film. Over and over again, never tiring to relive the minutes post- combat fatigue had erased from his memory. On the snowy mountains he took long solitary walks. That would have worried Vicki but for the forewarning of the psychologist.

Return from the skiing idyll brought back the reporters and a crush of after action reports. Paper towered on his desk as if FORSCOM had ignored the war. He called Greco to see if he had a similar paper mountain to climb. They agreed that they'd wipe their slates clean, if only to get down to what was important: any document predating homecoming went into overflowing wastebaskets.

Vicki felt even more acutely that there had been no interim between the Gulf and the paper war. She was losing her husband again even before she regained him. Repeated in various forms throughout Ft. Campbell and the summer, an incident brought new relations to denouement.

For some forgotten reason, she visited 1-101's headquarters where she had often presided over the battalion's support group. The halls now swarmed with aviators where high heels had echoed in loneliness during the past months. Vicki's friends in the rear detachment were no longer at their familiar desks but reintegrated into the unit and out training. Not a trace, not a memory of the home front's vigil here. That seemed to have been ignored, and the headquarters transformed by indifference. Now the building was so bustling, so different— including her husband when she entered his now cluttered office and found him puffing a cheroot.

Cody had fulfilled his incredible public promise to bring all his guys back alive despite brownouts, triple A, SAM's, ground fire and MIG's. But he had also made a personal promise to Vicki—he'd stop smoking for the family's sake, and until he deployed he did. In postwar pillow talk he confessed to backsliding. The war had been pretty tense at times, smoking helped keep him alert, and the guys sort of viewed his cheroots like Patton's pistols. Good for morale, you know...

In the honeymoon of homecoming Vicki forgave. But now here he was, surrounded by war souvenirs, at the once neat desk where Vicki had toiled with the bills of lonely wives whose husbands had been off flying up a desert storm and, she suspected, having a great time.

"You're a liar, Dick Cody!" He gazed guiltily at the smoke plume from his cigar. "I didn't wait for you to come home from the war so you could kill yourself with cigars!"

She slammed the door loud enough to jolt Davis from his swivel chair in the next office. Vicki stormed down the hall, while eyes peeked out to see if a Scud had hit the CO. Someone murmured "expect no mercy," then doors quietly closed as veterans contemplated their own spousal readjustments.

Cody quit once more. If there were some pains of readjustment with his wife, he found compensating stature in the new regard from his boys, Clinton and Tyler, and this was typically true for desert stormer children. Dad was a celebrity, beseeched to speak at schools and civic clubs, lionized by the press and put on parade. Kids looked up from their MTV's to see him with new eyes.

Foretelling that his days in command were numbered, Peay denied himself the three week leave bestowed upon the rest of the division. He had too much to do preparing for succession of command, and deploying the Screaming Eagles in as far-ranging operations as he had during Hail Mary. Cities clamored for troops to march in victory parades. Brigades flew off to Memphis and Chicago, battalions to smaller cities, all as prelude to the nation-stoppers in Washington and New York on successive weekends in June 1991.

Peay remembers New York as a "happening." The canyon streets crowded marchers and spectators close together amid a *schmall* of ticker tape. For the troops, Gotham's reputation for cynicism will no longer be believed. New Yorkers expect the best in their town; they're merciless when it's not delivered whether by a deli or the Mets. Comity is a mark of those who can't compete. "Expect no mercy," could be the city's motto as much as 1-101's. The marchers didn't know what to expect from New York. What they got, what they heard in half a million voices, was rumbling recognition that they were the best in the ultimate competition called war.

Washington sniffed at New York's earthy outpouring. The capital event would be classy (at a classy price of $8 million), anything but crass. Hold the confetti, Washington's buildings aren't high enough anyway. The town prepared with a sense of history, editorials recalling for comparison the two day parade of the Grand Army of the Republic in 1865. There would be no tight squeeze for the marchers on Washington's broad boulevards. The hundreds of thousands of spectators stood back and were orderly as if to give the nation a better view.

Just before adjutant's call came the fly-by of dark, unmarked warplanes from the desert, looming over the Washington Monument then paralleling the route of march toward the Lincoln Memorial and The Wall. Slow aircraft, like the Apache, led the procession with the supersonics throttled down and wobbling to prevent stall. From the opposite direction, towing a banner, came a biplane hired by local Screaming Eagle vets. Most eyes were elsewhere, but the banner's message was legible from the Iraqi Embassy: "101st A/B—150 mi. from Baghdad."

Afterword & Acknowledgments

This history was begun almost as the dust of Desert Storm settled. I'd met Binnie Peay when we both made speeches at a 101st banquet during the 50th Airborne Anniversary celebrations described in the Introduction. When the Gulf war broke out a month later, I importuned him to arrange my assignment with the 101st as they conducted the covering force mission. He was willing enough but ARCENT was not, the most valid reason being that I was a colonel (in the reserves) and the organizational structure called for but eight colonels in the division. Anticipating battle casualties, it had been raised to over strength in sergeants and lieutenants, but an extra free floating colonel was deemed unnecessary, though Peay had two special projects in mind for me. The first was as liaison with the Saudis because in the early 1980's I had worked for a Saudi royal commission in the kingdom.

He also wanted my help with the text of a 'yearbook' for the troops. This largely pictorial history, *North to the Euphrates*, was duly published by the Tennessee-Kentucky Chapter of the Association of the US Army in the summer of 1991 before most of the desert veterans departed for new assignments. Peay's request was before the ground war began, so my involvement with the yearbook was restricted to deployment activities such as POR and the convoys to Jacksonville described here in chapters I and XV. This was accomplished during a two week assignment at Ft. Campbell I finagled that coincidentally ended the day the ground war started. Like everyone else there, I was entranced with CNN whenever I was not at work; indeed, work and the news were uniquely entwined: TV sets were on in every office, silently flickering, usually monitored by someone who turned up the sound if something topical appeared.

This fortnight tour ('ADT') was my first and last business in uniform at Ft. Campbell. At the end of the cover letter for the yearbook project, the last words I would ever write for the army, I waxed sentimental to the addressees that included Peay, Bolt and Seymour:

5. Nor can I praise enough the lavish support I've received for this project, especially from you who have been so helpful with your time and information. Indeed, without the influence of this headquarters, I would not have been allowed an ADT tour at all. From cookies presented by a support group, to meals at your homes, the generosity and hospitality of the Ft. Campbell community have surrounded me like a cocoon. I hope you sense my sentiment for this community in what you read here. If not, please tell me, because I want to tell the world about it as much as anything that happens in the desert.

6. Friday will be my last day in uniform. It was a pleasure and privilege to serve among you during my final assignment. It was a great fate to end my service with the unit that has meant the most not only for me but for two generations of Taylors. Air Assault!

Obviously my feelings for the Screaming Eagles are out front and unabashed. But hardly less so than the soldiers I interviewed, beginning with those I met at Ft. Campbell in February, 1991. Principally Melita McGrath, the division historian, who had returned from King Fahd because of a family emergency. She was replaced in the JOA by Cliff Lippard whose journal is liberally quoted here, especially in Chapter XXVII. Both McGrath and Lippard are out of the army now, she to help run religious missions in Georgia, he to run a Taco Bell franchise. The other vital contact from my first visit to Ft. Campbell was with the museum curator, Rex Boggs. Also recently returned from the JOA was an army civilian, Don Smith, who had spent a week photographing Screaming Eagles in the desert. His office provided dozens of photos that by war's end would be hundreds, and the prime source of pictures here.

There was a daily morning briefing for Seymour that I often attended. It began with the 'enemy situation' which for the first time showed me how Iraqi forces were arrayed. Though all persons at the briefings had top secret security clearances, the 'friendly situation' was not shown on any maps, so I remained uninformed of TAA Campbell's location. However, Peay had sent back word, common knowledge in the briefing room, that the division was "way out west." On the morning (Central Standard Time) of G Day, Rex and I huddled over a map and figured that TAA Campbell must be pretty close to Rafha. In daily contact with Bolt, both Seymour and Lynn probably knew precisely where TAA Campbell was but quite properly did not divulge the location to me as I had no real need to know.

Though the ground war had not yet started, good fortune put me in contact with a number of veterans from Desert Shield, most of whom were back for medical reasons. As soon as physically able, they were returned to duty which often began as gofers at the museum where I was working. It was from them that I learned details of life at Ft. Camel and the FOB's described in chapters III, IV, VI and VII. Of course the support groups were fully active, and I had occasion to talk a bit with Mesdames Lynn and Peay. Ft. Campbell was taut and tense, but the support groups had been tremendously buoyed by a visit from Mrs. Bush.

As a civilian in December 1991 I came back for interviews when, postwar, the significance of the maple grove was revealed to me. The heart-crushing casualty reports from the Vietnam years were too remote in time to impact on the Ft. Campbell community of the '90's. But Gander, in 1985, had been close enough to recent memory for the waiting families of Tennessee and Kentucky to feel the approaching spectre of deaths on a scale of hundreds.

Most of my interviews were at the Public Affairs Office. When I came in on the morning of December 12th, Maj. Gribben's secretary was palid, shakily smoking a cigarette. She looked so stricken I asked if she were ill. No, she replied, she was reliving the Gander crash exactly six years before. The pall had not dissipated for people who had been at Ft. Campbell during that ghastly Christmas season. They unforgettably realized that war is a ledger of death, each number an abstraction of utter grief. She felt that so deeply, it was easy to perceive how Ft. Campbell memories were also engraved by Gander as TV showed the ground war drawing closer and closer.

That visit in December 1991 was my third as a civilian. The first was in June and coincided with Peay's relinquishment of command. It was a most poignant period for him, so much so that I felt intrusive with many questions I could defer for future occasions. Good luck for me came when he was assigned to the Pentagon near my new home in Washington. His immediate absence, however, set the blueprint for this book. Instead of learning history from the top down, I'd work from the bottom up; that is, hear from the corporals through colonels before I talked at length with the generals.

But initially I simply followed Ed Gribben's recommendations as to who to interview to obtain both a broad and focused picture. In the first set of interviews were Adams, Hill, Purdom, Clark, Garrett, Cody, Vanantwerp, Huber and Riccardelli. Shelton and Bolt had already departed for new assignments in North Carolina and Alaska respectively. I never interviewed them, and this book is surely less for that, especially in the case of Bolt who received as many brickbats for his administration as Shelton did kudos for making complexities simple in the division's operations. Bolt's compensation comes from Peay's satisfaction with him. A chief of staff is meant to be Gen. Jekyll's Col. Hyde, a relationship for which none can fault Bolt's performance.

With the exception of Cody, interviewees below the rank of colonel were somewhat wary of what they should tell me though there had been a general declassification of war information. Nevertheless, a suspicion of journalists, engrained in desert sand, continued at Ft. Campbell and would have made my task tedious had not Peay advised Gribben that I was OK, sort of a close relative if not a current member of the Screaming Eagle flock. Thus I was allowed to interview without a PAO representative sitting in as had been the policy in the Gulf. I offered each soldier the option of either non-attribution or background. Few took it.

There was only one instance where I got a man in trouble with higher headquarters. This was because of a picture in the unit's yearbook showing troops on a bus, grinning with anticipation, over a caption that stated they were headed for Bahrain *again*. Bahrain, an island principality connected to the Arabian peninsula by a causeway, is as westernized as Saudi Arabia is strictly Islamic. In the Gulf war, Bahrain was synonymous with beer and the better things of life, almost as Bangkok had been in Vietnam. For Screaming Eagles to venture to Bahrain at all, much less in uniform and more than once, would have bounced Peay off the ceiling. But there was the picture, and the caption (which I didn't realize was facetious), so I mentioned the excursion in a draft submitted to a colonel two links up the chain from the unit. Though he had seen the unit's yearbook, he upbraided the commander and urged me to expunge mention of Bahrain. I readily did so when I determined the excursion never happened. Even if it had, I deemed it a prank in wartime, surely a bygone offense, no more than an amusing diversion from life in the field. That the colonel took it so seriously was one of the most startling contrasts between the jungle and desert. War stories from Vietnam commonly include military felonies such as theft of trucks from sister units!

Cody I expected to find jaded from repeating the saga of TF Normandy, but instead he relished the opportunity to polish his presentation. This was because, as I learned later, he was still on a mission: to have the Air Medals for his Normandy crews upgraded to Distinguished Flying Crosses. Cody felt that if this book publicised their exploit, the army might take favorable notice, but he did not succeed. Air Medals remained for the Apaches while DFC's (awarded by the Air Force) went to the Pave Lows.

Again to my good fortune, Cody was assigned to Ft. Eustis VA, an easy three hour drive from Washington. I was able to talk with him extensively there, becoming his friend and admirer. He is as colorful a soldier as I've ever met in the U.S. military, a man who can produce and, more remarkably, produce with flair. The stylistic counterpoint between him and Garrett was fascinating and surely will continue throughout their careers as both are ascendant stars in army aviation. No doubt they will occasionally clash in years to come, but resulting in a synergistic force like that produced by opposing muscles.

It was from Vicki Cody that I got the deepest glimpse of the war on the home front, a subject really deserving a book unto itself. It would include several chapters about Lettie Gingerich, the inveterate writer of hundreds of letters to soldiers up and down the line—'any soldiers' for the most part—a tireless, almost compulsive activity for a mother who lost a son in Vietnam. She is frank about her pay-off. Those who answer her letters, she wants to see.

"Then I can hug 'em and hold 'em as long as they'll let me. I close my eyes, then that warm body in my arms is Greg's."

There were not many Letties anywhere despite the relative popularity of the desert war, and I see her as a cup that primed the pump in the upswell of emotion that began to pour out in Bangor.

Concurrent with her letter writing, and part of its motivation, was Lettie's involvement with 'the mobile wall,' a transportable replica of the original Vietnam Memorial in Washington. Three replicas now crisscross the country in moving vans. Any town willing to pay for movement from the last site is eligible to display a wall for a flexible period, usually about a week. Walls are mounted and maintained by volunteers, many of whom come hundreds of miles to unload and erect. At this writing, walls are up in Angelina TX, Crawfordsville IN and Natchez MI, with Carthage MO, Greeley CO and Redondo Beach CA next in line. It is a long line, a yellow ribbon of back roads. Surely no two wars in American history, though divided by a generation, are more sentimentally connected than Vietnam and the Gulf.

While still in the desert after the cease-fire on 27 February 1991, the brigade commanders were directed to produce executive summaries covering both Desert Shield and Storm. Lippard compiled these into a bound document as required by 18th ABC where it was forwarded. This unadorned history, though well annotated and supplemented with graphics, was in my hands by July 1991, providing the spatial and temporal guideposts for the swirling sequence of events during the 100 hours which were jumbled even in Peay's mind so that two years later he had to reconstruct them.

Follow-on interviews awaited my acquisition of citations for bravery, a matchless historical resource because regulations require that the who, what, when, where and how of individual actions be clearly narrated and corroborated by witnesses. Acquiring this material was a surprising frustration. For some reason citations—read with fanfare at public ceremonies—thereafter become subject to the Freedom of Information Act, releasable only upon petition and payment of "search, review and reproduction" fees.

As division chief of staff, Tom Hill helped me shake citations out of the bureaucracy. Finally I received the desiderata, with a cover letter that said,

"Enclosed are sanitized copies of the supporting documents for those soldiers that you identified on the list accompanying your letter of 11 May. The social security numbers of those individuals, for whom narratives were provided, have been redacted in order to preclude a possible invasion of privacy. This is authorized in accordance with AR 340-21, The Army Privacy Program, para. 2-6."

I could have saved myself $84 by requesting the hometown press releases, written by the PAO when the medals were awarded. All were Bronze Stars for Valor.

To Ed Gribbens, head of Ft. Campbell's PAO, go my first thanks for scheduling interviews and letting me conduct them in private. Wendy Westlake of his office made the arrangements with many busy soldiers. Other principal benefactors I've already mentioned in this Afterword. To them—in approximate order that they appear in the book—I gratefully add Steve Weiss, now the command sergeant major at Ft. Sam Houston, TX.; Tom Greco, currently a student at the Army War College at Carlisle, PA; Mike Davis, whose journal of the hundred hours was a primary and invaluable source. He's now at Ft. Eustis, VA. Chaplains Adams (no relation to the general) and Kitchen provided fine insights into the outlooks of the Gulf and home fronts. Herb Kitchen went on to Ft. McPherson, GA where his song about TF Normandy, "The Night the Eagle Screamed," was recorded and briefly became a country-western hit. First verse:

On January seventeen, Cody got the word;
Loaded up his Hellfires and revved his mighty bird.
He lifted off into the night and headed for Iraq.

They should have known the One-oh-one wouldn't cut 'em any slack!

For his exhausting labors as G3 Ops, Keith Huber was promoted and took command of a battalion in First Brigade. His assistant, Dessie Greer, expects to leave the army with her husband Calvin. Myron Yancey (a nom de guerre he picked) is also out, driving an eighteen-wheeler like the ones that rushed to the call for Jacksonville convoys. Ron Adams, like Hugh Shelton, was promoted to major general and works with Peay in the Pentagon as does Brig. Gen. Bolt and John Tilleli, CG of the 1st Cav during the scare at Hafer Al Batin. Phil Jones went on to Ft. Sill, OK. A VMI graduate, Jones was steered into the artillery by artilleryman Peay. Sarge and Agnes are still in the army, both promoted but neither any longer at Ft. Campbell.

Unmentioned so far is the fact that Ted Purdom's wife (a lieutenant colonel) was an army nurse stationed near King Fahd as Lori Gabram had been. At KKMC, Lori treated more Iraqi casualties than American. She caught up with Doug after the cease-fire; by coincidence, they returned home on successive days. Amid the festivities, he met Cody's father who as a Chevrolet dealer was also a member of the Corvette cult. He promptly bought Doug's '76 model and drove it back to Vermont. Doug will stay in the army (current assignment, Ft. Rucker) but Lori will leave because they have begun a family. As an army nurse, in case of another war in which they were both deployed, they would have to leave their daughter with grandparents, a prospect neither could accept so Lori resigned. Such a separation nearly occurred when her military hospital deployed to Somalia. Lori stayed behind only because of her pregnancy.

For similar reasons, Jorge Garcia left the army. Not yet a father, he felt the life of an army aviator would take too much time from parenting. He may have miscalculated by joining the FBI! Newman Shufflebarger went into the procurement field of army aviation rather than remain a line officer. Of the other members of TF Normandy, only Lou Hall is out of uniform. He retired and is now flying helicopteror the Dept. of the Interior in Nevada. Cody's XO, Howard Killian, explorer of the desert between Cobra and Viper, now tries to find his way around the

Pentagon. Tim Devito—in army aviation the surname has become an adjective like the Laffer curve in economics—now commands a company of Apaches. So too does Russ Stinger, the intelligence officer for the raid.

Quotations from Gen. Colin Powell are from correspondence. In a letter I asked him for a comparison of the Normandy raid with others in American history: Doolittle over Tokyo, Sonh Tay to liberate POW's in North Vietnam, and Desert One. I expected an answer that reflected less consideration than what I brought to the question, but blushed when I realized that Powell's insights—no doubt rendered from the top of his head—were deeper and fuller than mine: the essence of the Normandy raid was that it was integral to a larger whole, whereas the earlier raids were ends unto themselves. While saluting TF Normandy, Powell somewhat minimized their accomplishment. I would take exception, noting that of the four historic raids, Cody's was the only one entirely successful.

"Bastogne Night" is celebrated annually by a chapter of the 101st Airborne Division Association at West Point. On that occasion in 1991, I met Gregg Gile, former CO of Second Brigade and his XO, Dave Wood. Wood was an instructor at USMA and Gile the chief of staff of the 10th Mountain Division. That he retained a strong bond with the 101st was impressive as Gile is himself, all the more the wonder that he would have been eased out of his command a few months before the ground war. Peay assured me that wouldn't hurt Gile, and indeed he was promoted to brigadier general, and later commanded forces in Somalia. Gen. John Wickham (ret), a godfather of the 101st, continued in a civilian career near Washington and was a sometime TV commentator during the war. Later, after he moved to Tucson, he was very helpful in sketching in the evolution of the air assault concept.

Purdom was the most prolific writer among the brigade commanders. "Hail Fatima" is a very much boiled down version of his memorandum about the defense of Hafer Al Batin. Tallil also was principally his baby and worry; his operations plan, Desert Squall, for that formidable attack will probably become an air assault text and may be played out in a computer wargame to determine how costly it would be to send helicopters against heavy fortifications bristling with triple A defenses.

Montie Hess soon departed for a command in Puerto Rico, and I was sorry not to have interviewed him earlier as he produced a cornucopia of information, especially about the Baghdad Sequel, a subject that drew quizzical frowns when I asked the other colonels. They had been too busy fighting the war as Peay speculated about what could be the next and final phase. His confidant was Hess who briefed Schwarzkopf on the Baghdad Sequel.

Rhonda Cornum is the subject of her own book, so complete that I never interviewed her. She testified before the Congressional committee on women in combat whose conclusions were split. Peay, incidentally, was the next witness after Cornum. She was reunited with Garrett when he became assistant commandant of the Army Aviation School at Ft. Rucker. Currently she and Kory are in residency at Ft. Sam Houston, TX.

Frank Wilmoth, the commander of the division's aerial moving vans (Chinooks) provided the best picture of the nitty gritty problems of getting the division from here (TAA Campbell) to there (FOB Cobra). His battalion, 7-101, has written some errata for the book on the capabilities of cargo choppers. In the foreword could be the adage that an aircraft's ultimate limitation is the imagination of those who employ it. The book, as authorities wrote it, is but a guide for its users, always amendable by innovators like Fox and Pelletier.

Though I was only able to interview Jim McGarity (then a recruiting officer in Minnesota) by phone, his inspiration for TF Citadel is my favorite anecdote in the book. Even in the British Army, Arabists are scarce, and in the U.S. Army could fit into a Kiowa. Yet at the precise place, at a unique time, there was McGarity, who from private and nonmilitary reading recognized a topical exploitation of the experience of the 14th century Moslem adventurer, Ibn Batuta, a man who in the west is virtually unknown outside arcane academe. Leaping across the ages, the *Dub al Haj* became MSR New Market, an historical phenomenon shortly recognized by National Geographic Magazine.

Riccardelli continued to command the well educated MI

battalion. His daughter won a scholarship awarded by the 101st Airborne Division Association. By mail, I queried Gen. Schwarzkopf (ret) on several matters including the Baghdad Sequel, but through his secretary he begged off, probably because he was too busy writing his own memoirs, *It Doesn't Take a Hero*. Tom Drew achieved a double distinction by having piloted one of the first Apaches into Iraq (during the Normandy raid) as well as the first one to land in Iraq (during the Cobra recon). He flies on with 1-101. Broderick, the king of FARPS, now toils in the Pentagon. Alcus Davis, the busiest air traffic coordinator in the world on 24 February 1991, was promoted and remained with S&T Battalion.

Bob Clark relinquished command of Third Brigade in November 1992 to replace Hill as division chief of staff. Both colonels were promoted to brigadier general, Hill departing to the joint staff in the Pentagon. Purdom left a month earlier to Ft. Drum, New York, where he replaced Gile for the second time in two years; then both accompanied the 10th Mountain Division to Somalia where Gile was promoted.

Bob Johnson turned over his Black Hawks but again is working for Garrett, this time at Ft. Rucker. Bob Nichols, the New Age sergeant major, remained with First Brigade. Bob Vanantwerp, leader of TF Grader, is one of many Screaming Eagles going to school at Carlisle, PA. Sam, the mysterious Saudi, disappeared into the American population after his discharge from the US Army. Weiss believes he may have gone to Idaho.

Shelton, awarded a second star, went to Ft. Bragg to command the 82nd. Wearing shoulder patches from both airborne divisions, he attended Peay's change of command, Shelton's first visit back to Ft. Campbell. Promoted to lieutenant general in 1991, Peay picked up his fourth star early in 1993 and is now Vice Chief of Staff of the Army. Soon thereafter, Shelton was promoted to lieutenant general, replacing Luck as commander of 18th ABC. Luck, in turn, received a fourth star to command 8th Army in Korea.

John Seymour, "mayor" for nine months of Ft. Campbell, went to a special forces assignment in Hawaii, while the 101st's rear detachment commander, Dan Lynn, received a battalion in

First Brigade—a job for which he had been selected before the war. By the time *Lightning in the Storm* is published, all of the above assignments will have turned over once more. Thus do careers return to normal, and the game of musical chairs resumes. Desert Stormers are pleased to have 'sand in their file,' a plus when boards in the future consider candidates for promotion. The issue of veterancy came up immediately as promotion boards, delayed by the war, convened. One for aviation lieutenant colonels was chaired by Shelton and included Garrett. Shelton answered the question at the start and set the tone: what an officer did, not where he or she did it, would be the pre-eminent criterion.

Such were the steps taken to restore normalcy. Except for those about to retire, as Schwarzkopf did, or those pink slipped by defense downsizing, the Gulf war was no culmination but rather a spike in the normally straight line of military progression and concomitant careers.

The constancy has returned, though progress has narrowed and may even stall. The army has rarely overlooked its prospects, even when they were unpromising as after Vietnam. The army strives to understand its new role, in order to develop a familiarity with factors that can be rationally analysed and hopefully quantified. The national mood, the world situation, does not succumb readily to such analysis, but they do not discourage the effort. Today the military reconciles to inescapable realities. With reluctance, the army harkens back to that of the 1920's, and an old West Point ditty, "In the army there's sobriety, promotion very slow."

Yet the military mind is conditioned to look at the up side. Slow promotion means more prestige for less rank: a major can once again be a major officer, a colonel an awesome one like the captain of a capital ship in the navy. But selection for every grade of promotion will be by narrow margins. Talent is plentiful; positions promising advancement are not, raising uneasiness that the stultifying strictures of a zero defects army will recrudesce.

Amid such misgivings, the Gulf war is already taking on a sentimental patina for its veterans, that of a sunset of the good days, the last campfire of the army at its peak. As new routine sets in, the war is seen not only as a spike in military careers, but also something of a speed bump, a jolt. What matters now to Desert Stormers is the destination of the road so they can prepare for the end of their journeys. Preparation is based on prediction like that demonstrated in the exercise, Internal Look. So it will be a lucky army—and nation—to be as well prepared as were our forces in August 1990. Against Saddam, the army was all that it could be; what follows is rendezvous with clouded destiny.

Organizational location of persons during Desert Shield/Storm.

THEATER
★★★★

CENTCOM
Schwarzkopf

AIR FORCE	NAVY	ARMY	MARINES	SOCCENT
Gray				J. Johnson

CORPS
★★★

18th AB   7th
Luck   Franks
Akers
Yancey

DIVISIONS
★★

24th Mech.   101st AA   82nd AB
McCaffrey   Peay

HQ: Ron Adams, Shelton,
Bolt, Hess, Kitchens, Lynn,
Huber, Mixon, McGrath, "Sam,"
Lippard, Weiss, Dessie Greer

BRIGADES

(327th Regt.) (502nd Regt.) (187th Regt)
FIRST   SECOND   THIRD   AVIATION   ARTILLERY   DISCOM
Hill   Gile   McDonald   Garrett   Anderson   Gerald
McGarity Purdom   Clark   P. Jones
Nichols   Wood

BATTALIONS

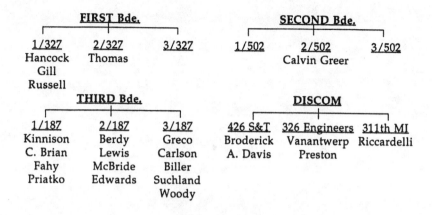

FIRST Bde.

1/327	2/327	3/327
Hancock	Thomas	
Gill		
Russell		

SECOND Bde.

1/502	2/502	3/502
	Calvin Greer	

THIRD Bde.

1/187	2/187	3/187
Kinnison	Berdy	Greco
C. Brian	Lewis	Carlson
Fahy	McBride	Biller
Priatko	Edwards	Suchland
		Woody

DISCOM

426 S&T	326 Engineers	311th MI
Broderick	Vanantwerp	Riccardelli
A. Davis	Preston	

AVIATION Bde.

1/101	2/229
Cody	Brilinski
M. Davis	W. Bryan
D. Gabram	Butts
Garcia	Cornum
TF Normandy	Dunlap
"Turbo"	Garvey
Killian	Godfrey
Morgan	Pacheko
Gilman	Stamaris
Stinger	

3/101	4/101	5/101
Curran	R. Johnson	Russ Adams

7/101	2/17
Wilmoth	Hamlin
Fox	Kranz
Pellitier	Rister
	Wyrick

Not shown: Agnes, Sarge

Glossary of Acronyms, Abbreviations and Gulf War Terminology

Note: Hyphens indicate that an acronym is pronounced by its separate letters. When written, no hyphens are used.

AA (or "triple A"): Enemy anti-aircraft artillery.

A/B: Airborne. Either paratroop or heliborne forces.

A-B-C: Airborne corps. There is only one, the 18th.

A-C-P: Assault command post. A small advance headquarters.

A-C-R: Armored cavalry regiment. About 5,000 soldiers in vehicles, mostly mechanized.

A-D-A: Air defense artillery. The friendly equivalent of triple A.

AFCENT: The Air Force component of CENTCOM.

A-F-R-N: Armed Forces Radio Network. Like a home town radio station for military personnel in the Gulf.

AFSOC: The Air Force component of SOCCENT.

A-K47: Probably the world's most famous assault rifle. Fully automatic, communist manufacture, the standard individual weapon in the Iraqi army.

A-P-O: Army Post Office, where incoming mail was received and delivered in Saudi Arabia.

A-P-U: Auxiliary power unit for starting helicopters.

A-O: Area of operations.

ARAMCO: Arabian-American Oil Company.

ARCENT: The Army component of CENTCOM.

AWAC: Airborne warning and control. A large aircraft stuffed with radar and radios.

A-W-R: Air worthiness report.

AVSCOM: Aviation Systems Command. The army agency that grants AWR's.

B-B-C: British Broadcasting Company. The international

short wave radio station from which soldiers in the Gulf received much of the world news.

Blivet: A large globular fuel container.

B-M-P: The standard Iraqi armored personnel carrier.

BX: Base exchange. An Air Force department store.

CAP: Combat air patrol.

C&C: Command and control.

C Day: The day on which movement to the Gulf commenced.

CENTCOM: Central Command. The multi-service U.S. headquarters reponsible for security in the Middle East.

C-E II: Camp Eagle II; aka King Fahd, Tent City, Fort Camel.

C-5A: The largest air force transport.

C-4: The standard military plastic explosive.

C-G: Commanding general.

Chem stick: A luminous baton.

Chin gun: The rapid fire cannon on an Apache. Also known as the chain gun, but most often called the 30 millimeter.

CINCCENT: Commander in chief, Central Command. Gen. Schwarzkopf.

C-N-N: Channel News Network (TV).

C-O: Commanding officer.

COL: Colonel.

C-130: The work horse transport of the air force.

CPL: Corporal.

CAPT: Captain.

CRAF: Civil Reserve Air Fleet. Airliners impressed into military service.

C-S-M: Command sergeant major. The highest ranking non-commissioned officer.

C-T: Counter-terrorism.

D Day: Day on which hostilities commence.

D-F: Directional finding by radio interception.

D-F-C: Distinguished Flying Cross.

DISCOM: Division Support Command.

D-Main: The principal headquarters for a division. See D-REAR and ACP.

D-REAR: Division headquarters for logistics and administration.

D-U-I/D-W-I: Driving under the influence (usually of alcohol). Driving while intoxicated.

E-A: Engagement area. That portion of an AO in which the enemy is expected to be taken under fire.

E-LINT: Electronic intelligence.

E-P-W: Enemy prisoner of war. See POW.

ERDE: "Eardree." Emergency deployment exercise.

FARP: Forward area refueling point, usually for helicopters, FARP can also be used as a verb.

Fleshette: A rocket for helicopters to attack lightly protected targets.

FLIR: "Fleer." Forward looking infrared.

F-O-B: Forward operating base.

FORSCOM: Forces Command. The largest army headquarters in the continental U.S.

FRAGO: A fragmentary order. Used to make a sudden change of plans.

G Day: When the ground war started.

G-C-T: Ground control team. The C&C at a FARP.

G5: The civil affairs staff section.

G-P: General purpose.

G-P-S: Geo-positioning satellite.

G3: The staff section at division headquarters or higher, responsible for operations, plans and training.

Gunship: Apaches or Cobras.

Haj: The Islamic pilgrimage to Mecca.

HEMIT: A rough terrain fuel tanker.

H Hour: The hour an operation commences.

Hind: A Soviet-made attack helicopter.

HUMM-V: High mobility multipurpose vehicle. Successor to the jeep.

I-D: Identification, friend or foe. An electronic interrogation.

I-G: Inspector general.

I-P: 1. Initial point. 2. Instructor pilot.

Inshallah: God willing.

JIB: Joint Information Bureau, CENTCO's media center.

J-O-A: Joint operations area. CENTCOM's theater of war, excepting Kuwait and Iraq.

Kevlar: Armored helmet worn by U.S. ground forces.

K-I-A: 1. Killed in action. 2. A person so killed.

K-K-M-C: King Kahlid Military City.

K-T-O: Kuwaiti Theater of Operations, including Iraq.

LRSD: Long range surveillance detachment. Pronounced *lurss-dee.*

LT: Lieutenant. The only rank spoken by its initials; e.g., L-T Jones.

LTC: Lieutenant colonel. Colloquially, "light colonel."

L-Z: Landing zone.

Mech: Mechanized.

M-I: Military intelligence.

M-I-A: 1. Missing in action. 2. Anyone so missing.

MOPP: Mission oriented protective posture. Attire worn to protect against NBC attack.

M-P: 1. Military police. 2. A military policeman.

M-R-E: Meals ready to eat. Dehydrated field rations.

M-S-R: Main supply route.

M-16: The standard U.S. rifle.

M-60: The standard U.S. machinegun.

N-B-C: 1. Nuclear, biological, chemical. 2. National Broadcasting Corp.

N-C-O: Noncommissioned officer; i.e., a sergeant.

N-V-A: North Vietnamese Army.

N-V-G: Night vision goggles.

Oh-deuce: 502nd Infantry Regiment.

O-P: Observation post.

OPLAN: Operations plan.

Pave Low: An air force SAR helicopter.

PERSCOM: Personnel Command.

P-F-C: Private first class.

P-J: Air Force paramedic.

Pod: Auxiliary fuel tank.

P-O-R: Permanent overseas replacement.

P-O-W: prisoner of war. A military captive of the enemy.

P-X: Post exchange. Army bases are called "posts." See BX.

P-Z: Pickup zone.

Q-M: Quartermaster.

R&R: Rest and relaxation.

REMF: Rear echelon personnel, a derisive term.

R-O-T-C: Reserve Officers Training Corps.

R-P: Release point.

R-T-O: Radio-telephone operator.

Sabkha: An intermittently dry lake bed.

SAC: Strategic Air Command.

SAM: Surface-to-air missle.

SAR: Search and rescue.

S&T: Supply and transportation.

S-C-I: Special compartmented information; i.e., super secret.

Scud: Long range surface to surface missile.

S-F-C: Sergeant first class.

SCT: Sergeant.

Slugger: Hand held GPS.

S1: Staff section responsible for personnel.

SOCCENT: Special Operations Command of CENTCOM.

S-P: Standardization pilot.

S60: An Iraqi SAM.

S3: At brigade and battalion level, the equivalent of G3.

Stealth: Nearly invisible to radar.

T-A-A: Tactical assembly area.

Tac: Tactical.

TAC CP: Tactical command post.

TACSAT: Secure tactical radio net served by a space satellite.

Tapline: Trans-Arabian Pipeline.

Team: A task force smaller than a battalion.

Tent City: Fort Camel.

T-F: Task force. A composite, ad hoc unit of company size or larger.

TOC: Tactical operations center, often synonymous with TAC CP.

T-O-F: Time of flight for a missile.

TOW: A wire guided anti-tank missile, either ground or vehicle mounted.

Triple A: Enemy anti-aircraft artillery.

U-H-F: Ultra-high frequency.

USAF: United States Air Force.

V-M-I: Virginia Military Institute, a small college.

Vulcan: An ADA weapon.

Wadi: A usually dry stream bed frequently encountered in the desert.

WO: Warrant officer. **CWO:** Chief warrant officer.

X-O: Executive officer.

Index